SATANAYA
AND THE HOUSES OF MERCY

Christopher Ryan

Satanaya
and the
Houses of Mercy

The Chronicle of a Circassian Girl

Christopher Ryan

"Because kitchen duty involves the total person,
it is vouchsafed only to those of evident virtue,
who manifest profound faith in the teachings of the Way
who have ripened and
are possessed of
a just and compassionate heart."

THE MASTER DOGEN

HAKAWATI PRESS
HAWICK

Published by Hakawati Press, Hawick, Scotland
email: info@christopherryan.co.uk
website: www.christopherryan.co.uk

First published 2018
Copyright © Christopher Ryan 2018

Cover illustration: Grace Connor – msgraceconnor@gmail.com
Map: Aliya Ryan – aliya@cantab.net

Designed and produced by Ged Lennox – gedlennox@me.com
Set in 10/13 Minion

Printed in the United Kingdom by Severn, Gloucester

ISBN 978-0-9569552-1-0

Quote from *Fusus-al-Hikam* – *by Muhyiddin 'Ibn Arabi*,
rendered into English by Bulent Rauf. Oxford ©1985 appears by kind permission
of Grenville Collins.

For further information: contact author at: info@christopherryan.co.uk

To Ottilie

ACKNOWLEDGEMENTS

Thank you to the many friends who assisted by accomodating this writer's needs for advice, retreat, friendship and encouragement: The Oxford posse: Sheila and Michael, David and Ros, and Charles and Denzil in the shires, for beautiful spaces to write. In Turkey: Meral Arim, for the generous loan of her flat by the Bosphorus at Beylerbey. Ufuk Değirmenci, cook, cup bearer and boon companion, dragoman and all-round fixer, and true friend when it counted most, with Kaz, and the denizens of the Mavi Kelebek: Hamid and Dilek, John and Bea, Pete and Joy, and all whose good cheer kept spirits high in Kayaköy. Prof. Dr. İbrişli and the cardiology and ICU team at Antalya Anadolu Hastanesi, special thanks for the Paça Çorbası. Nevin Halıcı, friend of Ateşbaz, and 'usta' of the Anatolian *mutfak*. Mustafa Elma and family, legendary hospitality and beautiful carpets in Konya ('come on Christopher, have just one more *alabalık*'). Bahar, Azim (*merhum*), Merve and all friends in Beshara Türkiye. In Israel, Rotem and Andrew, Noga, Limor, Tami, Yoav, Nur Anat and Ari in Gallilee, Akko, and Jerusalem, for showing me their land is still holy. Marzin and family and the Cherkess of Rehaniya and Kfar Kama. In Palestine, the sweetest *knafeh* cooks in Al Aksa Confectionary of Nablus. Keith Woolnough, publicist and sparring partner of Portobello Road. Julie Witford and the ever-helpful team at Cornucopia Magazine. Robert and Helga at Chalice Verlag. Tilda Johnson, whose untiring editing worked wonders and taught me POV. Ged and Grace for cover and production. Aliya for mapping. Zimmy and Mary Anna. And always the ever dear, patient Francisca, for never failing to insist 'you can't say that!' when really I shouldn't. And Bulent Bey, for bashing this chick pea back into the pot with such kindness and patience.

PROLOGUE

Cooks may come and go, but the good of their action remains. For after the obvious tastes have faded into comforting memories – the savourous smell of roasting meat lingering outside the kitchen door, the satisfying richness settling in the bellies, the deep hums of clove and cinnamon's warmth, the earthy scents of roots and wafting herbs, the sweet, the sour, the bitter and the salt – if the kitchen is a blessed kitchen, this goodness continues to bestow its benediction of nourishment and taste upon whomever it undertakes to serve with love.

Then every manner of sweet praise may issue from this kitchen, for the one whose heart is open. Whether she be cook or bottle washer, if love has arrived in the heart, and on the tongue, and through the hands, in whatever manner, and that love engenders the motivation to serve through the means – the 'meshiya' – of food then great things become possible.

In a time before the events related here, there was a cook who was a true lover. When eventually her time came to go, it was not the end of her influence in the convent's kitchen. A new cook took her place.

And when many years later that new cook became an old cook, a candidate was sought, an apprentice. Her name was Satanaya. She came from a Circassian village, Kfar Kama, near the Sea of Galilee in Palestine, and this is her story.

ONE

The Circassian Lady

London – 1975

HE WAS SO OLD by then, and I was still young and trying to make my way as a writer in a world whose soil was too rough for me to plough with the frail pen of my youthful poems and idealistic musings. It was late September, the end of a long, hot summer, and I was employed painting the exterior of houses in the Royal Borough of Kensington and Chelsea. I was standing atop a tall extending ladder, five floors up ('Health and Safety' was then a thing of the future) and wiping paint splashes from a cast iron rainwater pipe, when a voice from an open window hailed me; mellifluous, in an accent cultivated and clear, perhaps foreign but not alien, unheard as yet but instantly recognisable.

'Would you like to come up for a cup of tea when you've finished?'

It was not the voice I might have expected. I had been painting these flats for almost a week, and had already encountered most of the building's inhabitants, usually on their way to work each morning or on their return. The occupant of this flat was a writer. I knew that because I had seen him often enough scribbling at his desk as I passed his window when painting the gutters. He was called Mehmet. One morning I met him returning from his shopping carrying a brace of fat partridge from the Tachbrook Street market in Pimlico. He had recognised me in my painter's togs when I said hello and wished him 'bon appétit', and he had laughed.

'We shall roast them with butter and fresh thyme, and serve them in a sauce with white wine, cream and chanterelles.'

'And a nice bottle of Chambertin?'

'Ah, that would be nice, wouldn't it?'

We talked a little. It was a sunny morning and he seemed happy to pass the time in idle chatter. I mentioned I'd seen him writing, and asked if it was a novel.

'No. Novels are for inventive writers. This is history. The Ottoman Sultans. A lot of research, less imagination I'm afraid.'

He didn't appear surprised when I said that I, a painter in paint-stained overalls who spent his days seventy feet up an extended ladder, wanted to write; that I sometimes wrote poetry; even had a couple published.

'Yes, it's good to order one's thoughts, and express one's true feelings. Sentiment, without being sentimental,' he said.

Now we were putting the final coat of white gloss on the window frames. Mehmet must have known it was our last day on the job. But this invitation to tea did not come from the writer. It was a woman's voice that emerged from behind the yellow silk curtains.

This new voice remained a mystery until late in the afternoon. I rang the bell and a short while later came a cry from above, 'Watch out below!' and a large manila envelope sailed out from the fifth floor window and spiralled down to land on the pavement. It contained keys. I let myself in, and climbed the many stairs to the top flat. The door was opened by the writer, smiling, who welcomed me into the drawing room.

She sat in a low, old fashioned armchair, the kind with a wide firm seat and padded arm rests. The fabric of its upholstery once gold, was now faded to a dull pale ochre, worn thin in places, and tufts of horsehair showed at the edges. The lady who sat there, for she was a lady there was no doubt, was unassuming in appearance, though her presence was captivating. Yet I saw only the obvious: a long skirt, lilac and yellow Liberty print, white blouse with lace cuffed sleeves and high collar, and a pretty waistcoat also yellow.

'Now, introductions,' said Mehmet, and turning to the occupant of the armchair, 'This is the Lady Satanaya. Or should I call you Countess?'

'If you do, I'll start calling you Prince. Stop it, Mehmet.' She feigned crossness, then, smiling at me, said: 'Now, who are you, young man?'

'I'm Jacob.'

'Like the ladder?'

'That's meant to be my line,' I complained.

'Ah, you'll have to be quicker than that.'

Yes, I was slow. And she was... beautiful, fascinating, intelligent, quick... and not so much old as strangely timeless, a presence of ancient persisting. Not quite the sphynx. The desert perhaps. I found out later she was in her nineties. Not that you would have thought it. Satanaya seemed to be held in a private energy stream, the kind of energy within which a very self-contained child, a happy child, exists. Her movements – at one point she rose to fetch something from the desk – were smooth, as if floating in her own hover-field.

She was perfectly charming. And we talked such nonsense that afternoon. Apparently she had returned to London from somewhere in 'the Levant' to put her affairs in order. Her husband had died some years before, and now she wanted to deal with the last threads of inheritance for her extended family, whose members were, it seemed, spread across the four corners of the globe.

The conversation was a peripatetic of happy reverie, circling events *recherché*, from a world not yet altogether lost, revived in the nostalgic references and reminiscences of this strange pair. Mehmet must have been at least sixty years old at the time of our first meeting. He had emerged latterly in the London antique trade, mysterious as a rare manuscript from some arcane library of esoteric lore, yet well able to translate himself in the open parlance of that time. And Lady Satanaya? Who was she, I wondered. A greater mystery? Or none at all? Inscrutable, unthreatening, she was strangely motherly, like the Tao, 'the mother of all things'.

Later, downing pints with friends in the evening sunshine outside a pub on Portobello Road, I had to ask myself, had I been dreaming? The afternoon had passed like an old movie, intelligently scripted, considerate, and tastefully nuanced, without being mannered. Something had captured me. Not their personalities, but a quality, a presence both she and Mehmet inhabited and which drew me in. A quality of complete security, a natural certainty. A kind of quiet joy. And the food. Perhaps it was this, the happiness of the shared meals which made me return. I hungered for this. I wanted to find it's source.

I met Lady Satanaya just a few times in the next few years. A select coterie had formed around Mehmet, who held regular afternoon gatherings to which I was invited. Lady Satanaya joined us whenever she visited London. We were a motley crew who climbed the stairs and assembled in the drawing room with the yellow silk curtains, for tea and conversation: an antique dealer, a practitioner of healing, a believer in extra-terrestrial visitors, a young aristocrat with a serious drug problem, a rock empresario, and a Hollywood actress who sought enlightenment, but could only spare half an hour. Our conversation ranged from the most sublime mysteries to the ribald and ridiculous. Laughter was our leveller. I was always last to leave, then Mehmet would insist I stay for supper. He was a perfect host and on occasions, with him in the kitchen and Lady Satanaya calling suggestions from the drawing room, some extraordinary meals were enjoyed.

Though I tried often to bring the conversation round to her origins, Lady Satanaya preferred to speak of the topics of the day, occasionally referring to her recent (post-war) activities, rather than what she termed her 'ancient history'.

'Jacob, why are you *always* trying to dig up the past? Do you want to know about my lovers, is that it?' She laughed at my embarrassment. 'Well, they're all dead now, and the dead don't speak, do they? All our loves turn to dust in the end. But love itself remains. Isn't that right, Mehmet? Isn't that what you are always saying? And I shall be dust soon enough.'

She passed over her life as if it was of no importance. Perhaps at ninety years that's how it seems, but I was sure she was hiding something, some story that wanted to be told, but she wasn't letting on. Our conversation was like a friendly game of tennis where it is more congenial to continue the rally than to score points. While I freely revealed my meagre past, she only threw me crumbs: the mention of far-off cities, long dead rulers, countries which no longer existed; but only as asides while discussing a dish we might be eating, or likening something or someone to a past memory. She referred to herself variously as Circassian, Palestinian, even French, which she spoke fluently. And Turkish of course – Ottoman Turkish that is. And somewhere along the way there were South American cousins.

There was a story here, somewhere. And the urge to unravel this attracted me as much as the character herself.

Then one day I heard she had died. Shortly afterwards, a huge parcel arrived from a firm of solicitors in Paris. Inside was an ancient tinned copper cooking pot in which, wrapped in a blue woollen cloth, was a bundle of papers and letters, notebooks and diaries. Some were in Arabic script, some in Old Turkish. Most were in French. An accompanying note confirmed that the old pot and contents were from the Lady Satanaya 'for Jacob, who always enjoyed digging around in my past'.

Over the years I browsed the old manuscripts, and others that came to me in time. I learnt enough Turkish to make my way in some of the diaries. The French was easier, mostly letters with recipes, and some stories; but some of the diary entries, well, without being indiscreet, these did show Lady Satanaya to be very much a woman of the world, in fact of many worlds. But, it was all so long ago. Somewhere along the way in the many moves, the manuscripts vanished. Faded away more likely, but enough was gleaned to piece together a sort of story of memories, which seem as valid to me as any history where the players have all gone away long ago. Perhaps not simply to dust. And we hope not beyond memory. To love, perhaps – who can tell?

Jacob Merdiven de la Scala
Baños, Ecuador.

TWO

It came as fire

Convent of Seydnaya, near Damascus, Ottoman Governate of Syria, 1896

T CAME AS FIRE. It would end as light. Fire that swept away all remnant of her brief past. Light would come, as knowledge, brilliant in the end, but for the present it shone dark, invisible, deep from an unknown future.

The fire that surrounded Satanaya now, consuming her kitchen, was truly consuming all her hopes. Leaping like a mocking witch's cat, from stove to table, spilling wickedness upon the stone floor, devouring and laughing at her helplessness. She fled. Outside the kitchen door she collided with Mother Superior, fell, picked herself up and continued running until she was outside the convent. She didn't stop there, but ran on down the great steps and past the small encirclement of shops and houses, beyond, into the fields below. She didn't stop until she reached the stream, now big and brisk with early autumn rain. Only here, stepping straight into the water, did some of the heat in her begin to cool.

As Satanaya's feet began to numb in the chilly stream water and her breath calmed, she looked back over what had just happened. The kitchen was not her kitchen, but her place of work, the kitchen of the convent of Seydnaya. She wasn't even the cook. Not yet.

And that was the problem, she knew she was meant to be a cook. She had dreamt of it since she was seven years old when she had come with her mother on a pilgrimage to venerate the convent's holy icon. There she had been overcome, not by the odour of sanctity (as had her mother and all those devout ladies chattering novenas beneath the star-studded blue ceiling of the candle-lit chapel where the sacred image of the Virgin and Child, veiled beneath a cascade of *tamata*, peeped out upon the faithful) but by the sweet and savoury scents emanating from the convent kitchen. She had crept away unnoticed from beneath the congregation's fervent expressions and profuse tears, and by following her nose along the labyrinth of stone steps and passages found herself at the kitchen door.

She had stood there, gazing into an inferno of activity. The kitchen air was full of steam and smoke and the whirling flurries of flour caught in beams of sunlight sliding through a back door. Two hefty women, covered head to foot in white flour, white kerchiefs and aprons, tossed and kneaded piles of dough upon a big board. They formed little balls of dough between their plump hands, then pressed the dough balls upon a sieve and placed them on well-oiled fire-blackened trays, with an almond atop each. As a tray was filled, it was slid into the glowing cave of the wood-fired oven. Trays of cooked cakes were brought out and left to cool awhile. Then one of the hefty women with thick arms picked a saucepan from the stove and poured syrup over the cakes while they were still warm. Seeing little Satanaya standing there, eyes agog, the lady took a dish and picked out one of the smaller cakes which had expanded to the edge of the tray and lost its round shape. She called the girl over, offering the dish.

As Satanaya entered the kitchen something in her woke up.

'Yes please. What is it?'

'Cake. Try it. It's called '*kalbura bastı*', it's Turkish. It means 'pressed on the sieve'. See the little pattern it makes on the cake, from the wires in the sieve?' The cook spoke in heavily-accented Arabic, like the people in Satanaya's village.

'I think I know these – my grandmother used to make them for us.' Satanaya answered in Adige, the language of the Circassians. She broke off a little piece of the warm cake and tasted it. Her eyes lit up. 'Mmmmm, delicious. Better than...than...' she stuttered and stopped, realising her impending disloyalty. The cook smiled and they began to chat in their own language.

'It's the honey in the syrup, and we add a little ground walnuts to the mix.'

The other lady, looked on bewildered so out of politeness they switched back to speaking in Arabic.

One taste, they say, is enough. The child Satanaya stayed in the kitchen all that afternoon, watching the two hefty ladies mixing this and slicing that, and feeding her little tidbits of fried meat, oily vegetables, soft fresh bread with crispy crust, and always more cake. It was late when her mother finally caught up with her. She too had been having significant revelations of a deeply emotional kind in the little sanctuary of the holy icon, the 'Shaghoura', and had quite forgotten both the time and her little girl. Now she was relieved to find her daughter well and well-fed, enjoying the hospitality of the large and open-handed cooks of Seydnaya.

For the rest of her stay, Satanaya was completely absorbed in the activities of the kitchen. Sitting up on a high stool, she watched, and occasionally helped, the two stout and hearty ladies as they prepared endless dishes of meat and vegetables, baked bread, tasty breakfast rolls with egg in the dough and spotted with nigella seeds, buttery 'sanbusak' pastries that crumbled in the mouth, filled with cheese or mincemeat. She even tried her hand at making 'koubeh', the little egg-shaped bulgur rissoles filled with savoury lamb and pine kernels.

A week later they returned by way of Damascus, down through the Hauran, where they lodged among fellow Circassians, and on past the Sea of Galilee to Kfar Kama, by which time seven-year-old Satanaya had made up her mind to become a cook. Yes, she would become a cook with the two generously-girthed ladies in Seydnaya. She would become a cook even if it meant becoming a nun! Such are the dreams of children and youth, before nature has its sway.

Yet the dream persisted, and Satanaya, through the kind of concentrated resolution that only childlike certainty can bring to bear, eventually had her way, in spite of family objections.

Satanaya was the first child of her parents to be born in Palestine. Her father, Mansur, a Muslim, had met Gülay, a Christian, in Kayseri in central Anatolia. Both their families had fled to Turkey following the Russian purges which had driven most of the Circassian population from their tribal homelands in the Caucasus mountains. The Ottoman Sultan Hamid II had designated villages within the Empire for the resettlement of the Circassian refugees. The two families then travelled on to Palestine, to the village of Kfar Kama by the Sea of Galilee where Satanaya was born in the last days of 1881 of the common era.

Satanaya arrived in the world with a strong sense of her own being, an attitude which some interpreted as wilful or stubborn. Nowadays perhaps she would have been called a wild child. Not that she was consciously disrespectful to her parents and elders, but the demands of her nature tended to brook no opposition. When the young Satanaya saw the village boys riding horses, she had to ride too. No one could convince her that a girl should be content to spend her time in the house. When her father caved in and gave her a small pony, she was off from dawn to dusk, exploring far and wide, and causing her mother to curse her for a Cossack for the worry she caused.

But the fire that consumed Satanaya now, temporarily extinguished as she stood in the waters of the stream, was no simple kitchen fire to be dowsed so easily. That fire of the cooking hearth, in submission to the hand of the cook for the transformation of the raw ingredients into the finished dish was but a shadow of the fire that sparked inside Satanaya. For her heart had become the crucible of an elemental descent from pure light, where the base ore of her ignorance could be refined to the pure gold of self-knowledge.

The fire had not begun in the kitchen. Where then? Was it kindled in those moments of dissatisfaction that arose when the girl began to bloom, as her mother had before her, into the perfect flower of Cherkess woman-hood? When she first felt the pleasure of lying alone among the sweet smelling grasses and wild flowers of the meadow, her body warmed by the sun and feeling the earth's pull; knitting, weaving, threading its quickening energies through her skin and into her blood, warmth which flowed up from the soles of her feet and mingled with her breath somewhere between her chest and her stomach, gently, until her whole being bathed in tender delight.

Initially her malaise was towards her sisters. For the first time in her life, their childishness really bothered her. Oh yes, they had been annoying before. Always. Those raggedy scamps running and screaming about the place, crying at the least inconvenience, though she loved them for that. Now she felt irritated by their noisy boisterousness, by their innocent, inconsequential banter, their mess, their inability to recognise boundaries. Simply, their presence. It impinged on… what? That deliciousness of lying in the field, cocooned in the feeling of herself alone. Her gorgeous solitude. When she barked at them to shut up, her mother Gülay noticed the differ-ence in her tone. She gazed fondly at her eldest daughter, and remembered days among the Bulgarian rose fields, lying in the soft Balkan soil heated by the summer sun, when she too had woken to this connection with her body, with earth, and the changes that inevitably ensued.

But her frustration was not limited to petty sibling annoyances. Although she was happy helping her mother in the little kitchen in Kfar Kama her thoughts harked back to Seydnaya, and she began her pestering again. What Satanaya didn't know was that Gülay and the Mother Supe-rior, and Seydnaya's now aging cook, had kept in contact since that day seven years earlier when Satanaya had tasted the hefty ladies' sweet flour and semolina 'kalbura bastı' cakes topped with almonds and drenched rose-scented honey syrup. It had been agreed and arranged. Satanaya was to become apprenticed to the old cook. No mention was made of her taking the nun's habit. With three daughters, and no sons as yet, while Gülay accepted the practical necessity of one less mouth to feed, and though sad to lose her young companion, she knew Satanaya would learn a good trade which would only improve her marriage prospects.

For the past two years Satanaya had taken her place blissfully before the preparation tables, the big ovens and kitchen range of the convent, and she worked as hard as the two hefty ladies. The Circassian cook was called

Beulah, a name given her by an old Jewish midwife, as she had been one of the first Circassians to be born in Palestine. Her sister-in-law Ayşe was most likely a muslim but nobody seemed to know, or care, as she regularly lit candles and prayed before the icon of the Virgin and Child. For it is widely accepted among knowledgeable people of the latterly bloomed third of the single stemmed tri-floral faith that comprises the people of Moses, Jesus and Mohammed, that both Mary and her son Jesus are sainted prophets.*

But what of this fire that threatened to consume, not just the kitchens of Seydnaya, but the fabric of Satanaya herself? Simply put, Satanaya was in love. Well, the prurient might call it lust, but for all the pure and innocent virgins of the world, when cupid's arrow falls, it scores equally on the animal soul as upon heart. If this were not so, the indivisible light of pure beauty appearing in the diversity of humankind might never have descended below the sphere of the angels and gone forth into the mud of earthly existence and multiplied. But it did and it has and for Satanaya she is about to gain her first taste of what it means to become a daughter of time.

---

* A tradition states that when Mohammed entered the Ka'aba and ordered the removal of all the idols therein, the prophet placed his hand over the ikon of the Virgin and child Jesus, both an act of endearment, of affection, whilst at the same time hiding from view the shocking fact of similarity between the features of Christ and Mohammed, a metaphorical similitude stemming perhaps from their brotherhood as envoys of God; and the Virgin herself arising forty generations from the bosom of Abraham, however distant a cousin to Mohammed, yet in essence so close.

THREE

The Young Goatherd

Seydnaya, Syria

HE YOUNG GOATHERD who brought the milk each day to the convent's kitchen door was so far as we are aware no relation of the noble goatherds of Mount Kassioun (one of whom, with his billy-errant, Shams the Goat, by valiant self-sacrifice brought peace to the flock and prosperity to the convent of Seydnaya in hard times long ago). Nonetheless, he was a boy of some heart, good looks, and surprisingly clean habits for a lusty young goatherd. And although it was some time before Satanaya fully comprehended the import of his leaning and lingering by the old Cyprus tree, chewing on a stalk of grass, with his pretty Canaan puppy playing at his feet, during and after delivering the daily supply of milk to the kitchen, when the piastre dropped it was too late to prevent the inevitable.

To begin with, passing the time of day with this interesting creature who was neither a woman nor a nun, Satanaya found herself enjoying the same warm feelings she had experienced lying in the fields by Galilee's shore; and the same stored heat of the sun now penetrated her body as she leant against the old stone walls by the kitchen door.

It wasn't so long before she was taking walks in her free time. If she saw the goatherd, with his flocks, away on some distant hillside, she noticed her mood would change from anticipation to happy excitement. Soon she found herself seeking him out on her walks. In time she simply went to where she knew he would pass. And he would greet her, and she would answer.

On a warm summer's evening, a few weeks after their first meeting, Satanaya was sitting waiting for the goatherd to come by. It was a hillside out of view of the convent, yet high enough to watch the sunset when the land around was already in shadow. The boy came by as expected with his herd of dark reddish-brown, shaggy-coated Damascus goats. This time he stopped, came over and sat down near her.

'It's my favourite place to watch the sunset,' Satanaya said.

'Me too. I often come by here. I love it here.'

He paused, then very quietly as if in confidence, he said, 'Sometimes, when it's very quiet, I hear songs.'

'What do you mean, songs? who sings these songs?'

'I don't know, they're just out there, and they come to me. I hear them. Then I remember them and sing them to myself during the day.'

'Couldn't you write them down?' said Satanaya. She had been taught to write and read by her father and imagined everyone could read and write.

The goatherd looked a little puzzled. 'Why?'

'So you don't forget them.'

He laughed, and studied her with his big dark eyes, dark and wide as the kid goat nuzzling the bag hanging from his shoulder.

Then he became serious. 'I don't forget them.' he said. 'Why should I forget them? I wouldn't forget you, now I've seen you, would I? How could I forget you? I might just as easily forget myself. No, once the song arrives, it stays.'

Satanaya thought he was funny, but she liked him too.

'Ha ha! I bet you say that to all the girls,' she teased.

Yusuf looked upset at her words, so she softened and said, 'will you sing me a song? That way I'll know you won't forget me. And I'll not forget you.' This time it was Satanaya who with her deep blue Circassian eyes gazed at the boy, his face tinged golden brown in the evening sunlight and she felt herself drifting in the comfortable earth of her being.

The boy shaded his eyes and peered towards the sun, now low above the distant hills. Then he began to sing in gentle lilting tones:

swallows dancing the valley skies
searching for a place to nest
when the bitter weather ends
will they find a place to rest?

swallows searching the hills below
waiting for the snow to go
only where the valley's warm
will I bring my babies home

swallows diving in the evening light
catching insects in their flight
when they're strong enough to fly
my babies leave me by and by...

He had a beautiful voice, soft and deep. He trailed off his singing in the last verse, his voice getting quieter and quieter. The sun had set and night was falling.

'It's late. I must go. What's your name?'

'I'm Satanaya.'

'What a strange name. Where does it come from?'

'It's Circassian. It's a flower, and a long story, too long to tell now. I must get back also,' and she ran off a little way down the slope, stopped, and called back, 'Hey, I don't know your name.'

'Yusuf. I've got a lot of brothers.'

She laughed and turned back to the convent, leaving the night to the goatherd calling his dogs, and the bells of the goats clanging through the valleys.

And so it went. The meetings on hillside. The gradual step by delicious step of falling in love. And as the slow revealing of colour accompanies the growing warmth of spring, so too their relationship was accompanied with tentative contact. A brushing of hands when Yusuf offered her his water flask one evening produced an effect in Satanaya not dissimilar to that sweet cake, *kalbura bastı*. Not content with a mere glancing touch, the next time they met, she took both his hands. She then repeated what her father had once told her:

'Look at your hands,' she said, and traced with her finger on his palms, the lifeline, the head line and the line of the heart, which formed the Arabic numerals – ١٨ and ٨١ – in his right and left hands, cut through from top to bottom with the line of destiny, the past and the future present in both hands.

'You see, look at the lines, mirrored in your hands. 18 and 81, making 99, the sacred number of the Names of God. 'Now join your hands – all the opposites disappear in one hand – is it right? or left?'

Yusuf had never learnt to read, and blushed in the face of Satanaya's cleverness.

'But you know,' he said, 'there is a hundredth name, that only the camel knows,' and he placed his hands in hers. 'Maybe it's hidden in there, when we hold our hands, and it escapes when we let go.'

Neither spoke for a while as each wondered on this hidden name. Satanaya broke the silence.

'Anyway, the point is, I was born in 1881, which father said is a year of great significance. At the end of the year, on the cusp of the sign of the horse and the goat. He said I have the fire of the untamed horse, and the stubborn determination of the goat.'

'To me you are like a bird, a beautiful bird that flies free.'

Then Yusuf let go her hands and closed his eyes tightly. Satanaya looked at him.

'What's wrong?' she asked.

'Nothing. I don't know. It's just, well, I hear a song, it's so beautiful, and yet its so sad.'

'Then don't sing it to me. I feel happy.' She squeezed his hand, and the boy opened his eyes and smiled.

'You're still here!' he said

'Of course I am, what did you expect?' she laughed at him.

'Nothing, it's just... the song... oh never mind.' And they sat there holding hands until the sun had disappeared beyond the distant Jebel Lubnan, and then they parted.

How did Satanaya know she was falling in love? Very simple. In the late summer, when all the she-goats gave birth and the hills were resounding to the bleating of the newborn kids, the young goatherd Yusuf accompanied all the other herders and their flocks into the high pastures many days distant. For weeks and weeks there was no sign of him. She still came out to their favourite meeting places. She would lie in the warm grass, enjoying the sun's caress and recalling his image. She found herself humming his songs, picturing herself together with him, talking to him, making scenarios where they were doing everything together. Every time she brought his face to mind she felt a kind of bliss.

When he finally did return, one evening at the end of September, and she saw him bringing his flock round the hillside just before sunset, she let out a tiny squeal, jumped up and ran towards him. Yusuf, who was still a shy lad, didn't run, but his face lit up in a way she had never seen before, brimming with happiness. He caught her in his arms and hugged her tightly, humming the melody of the song of the swallows, holding her close, cheek pressed to cheek, just as she had seen him hug the little kid goats that had lost their mothers, and stroking her back as if to calm her. And then he started kissing her, gently, near her ear at first, on her neck, then her cheek. He was shy, but finally he let his lips graze hers. She held herself still, wanting him to leave his lips on hers, and for a brief moment – oh how do we talk about this first kiss, this impossibly delicate meeting of sweetest intimacy, the breath to breath, soul to soul, of first love, of spirit meeting itself in the mirror of another? For a brief moment as time submitted to love, that kiss took on the mantle of eternity, and for all and in eternity it would remain, no matter what time tried to hide in its dark cupboards of forgetfulness.

The bells from Seydnaya rang out over the now-dark valley. Those two in love lingered, bodies close, sharing the lovely scent of each other's skin, pulling themselves apart, only to embrace again, until Satanaya took a deep breath and ran off, fearful of being locked out of the convent at night.

What had begun as gentle warmth in the spring had become a flame in autumn. A single thought now possessed Satanaya, to gaze forever into the deep brown eyes of her Yusuf, to hear his songs of snows and swallows, to be held in his arms and feel his sweet breath mingling with hers.

But it was not to be. It would have been hard, nay, impossible, for their trysts to remain secret, as they would wish – they were both young and naturally shy, and would be embarrassed should their feelings for each other become public knowledge. Marriage was far from their thoughts. But love, first love, possesses a quality of absoluteness, a sense of an immeasurable vastness in which time as we know it disappears.

A nun whose task it was to bring in the washing strung from the high flat roofs of the convent, had noticed young Satanaya's evening walks and her regular disappearance behind the same hill, and the subsequent approach of the goatherd from the opposite direction, he also vanishing from view, and neither of the pair emerging as one might hope, or expect, within a respectably brief interval.

In fact, the intervals had become longer and longer, until the day of the young goatherd's return, the very day of this historic timeless kiss. The conscientious lady of the cloth, frustrated perhaps at her own inability to find amorous satisfaction in the interior life, or maybe she was just a thoughtless gossip, this strict observer could not bear the suspense and set out at sunset to spy upon them.

Rounding the hillside where she has seen the couple disappear, by now almost in darkness, the dark-habited spy came bang up behind a huge black billy-goat having its way with a silky-haired female of his harem. At that instant the billy neighed loudly as he descended the rump of the she-goat. The observant nun saw only what she wanted to see. Her fervid imagination transposed the subjects of this animal coupling into the objects of her own expectation, those innocents in love, Yusuf and Satanaya. Now she really believed heaven had fallen and the very fires of perdition made manifest just beyond the holy gates of Seydnaya. She ran back to the convent and blurted out to all and sundry that the little kitchen maid had been taken by the evil horned devil himself.

The story reached Mother Superior's ears. A wise lady, and not one to be fooled by emotional outbursts and unbridled imaginations, she brought her distracted crew under control with a decree of silence for that night, delivering to the informant a withering lecture on the dangers to the soul in prying into other's affairs and giving her a purifying penance of Stations of the Cross with immediate effect.

Satanaya, floating within the blissful nimbus of that kiss, returned to the kitchen to find Beulah the cook supervising the novices serving supper in silence. The quiet of the convent was soothing after her earlier excitement. Alone with the washing up, she scrubbed away merrily, unaware of anything untoward.

Yusuf meanwhile was experiencing a strange homecoming of his own. One of his brothers had noticed him often coming in late of an evening, and had also decided that day to follow him and see what he was up to. From an opposite hill in the west, hidden from the couple's sight by the lowering sun and the fact that these two had eyes for none but each other, Yusuf's brother spied their embrace with concern and some degree of envy.

Yusuf's family were nomad goat herders, Kurds who had drifted south from their Anatolian tribal lands in search of pastures new. Over the years the convent's own herds had grown considerably, so when that mysterious figure Daud the Arwadi, of whom much has been written elsewhere, had grown too old to make the yearly trek from his home above Damascus on Mount Kassioun to arrange the herd's tupping, the Kurds had taken on that role.

It was a lucrative contract for which they received half of the herd's produce: kids, milk, skins etc., a contract for life, it seemed, and one which meant the Kurds could look forward to a secure settled existence in their new home. They bought land in a nearby village and built a house, and began making solid alliances within the local Kurdish community, marrying off their numerous sons and daughters, so that Yusuf's father could now call himself a tribal sheykh.

Yusuf lifted the latch to the door of his family's cottage and entered. Inside it was silent. A fire burned in the hearth where the evening meal bubbled gently. His family sat still on the low cushions which lined the walls. No one was speaking. His mother was not to be seen.

'Here you are at last,' his father hissed, as he rose and grabbed Yusuf by his collar. 'So, you think you can go and mess with the ladies of the convent do you, like some randy goat. I'll show you.'

In the corner of the room, the informant brother grinned. 'Give him the stick, father, like when you break in horses.'

'Who does he think he is to ruin our business with the nuns?' said another brother.

'He'll find out soon enough when he has to fend for himself.' said a third.

It was evident that the family had already heard the informant's evidence and passed judgement on the affair in Yusuf's absence. His protestations went unheard. The sons cheered as their father administered a brutal thrashing such as angry, uneducated men give to animals they feel compelled to dominate.

The father's arm eventually tired of beating. He threw the stick into a corner and spoke with bitterness.

'Now, get out of my sight. Tomorrow you go to Damascus, and you won't show your face back here unless I send for you. Now go!'

The boy was too shocked to argue with his father. And his brothers just laughed at him. They had never understood this gentle soul. Yusuf was a soft one, they said, and now he was out of the way, their slices of the inheritance would undoubtedly increase.

It was a dejected young lad who, before daybreak, saddled the oldest donkey in the stable and set off on the road to Damascus. As his weeping mother bade him farewell, she told him of an old relative of hers, a curer of furs and hides and a drum maker, a dervish who kept a shop in the Street of the Apothecaries, who would look after him.

Poor Yusuf. His world had collapsed and he was broken, not just by the beating, not even by being banished from the family but by the thought that he would no more see Satanaya. He had been forbidden to pass near the convent, and as he looked back and saw the high walls receding slowly in the distance, his heart cried out. Now the saddest of farewell songs arrived to his ears, but whenever he opened his mouth to bring it to tune, he only choked on his tears. But he remembered the words and sang it often in the years to come.

We kissed but once and then we parted
held our hearts out to each other
embraced in love upon the hillside
such a kiss I'll ever savour

May all our first loves be our best loves
first and best before the rest love
what befalls us from now on love
let it never come between us

Driven from my home and mother
Cast aside by father, brothers
I shall roam the whole world over
knowing that my heart once knew her

Satanaya is my first love
Satanaya you're my last love
Better to have loved and lost you
Even if my life it's cost me.

There was more to this song, which came to him in time. Not all of it was doom and gloom, nor was it unfavourable to the poor, heartbroken, young goatherd, but he was too miserable to pick up on it then. The wind blew upon his back and covered his departing tracks with the dust of the day.

FOUR

Kazan Dibi – Burnt Bottom Pudding

Seydnaya, Syria

 DREAM IS NOT ALWAYS TRUE. Unless its truth is in its opposite, as a mirror which shows the image reversed. That night Satanaya went to bed still ignorant of the thunderheads rising upon the near horizon of her destiny. She closed her eyes holding in her memory the image of Yusuf's gentle face, and the scent of their sweet embrace. She dreamed of her love with his eyes dark as deep water, his strong encircling arms, his soft cheeks, and she drowned in the annihilating breath that came with the touch of his lips upon hers. The barest touch, but it was a flash of lightning whose spark struck deep, and she vanished into fathomless sleep.

All next day she breezed along, carrying out her duties in that light-

21

ness that new love brings. In late afternoon she went to their accustomed trysting spot. She waited and waited, and when the sun went and he still didn't come, she began to fret. Why was he not there? Was he alright? Why is he late? Maybe he is hurt. Then, as darkness fell and she was wondering whether to wait any longer, a figure emerged from the gloom towards her. 'Yusuf at last,' her heart leapt and she rose to meet him. But wait. Was it him? The figure looked like Yusuf, but something wasn't right. She stopped and started to back off.

'So, little girl, you like goatherds do you? I'm afraid Yusuf's gone and he won't be coming back. But I'm here instead. Why don't you come here and give me a kiss, and something else maybe…'

Satanaya was shocked. It was one of Yusuf's elder brothers. She had seen him before, bringing cheese to the convent with his father at Easter. She had thought at the time the goat cheese had smelt pretty strong. Now as he approached, she realised it had been the smell of this man, a sour old goatstink fellow, not the cheese, and not at all like her sweet smelling Yusuf. This odour made her want to throw up. She panicked and she turned to run away. Confused and afraid, Satanaya stumbled and in an instant the man grabbed hold of her.

'Come here, girl. You had my baby brother, so why not me? I'm a real man. After all, now he's been sent away, it would be a pity to waste all this.'

She felt his arm tighten around her, moving south and gripping her behind. That was it. Enough!

'No!' she screamed. The indomitable spirit of her Circassian name-sake, Satanaya heroine of the Nart sagas, awakened. No longer was she just a little girl playing in the meadow. In a flash she understood that she was a woman, and not a plaything. She knew what to do.

'No!' she cried again, then, twisting round: knee to the groin, nails to the face, fingers in the eyes and push. It was a game she had played with the Arab girls in Kfar Kama, called, 'How to deal with your brother's friends.' But this was no game. Somehow, as if possessed of a power not her own, she found the strength necessary to heave the man away from her. Then she ran. She ran like the wind that comes down from the high forests of the Caucasus and storms across the Black Sea coast, battering and blowing and making fisherman afraid. She ran until she reached the back door of the convent. Only there, within the safety of the cloister did she turn around to look, but no one was following her.

The next week was hell for Satanaya. The autumn rain arrived unseasonably early, and for days it poured down. Within Satanaya the waters of her heart poured out: first tears, so many tears, then worry, anger, worry, fury at that brother, worry, concern: 'Oh my Yusuf… where have you gone, why don't you come…' she cried to herself. And self-pity: 'If this is love, I don't want this. No. no. no. I want to go back to how it was before, just walking on the hillside, lying in the grass alone.'

But love is not all sweetness and light, and Satanaya was just beginning to discover other faces to this mystery. Yet, even with the worry, the anger, the confusion, and a big purple and yellow bruise on her backside where the brute had grabbed her, she still found herself returning to love, to the memory, to the face, to the breath, and she would find herself imagining that moment when all the pain, all the awkward separation would fall away. But the moment never came, and she would end up caught in a longing that threatened to eat her up; that hollow pain stabbing her from deep below the ribs, that desperate hunger of the soul when it has been ripped by love, torn by separation from home, from family, from the object of desire, from all that made her whole. In the end though, it was too much, it had come too quickly, she had been unprepared and it showed. Her work in the kitchen began to suffer, pots were left to boil dry, she put too much salt in a dish, or none at all; the bread wouldn't rise, the yogurt wouldn't set, the mayonnaise curdled and the curd cheese wouldn't separate from the whey and float in big fat lumps as it ought.

And then the fire. Oil in a pan, a big, old *kazan*, left untended over the flame. Satanaya had been drying the aubergine slices before frying them, standing by the kitchen window. She was watching swallows dive and skim the air by the big old cypress tree, and for an instant she caught a scent, a shred of a song on the breeze: *'when they're strong enough to fly my babies leave me by and by…'* At that point she smelt burning. She turned around to find the pan aflame. She rushed over, grabbed the handle to move it outside, but in her hurry she tripped. The burning oil spilt across the stove and onto the table. Flames from the open range leapt up, and in seconds a conflagration had begun. Satanaya screamed. Her feet were burning, but she had enough presence of mind to grab the sand bucket and throw it over the table to stop the fire spreading. Then she fled, almost knocking over Mother Superior on her way out. And that was how she found herself stood, trembling, in the pouring rain, up to her knees in water, letting the cool flow of the stream ease the pain of her burned feet.

By the time Mother Superior arrived, Satanaya was sitting on a rock, her skirts up over her knees, both feet still immersed, drowned in the light reflections of the rushing torrent.

'I suppose it wouldn't interest you to know that the fire is now out?' said the nun.

Satanaya looked up. She didn't know what to say. The shock of the fire, her burns, it had knocked something right out of her. She just stared, and mumbled, 'I'm sorry, really, I am.'

'Look, these things happen. But they can't go on happening. Something has to change. It's up to you. I understand there was something between you and the boy who brings the milk – what's his name, the Kurd's son... Yusuf?'

Satanaya was about to protest, but hearing his name spoken, she burst into tears. The elderly nun was firm, but solicitous.

'Whatever may or may not have happened – and I suspect very little actually did happen – it has caused something of a disturbance, both in the convent, and with the Kurdish family. Now, some choices have to be made. The family have sent the boy away – they don't want to lose their contract with us; but more than that, the old man's pride is hurt at the thought of one of his sons getting involved with a Christian. If indeed you are a Christian – I've never been quite sure.'

Here Mother Superior paused.

'As I said, choices. If you go back to your family, I understand a marriage is almost arranged, so with the skills you've learnt here, you would make a very sought-after bride. As for remaining with us – well, I have a job to do, and something like this does upset the general temper of the place, which is, after all, for quiet contemplation and retreat. Not that occasionally a little thunder and lightning doesn't help to keep us in touch with reality. But now I hear that one of the old Kurd's sons is spreading stories about you, which, if they were true – and I'm quite certain they are not – there would need to be at least dozen Satanayas roaming the hills between here and Maloullah to account for all the accusations of goatherd seductions being levelled at you.'

Satanaya's face now wore a look of such indignation as would have felled a tree.

'He would have raped me!'

'Ha! Yes, I did notice the scratches on his face,' Mother Superior laughed. 'He claims he was fighting off a wild marten that was attacking one of his young kids.'

'Well, he should have known better than to mess with a Circassian girl.'

'So you see, your remaining here has its complications. There's another possibility, temporary perhaps, but who knows? An old friend of ours who lives outside Beirut. She has a small farm, entertains a lot of guests. I'm sure she would be able to make use of a strong young girl who can cook – more or less. Although a little less salt, and more attention to controlling the fire – of the hearth and the heart – would not go amiss. Now go back in and have cook attend to those feet. We'll speak again when you're better.'

It was only afterwards that Satanaya thought what a strange and wonderful conversation it had been. Her burned feet had taken her mind off her broken heart, and now Mother Superior's words had taken her mind off the awful burns. She spent most of the next week in her room, being tended by the hefty cook Beulah who dressed her wounds, applying cooling salves and wrapping her feet in healing herbs.

While she convalesced, she thought things over and over. She'd burnt her bridges here at Seydnaya, literally. She didn't want to go home, not now. There would be too many questions asked. And besides, she only had marriage to look forward to there. That was her mum's plan, for sure. Her father, well, he had a different understanding about life. He always respected Satanaya's will in serious matters; it had been he who had agreed to her request to come to Seydnaya in the first place, and her mother was only persuaded because of the honour of having her child accepted in this prestigious convent. That she was only a cook's assistant had been no matter. But marriage? To someone she barely knew, if at all? This had never been part of Satanaya's plan. No. The farm outside Beirut, with this mysterious old friend of Mother Superior – and as it happened, a friend of the cook herself – sounded much more interesting. She knew she would have to face her family eventually, but that would come later.

FIVE

Exit, Pursued by a Cooking Pot

Seydnaya, Syria

HEN SATANAYA WAS well enough to travel, Mother Superior summoned her to her quarters, high up in the fortress convent. The view from there gave out over the village and pastures below, across a wide valley, yellow in autumnal dryness, to blue hills beyond.

She climbed the stone staircase and knocked on the broad oak door.

'Come in.'

The apartment was a very simple affair, just a living room with a desk beneath a window and a small area for sleeping curtained off against a far wall. The old nun sat in a small straight-backed armchair, and beckoned with a wave of her hand to the other chair.

'Come in, dear, and sit down. I heard from cook that you are much better, and have been considering the Beirut option. I wanted to hear it from your own lips so I thought we'd have a little chat. Now, how do you like your tea?'

On a low table between the chairs was a small brass samovar and a tray laid with tea things and some cake. Mother Superior poured a little strong, dark tea into each glass from the pot atop the samovar, and topped up with hot water.

'Sugar? Two?'

Satanaya nodded nervously. She had never been served by any of the nuns, and certainly never invited to tea by Mother Superior.

'And cake? It's seedcake, my favourite. Well, you know that, of course. You probably made it yourself. It's quite delicious.'

Satanaya smiled and began to relax. 'Thank you.' she said, taking a piece. She had indeed made the cake. Cook had shown her how, and now she made one cake every week which was put in a tin and taken away. She had always wondered where it went.

'So, Beirut it is then?'

'Yes... I really thought about it a lot. I even went to the icon and prayed. After that, well, it just became clear. I could see myself in Beirut, cooking and working in the garden. Cooking all the things I learnt here and more. Cook tells me the lady has wonderful gardens there, with all kinds of vegetables and fruit; and fish are brought up from the coast. But she only keeps three or four goats, so there isn't need of a goatherd. I just don't feel ready to return to Kfar Kama just yet...'

'Look, my dear Satanaya, if you are still thinking about the young man, well, that is quite natural. But you are an intelligent girl. You must know that's over. He has been sent far away, and if my instincts are right, he will not be coming back. That kind... well, he had that faraway look in his eyes. I met him too, a number of times. A lovely lad, handsome – but a dreamer, certainly. It would be a very long time before he settled down into what you would consider suitable husband material. If ever. He has a poet's soul, and will be a wanderer. If he's lucky, he'll make his way eventually, find a trade, make a small living, but for now he is quite raw, and needs much cooking.'

Satanaya looked down. Try as she might to control her feelings, at the mention of Yusuf, tears began to well in her eyes. Although she dearly wanted to pour her heart out to someone, she was too shy, in awe even, of

Mother Superior. She felt all tied up inside and couldn't find the words.

'Wha… wha—' she began, but instead of speech came a pitiful wail and floods of tears.

Mother Superior, in spite of her firm reputation, was the soul of compassion when it came to understanding another's pain. She beckoned the weeping girl to her and embraced her fondly as any mother.

'There, there. Let it all out. You know crying is the soul's way of growing, as long as we know when to stop. Tears for love will burn away your shortcomings.' Satanaya began to relax. The nun hugged Satanaya again and giving her a handkerchief, smiled. 'Now, tell me, what is it you want to say?'

'What I don't understand, Mother Superior,' said Satanaya, wiping her eyes and gazing out through the window to the distant hills, 'is, just what happened. One minute I was happy in the kitchen. I really loved it, you have no idea, I didn't mind the work at all, even though it was really hard when we had a lot of visitors. I loved being in the middle of all the wonderful smells and tastes, and seeing the food all plattered up and going out looking so beautiful. And when Yusuf came, he completely took over my mind. I couldn't think of anything else but him. It was also wonderful, just like the cooking. In fact I enjoyed the cooking even more then. I was so happy.' She stopped and looked down at her hands. Then she turned and looked directly at Mother Superior.

'Was it love? Was it really love? Because if it is love, then how can it stop just like that. I wanted to love him forever, for always. So why does it hurt inside so much? When I used to think of him I was so happy. Now it just hurts.' Satanaya's tears were flowing again, a silent, sobbing stream pouring from her blue eyes as she looked helplessly at the old lady opposite her.

'Love. Ah! yes, love… Love…' Mother Superior repeated slowly, and closed her eyes for some moments, as if gathering herself in some deep place within.

'Love is such a big thing. And we are so small. How can we understand this? If we open ourselves to Love, we are opening up to something very big. If we are to reach its full measure, we must expect to be expanded with it. When we are given a little taste, too often we want to keep it within this small place. We call it ours, and we try to make it into something it isn't. But it can't all fit into a small place. So when the person we love is no longer with us, we think love has gone. That's when love stretches us, that's when we feel the pain of love.

'But does it have to hurt so much?' asked Satanaya.

'Love moves us, it makes us grow from the inside. Something new is being born in you now. Like a seed breaking open and pushing through the earth. Of course it's not easy. It's your soul being born. You do understand what I mean by soul?'

Satanaya nodded. Her father had often spoken of such things, but her understanding was vague.

'I think so, sort of,' she hesitated. 'Doesn't it have to do with things deep inside me, to do with my feelings, how I comprehend the world, how I see myself?'

'In a way, yes.'

'But what has love got to do with it? '

'Love is the soul's food. Look, we plant a seed, and when the sun comes a plant grows. If we deny it proper nourishment, will it come to bloom? We are not so different. Life is a journey for our souls. Once we begin, we need to keep on to the end. Love will always move us forward if we let it. As you've discovered, it isn't always easy.'

'Yes,' said Satanaya, 'but what *is it*?' Satanaya was feeling confused. The idea of love, once she began to think about it, seemed veiled by some opaque sky of emotion. Nothing was fixed or certain anymore in her mind.

Mother Superior sighed patiently, picked up her tea and sipped slowly before continuing:

'Look, before we can really talk about love, we need to ask ourselves, "who is this that is loving?". "Satanaya", you say, "It is Satanaya who is loving." And what is Satanaya loving? What it is that you loved in this boy. Is it real? Is it that big thing, the thing that is not limited by this lovely face, his body, even the presence of this boy? If so then his absence will not take away the joy, that sense of wholeness and homecoming you felt being with him. We have to discover what is the real object of our love. But for that Satanaya has to become as big as love itself. Satanaya has to find her wholeness.'

A sudden sense of vastness began to overwhelm Satanaya, as when the clouds part and light enters. She had stopped crying and was concentrating on Mother Superior's words, trying to take in this idea that love wasn't just something she felt for her young goatherd, which ended when he was

gone; that it was there all the time, just as the sky was always present in its
vastness.

Mother Superior continued: 'You two were mirrors for each other, for
your souls to grow. But while discovering yourselves, you were overcome
by the other's image. You loved a boy, a beautiful boy, but could he return
that love? He was so young, lost in his songs, lost in the beauty he saw in a
young girl; he wasn't big enough to stand up against his father, his family,
his tribe. He couldn't provide you with the kind of mirror that Satanaya
needs for her own heart to grow.'

Mother Superior stopped, sensing that Satanaya had something to say,
but was finding it difficult. Eventually, blushing all the while, Satanaya
spoke.

'You know, we kissed. And something happened. This feeling through
my whole body. I don't know how to explain, but it was extraordinary. I felt
I was floating. All the edges to myself seemed to disappear. And the feeling
remained with me for ages.'

The old nun smiled. 'Now, you are young,' she said. 'Your body is
becoming a woman. Your feelings are strong – that is natural – stronger
than your mind at times. And when those feelings are there, everything
inside you is pulled to earth, while your heart is flying in the seven heavens.
It is natural. Do I need to spell it out to you?'

Satanaya blushed again as she made the connection, and something of
her innocence fell away.

'So that is also love?' she said.

Mother Superior laughed.

'Of course, and it has a purpose. There are parts of a person that are
not there when we are born, that come later, as we grow up. I don't need to
explain: you've seen animals, how they breed, and produce more animals.
It is necessary. We have that in us and it is a part of love too, a very important part, it helps connect us fully to this earth which supports our bodies,
and connects us to each other. How else would we learn to care for each
other? Without this human-animal love, we humans would disappear
from the earth.'

'So, falling in love is natural then.' Satanaya smiled at the realisation.

'Why not? When we fall in love, shouldn't our bodies fall in love too?
And when bodies fall in love, they long for each other, long to become one
with each other. Then when they separate, they feel pain, like the pain you

are feeling right now. But this is temporary. This is the love we call passion. It binds us all together: families, lovers, children and parents. And it is why death is painful to those left behind. We are all held together by the actions we share, everything we do in time and in this world we live in. Really, Satanaya, it's good that you look at this now, while you are still so young, so you will not be disappointed too often in the future. You will be disappointed, I assure you, but hopefully you will learn to see the signs and let love move you on quickly to a bigger perspective.'

Mother Superior stopped speaking, picked up her plate with its slice of seed cake and ate a small piece. She took a long sip of tea and replaced her glass on the table. She looked carefully at the young girl before her. Was the cup of her soul full yet? The thirsty look in Satanaya's eyes told her to continue.

'Romantic love is what joins these two things, the love of your body, to the love of your heart; but the love of the heart brings an added joy that goes beyond the pleasure of the kiss. And it brings light beyond the fire that comes with the embrace of bodies trying so hard to be one, but that union is subject to time and always falling apart in the end. Romantic love, true love, the love of the heart – this can lead to another kind of love altogether, as long as it doesn't become tied to one particular form. But this is a long road and not an easy one, and everyone isn't prepared to go on that journey. This is love's own journey to itself.'

Satanaya was no longer simply listening with her mind. Something had woken in her that was hearing beyond the mere words; as if she was somehow tasting what they were talking about. She couldn't explain to herself this idea of love's journey to itself, but somehow she knew this to be true.

'So, love is here all the time.' Satanaya said, 'even right here now, in this room.' She looked around, amazed, as if seeing the walls for the first time, newly formed and strangely alive. 'So, is everything here for love?'

'Yes, the love of the heart. The heart too has its dimensions. What we think of as our heart, our loving heart, is barely a heart at all, it's mostly the reflections of strong feelings and emotions in our mind which produce effects in the body. Most of these desires are our own creations. But it's what we have to work with, and they point to a heart of greater, even *great* dimensions. This great heart is not just loving, but it is a knowing heart. It too desires, but unlike our little heart which yearns for this person or that thing or idea, this heart's desire is total, and not partial; so its love is complete.'

Although much of Mother Superior's speech went over her head, it had carried something, a certain sense that, while not easy to grasp with her mind, nonetheless went some way to ease the pain Satanaya felt. Perhaps it was simply the kindness with which the old nun spoke, how she opened her heart to the young girl, a heart that was certainly full of this bigger love. Satanaya left no longer worrying, and perhaps just a little less in hopeless agony over her first failed attempt at love. But no. Not failed, she told herself. It was what it was. It had something real to it: a taste, a glimpse.

She was not yet ready for the full onslaught of love.

The day of Satanaya's departure from the convent dawned heavy with clouds, certain of imminent rain. Wearing the heavy woollen shawl her mother had made, Satanaya stood looking at her pitifully small swag, the sum of life so far – a few clothes, some jottings of recipes and notes on ingredients from her two years in the convent kitchen.

A bold knock at the door, and Beulah the cook entered the room.

'Now you didn't think you'd escape without saying goodbye, did you?' said the cook, beaming, 'especially as I've got a little present for you.'

Beulah handed over a fat notebook and a pile of handwritten papers, some with food stains, all evidently well-thumbed. Satanaya was stunned. This was the kitchen's holy writ, that Satanaya had been forbidden to touch. It was kept on a high shelf for the use of the initiates only. To be handed this manuscript was akin to being anointed into a priesthood. She was speechless.

Then from behind her back the cook produced a partly-blackened cooking pot, the very one in which Satanaya had been about to fry the aubergines when her world caught fire little more than a week ago.

'I've had the inside re-tinned, and cleaned it as best as I was able. It belonged to the cook who trained me. Her name was Takla, and this was her favourite pot. She said someone would come for it one day, she was certain of that, and I was to keep it, and her cookbook, for that person. She called it her lucky pot, it was a wedding present from the Cairene, an old Egyptian gentleman she called her *'usta'*, her master. She said her stews always came out tasting better when she used this pot.'

The pot seemed nothing in particular. It was what they call in Turkish a *kazan*, made of copper, about 15 inches in diameter at the top, and flaring out to maybe 18 inches or more at the base. The base was slightly concave, so that it would neatly plug the circular hole of a clay or iron stove, or sit on an iron tripod over an open fire. It was perhaps 10 inches deep, and had a wooden lid which fitted neatly over the top. The pot had rings fixed on either side, connected by a curved brass handle for lifting or hanging, which could swing down to sit snugly round the outside rim of the pot. Around its blackened base ran some Arabic script, barely visible, the words mostly obliterated by the baked-on soot and grease.

Again Satanaya didn't quite know what to make of it.

'But how do you know it's meant for me?' she said, looking imploringly at Beulah. The cook just smiled, rocked her head a little, but said nothing.

Satanaya took the pot in her hands and experienced a strange sensation, a queer sense of ownership, familiarity, as if the pot had always belonged with her and had just been returned.

'Oh, and you're meant to have this too.' said Beulah.

From somewhere deep within her voluminous skirts, the cook extracted a battered old wooden spoon. 'I suppose if nothing else, you can bang the pot to announce dinner is served. Which reminds me, I've got work to do, and a new assistant to train, so...' she took Satanaya in her big round embrace and hugged her tight. 'No crying now,' said the cook as she left, trying to laugh while her own eyes brimmed over with tears. The sight of cook laughing and crying into her apron at once made Satanaya see the absurdity of the situation, and she too laughed through her own tears.

Alone in her room, she looked at the *kazan*. She held it up and tried to read the script around its base, but she was puzzled. She couldn't make any sense of the few words she could decipher. She had heard stories of the old chef Takla – how as a young girl she had taken on the kitchen at Seydnaya and made its feasts famous throughout the land. She felt a strange thrill to be holding Takla's pot, and wondered if she would ever inherit, not just the pot, but the blessing of all the great dishes that had come out of it. She felt inspired and, taking the *kazan* in one hand and the wooden spoon in the other, she jumped up on the bed, and banged the pot with the spoon, like a drummer with a drum, and announced,

'Now hear this, all you humans and spirits, angels and djinn, wherever you are in this world: I, Satanaya, though wounded in love, am thankfully not dead. And by the power of this noble cooking pot of the great cook Takla, and the strength of her esteemed wooden spoon, I dedicate my life to cooking with love, for love and in love, with God's blessing and the help of His Saints. And by the generosity of the Almighty Providence, may no one ever go hungry as long as this pot can hold food and this hand can hold this spoon. Amen.'

It was a grand gesture, even if seemingly in jest, but words carry their meanings whatever the speaker may think. For now, though, it was just the fillip, self-administered, that Satanaya needed to take hold of herself, with courage and her luggage, and bid farewell to Seydnaya. Shortly afterwards, with two accompanying sisters, loaded with provisions and their bundles, and all in heavy woollen capes, they mounted donkeys and set out upon the road to Beirut. Moments later the rain came gently folding in upon them from the mountains of the Lebanon.

SIX

Le Petit Château de Misèricorde

Lady Gülbahar's Farm (Beyt'ur-Rahma), above Beirut

 NIGHT SPENT IN A FUNDUK somewhere on the Damascus road, a night in a convent near Beirut, and then the steep climb up into the hills from the city by the sea. It was late afternoon when Satanaya reached the jasmine-clad walls surrounding the farmhouse of Lady Gülbahar.

She rang the old goat bell which she saw hanging from the gatepost. A gentle, hollow clocking sounded, no different from the sounds she knew so well as the goats made their way round the hills of Seydnaya. She swallowed her feelings, even as tears came to her eyes, and tightened her grip

35

on the old cooking pot that now held her small bundle. A minute or two later a young girl appeared, a slender Abyssinian maid.

'Welcome, welcome.' said the girl. 'We have been expecting you. Follow me, please.' She led the little troupe on a track around the outside of the wall, through another gate and up into a yard at the side of the farmhouse. There a table had been laid with tea, bread and cakes for the nuns who were continuing their journey. Then she took Satanaya's hand, saying:

'Madame wishes to see you straight away.'

'Oh well, this is it, I suppose.' Satanaya managed a grin as she bade farewell to the two sisterly escorts.

The maid took Satanaya back to the first gate which she pushed open. 'Now, go on up.'

She heard a faint cry, 'Yoo-hoo!' and looking up she could just make out through the greenery a small hand waving from the terrace of the large farmhouse above her.

The eccentricity of this welcoming call banished her initial apprehension and the strong evening scents wafting from the garden soothed her nerves. It was a delightful garden, full of faded roses amid burgeoning shrubbery which while no longer in full bloom still gave off delicious aromas of lush herbage. Rosemary grew in strident clumps, a sign that women were in charge here. A sharp scent of citrus from camomile crushed underfoot rose from the warm stones of the path. Fat berries turning green to purple weighed down the branches of some horny-trunked olive trees, and lemons, still dark green, showed future promise in their plumpness. The path wound lazily back and forth so that her ascent though steep was in no way laborious but had the quality of a gentle evening stroll. A huge fig tree spread a canopy over one turn – cream and black skins littered the ground beneath, while among the branches bulbous fruit burst purple skins rimmed ivory to red and oozing honey golden seeds.

Again the woman's voice descended from the balcony above: 'Hello, my dear. You must be Satanaya. Forgive my dreadful manners for not coming down to greet you, but I was so comfortable here, and the sun is just the right temperature now, don't you think?'

Satanaya climbed the steps to the wide terrace that surrounded the farmhouse. There, upon a chaise longue amply arrayed with soft-looking cushions of embroidered linen and satin, a patchwork knitted rug over her knees and a glass of red wine in her hand, reclined the châtelaine, Lady

Gülbahar.

'Have a little wine, dear, won't you? And sit down a moment. Let me take a look at you.'

Satanaya nervously presented the letter from Mother Superior, and stood there clutching her bundle.

'Do sit down, I won't bite.' said the ancient dame in Arabic.

Timidly Satanaya sat on the edge of the chair nearby.

'And some wine. Go on, you've been travelling for days, it will do you good.'

Satanaya hesitated further before accepting a glass of deep red wine. It was luscious, long-flavoured wine, leather and oaky as an old bookcase, warm with the ripeness of autumn fruit and bright as the sunlight streaming across the distant sea. She felt a flush down to her toes, which reminded her of... No, she stopped herself and changed her thought. *This is now and I'm enjoying this.*

Lady Gülbahar put down her glass. She took up the gold-rimmed lorgnettes which hung from her neck and investigated the letter. Satanaya observed her host. A lady of some years, venerable even, but from behind those deep aged lines emerged a beautiful face, well-loved, experienced; a gently weathered face, finely graven with soft lines of humour and tolerance and still glowing with the irrepressible blush of a child, a rosy complexion that shone with inner vitality which time had not diminished. When the lady spoke, it was as if behind those faded eyes and small mouth, a harp or lute played, shaping the words upon the parchment of those still-red lips as musical notes, as the melody of a generous soul.

Lady Gülbahar folded the letter and placed it inside the book she had been reading. She gazed at Satanaya.

'Mais, ma petite cherie, tu es belle! Si belle. No wonder. No wonder at all...'

She then enquired after Mother Superior, and how things were in Seydnaya, and how Satanaya's journey had been. Small talk to put Satanaya at her ease.

'You must be tired from travelling, so why don't you take yourself and your little pot of things and go and find your room – Pelin will show you – and take a bath.' Here Lady Gülbahar rang a little bell. 'Then have some supper. Tomorrow we'll talk. I just can't wait to hear all about him. Mother Superior says he was very good looking. Now, off you go.'

As Satanaya was led away by the sweetly-named diminutive servant girl, Pelin, who had met them earlier. Lady Gülbahar's soft, clear voice followed: 'You don't happen to play bezique do you?'

Whatever prior thoughts Satanaya may have entertained about her new mistress had been blown to the four winds during those strange but uplifting fifteen minutes in her company, drinking red wine as the sun sank into the glinting sapphire sea. That night as she lay in bed wrapped in soft linen, all warm and clean and relaxed after steaming in the *hammam*, hunger sated with a bowl of thick vegetable soup, she mused, 'I think I might be really happy here.'

Satanaya woke early. Her bedroom was behind the main house, across a small garden behind the kitchen, and had a window facing east. It was in a wing which as well as accommodation, included a hammam, an ice house, and a wood store. Further up the slope were the winery buildings. In a separate area across towards the west were animal sheds and other farm buildings.

She was sharing the room with little Pelin, who was already up and about. Wrapping herself in a woollen cloak, she went outside. The air was fresh, dew hung from bushes and herbs in the little kitchen garden, and a light mist was fast disappearing off the hillside. Nearby a cockerel sounded, clearing its throat. Once its reveille finished, the air became quiet and still. Satanaya washed, dressed and went back across the garden and into the kitchen through the back door.

Behind a large table, within a fine mist of billowing flour backlit by the sun, stood an apparition all in white. Sleeves rolled, and kneading up to her elbows a large pile of bread dough, her bun-like form enfolded within a large white apron and smiling beneath a lace-trimmed bonnet stood the cook .

'Bonjour! Merhaba! Sabah-al khayr!'

Satanaya was not at all sure what language this strange apparition spoke, so she stuck with Arabic:

'Sabah-al khayr'.

'Sabah an-nur. So you are my new helper. *Ahlan wa sahlan* – welcome. At least I don't have to try that Circassian *langue* the Mistress slips into sometimes, quite impossible; and she isn't even aware when she does it!

Don't worry, we'll have you speaking French soon enough. It is the language of the kitchen after all. Now, why don't you run along and say good morning to the Mistress. She's having her morning coffee on her terrace. She said to send you up when you appeared. Come on, I'll show you.'

The cook, whose name was Clotilde, covered the dough with a cloth and directed Satanaya through into the main hall of the house.

A wide central staircase rose up in the centre of the hall, dividing in two at a landing and turning back on itself. The landing gave onto a small 'cumba', a suspended seat set in an oriel window which overlooked the paved courtyard at the back of the house. Each arm of the now bifurcated staircase continued to an upper landing, which opened onto an enclosed balcony – a kind of small conservatory – which could also be accessed from the two bedrooms that led off either side of the landing. As she entered the balcony Satanaya found Lady Gülbahar sitting in a pale blue and white striped quilted dressing gown. She was reading a newspaper and drinking coffee from a china cup decorated with pale blue dragons. Pelin who was also sitting having breakfast greeted her new room-mate and slipped away, leaving Satanaya alone with her mistress.

'It's impossible to know what to think, and even less what to believe.' said Lady Gülbahar, putting the paper down in mock exasperation and letting her lorgnettes drop. 'Such lies this paper prints. But then, what else can they do. If they printed what was actually happening, either the Sultan would have the paper closed down, or the people would rise up in revolt, like the French. So we learn to read between the lines. Now, my dear, sit down, won't you? There are brioches, and coffee, figs and walnuts – the walnuts are fresh, this season's, from our own trees of course. Quite divine with just a little salt. And white cheese if you wish, and honey. And brioches. Did I just say that? Oh well. Come on now, take a plate and help yourself.'

Satanaya sat down and took a brioche. It wasn't exactly a brioche, but a Turkish *açma*, similar, but different, with tiny black nigella seeds covering its thin golden crust, and inside sweet and soft like the *cholla* bread her Jewish neighbours used to bake on Fridays in Kfar Kama. She took some curd cheese and fig jam, and poured herself a cup of coffee. She broke off some bread, spread it with cheese and jam, and put it in her mouth.

'So, here you are! All the way from Seydnaya. And you came by Beirut?'

'Yes, Ma'am.'

'Have you seen the sea before?'

'Oh yes, Ma'am. We live near the Sea of Galilee.'

'Yes, of course. How nice for you.' Lady Gülbahar smiled indulgently, and continued making inconsequential chit-chat, while Satanaya between mouthfuls of breakfast spoke of her childhood in the Circassian village and how she had wanted to become a cook at Seydnaya.

'It was so wonderful in that kitchen. Until...' Satanaya stopped, and couldn't go on.

'So, you had a little taste of love, and the nuns got all excited.' said Lady Gülbahar. 'Well, that's not so surprising is it. But tell me, what of the boy? What's happened to him.'

Memories flooded back, bitter and sweet as the tears that began to well up in her. She explained the problem with Yusuf's father, the Kurdish goatherd, and the brutish brother.

'I don't think I'll see Yusuf again. His father sent him off to Damascus and won't let him come back. '

'Maybe he doesn't want to go back to his father. Maybe you did him a good turn.'

Then the old lady fixed Satanaya firmly with her steely blue eyes: 'Look, Satanaya, you're young, you've had a little affair and your poor heart was opened wide. It had a small taste of something bigger than itself, and then that small thing was taken away, just when it wanted more. Well, all in good time. Hearts need to break now and then if they are to grow big enough for love. The best thing for your little broken heart is not to sit around moping, but to get out and do something.'

Satanaya didn't quite know what to think. Somehow she had hoped for a little more sympathy from this lady who had been kind enough to take her in, unseen, from the convent. She was still somewhat fragile, and was upset that this love affair, so important to her, seemed to have been dismissed so lightly. She fought back the tears but to no avail. They just poured out of their own accord. Then, biting her lip, and swallowing her dented pride, she managed a few words, chokingly, in response.

'I'm so sorry. It's just hard sometimes to forget. I'm really grateful to you for letting me stay here and... and...' her voice trailed off into a ruffle of sobs.

'Oh my dear, you won't forget. You absolutely mustn't forget. After all, first loves are the sweetest, truly. But that's what they are, first loves, of many to be sure. So don't dwell in the past. Moping doesn't suit your beautiful face. Look at young Pelin, do you imagine she hasn't something to cry about? She lost her mother and father, in fact her whole family at such a young age, she nearly starved to death in the desert and was rescued from being raped in the brothels only just in time. When she came here you wouldn't have recognised her. So thin, so silent. But good food and lots of hugs – and just look at her. You're here now, that's the main thing. From what Mother Superior says, you really want to cook. So you shall cook. We can come back to love any time we like. Maybe I'll even tell you about some of my little affairs.'

With that Lady Gülbahar gave a little laugh and drained her coffee in one go. Satanaya managed a brave smile and wiped her eyes with her napkin.

'That's better. Now, come and give me a hug and then we'll go down to the kitchen and see what's cooking.'

Satanaya went over and embraced her new mistress. She was already feeling much better. Then Lady Gülbahar took her arm and together they descended the staircase, crossed the hall to the drawing room on the left, through the adjoining dining room, and into the kitchen. The dining room Satanaya now noticed was a considerably larger space than it had seemed at first, as it was divided into two areas by panels half-way along which folded back into the walls.

Little Pelin had reappeared as Lady Gülbahar and Satanaya finished talking. She cleared away the breakfast table, taking the loaded tray to the scullery, which was off to the right between the dining room and the kitchen.

'Bonjour, Madame.' Clotilde curtsied while continuing to shape bread dough into little rolls.

'Bonjour, Clotilde. I gather you have met our new helper. What's on the menu today?'

'It's soup for lunch. I thought Satanaya could make it, so we'll see what she's capable of. Or not.' said Clotilde.

SEVEN

Takla's Cook Book
and Uncle Mesut's Lentil Soup

Beyt'ur-Rahma, near Beirut – 1896

 ATANAYA FOUND HERSELF in unfamiliar territory. Back in her room she sat on her bed and undid the bundle containing the soup pot and the cookbook and the wooden spoon. She stared at this strange assortment. How could she cook soup just like that, on her own? In the convent she had always been given strict instructions by Cook. Every measurement, every ingredient, checking the fire, everything had to be done exactly the way Cook said. Then Cook tasted it and sometimes adjusted the seasoning, though more often of late she had just nodded, making a somewhat non-committal 'mmm…' and let the dish be. Now suddenly Satanaya had to do lunch without any help. She looked at the pot. It was Takla's pot, the same one she had burnt, now re-tinned, and cleaned well enough though still pretty black. It was a good pot, with its brass rings like earrings on either side, its curved handle and wooden lid. And the big wooden spoon was a fine piece of olivewood, well worn in over many years, with a notch cut in the end to catch the rim and not slip into the pot.

Inside the pot was a fat old notebook bound in thick soft leather with the title 'Takla's Cookbook' tooled roughly on the cover. She flipped through the yellowed pages, stained where a greasy thumb had left its print, or a splatter of meat juice from a pan had found its way over to smudge the ink and add a dot to a ta (ت) to make a tha (ث), or even three dots to turn a sin (س) into a shin (ش). But it was mostly readable. Many of the pages appeared to be correspondence ending with an indecipherable signature, old letters which had been tipped into the book carefully by hand.

The first few pages were in Aramaic, titled 'The Art of Cooking', evidently added later into the original binding. Further on, where the recipes began, the text showed a mix of different languages, but the ingredients were usually understandable.

She looked at the Aramaic, and found it not so difficult. She slowly worked her way through the first paragraph. It began:

'Cooking is an art. But it is more than that. It is no less than the education of the soul. Cooking is like breathing. The cook is the body into which the breath of this art is blown. Perhaps it is like this: we take an empty sheep's bladder, attach to it pipes which have holes at certain known places, and we pump in air. Then while squeezing the bag we release the air in measured amounts at regular intervals. In this way, if we know when and where to stop or unstop the holes, we may produce music. If the displacement of the pipes is not correct, holes in the wrong place, the pumping too strong or too weak, the resultant sound will be off-key, discordant, or too loud or too soft, a raucous cacophony, or a barely audible whimper bereft of melody.

   Cooking is like that. It is a matter of allowing the correct measure of ingredients, the right balance of seasonings, and the harmonious arrangement of the various components, so that they present an overall *unity, while at the same time allowing each dish its unique taste or combination thereof. But like music, like all art, it begins with the breath, for the breath carries the spirit, and it is the spirit that carries the essential vision or knowledge of taste which transforms what otherwise might as well remain as raw meat or unground corn, turning it into something not merely digestible, but, like the well-played song, something to enjoy, to savour, and which may transport one to hitherto undiscovered pleasures.*

'Remember also that the sense of smell is intimately connected to breathing, by whose agency the delicious odours and scents of well-cooked food are received so that a dish may be elevated from merely, salt or sweet, bitter, sour etc. to a different level of taste altogether. The sense of smell is apprehended directly by the soul, without the intermediary of the relative mind. So in cooking as in life, pay attention to the breath for what may be given of this direct taste – for the education of the cook is in the taste.'

Satanaya flipped through to the end of this introduction, to the last line which said simply. *'From letters to Takla by the Cairene containing hints and explanations, and recipes from his Bolu Cook and other notable masters of the kitchen'.*

Next came a title page in Turkish announcing *'Çorbalar'* (Soups), in red ink; the rubric on the page following, also in Turkish, read: *Mesut Amca'nın Mercimek Çorbası* – Uncle Mesut's Lentil Soup

As she read through the description of the dish and its preparation, she experienced an extraordinary sensation. As if tasting the dish itself, she felt its thick warm creaminess coating her tongue and the roof of her mouth, and the tang of fresh lemon – the scent of citrus zest upon her fingers as though she had just squeezed a lemon. Then she recalled the lentil soup she had eaten when she had returned to Seydnaya to join the kitchen brigade. The journey had been long and tiring in bad weather, and it was late at night when she and her mother had climbed the steps to the convent gate. The community had eaten and gone to bed, but Cook had waited up and fed them in the kitchen with big bowls of this hearty yellow pottage, with quarters of lemon and some of the morning's bread toasted. In spite of being tired and nervous she remembered how content she had felt afterwards.

There followed a brief explanation concerning the provenance of the recipe and some further notes. Evidently the aforementioned Cairene's Bolu cook had an uncle called Mesut who was the cook of an Armenian merchant from Antalya. Satanaya knew that Mesut was the same in Turkish as the Arabic name Masud, meaning 'happy'.

'Hmmm.' she thought, 'Happy? why not?'

She read on:

Lentils are very good for grounding oneself after extremes of exertion both spiritually and mentally, for anchoring those of feeble mind inclined to flights of fancy or with tempers fractured from the extremes of love-sickness, and provide good energy for those engaged in heavy physical activities where meat is either unaffordable or undesirable. Not suitable for nuns while engaged in spiritual retreat, but most efficacious in returning them to the mundane life from their celestial soarings.

She looked at the list of ingredients: red lentils, onions, carrots, potatoes, green peppers, tomatoes, flour, butter, meat stock (or vegetable stock), oregano, thyme, parsley, salt and pepper. 'Looks simple enough.' she thought.

Satanaya returned to the kitchen where Clotilde was bringing in the bread baked fresh each day outside in a wood-fired clay oven. The oven was built into the corner of the kitchen garden where the hammam abutted the kitchen. The fire of the oven was flued in one large chimney stack together with the fires from below which heated the water for the hammam, and those of kitchen stove.

'I thought of making lentil soup.' said Seydnaya. 'Where will I find the ingredients?'

'I'd better give you the proper 'Cook's Tour', hadn't I?' said Clotilde as she stood in the doorway to the garden and shook the flour from her apron. For the next half hour she showed her new apprentice over her domain.

'Everything has its home, so make sure you always return things to their correct places.' she said, pointing out the pot where the wooden spoons lived, the rack for the knives and the stone for sharpening, all the ladles and sieves and skimmers hanging handily to the right of the stove, the drawer with all the special kitchen tools like mandolins and apple corers and other innovations that had not yet made it to Seydnaya but were commonplace in European kitchens.

'All the glassware and table china, dinner services and cutlery are kept in the scullery of course.'

Outside the back door of the kitchen they entered a cool stone building where onions hung from strings and old tea chests filled with dry soft earth contained carrots, potatoes and other root vegetables; apples wrapped in paper lay neatly on slatted racks.

Next door was the game larder, a little building built partly into the hill with thick stone walls and a very high domed ceiling.

'We don't have much call for this since the Ambassador departed', Clotilde said. 'He was a keen huntsman and bred his own pheasants, quail and partridge, but now it's only my husband who can use the gun, and he occasionally brings in a few rabbits if he finds them among the vines. But we have plenty of ducks and chickens, and we can usually buy game from the local hunters or from Beirut.'

'Your husband?'

'Yes, Gérard. He's the winemaker. You'll meet him at lunch. He likes lentil soup, so we'll keep our fingers crossed, eh?' Clotilde chuckled. She seemed a very equable lady, and didn't seem to be particularly possessive with regard to her kitchen, which was a relief to Satanaya. There had been quite a strict order in the convent kitchen, where every responsibility was carefully delineated, and she spent most of her time doing 'parts' of meals, and rarely was she left alone to do a whole dish, unless it was the breakfast porridge. In spite of this, she had managed to build up a small repertoire, and she was faster than any one else when it came to peeling vegetables and slicing onions ever so thinly.

Back in the kitchen Clotilde lifted up a trapdoor in the far corner revealing a dark and indeterminate space below.

'This is where we keep the preserves. Mind your head, now.'

She led the way down a wooden staircase into a low barrel-vaulted cellar, its walls lined with jars and casks, containing various preserved comestibles. Pale pears, pinkish-orange quinces and crimson plums peered out through syrup within their glass containers; fat olives, green and black, sat in vats of oily brine next to tubs of tomato puree and paprika paste, the darker pepper paste distinctly labelled 'HOT' and the lighter-coloured one 'SWEET'. All manner of vegetables too had been preserved in jars: celeriac, white beans, tiny artichoke hearts and large artichoke bottoms. A whole wall was given over to wine, neatly stacked in stone bays, with labels hanging from the necks of each dark green bottle giving the year of vintage and the row of vines. Boxes of champagne were stacked nearby.

'That's the wine we will use in the house this year.' said Clotilde, 'the main production is cellared below the winery.'

Back in the kitchen, the cook pointed to a row of large earthenware pots standing along one wall. 'Here we keep the grains, pulses and flour, and on the shelves above: nuts, dried fruits, spices and other condiments. We use fresh herbs from the kitchen garden as much as possible, or from the market in Beirut. Now, is there anything you haven't seen which you'll need for this soup?'

'Do we have any stock?'

Clotilde laughed and pointed out a huge pot on the stove where every few seconds wafts of steam lifted the edge of the lid with a gentle puff and clink. 'All you'll need there, I think.'

'And how many are we cooking for?'

'About twenty. You can never tell who'll turn up for lunch. It's mostly the farm workers. As well as the vineyard, Lady Gülbahar has land down in the valley and further up the hill and we usually feed the labourers when there's work going on. Today they are ploughing some fields before planting winter barley, so they're bound to have good appetites.'

And so Satanaya began her first day's work in the kitchen of the *Beyt'ur-Rahma*, by making Uncle Mesut's Lentil Soup, from the recipe in Takla's Cookbook*.

Lady Gülbahar patted her lips with a small lace-trimmed napkin, took a sip of water. Gérard the winemaker gave a satisfied belch, patted his stomach, and smiled at Satanaya. Satanaya looked around nervously, wondering, 'What do they think? Was it ok? Did I pass muster?'

Clotilde the Cook noticed the exchange and smiled to herself. Then Lady Gülbahar looked down the table where more than a dozen farm workers, men and women, were wiping clean their bowls with hunks of Clotilde's bread.

---

* see Appendix I – Recipes

'Well, you seem to have the approval of this table. Uncle Mesut's lentils are evidently a success.' the châtelaine said, 'Now, what can you come up with for our Friday evening dinner. We have guests coming up from Beirut, and not just locals. There may be some Europeans as well, we'll see.'

Satanaya's brief moment of relief turned quickly to trepidation. Cooking a hearty lentil soup for hungry farm-workers was one thing. A dinner for the society of the city quite something else. Then Lady Gülbahar gave a reassuring laugh.

'Don't imagine you can have our kitchen to yourself, we'll all be there.' And she was true to her word.

EIGHT

The Anonymous Fish Restaurant

Beirut

ARLY MORNING MIST mingled with the smoke of breakfast fires, filtering the hazy sunlight streaming through the valleys of Mount Lebanon. The light lay in patches on the dappled bark of the old plane trees, their green leaves now turning to late autumn gold. Satanaya felt the freshness of the air, not cold but sharp as lemons. A week earlier she had come this way, wrapped in the cloud of her sad mood. Now her vision was renewed. As the land rolled down, she saw unveiled between the pines the bright vista of a city set within orchards, and beyond the sparkling blue waters of the Bay of St George.

The teahouse half-way down the road into Beirut was well known to Clotilde. She greeted the owner who sat smoking a pipe by the entrance and tied up the horse and cart at a water trough. But instead of going inside for refreshment, she took a basket in one hand and with Satanaya following, she headed around behind the building.

'Don't worry, we'll have tea later. We've work to do first.'

Clotilde strode ahead into a pine forest on a small path. After fifteen minutes, they left the path, ducking under low branches, and scrambling over the soft cushion of strewn pine needles for a few hundred yards until they emerged below a small ridge. Here the view was clear over the tree tops, to the harbour, busy with craft of all kinds; big steamers and tall-masted sailing ships lined the quays, other vessels made their way in and out of harbour, and dozens of smaller craft fussed about. A little further along they could make out the fishing harbour which sheltered rows of caiques caught like so many sardines upon the line of the tidy breakwater. The city itself seethed under a flat cloud of woodsmoke as the day got underway.

'We didn't come here to admire the view, Satanaya, but for these little beauties.' Clotilde pointed up into the woods to her left. Clustered beneath the pines, poking out among the roots and needles were dozens of what looked like little saffron yellow flowers. Closer inspection revealed them to be mushrooms.

'Chanterelles, and what a good crop this year. Just what we need for this weekend's menu. Come on, let's get picking.' And with that she dropped to her knees and began to lift the delicate little trumpet-shaped fungi out of the needles and lay them in the basket. Satanaya knelt down and together they worked away for about fifteen minutes, choosing in preference the larger mushrooms, leaving the tiny ones to grow some more, until the basket was heaped high. They had barely made a dent in the crop.

'We'll have to pick them again next week, before the rain comes and spoils them. We can dry them above the stove and use them through the winter.' the cook said. Then, carefully covering their golden treasure with a light cloth, they made their way out of the woods and back to the tea house.

'But how did you know where to find them?' asked Satanaya. They were sitting outside enjoying little glasses of sweet black tea in the warming sun.

'Ah well, either you're lucky, or someone tells you. In fact it was the old

Ambassador who discovered this patch. It was during his hunting days. He was after some gamebird or other and followed his dog after it, and here he found the wounded bird lying in a whole fanfare of chanterelles. He didn't pick the mushrooms then. He didn't want the other hunters to know. Later he returned with Gérard and me, under sacred oath to keep secret the location. It's a tradition among mushroom gatherers, they never divulge their sources. Of course, other people may come across this patch, though I doubt it, it's so far off the track. Anyway, there are plenty to go round and I know other places. And other types of fungus too, morels and truffles, which I may show you in time. We've never had a shortage of delicious things at *Beyt'ur-Rahma*. Now, drink up or we'll miss the best choice in the market.'

It was Saturday, and the hubbub of downtown Beirut was quite distracting for Satanaya, but Clotilde remained focused. They parked the horse and cart near the vegetable market and headed over to the Women's Market, where ladies from the villages came each week with the best and freshest of their wares. Thick bunches of fresh herbs, dill, parsley, sage and mint were stacked up alongside all manner of greens, beet tops, purslane, some still with their roots. Bottles of thick, opaque olive oil, first cold pressing from some ancient stone press turned by a donkey in the hills nearby; and pomegranate molasses, a reduction of the fruit into a thick dark syrup, sat next to small bowls of aged lemons, tubs of homemade paprika and tomato paste, and boxes of dripping honeycomb.

'It's just some herbs and greens we need now, we never seem to grow enough in our patch to cope with the big dinners.' Clotilde was ruffling through the pile in front of a severe looking lady with a large mole on her chin and thick eyebrows, dressed head to foot in black who appeared to scowl at anyone showing interest in her produce. But this didn't put off Clotilde and she went on picking out what looked to be the freshest bunches of parsley and dill, as well as rocket and purslane. She paid the dark lady who finally smiled when the money was in her hand, and on they went with their shopping.

In the fruit section of the market they spied tangerines, just coming into ripeness. Clotilde picked through them, choosing a few dozen that she could feel were becoming loose between the skin and the fruit, and likely to be sweet. 'The locals are used to eating them when they are still tight and tart, but I know Lady Gülbahar will only serve them when they are quite sweet. These must have come from quite a way south, probably down the coast near Jaffa. Ours are still quite sharp.'

They stopped at a vegetable stall run by a character called Mr Jemil. He was a big man dressed in voluminous black *shalwar*, a long striped and collarless shirt, black waistcoat and thick, grey hair tied up in an old ragged *keffiyeh*. His beard, a pepper pot of white, black and ginger sprouts could not compete with his enormous moustache which stretched fully to either side of his wide grinning face, above a mouth arrayed with a jiggle of not-unwhite teeth skewed and gapped at impossible angles, reminiscent of an ancient and abandoned graveyard. He boomed out a welcome to Clotilde, took both her hands and pouring out profuse kisses upon them, addressed her in a strange mix of French and Arabic, calling her *Ma Bonne Femme de Motfaq al Beyt'ur-Rahma*, and adding some obscure (to Clotilde) endearments that seemed to have a lot do with henna-tipped fingers, young gazelles and gazing with nostalgia at the cold ashes of abandoned campfires. Mr Jemil was nothing if not poetic in his enthusiastic greeting. He was more restrained with Satanaya, muttering quietly, '*Allah, allah! si jeune, si belle, ya jamal, jamal!*' while with hand on chest he gave a small but dignified bow.

Satanaya stood back, not quite sure how to deal with all this bonhomie. But Clotilde was equal to the situation.

'Ah, you old rogue Mr Jemil, how many glasses of arak have you drunk already this morning, eh? I hope you're not going to mix up my order again like last time, when you sent me all seed potatoes, instead of the Sayid's potatoes. Flattery will buy you a smile, but it won't excuse a wrong order.'

Little wooden stools were produced, coffee arrived in tiny porcelain cups, and the Bonne Femme Clotilde produced a list for Mr Jemil who read this out to a small boy. The boy began packing wooden boxes with basic vegetables: potatoes, carrots, leeks, onions, etc., which would all be delivered to their cart before they left for home.

Next they headed down to the seafront to view the morning's catch. Among the wrathful wriggly-faced rascasse and humdrum grey-suited mullet were sleek and steely-blue loup de mer, pink and silver-scaled bream with blunt heads and bewildered eyes, sticky little squid and live lobsters claw-tied and waiting for a pot. There were shark, octopus and huge prawns, and sardines graded in various sizes.

Clotilde liked the look of some big fat-bodied bonito which were just being delivered.

'What do you think, Satanaya?' she said.

Satanaya felt the flesh – firm not hard, and bright of gill and eye, just as she had read in Takla's cookbook how fresh fish should be.

'They seem good to me,' she ventured cautiously.

'They will make splendid kebabs with a little pepper sauce.' said Clotilde, as she paid the fishmonger.

'Now, I don't know about you, Satanaya, but I'm getting hungry.'

'Me too.'

'Come on then, I know just the place for an early lunch that will see us right for the journey home.'

Clotilde led the way into an alley one block back from the seafront where a small painted sign in the shape of a fish hung above the doorway of a little cookshop. It may have been a John Dory, the shape was right, more or less, but the sign was old and much of the paint had flaked. Where would have been the thumb print of the saint whose handling of this fish endowed it laterally with that mysterious black dot, and thus its name in French, the Saint Pierre, there was only bare board. Fishermen were sitting at plain wooden tables outside in the street eating soup. Inside a few more tables were filled with customers all eating soup. In fact soup was all the establishment served, and only one kind of soup at that, more of a stew really – a real bouillabaisse.

Now, it is a myth wide-spread and not without its true believers that there are as many real bouillabaisses as there are cooks in Marseilles. But that is not so. In fact there is only one real bouillabaisse, and depending on the skill, the education, the love and passion of the cook, that 'real' bouillabaisse' is either attained, or it is not. Certainly it may come in a variety of guises, a slight variation of ingredients dependent on season and the prevailing weather, the state of the sea, the phase of the moon etc., but in so far as we are concerned with good taste, there is only one. Many aspire, and some hit the mark, some often, some occasionally, and some accidentally; and some cooks die before they attain satisfied rest in their search for perfection. But it is believed that in the end all who sincerely desire to achieve bouillabaisse are not disappointed. The restaurant with no name just off Mina Street in Beirut in the 1890s was in the upper echelons of those establishments which have reached this excellent station. But it was a station hidden to all but the fishermen of the Eastern Mediterranean.

One of the great unknown cooks – no, let us name them according to their true achievement: 'chefs', for we are discussing the *summum* of those gifted with true knowledge of taste – a little lady of Marseilles, had been cooking her bouillabaisse under the sign of the anonymous fish for as long as Clotilde could remember. No one knew how she came to be there, it was so long ago. Some say that she had followed her husband who had come to work on the building of the Suez Canal nearly forty years earlier. While docking in Beirut, the husband had succumbed to a singularly virulent intestinal condition which ultimately proved fatal. Down on her uppers, so to speak, she was not one to let herself sink. She rather liked the climate of this polyglot port where French was widely spoken, so she did the only thing she knew. With the small change that remained after selling her husband's belongings, she set up a food stall near the fish market. She scavenged the market each morning for fish heads and bones, which with a few bits and pieces from the left-overs of the vegetable market from the previous day, she concocted a sort of stew of a soup which she hoped to sell to the fishermen returning hungry each morning from their work at sea. It was make or break for her as the only alternative was to sell herself there on the quay – easily done she knew, she'd seen it in the docks of Marseille and it was the same here.

The little widow of Marseille put her heart and soul into making the best soup she could from such meagre ingredients, setting up her table and charcoal brazier beneath a little canvas awning. She promised the local *zabıta* – the market warden – a bowl of her soup if he would look the other way while she got her business going. It didn't take long at all. The scents of rich fish stock seasoned with fennel and saffron wafted along the quay, and once the first few punters had tried her soup, the word quickly went round. She had so many customers that soon she could afford to purchase whole fish and other seafood, though she still made her stock from the day's unsold odds and ends of seafood and unwanted heads and bones. To begin with she worked and slept beneath her little awning, but in no time at all she was able to rent a small shop, which she eventually bought, and there she hung up the wooden sign of the fish.

Satanaya and Clotilde found a small table within the shop. The old lady patronne, La Veuve du Poisson Anonyme, came over and greeted Clotilde, quietly shaking her hand, then disappeared behind a lattice screen which hid the kitchen area. She returned with two bowls of steaming broth out of which arose a veritable cornucopia of seafood. A plate of bread and a dish of mayonnaise was the only accompaniment.

Whether it was the splash of arak the cook put in to strengthen the fennel, or the creamy innards of the sea urchins in the sea-rich stock, or the combined flavours of the scorpion fish, the conger, the firm pieces of monkfish, the delicate fillets of John Dory simmered with bay leaves and thyme – the essential herbs of the Mediterranean – or perhaps the kindly look of grace upon a poor widow from the spirit of the icon of Mar Boutros, patron saint of fishermen, hanging inside the kitchen door, all conjoined to produce an effect not merely upon the palate of Satanaya, but in her very being. It was unlike anything she had ever tasted. She was completely blown away. In a flash she understood: the information was in the taste. She saw with each mouthful how the soup was made, how it was structured, and she found herself differentiating the flavours, the textures, even the cooking times of each component. Of course, none of this would have been possible were it not for those years of preparation in the kitchen at Seydnaya. But now something new was happening. She saw how the real cooking began with the taste, from where one had to work backwards, so to speak. She remembered something she had read in Takla's Cookbook, something about the cook being the place where knowledge of cooking is revealed:

> "The true cook doesn't acquire this knowledge through her own efforts or her cleverness. The cook who discovers through experiment, through a process of elimination, comes to a knowledge accidentally. The true cook, who discovers by taste, enters a different order of relationship with food: knowing the taste in herself. But for this the cook needs first to be hungry, not just stomach hungry, but soul hungry, so that she is disposed to receive the dish as it is, without adding anything of her own invention. Then the dish itself will teach the cook, for no other reason than its own love to be known, tasted and consumed."

Now as she chewed and drank, with each mouthful information was being given. She savoured, she tasted, she distinguished, by all her faculties, not just within her mouth, her tongue, her teeth, which gave her descriptions of the textures and sent her messages of shape and consistency which conformed to pictures in her mind of this fish or that mollusc,

and the combinations of sweetness, sour, bitter and salt which told her of
the character and relationship of the ingredients to each other, but also the
sweat of the steam spoke of peppers, the scent of the broth revealed sweet
herbs, so that her eyes took in the whole generous arrangement of the plate
as an integrated whole.

They ate in silence, in respectful awe before perfection, paid gratefully
and vacated their table to others waiting outside, eager to lunch. They
returned to their horse and cart, which had already been loaded with vegetables and the bonito, now wrapped in newspaper and packed in ice, and
set off homewards.

Following the harbour road they passed the main docks where a large
steamer, newly arrived from America, was disembarking passengers. Satanaya was leaning against the back-board, relaxed in a state of deep
satisfaction from her meal. She gazed at the people disgorging from the
gangplank. Ladies in gay white dresses holding lacy umbrellas, men in
striped suits and derby hats, it was all so unfamiliar.

'Look at them, they think they are Europeans!' laughed Clotilde, 'or
Americans perhaps, but they are Syrians just like us, so mixed up we are,
trying to return to our roots.'

Satanaya looked but her mind was elsewhere, digesting the thoughts
and feelings that had been with her since lunch, contemplating its revelations of taste. When she finally focussed she became aware that her vision
had alighted upon the face of a young man, not much more than a boy
really, a pale creature with long, dark hair, wearing an ill-fitting suit, who
was returning her look with a disturbing intensity as he was drawn in the
tide of the arriving throng across the quay. Then as the crowd entered the
customs shed he was lost to view.

NINE

Soirée at Beyt'ur-Rahma

T A DISTANCE the coppiced pomegranate tree behind the kitchen garden appeared as an old arboreal empress; autumn gold garlanded the dark tresses of her splayed branches, bejewelled with ruby pendants of late ripening fruit, and a largesse of wind-scattered leaf gilded the brown earth beneath. Above the hillside clouds scudded in from the west, high and light, and rain was not expected. Satanaya left off her early morning meditation and went into the kitchen.

Some weeks earlier Gérard had put the word out among the local hunting fraternity – which meant basically anyone who owned a gun in these parts, so, most of the men with any land, and a few old soldiers – that pheasant would soon be on the menu at the Beyt'ur-Rahma. Since the Turkish Ambassador's demise, pheasants were no longer bred at the Beyt. However, a few wily birds had escaped the gun over the years, and small colonies of wild birds even managed to survive the indiscriminate slaughter which hunters in these parts generally visit upon the local fauna. So, greeting Satanaya now on the kitchen table were a dozen brace of gorgeous birds in full plumage awaiting her attention.

The menu for the evening feast was pinned to the wall with a list of the ingredients needed for each dish. It had been discussed beforehand by Lady Gülbahar and Clotilde, but even at this stage Satanaya had been consulted as to what might make a nice appetiser, something that could be eaten by the guests easily with their fingers, before they sat down to dinner. She suggested the 'Gül Böreği'. She had been allowed to make these little pastries in the convent, particularly because of her slender and deft young fingers. The dish also happened to be an old favourite of Lady Gülbahar, and so it was agreed.

MENU

Gül Böreği
(pastries of goat's cheese or minced lamb)
∗
Consommé
∗
Bonite en brochette
(bonito, bay leaves, red onion, sweetpepper sauce, green peppers)
∗
Faisan à la crème au Chanterelles
∗
Sorbet de Grenade
∗
Fromages de Chèvre et de Brebis

les vins:

Veuve Cliquot 1889
Petite Miséricorde Blanc de Blancs
Domaine Beyt'ur-Rahma. 'La Châtelaine'.
∗
Brandy de Maison
Arrack de Maison
∗
café Arabe
∗

Clotilde was already arranging the necessary ingredients for the dinner. Lady Gülbahar strolled in after breakfast, a string of onions in one hand, and in the other a slender ebony holder in which a cigarette of sweet Balkan tobacco smoked away. She was dressed in blue smock and baggy pink *shalwar* trousers, and a dainty full-bibbed white apron. Pelin slipped in behind carrying her mistress's coffee. A woman from the village arrived to make the thin *yufka* pastry for the *börek*. She carried her own pastry board – a large circular table with very short legs, and her rolling pin – a long thin wooden dowel.

'Now who wants to pluck and who'll do the onions?' announced Clotilde, then everyone rolled up their sleeves and set to work.

Satanaya was well used to plucking game from her time in the convent, and she knew speed was of the essence, as often the birds were hung a long time and were rather smelly. These pheasants were for the most part cleanly shot, and two weeks hanging in the well-ventilated game larder had tenderised them without any undue putrefaction. At any rate, she took the birds outside into the open area beyond the kitchen garden where any loose feathers and shifty odours would be blown away by the wind.

Placing the bird head down in the opening of an old sack on her lap, starting at the neck, gripping small tufts of feathers with quick sharp pulls she plucked away from herself into the sack. With Pelin helping, they had the birds plucked and gutted in little more than an hour. They covered the birds in a damp cloth, and put them in the icehouse to keep cool till the time came for cooking. The livers and hearts had been put aside and would later go into a terrine along with any meat left-over from the dinner.

Everyone helped in preparing vegetables. The pheasant would be served with *pommes duchesse,* and white cabbage cooked with apple, raisins and caraway seed. Lady Gülbahar supervised the soup, a delicate beef consommé flavoured with a hint of tarragon and the merest suspicion of *clou de girofle*, with stock clarified with egg white and mince.

Gül Böreği – Rose Pastries

The village lady sat straight backed on a thick blanket in a corner of the kitchen, her legs out at ninety degrees and a checked cotton cloth spread upon her knees. She dusted the board with flour, then pulled a small piece from the dough she had prepared, of plain flour, water and salt. She flattened the dough, turning it with the palm of her hand and began to roll it out with the long thin rolling pin. Then wrapping the flattened dough around the wooden pin, she lifted it and with a deft movement flipped it back onto the board, stretching it a little as it unrolled. She repeated the action, rotating the piece a little each time, until it had expanded into a large flat circle, increasing in size as it became thinner. While lifting the sheet of dough she would dust the board with more flour. When the dough had become a wafer-thin sheet covering the circular board she flicked it onto a floured tray beneath a clean cloth. The whole process had an easy timelessness to it, as if she was connecting to an age-old rhythm when her ancestors had first gathered grasses and grains to grind into flour, and begun to bake. She continued rolling and dusting, flipping and flopping, until the dough was all used up and the tray was stacked with more than a dozen sheets of *yufka*.

Meanwhile, Lady Gülbahar and Satanaya made fillings for the *börek*. For the meat filling, they sauteed finely-chopped onion in butter, then added some minced shoulder of lamb, turning it with the onions until all the pink in the meat had disappeared. This they seasoned with a little salt and pepper, just a small amount of tomato paste, a dash or two of pomegranate molasses, a touch of sugar and some *kibbeh* spice. This fragrant spice mix Satanaya had brought from Seydnaya, prepared for the convent by a merchant at the Salihiyye end of Abdul Ghani al Nabalousi Street in Damascus. They added lightly toasted pine kernels, some pre-soaked tiny little 'bird' currants, and some finely chopped parsley. The cheese filling combined fresh goats cheese with finely chopped dill and parsley, a little lemon juice, salt and a sprinkling of chili flakes.

The name *gül böreği* means 'rose pastry', on account of their flower-like shape, and would not be cooked until afternoon tea time, when the guests were arriving. The pastries were to be served on the terrace as a canapé, with champagne, as the sun went down. But so as not to disconnect the parts of the process, here is the remainder of the recipe: first they prepared a glaze mix of whole egg, olive oil/clarified butter and milk in equal parts. The circular sheet of yufka was cut into triangular segments like slices of pie, from the centre outwards, so that each sheet was divided into ten pieces or so.

'In the old days in Beirut,' said Lady Gülbahar to Satanaya, *sotto voce* so as not to scandalise the village lady, 'we called them *Orospu Böreği* – Whore's Börek. We would buy the yufka already prepared, and add a little garlic and paprika and a spoonful of yogurt to the glaze mix; we'd sit together folding the pastries and laying them onto a tray, and take them to the baker next door to be cooked. It was easy to prepare, something to snack on between clients, and get back on the job again.'

Then sitting with the glaze mix between them, and each with a buttered tray to hand, Lady Gülbahar taking the cheese mixture and Satanaya the meat, they began to fill and fold the little pastries.

Dividing a sheet of yufka from the centre into long triangles, they spread a light teaspoon of the mixture, meat or cheese, across the short edge of the pastry. Taking the two lower corners between the finger and thumb, they folded over perhaps three inches of each side, to stop the mixture escaping, and rolled it up, very loosely. It was just like rolling up a carpet in miniature, if a carpet was shaped like a long isosceles triangle. Just an inch or two of pastry was left unrolled where it tapered to a point. This loose flap was dipped into the egg glaze mix to seal the roll. At this stage it looked like a simple 'sigara börek'. Now with a deft twist of the fingers, one end of the pastry roll was tucked in, and rolled up lengthwise on itself, and the other end was dipped in the egg mixture to fix the pastry in its spiral shape. It was then placed on the greased tin, leaving a small gap between each.

Once the trays were filled, they brushed them with the glaze, dribbling the remaining mix generously over the lot. The pastries were baked in a medium to hot oven. Later Satanaya found the recipe in Takla's cookbook, and noticed a remark written in the margin: '*It is important to fold the börek loosely, so that while cooking they bloom, with space to expand their petals.*'

The guests began to arrive in the late afternoon, in time for tea and to watch the November sunset from the terrace. Dusk approached, the western sky glowed, the eastern horizon glowered, and fine vintage champagne, 1889 Veuve Cliquot, was poured. Eventually, when the vanished sun presented its rosy reprise somewhere above the Syrian desert, Satanaya presented the *gül böreği* on a silver tray, while Pelin handed out napkins. The guests were delighted and the conversation quickly turned to food.

Intense but good-natured arguments began over the various merits of French mille-feuille and Turkish yufka pastries, of boeuf-en-croûte and baklava, and the origins of croissants. Lady Gülbahar's protégés were always invited to take part in her soirées, and the guests all agreed what a delightful addition was the new assistant cook and a lively toast was drunk to her. Thrust momentarily into the spotlight, Satanaya was all blush and coy on the outside, while inside she felt so happy.

The guests were mostly old friends of Lady Gülbahar from Beirut's artistic set – a mixed bag of poets, painters, some classical musicians and a large lady nightclub singer. Satanaya found them an easy group to be with, and although she was busy serving and clearing, she couldn't help notice the attention which the men, young and old, paid her with their eyes.

As evening's darkness cloaked the land the party moved into the dining room. Light from several branched candlesticks illumined a field of linen covering the long table and gleamed and sparkled in the polished silver and chinaware brightening the whole room. Pale damask roses spilled from their vases in studied abandon – the handiwork of little Pelin. Pelin, who had known the pain of absence of flowers so much in her earlier life, had developed her aptitude for flower arranging with an enthusiasm verging on obsession. She abjured the convention of symmetry in her creations, preferring to let flowers and foliage settle according to their own natural inclinations, so that unsuspecting visitors, if left alone for long in the drawing rooms of Beyt'ur-Rahma, would find themselves transported to wild mountain valleys, rocky cliff tops and romantic ruins as they daydreamed amid her floral creations.

The consommé calmed their palates after the excitement of the champagne, and with their glasses replenished with the white wine of the maison, *Petite Miséricorde*, they tucked into the spicy bonito kebabs, with gratitude for all mercies great and small.

The pheasant was tender and moist, and the crisp flounce of the pommes duchesse made the perfect fop for mopping every last delicious drop of sauce, creamy and fragrant with the sweet-scented chanterelles*. All agreed it was a magnificent dish and again glasses were raised of the deep red cuvée, a Rhone-style blend with a local varietal, which the

---

* for recipe see Appendix I

Ambassador had named 'La Châtelaine'. For the pheasant, the plaudits were to Clotilde, who beamed a wide Provençal smile, and bowed daintily.

The dinner service for the evening was Lady Gülbahar's favourite, the fine Sèvres *'bleu celeste'* which the Ambassador had acquired during a stint in Paris. Each gilt-edged dinner plate was decorated with a different hand-painted bird within a border of deep cerulean. Once the diners had cleaned their plates – for at Lady Gülbahar's feasts, little ever remained for the chickens – the guests amused themselves with a party game. Each reciting poems and songs, fantastical tales improvised on the spot inspired by the particular avian subject of their plate. When someone called upon Satanaya to do a turn, she blushed again. She had not expected to have to perform in public like this, and looked uncertainly to Lady Gülbahar. Lady Gülbahar just smiled at her, as if to say, 'well, go on, tell us what is on your plate?'

Satanaya looked down and saw the most beautiful bird with feathers of every colour, but she had no idea at all what it was called. Even as she gazed, it began to change shape until it took on the appearance, just for an instant, of a hoopoe, before reverting to its wondrous paradisical glazed form. She remembered the stories her father had read to her, from the Qur'an and from the Persian poet, Attar, in his book called 'The Parliament of the Birds'. It was a story of the Hoopoe bringing a message to the Queen of Sheba from the great prophet-king Solomon. She stood up and found herself extemporising a poem on this theme. Afterwards Satanaya couldn't work out where these words had come from, they just seemed to flow magically from her, from a picture, both in her mind, and on the plate before her

> *'My bird's a song of love and longing*
> *far across the deserts flying.*
> *From King Solomon, it's crying:*
> *"I am beauty's messenger*
> *sent to Abyssinia.*
> *In God's name these words I bear*
> *To Bilquis your fair Queen.*
>
> *I know I seem to all but you*

as just a little brown hoopoe
of plain and simple dusty hue
but with my little crested crown
I hint to those with inner eyes
for I am clever in disguise
and show myself to you alone "

'And then Bilqis, but only she, beheld the bird in its original paradisical form. She received its message with love and submission in her heart, so that when she arrived at King Solomon's court, he recognised her, and in spite of all the hearsay, about her appearance as a she-devil with hairy legs and other such nonsense, and that business about worshipping the sun, Solomon knew the real beauty hidden within, and loved her accordingly.'

Satanaya smiled shyly and sat down.

'Bravo, bravo ma petite!' Lady Gülbahar clapped her hands in delight, glasses were raised all round. Satanaya blushed again and together with Pelin cleared the plates for sorbet. This was followed by the cheese, the arrack and the brandies. Then leaning on Pelin's arm, Lady Gülbahar rose from the table and bade all goodnight. But the night had just begun. The night club singer and the musicians broke out into endless love songs, for as one refrain died away, another took its place with barely a minim or a breve of pause. Most of the guests were familiar with the lyrics and joined in, while Satanaya set about clearing the table and carefully washing the precious china. Clotilde and Gérard danced together out on the terrace, others sat smoking narghilehs. When eventually the musicians' repertoire began to wane, carriages were called, and the party, happily but sleepily drunk, were arranged comfortably with blankets and waved off in convoy down the hill to Beirut.

TEN

Pelin's Story

OW DID YOUR FARM get its name?' asked Satanaya, over coffee one morning shortly after the soirée.

'You mean *Beyt'ur-Rahim* – The House of the Womb?' said Lady Gülbahar.

'That was the address Mother Superior gave us. When we asked directions from Beirut, everyone seemed to know it.'

Lady Gülbahar sipped her coffee and sat back.

'One day,' she began, 'a herdsman heard the bleating of young goats coming from high above the farm. He climbed up and was just in time to see a newborn kid goat, and then a second, emerging from a narrow crevice between two smooth, tall stones in the hillside. They were both still wet from birth and trailing their cords. No mother goat was to be seen anywhere – the slit in the rocks was too narrow for a fully-grown goat to pass, especially not a pregnant nanny – and no goat was missing from the goatherd's own flock. Perhaps the mother had been taken by a wolf, or died and carrion birds made off with the corpse. Afterwards the place became known as the Womb of the Goats. The farm has always been referred to by the local villagers as '*Beyt'ur-Rahim*', The House of the Womb.'

'But we call it *Beyt'ur-Rahma*, don't we?' butted in Pelin.

Lady Gülbahar smiled. It was true. By the time of Satanaya's arrival, due to the unrestrained kindness shown by its mistress to certain young ladies in need, it became known by those close to Lady Gülbahar as '*Beyt'ur-Rahma*', the House of Mercy; for is it not said that *rahma* – the compassionate mercy – is the root and womb from which all potential existences are delivered into being in this world?

As Satanaya subsequently discovered, the young servant Pelin was one example of the good lady's beneficence. This little frizzy-haired black child had walked the desert sands of the Horn of Africa from her homeland in far-off Ethiopia, to the very shores of the Red Sea. The Jews of that land had maintained a belief for thousands of years that they were the last of the people of Moses who were left after the flight out of Egypt, and that eventually they would reach the promised land. One day an itinerant anthropologist from Europe astonished them, bearing news of a community of Jews in Palestine.

Pelin's family, eager to rejoin their long lost brethren, set out with a group of Ethiopian Jews on the hazardous journey to their homeland. The pilgrims' numbers dwindled as the hardships of the road – the depredations of bandits, and lack of food and water – took their toll. Little six year old Pelin watched as her mother grew thinner and thinner, and was unable to feed her baby brother, who clung to his mother's breast, now dry of milk even as the springs and watercourses of the desert were dry of water. When robbers took the last of their animals, the pilgrims were too weak to resist their assailants who didn't even bother to kill their victims, abandoning them to the sun in the day, and the hyaenas at night.

No quails or manna fell from celestial heights to ease their plight. But Pelin was tough as a nut. When her mother died with her dead brother in her arms, she didn't cry. She knew enough of the scriptures even at that young age to know that they too would reach the promised land in their own way. She had to preserve what little strength she had left to continue her journey. Pelin was an unusual child, her beliefs reflecting the stories her grandfather told, stories based on observations of the world around her; nature for her was the unstinting source of all life, equal in its aspects of beauty and of rigour, whether evident, like the rain, or hidden, like the springs beneath the earth. She saw that only the behaviour of humans who had lost the connection with this original providence, who ceased to humble themselves to the earth from which the crops sprang and the animals fed, brought about such breakdowns as the pilgrims were experiencing now. But it didn't shake her certainty in the essentially generous and life-giving nature of her world.

When one by one her travelling companions fell by the wayside, and she was left alone but alive, she stayed calm and climbed a hillside where a single tree clung to life in the barren wilderness. She curled up in its meagre shade, remained still, and with her whole being questioned her soul, her own portion of this great nature, asking 'What now?' It wasn't a question that would be answered in words, but looking around it occurred to her that something must be feeding the tree, and whatever it was would feed her too. Behind the tree in a shady part against the rocks a hoopoe appeared, a bird blessed with the power to divine water underground. It vanished from view and soon after the clacking of its wings evidenced its departure. She crawled over and discovered a patch of sand all damp and scratched up with claw prints where the bird had been. Scraping away the sand she dug. As she dug the sand became wet. And when she had dug as deep as the stretch of her arm, water began to pool in the cup of her hand. She drank and she revived. For three days she hid in the rocks, sharing the water with a variety of animals that came by, a desert fox, a parade of rock doves, and on the morning of the third day she awoke to find a goat standing above her, a female goat with a full udder of milk, and not a kid to be seen anywhere. It was the most natural thing in the world for little Pelin to reach up and suckle at the teat of this mother goat. When later that day another band of pilgrims searching for the promised land came by, worn out, parched with thirst but still retaining some food stocks, she invited them to her wellspring, and adding her milking nanny to their own miserable supplies, joined their caravan.

When those few remaining faithful souls reached the Red Sea, the waters didn't part, but a great ship of Muslim pilgrims journeying to Abraham's black stone shrine of Mecca, ignorant of the language of this strange, silent, sandblasted community which had emerged from the desert, and not recognising them as anything but fellow pilgrims, offered them hospitality and passage to Yenbo. On arrival upon the coast of Arabia, however, fortune favoured them strangely. This lost tribe of Israel, anciently freed of Pharoah's chains now completed their journey to Jerusalem as manacled slaves. At Yenbo the ship's captain had revealed the true motive of his earlier generosity when he sold his human cargo to Arab merchants on the quayside. It was thus with a sense of irony that they broached the Mount of Olives and beheld before them the great walled city of peace crowned with the grey dome of the Haram al-Sherif. Pelin's compatriots were disheartened to discover that the streets of the city no longer flowed with milk and honey as their scripture had promised, but were filled with touts and hawkers, cruel soldiers on horseback and bad tempered clergy. Pelin, however, was not disappointed in the compassionate nature of her universe, which in its infinite kindness had quenched her thirst, fed and clothed her, and now delivered her to her goal.

Pelin's original name was Hirut. She was renamed by her erstwhile masters, Bedu tribesmen who brought her to the Holy City and sold her to a brothel. This renaming completed the transformation which had begun weeks before in the desert, when her past had seemed to die. And with this rebirth, a new name.

Pelin was too young to serve the brothel's clients in the customary manner. As a virgin she was a valuable commodity, and she wasn't abused. In fact she was looked after most carefully. One punter, however, a trader from the Mediterranean coast, took such a fancy to her that, with an eye to future delights, he bought her from the brothel and had her installed in his local whorehouse in Beirut where she would work as a cleaner and scullery maid. 'Until her fruit ripens,' as the trader put it.

There she was soon spotted by one of Lady Gülbahar's scouts; the Beiruti pimp was paid off, and she became a maid at *Beyt'ur-Rahma*. The dust was scrubbed off, her hair washed, untangled and braided, and when Lady Gülbahar saw such a picture of cherubic innocence she immediately fell in love with the child and formerly adopted her as one of a long line of apprentices and daughters.

Pelin, whose life had mostly been a struggle until then, took a while to realise that she had reached a place of real safety. For the first few months she didn't even speak. She hardly knew what language was being spoken anyway, and was afraid that if she said the wrong thing, if people realised she was Jewish, she might be sent away, sold again or worse. Gradually she understood that this place was different, and slowly a bond of trust grew between Lady Gülbahar and the little Abyssinian maid. Although notionally Pelin was there simply as general helper in the house, kitchen or garden, bit by bit she attached herself to her employer with such devoted attention that before long she became Lady Gülbahar's personal coffee maker (Pelin insisted that as an Ethiopian, she would best know how to prepare coffee, and indeed this proved true); she learnt her mistress's breakfast preferences and took on preparing the tray each morning with fresh flowers; she brought the evening wine on a silver salver, pouring it carefully into the precious Bohemian crystal glass with the dignified hauteur of a Parisian sommelier – Lady Gülbahar chuckled inwardly at the seriousness with which the little girl performed this task. Pelin was the soul of attention, so that it seemed the châtelaine merely had to think of the girl and she would appear like the proverbial genii of the lamp.

As she gained confidence, Pelin developed an endearing style of speech incorporating a wide variety of languages: a little Arabic picked up on her travels, a smattering of Greek mixed in with Turkish from her time in Beirut, and strange phrases in French overheard from Lady Gülbahar and Clotilde the cook. And all threaded upon a string of Amharic syntax. Even if one didn't understand all the words that tumbled from her small dark lips, the meaning conveyed through the deep pools of her Abyssinian eyes, as unblinking she addressed one in pleading tones, ensured that whatever it was she wished to convey, the sense was eventually discovered and responded to.

With Lady Gülbahar's help, Pelin eventually learnt to write in Arabic as well as in the Latin alphabet. Then with the help of the Turkish Ambassador and a couple of the more literate patrons of the salon evenings – a French doctor and an Egyptian judge – Pelin undertook a systematic study of Arabic, French and Turkish. When she finally untangled the linguistic bunch of grapes in which she had initially garbled and gambolled with such abandon, and was able to communicate correctly in each tongue, Pelin was also entrusted to take dictation for the vast and varied correspondence that Lady Gülbahar dealt with most mornings, taking copies of all her missives for future reference should the need for clarification ever arise. Pelin began to love the written word. She understood its power, and hence its value, and gave it due respect. And Lady Gülbahar, whose own spoken language could be quite colourful, relied on Pelin to temper her over-enthusiasms on paper, to correct mistakes as well as censor the occasional indiscreet usage of street language, preventing it from slipping into the bureau of official post; or editing what might pass as a humorous 'bon mot' in speech but in print might imply inappropriate intimacy rather than as intended irony for a particular addressee.

Those readers who may have encountered Lady Gülbahar in her earlier life will know that she too had been a victim of the sordid world of Beiruti harlotry, before being rescued by the noble Daud the Arwadi. He it was who paid for the farmhouse where he installed her as his erstwhile mistress until he went off and got involved with a lot of goats – an altogether different tale*. Since then she had married the widowed Turkish Ambassador, a late but happy love for him and a secure pension for her; and the farm became both a home and training school, and hence the means to a legitimate livelihood, for a number of young ladies saved from the mean streets and the waterfront of the city below.

The Ambassador spent his retirement developing the farm's vineyards, while Lady Gülbahar played host to old friends and new with regular banquets and soirées attended by the steady troupe of dignitaries and intellectuals, literati, travellers and exiles from east and west, who arrived at the gate of *Beyt'ur-Rahma* on recommendation; her table was known to rival that of Seydnaya, and perhaps due to the establishment's limited accommodations (only the most favoured guests, those she referred to as 'family', ever passed the night beneath the farmhouse roof) it was never mentioned by Cook's Tours. Yet neither Shepheards in Cairo, nor even the Pera Palace Hotel in Constantinople, nor the Baron Hotel when it opened a few years later in Aleppo could boast a more distinguished guest book. Not a few future heads of state, and heads of future states for that matter, learnt a particular discernment of taste for fine wine and delicious food at the table of the Beyt.

---

* *The Story of the Damascus Drum*, Hakawati Press, 2011.

Lady Gülbahar had become something of a fine amateur in the kitchen. Over the years she, Clotilde and the assorted staff of the Beyt had developed a quite unique cuisine. Depending on the particular hue of the guest list, a menu would be chosen from the best of French provincial food, the Ottoman refinement of vegetable cooking and the subtly spiced dishes of the Middle Eastern table. The weekend soirées were generally limited to between six and ten guests. Unless it was a party, when numbers dictated buffet service *en plein air*, with a charcoal grill for cooking beef steaks, spatchcocked poultry and gamebirds, and kebabs of lamb or fish.

Many were drawn to the Beyt on account of the wines. The cool breezes from the Eastern Mediterranean which blew each evening into that cleft of the Shouf mountain range as a balm from the summer heat, and the well drained slopes of chalk soil found only in that little nook, produced the perfect *terroir* for the local vines as well as those which had been given him by his friend the French Baron. Indeed, the Baron, whose renowned vineyards in the Girondais produced long-lasting wines *sans pareil*, was now engaged in promoting viniculture in Lebanon and Palestine, and had spent a lot of time with the Turkish Ambassador advising and helping turn his *'petit château de miséricorde'* into a budding *'premier crû'*.

Then came the year the Ambassador called 'the great vintage', when his small acreage of terraced vines had benefitted from good early rainfall, a long hot summer with just enough late precipitation to bring volumes up to a good level. Sugar levels perfect, great acidity, plenty of tannin to be smoothed out over the years. It was a big crop, more than any of the earlier years. Although too old now to take part in the actual physical production, he still took pleasure in discussing and mulling over each stage with his winemaker, Gérard. This former sailor from Provence had stumbled into the farm one spring day having jumped ship in Beirut. The sight of the warm green hills rising up off the Mediterranean had provoked pangs of homesickness for his family's farm near Vence. Together Gérard and the Ambassador had uncovered the ways of the grape, they had worried like parents with unruly offspring over the vagaries of the seasons, become jointly drunk when early tastings proved their efforts, and commiserated when things didn't go right.

Now the Ambassador watched with joy as this magnificent crop was trampled underfoot by the local villagers barefoot in the big tank by the cellar doors, he swooned over the vats as the must fermented; and his eyes filled with tears as the raw wine was poured off into the oak barriques, for he had divined in that moment of supreme satisfaction that he would never live to taste this vintage in its prime. It would take decades until it reached maturity in the cool, dark hermitage of the cellar dug deep into that rocky hillside. But it was enough for him to have seen it this far. Time would do the rest. He had done his best and achieved more than he'd hoped. There was wine enough laid down to keep the tables of the Beyt groaning with good cheer 'til well beyond both his and Lady Gülbahar's lifetimes. And anyway, he felt tired.

And that was how they found him, seemingly asleep by the barrels as if their fumes had closed his eyes in dreams. But he had drunk more deep than any wine of this world's keep; he'd supped on honeydew, and now was tasting paradise. They laid him to rest in a modest tomb above the vineyard, from where his spirit mingled with the sea breezes and continued to bring a refreshing coolness to the eyes of all in the farm below after the heat of the day.

ELEVEN

Girl Talk and Superheroes

Beyt'ur-Rahma, Lebanon, 1897

HE MONTHS PASSED, the seasons progressed. Winter was brief. Snow fell in the hills and the fire in the hall burned throughout the day. Satanaya and Pelin were kept busy preparing braziers which they took to the rooms each evening to take the chill off the night.

As with the seasons so the menus changed. Almond blossom and green plums heralded spring and sweet young vegetables appeared in the market. At Eastertime milk-fed lamb was prepared. With summer the kitchen was busy preparing feasts for the regular soirées. Before she knew it, autumn returned. She had passed a happy year in the Beyt'ur-Rahma. While Satanaya's culinary education continued apace, her mind was now being developed in other ways. She had a natural aptitude for languages. Already fluent in the Adige language of the Circassians, she spoke Arabic, could get by in Aramaic, and was slowly finding her way in Turkish. Now Lady Gülbahar started her on French:

'Vraiment, c'est très facile, and once you can speak it you will have an entry into a whole new world, the world of Europe, the modern world.'

As Lady Gülbahar spoke her own unique blend of Arabic, Persian and Turkish, and occasionally Greek, in a charming approximation of the Ottoman language, spiced liberally with French – as well as Italian, English, German, and and her native Adige as the occasion demanded – Satanaya quickly built up a basic vocabulary as well as acquiring some curious archaic aphorisms.

French had been an essential tool of the trade in Lady Gülbahar's earlier career, when a fluttering of her long eyelashes above rouged cheeks, and a coy little 'voulez-vous coucher avec moi' whispered in low tones from her pert cupid's bow lips proved a marketing advantage which raised her earnings over the other street girls. The Turkish Ambassador had command of the three languages of the Ottoman court and had spoken the diplomatic language fluently, so he had been able to iron out some of the coarser expressions with which his wife seasoned her conversation. With the châtelaine's encouragement, and with Clotilde chattering away in the kitchen, and correcting her accent, Satanaya quickly became proficient.

Lady Gülbahar not only encouraged her ward's language skills, but took pains to stimulate her interest in the wider world. She saw a great future for this young girl who reminded her so much of herself at that age. Satanaya was intelligent, independent, beautiful, somewhat headstrong, but with the fearlessness of youth living in the moment. These traits, neutral in themselves, could get a girl into trouble if not judiciously guided to bring out the best of her potential.

'There are two kinds of women, Satanaya, and we carry both inside us' said Lady Gülbahar one day. 'Most of us tend to see only one side, the woman we act out in front of people, and many of us believe it to be the real woman. This is the poor, weak, dependent creature who submits to her man, follows his orders, takes his advice, all those things our culture expects her to be; she bears his children, works hard in the home, tries to do her best for her man, accepts his anger as well as his love. She suffers, she is humble and faithful to the lot of Providence, without complaint; in this way she develops the strength and resilience to carry her and her family through the terrible difficulties that life throws at us. She's a saint really, although in her natural humility she will believe she is nothing.

'Then there's the other woman. She is not weak, not tied up with emotions. Quite rational and mentally strong, she is capable of anything. But this second woman lives only in the imagination of the first. Sometimes in moments of crisis she escapes the mold and takes control, but as soon as things calm down she quickly withdraws. Mostly we deny her. She remains a hidden creature, dark and mysterious; perhaps even we are ashamed of her, and pretend she doesn't exist. But she is really a hero. We don't like to admit that she is there, it is easier for us to remain passive, to keep silent and let men do all the important stuff. But she is in us and she will out, if given the chance. And given the chance, these two women can make friends, and see they are really two sides of the same person, then that person, the real woman – well, believe me, that woman is unstoppable.'

The old lady paused. Satanaya was intrigued and hanging on her every word. She recognised how most women were as Lady Gülbahar described: the village wives in Palestine; the nuns (except Mother Superior, of course, she was altogether different, anyone could see that); even Clotilde was quite a wee wifey (although she suspected that the jolly French cook didn't submit blindly to her husband Gérard – they seemed quite an equal partnership), but most of the women in the farming community around Beyt'ur-Rahma, while undoubtedly strong, submitted to the order of a society where men completely dominated.

'But isn't that the same everywhere, Lady Gülbahar? I mean, isn't that just how it is?'

'So it would seem. But you know, it hasn't always been like that. You remember the story of your namesake, don't you?'

Satanaya knew well the Legend of Satanay, the great heroine of the Adige people – the Cherkess, or Circassians as they are generally called in the wider world.

The ancient Circassians were known by the name of Narts. Their epic legends of their origins in the North West Caucasus date back three thousand years and are in the many stories and songs called the Nart Sagas. Paralleling the legends of their neighbours in Ancient Greece, these tales relate tell the deeds of marvellous beings, gods and monsters, heroes and villains, and heroines too, exemplifying the chivalric qualities held dear in Circassian culture. And the heroine pre-eminent among such was the Lady Satanay. She is known as the Mother of the Narts. She is named for a plant with small white flowers, known also as Filipendula or dropwort, the flower from which she was born.

In the land of the Narts there was no one more beautiful than the Lady Satanay, and the Nart gallants were literally queueing up to marry her. She was so beautiful in fact that within her presence men lost their self-control. So great was the attraction young men felt for her that it is related that when doing her laundry at the river one day, she hitched up her skirts to avoid wetting her clothes, exposing her delectable and well-formed nether parts. A young herder by the name of Zhemix'we who was passing on the opposite bank just could not contain himself; and nor could he contain his seed, which involuntarily ejaculated itself with such force that it bridged the stream and landed on the very rock where Lady Satanay was scrubbing her smalls. Responding in accord with the intensity of Zhemix'we's expressed desire, the stone became receptive as womb to this broadcast of seed and subsequently gave birth to Lady Satanay's son, Sosriqwe.

Lady Satanay was fertile in other fields, being blessed with qualities of creative invention when the secrets of viniculture were revealed through her to her people. She became the repository of great wisdom and prophecy to be consulted by the Narts in struggles with their enemies, and by following her wise advice the Nart nation survived. But she had her naughty side too, and like any semi-divine mother of mythology worth her salt, she was not averse to using a bit of magic if it would further her progeny's career.

'And so you know that a Circassian woman is the equal of any man, and more than equal at times?' said Lady Gülbahar

Satanaya laughed. Hearing Lady Gülbahar speak like this had a wonderful effect on her.

'But what about men? Do men have two men inside them too?'

'Well, yes, I suppose in a way they do. A bit like our hidden woman, but the opposite. They like to appear strong and in control, forceful, always right, never surrender. Perhaps that's why they often appear hard. And we respond to this, we women, by being the soft to their hard, so to speak.' Lady Gülbahar gave a slight giggle. 'But you will see, they also have their gentle side which they don't like to show. Which is a shame, because it can be quite beautiful, quite poetic. In fact, that's why I so much enjoy having artistic people at our soirées. These artistic ones are not so afraid to show their sensitive sides, they seem more able to let their two sides talk to each other, negotiate; they express their feelings as well as making intelligent conversation. Even so it's rare for them to find a real balance, they place such importance on their self-identity.

'The Turkish Ambassador had this balance, and more so as he got older. In fact, I'm rather glad we met later in life when he'd obviously worked out these two sides.

'Sometimes he expressed himself with such a powerful sentiment, and his words came from somewhere so deep, as if a bigger, a truer self was speaking. It wasn't simply an amalgamation of these two sides, but – how can I say? – it was as if he became a real man. I think working with the vines showed him that balance, having his hands in the earth, doing something he loved and knew would benefit others more than himself.'

'I'm sure you had something to do with it.' said Satanaya, thinking that Lady Gülbahar herself was no ordinary woman when she spoke like that.

'Ha ha. But you know,' said Lady Gülbahar, 'the world is changing and there are women out there, in Europe and America, who are changing it, and changing themselves with it. They want to have a say in deciding their own lives, who they will marry. If they will marry. To own their own lives without having to get the permission of any man. In some countries, where they do such things, they are even demanding to vote in elections to parliament. Now, there's a thing. One day, Satanaya, you could be one of them, who knows?'

'Not if my parents have anything to do with it; or the Turks; or the mullahs or priests for that matter.' said Satanaya, 'And anyway, we don't even have a parliament.'

Lady Gülbahar continued: 'There's one area where we women are really quite different: love and compassion – these qualities are central to our nature in a way few men understand. How else could we be mothers? For that matter, how else could we suffer the whole matter of giving birth and raising children?

'And we don't even have physically to produce children. Look at me – I've never given birth, but I've still been burdened with the whole business of bringing up children – and I include some of the men in my life among them. But I don't regret it. It couldn't have been any other way.

'For men, it's different. Of course they have these qualities, and just occasionally they are able to bring them into focus in their lives in a very powerful way, and often they are the ones the world makes a song and dance about, the great poets and writers on love for instance. The revolutionaries who give birth to great ideas and movements. Prophets, kings. But let me tell you, they aren't saying anything we women haven't known all along. Love ultimately holds us all together, and for us women, love is about sacrifice. If we women know anything at all, it's sacrifice.'

Lady Gülbahar paused and reflected.

'Ah, yes.' she said, 'That reminds me, I've heard from your family. They're all well, and your father is on his way here. I imagine he will want to talk to you about your marriage.'

Satanaya gasped. She was dumbfounded.

'You can't put it off forever.' Lady Gülbahar continued. 'Do you want to go away with him? Much as I love having you here, I can't go against your family's will.'

Satanaya was really stunned. She had been living quite happily – blissfully even – at Beyt'ur-Rahma for the past year now and had managed successfully to push all thoughts of the future from her mind completely. This was not welcome news. Of course, she loved her father, and knew he would listen to her wishes, but it was doubtful whether they would be able to convince her mother that her life here was for the best. In fact, Satanaya had not even discussed these matters with Lady Gülbahar. Time had just flown by and the question of her status had never arisen. But now that it had, something broke inside her.

'No!… NO. NO. NO. I can't. I won't! I would rather die. There must be some way out of this.' Satanaya's outburst was so sudden that it even disturbed the lake-calm equanimity of Lady Gülbahar.

'But surely your parents won't make you marry someone unsuitable. From what you have told me, your father seems an honourable man, and well-respected. I'm sure he will have found a good match for you.'

'I'm not worried about father.' Satanaya was crying now, and between her sobs she explained: 'It's mother, you see… She… well, she sees things differently… It's all about the wedding, and grandchildren and all the traditions. Her own wedding was such a hurried affair, it was during the time of the migrations, and it was more important to start producing children than worrying too much about impressing the tribe.' She took a deep breath. She was feeling calmer now. 'To be honest, Lady Gülbahar, I just don't feel like getting married. Not to any one. At least, not at the moment. My life is only beginning.'

Satanaya was besides herself. It was true, her parent's marriage had been a sudden affair. A love match, in fact, and unusual under normal circumstances.

They had met and fallen in love in Kayseri, an important agricultural market and busy commercial centre in central Anatolia, famous for its gold ware, carpets, and its preserved comestibles. Kayseri's half a million Muslims, Orthodox and Armenian Christians lived and worked side by side as they had done for nearly a millennium. In spite of the hardships of the time, her mother would fondly recall the city's spicy buffalo meat sausage called *sucuk* – and the *pastırma* – dried beef fillets encased in thick spice paste. Here Mansur's family set up as butchers, adding Circassian meat traditions to a town famed for its viands.

One day, in the Kayseri sheep market, the slender (as refugees must be), blue-eyed shepherd's daughter Gülay, had caught the brown eyes of Mansur. This young man, the quiet grandson of a renowned Circassian Sufi sheykh, was purchasing lambs for the family butchery. And her glance was met and returned. The exigencies of their situation, as strangers in a foreign land, the importance of continuing family lines and maintaining tribal strength, facilitated the waiving of some of the more restrictive customs of their related culture and religions. Marriage was effected and shortly afterwards they continued on to Palestine.

But that was then and this was now. Why did Satanaya have to go back to the old ways? Such were her thoughts, as she saw the magnificent bubble of hope for a different kind of future that her brief sojourn in the Beyt had created burst when it had barely begun.

'Well, maybe you can convince your father. You are welcome to stay here, of course. But only on the condition that both your parents are agreeable. Let's wait and see. Don't worry, *ma cherie*, we'll come up with something. *À barque désespérée, le Dieu fait trouver le port.* Now, let's go and see what's happening in the vineyard?'

TWELVE

Ride to Sidon

Sidon, Palestine, 1897

ATANAYA AND HER FATHER Mansur took the coast road south from Beirut, through small villages, buried among dark-leaved groves of orange trees bright with ripening fruit. To their right the Mediterranean, glowed pale and milky blue in the morning light. Herds of swarthy goats and dusty sheep drifted over distant hillsides. Far beyond, soft-shouldered mountains floated, half-hidden beneath snow and a hazy sky. A fresh breeze warmed as the day wore on. Perfect riding weather as autumn turned into winter.

For Satanaya it was a journey back in time. For hours they tramped in silence in sight of the shore. She thought of the home to which she was returning. So much had happened, so much had changed in her during those few years away that her memories of childhood seemed to be of another person. The connection was there, of course. The moment she had seen her father she became a little girl again. She adored him and had run down the path from the terrace to greet him, flinging her arms around him as she had done as a child. They had talked for ages together, and she had heard all the news of her siblings and friends in the village. But once she had extracted all the gossip of home, inevitably the subject of her marriage came up. Then an atmosphere of gloom invaded their conversation as she tried to accommodate this dreaded subject in the new and awakening Satanaya she now felt herself to be. In the end, after much tears and several outbursts which always resulted in her apologising for her temper, she had agreed, much against her own feelings, to return home and meet the intended boy. Only if she felt happy with the situation would she consent to the marriage. If not, and if no evident alternative appeared, she might return to Beirut on a permanent basis.

It was not the traditional way among the Adige people. The preferred method of betrothal was for young people to be introduced gradually to the opposite sex through the medium of staged social events. They would become familiar with each other through a gradual process, not through talk and touch but by taking part in traditional dances. Here the boys would try to out-do each other to impress with their haughty attitudes and fancy foot work while the girls, equally proud and full of disdain, would play hard to get. The real intercourse, meanwhile, took place with the eyes, mirroring their true feelings without words. In this way, couples chose each other, and although the various parents might not agree, invariably love won out. However, following the massacres by the Russian army and subsequent expulsions from their Caucasian homelands, in the great scattering diaspora the cultural integrity of the Circassian peoples was under threat. Many marriages, like her parents own, had occurred outside the accepted pale of their traditions, and the need for some degree of 'arrangement' to strengthen bonds within the tribes had crept in.

'So, what's this fellow like, papa? I don't remember him from before.' said Satanaya.

'No, you probably wouldn't. His family arrived in Kfar Kama around the time you left for Seydnaya. His father – his Adige name is Dzagashta

– was a blacksmith, but later joined the Turkish army like many Circassians and fought against the Russians and Rumanians when they entered Bulgaria in 1877. It was a terrible time – the Siege at Plevna, you've heard people talk about it... '

Satanaya had certainly heard of the great siege of Plevna. Following the heroic defence and eventual defeat of the Turkish forces holding the Bulgarian town, and the subsequent arrival of the Russian army a few miles outside of Constantinople, the Great Powers of Europe had been moved to intervene on Turkey's behalf and to engineer a diplomatic solution. When the fate of the great city, and that of the Ottoman Empire itself, hung in the balance, the British navy had trained its guns on the Tsar's army, halting the Russian advance, thus preventing the city's destruction, bringing about a truce and peace at the Treaty of Berlin. Every Circassian knew such affairs were also intimately connected to their own fate, and were among the reasons they were received with such favour into the Ottoman fold after suffering near-genocide at the hands of the Russians in their own lands*.

Satanaya's father recalled that the girl's intended father-in-law, Dzagashta, who was a sergeant, had been given the Turkish name Kiliçzade – 'Son of the Sword' – on account of his exploits at Plevna.

'Yes, he was quite a hero, and he saved many men by his bravery. His commander and some officers were cut off by a group of Cossacks during the final attempt to break out of Plevna. Kiliçzade fought his way back through the Russian lines with his men and rescued the officers. His unit was one of a few which succeeded in breaking out and escaping capture. His son is called Timur. He's a blacksmith, just as Kiliçzade was before he was driven out of Shapsug lands. But Timur is quite different from his father. In spite of his age, Kiliçzade is still a big bull of a man, just as you might expect a blacksmith to be. Timur is a gentle soul really. He's still young, and they say he uses a much smaller hammer than his father. But he does good work. Anyway, your mother likes him.'

That last remark brought a grunt from Satanaya, and she glanced wryly at her father.

'Yes, well, that's the important thing I suppose.' she said, and they both laughed. For form's sake it had been agreed that after her return, dances

---

* Appendix Two – The Russo-Ottoman War of 1877-78

would be held. Satanaya's father as a respected elder, would be expected to host the usual social events which precede a betrothal.

In spite of her headstrong attitude, her father was secretly proud of her. As a child, once she had mastered her pony, he sometimes let her accompany him on long rides to visit other groups of Circassian refugees, many of whom were his *murids*, pupils in the way of *Khabze*.

Mansur had inherited spiritually from his grandfather, a Sufi sheykh, the ancient Circassian traditions of *Khabze*, with its rich and deeply chivalric code of conduct based on responsibility to oneself, to others and to the world around one, in concordance with a 'Higher Mind', the Mighty *Tha*. For the sheykh, the way of the Prophet Mohammed was simply a further expression of the same eternal truth. He found no contradiction in uniting within his own soul the various strands of ancient and recent lights in a single seamless vision. This manner of vision he bequeathed to his grandson Mansur, when as a young lad he accompanied the family on the long journey of sacrifice and adventure into Ottoman lands.

And in the same way Satanaya too came to absorb by a kind of osmosis, a portion of this wisdom. As a child sometimes, she would sit quietly in the background, listening to her father counselling the men, young and old, on how to behave in this mixed environment, where now they rubbed shoulders with Jews and Druzes, Orthodox, Catholic, and Armenian Christians, as well as Alawite Muslims and Bedouin of Sunni persuasion. His advice was quite simple, 'Remember, there is only ever one thing, and it is our task to build into that; whether we come to it by religion, or simply by our way, our way of life – our task is to know who we are, and to recognise the single source of our being. That is our journey in this world. So, be helpful to everyone, for we are all of that single being, do not harm anyone, and keep everything clean.'

Of course, for Mansur as a recognised 'elder' there were many established traditions to be passed on and maintained, and he didn't deny the importance of these in helping the little groups of the Cherkess diaspora maintain their cultural identity within a refugee society. But he believed strongly that for each person, or at least for any one in whom the question of knowing oneself arose as an imperative, establishing a direct link to his or her essential being was possible and necessary. Satanaya just sat, and listened. Her father knew all the old tales of the Narts, as well as the Koranic and Biblical stories, the Persian poets and traditional tales of the Adige people. When people came with questions, he would draw on this deep well of stories to illustrate the problem in hand, hoping to elicit a response from the questioner, to allow the person to reach his own conclusions, to help him discover the answer for himself. This was his preferred way, rather than preaching a fixed rule, which would only make between them a relationship of dependence. He too became known as a sheykh and a Sufi. Mansur didn't call himself anything.

Their journey from Beirut took them down the coast, and by evening they reached Saida, the ancient Phoenician city known as Sidon. Pretty gardens and orchards of bananas and palms gave way to narrow streets surrounding the old souk. They emerged at the seafront opposite the harbour where, beyond a breakwater filled with fishing boats bobbing at their moorings, rose an old castle on an island. Saida has been involved with the fishing industry since Phoenician times. Even the name has its roots in the Semitic word for fishery. Home to navigators and shipbuilders, the original ancient mariners of the Mediterranean, the city became synonymous with the people themselves, and was known as 'Mother City of Phoenicia'.

They put up at a nearby *khan*. A streetfood vendor had set up his cart within the walls and they dined on a simple dish of *mujaddara*: rice and lentils, spiced with cumin and topped with a heap of caramelised onions. Afterwards father and daughter took a digestive evening stroll. The sea was calm and fishermen were taking their ease; muscular young men with sun-darkened skin, bare to the waist, sat mending nets, strung between tall palm trees, stretching the skeins from their big toes.

Back in town, in a narrow backstreet they came across the glass-fronted patisserie of Sheykh Mustafa Sinoura. Multicoloured sweets in tall jars with gleaming brass lids lined the high counter below which trays of variously shaped biscuits, pistachio pastries and syrupy almond confections were displayed.

Here they discovered Sidon's renowned shortbread called 'Seniora', invented by Sheykh Mustafa some forty years earlier. On a small table they nibbled the delicious crumbly biscuits, slightly hollow inside, and sipped small cups of stomach-soothing coffee. Although tired from a long day in the saddle, Satanaya, wishing to add to her *repertoire de cuisine,* insisted on seeing how the biscuits were made. Leaving her father to talk with the Sheykh, she was led away by the proprietor's son who was only to happy to show off his kitchen to the beautiful Circassian girl.

As cooks will know, the best dishes are often the most simple, and Seniora biscuits are of this class. But the Sheykh's son, keen to impress a fellow cook, especially one as as charming as Satanaya, managed to make the whole process sound like a mystical treatise being imparted to one of the elect.

'Take the finest confectioner's sugar, what we call 'sucre glace'.' he began, while pushing a scoop into a large container, lifting out a mound of pure white powder and waving it under Satanaya's nose. 'Then butter. It must be the freshest butter, from cows fed on the rich sweet grass of the high pastures. The butter and sugar are then mixed for at least two hours so that the sugar is completely dissolved in the butter which becomes like sweet cream.'

'And here…' He paused as he uncovered a large mixing bowl of what looked like thick whipped cream or yogurt, 'Look, we have just finished this batch.'

He dipped in a spoon and proffered it to Satanaya at the exact moment she leant forward to look, resulting in a great blob of sweet sticky mess landing on her nose. The young man was startled and blushed with embarrassment. And then fussing about with a napkin he only succeeded in wiping the mixture further across her face.

Satanaya just laughed and licking the mixture from her lips took the napkin from him and cleaned herself up.

They moved to another room where men where hard at it, mixing away.

'When the butter-sugar mix is ready, we add flour – the finest, most refined flour, sieved of course – and mix well. The biscuit dough is then left over night, and as we all know,' and the sheykh's son gave Satanaya a knowing glance, 'night is when the best magic happens.' He was getting into his stride now. Normally a shy lad, something about Satanaya, her look of fascinated interest when he spoke, had drawn him out of his shell. And she, for her part, was flattered by his enthusiasm, and wondered whether he would have been so forward had his father been present. But she was not going to let a little innocent flirting put her off discovering this new culinary process.

'Now, in here…' and he led Satanaya through a door into a room lined with tables. Here amid a snowstorm of flour and sugar, a team of white-aproned men and women were busy with rolling pins, doughs and other ingredients. He pointed to a woman who was rolling out some dough into a long sausage.

'Look how she first flattens the sausage slightly before cutting it into little diamond shapes.' he said.

The woman, who could have been a double for Beulah, the cook at Seydnaya, nimbly laid the little pieces of raw dough in a spiral on a large circular tray and placed a pistachio nut on each. The tray, when filled, took on the appearance of seeds in a great sunflower. Then on into another room where two men sweated before a couple of large, wood-fired brick baking ovens.

'It is important to get the fire very hot before we put in the dough. And we turn the tray a little every few minutes so the biscuits cook evenly. They are done in no time at all.'

He picked up a biscuit which was cooling on a tray nearby, and bit into it.

'Did you hear the crack? And look at the slight hollow inside. That's why we get the oven so hot, to get the biscuit to open up, to get that crack in the mouth.' The sheykh's son turned to Satanaya, but she was too busy scribbling in her notebook to notice the shy devoted look in his eyes. They returned to the shop where Mansur and the old Sheykh were busy in conversation.

'Papa, that was amazing,' said Satanaya, 'but I'm so tired now I can barely keep my eyes open.'

She knew it was really her father who was tired, but she knew also that he was too polite to break off talking with the Sheykh of his own accord.

'Yes my dear, I know, we have another long ride ahead of us. Perhaps we better call it a night.' He thanked the Sheykh and they made their farewells. The sheykh's son saw them to the door and stood following with eyes of fondness and longing the form of Satanaya disappearing down the street.

They returned to the khan. It really had been a long day in the saddle, and Satanaya, who had spent many hours brooding over her immanent future, now quickly drifted off with a vision of endless spirals of golden lozenge-shaped biscuits passing before her eyes, and entered a dreamless sleep among the ghosts of millennia.

THIRTEEN

Hold Fast to the Rudder of the Ship

Tyre, Palestine, 1897

 SALT TANG and the scent of oranges on the morning breeze quickened the riders' spirits as they rode through endless citrus groves south from Sidon. They reached Tyre before sundown.

Tyre was once an island floating happily off the coast. In order to subdue the Tyreans, Alexander the Great built a causeway to join it to the mainland. For two thousand years the sea dumped sand with every tide until it formed a permanent peninsula. Tyre … *'Thou, O Tyre, hast said, I am perfect in beauty…'* but where was its beauty now? Ebbing and flowing with the sands of time, no more were the patricians of Rome born into the purple of its crustaceous trade; the city receded into a backwater as empires marched west with the sun. Mansur and Satanaya walked their mounts through the outskirts, along rubbish-strewn streets of tumbledown houses and onto a beach leading to the causeway.

'The story goes,' said Mansur 'that the city of Tyre got its name from Tyrus, who was a nymph, a kind of female jinn in the mythology of the ancient peoples of the Mediterranean. She was the beloved of Heracles the Hero, son of Zeus the king of the gods. Anyway, they were walking along the beach one day – maybe this very beach – when Heracles' dog bit into a shell lying in the water, and his mouth became stained with the most fabulous purple colour. Tyrus – she sounds like a bit of a trend-setter – insisted that Heracles get her a dress made from cloth dyed with the same purple stuff of the shell. Doubtless she got her way, because before long the island became famous for the purple dyes extracted from the shellfish the dog had bit. A gramme of the dye cost more than ten grammes of gold.'

Satanaya listened to the story and imagined this beautiful purple dye, and the dress that the capricious nymph insisted Heracles give her before she would let him enter her bed. Perhaps, thought Satanaya, she too could devise some impossible task to keep suitors at bay, just as her namesake in the Nart legends. Sadly, courting and betrothal had become just so prosaic and predictable in the world of mortals.

'There's another ancient myth,' her father continued, 'A king of Tyre called Agenor had a daughter called Europa, who became enamoured of Zeus (who else!). Zeus just had to have her. As Europa was walking along the shore, the god appeared in the shape of a beautiful white bull with shining horns. Europa fell for the bull's beauty, and its unthreatening expression and peaceful manner. She began to stroke the animal which responded by licking her hands, and eventually Europa climbed upon its back. All part of Zeus' seduction plan, because no sooner was she comfortably mounted than he wandered into the water. Before Europa realised, the bull was swimming away from the shore all the way to Crete. There Zeus took on a human form and had his way with her. '

'And that,' her father concluded, 'is how Europa, born in Asia, gave her name to the western continent.'

Satanaya was still pondering her own potential engagement. While there was nothing prosaic or predictable in the seduction of Europa, yet the story had annoyed her.

'These men – they really must have it their own way all the time.'

'Yes, but remember, Zeus was a god, what else could she do. I didn't hear you complain about the way Tyrus treated Heracles. All she got was the dress. Europa got three sons and a continent.'

'I'll take the continent, you can have the sons.' said Satanaya.

Mansur just laughed. 'And don't forget Dido, the very beautiful Dido. She was a princess of Tyre who set out from here to found Carthage.'

'Go on...'

'Well, she and her brother Pygmalion were joint heirs to the Kingdom of Tyre, but the king's subjects only wanted one ruler.'

'You mean, they wanted a man.'

'Yes, well, perhaps. Pygmalion was only a boy when his father died. He had Dido's husband who was extremely rich, assassinated.'

'Typical. I bet he was a spoilt little brat.'

'Probably did it for the money.'

'Always the way.'

'But he didn't get it. Dido and her supporters escaped by ship with her husband's gold.'

'Hooray! There's some justice, at least.' This pleased Satanaya. 'But still, she had to flee her home.'

'Yes,' continued her father. 'She ended up settling in Carthage, where Tunis is now. That's where she did the thing with the ox-hide. She asked that her party could be given a piece of land the area of an ox-hide, and when the locals agreed she cut a hide into one long thin strip, long enough to circle a parcel of land big enough for them to set up shop. Being Phoenicians, it wasn't long before Carthage had become a successful trading centre.'

Satanaya was warming to this enterprising female. 'And Dido?'

'She got tangled up with another divinely inspired adventurer wandering the Mediterranean in search of a country. This was Aeneas the leader of the Dardanians, from the Dardanelles. They were allies of the Trojans in the war with the Greeks. When Troy fell, Aeneas fled to Carthage and had a passionate affair with Dido. But when Jupiter sent his messenger Mercury to Aeneas, reminding him that he had a mission to found a new city, Aeneas snuck away with his men in the middle of the night, and sailed off to Italy to found Rome.'

'Typical. Another story of men taking advantage. And this obsession with founding cities – where does that come from?' said Satanaya.

'I suppose in some ways we are all looking for a home.'

Mansur's words resonated with Satanaya. Here she was heading back to the village of her birth, and yet her heart was fleeing elsewhere.

'And Dido?' she asked

'She killed herself.'

Satanaya thought this a bit extreme. She couldn't imagine anyone worth that sacrifice.

'Do people really kill themselves for love?'

'You'd be surprised. But not for love exactly, but it's effects can be strong. Anger, revenge, disappointment, hurt, unbearable pain.'

Satanaya began to feel uncomfortable and changed the subject.

'And does this mean that the Italians are really Turks? If Aeneas came from the Dardanelles?'

'I think the Italians would dispute that.'

They made their way to what remained of a once-fine caravanserai. A goatherd had corralled his goats at one end of the open courtyard. A fire burned at the opposite end where travellers had gathered around some street vendors who were preparing supper. As darkness approached, and the gates were closed, and all were well fed, the goatherd, a wild looking fellow in ragged apparel and unkempt hair, took a pose in the gathering and began to bang on a skin drum. He was a storyteller, apparently known in the region, and as soon as he had everyone's attention he began his tale.

Satanaya took out the notebook she had begun to keep ever since leaving Seydnaya, and the fountain pen which had been Lady Gülbahar's parting gift, and in the flickering light of the fire she wrote down his words as best she could.

Taking Hold of the Rudder of the Ship – A Fisherman's Tale

"Ilias dragged his boat down the beach and into the water. It was a fair day for fishing, the sea calm in the cool of the morning. As the sun warmed the air, a light offshore breeze barely stirred the water.

"Ilias gathered his net, his lines and a bucket of bait, and placed them in the boat; he raised the sail, and was soon gliding out over the barely ruffled sea. He headed up the coast to where he'd laid his lobster pots the previous day. He would lift these, and then cast his net, latching on to the coastal drift and let the current carry him out to where he could drop some deep sea lines and hope for a big fish.

"The day was opening like a dream. So still the water. And yet the air was moving strangely. How quickly the mood of the ocean changes. Ilias in his little craft was now moving beyond the limit of his accustomed sailing, far beyond the land, now a distant grey blur above the surf. And still the current drew him further.

"It is a fact that although one can drown in six feet of water, or perhaps much less, and death will take each one of us when and wherever it will, yet we fear the sea with a terror that increases as it deepens; in the same way does our sense of awe and trepidation heighten with every step beyond our familiar world into the depths of our undiscovered selves.

"Perhaps even more do we fear the depth of our mind, as we fear death itself. For what is this but another drowning, as we imagine the extinction of our relative existence? Do we ever and only begin to journey in the mystery of self when, like the ancient mariners, our desire to discover who we are overcomes this fear of drowning, when we sail beyond the shore of our known limits; and every breath revives and each breeze freshens our vision?

"Such were Ilias' thoughts as he watched his little boat being taken by the irresistible flow of the ocean. And then the sky too changed. Where before the opaline haze of dawn had promised another bright azure day, now great blooming billows of grey rolled in from the east, transforming the cobalt sea to dull pewter. Beneath this vast and limpid stretch of undulating blackness the water seethed as if some vast monster was rolling over in its sleep, turning and awakening.

"The storm, when it came, did not show immediately in the expected bluster of wind and rain, but in the slow compounding of heaving seas, sinking and swelling as if the earth itself rocked back and forth, and the sea responded like water splashing in a carried pail, in vain attempt to regain the cradle of its lost horizon.

"In such a situations where the power of nature expressed itself *in extremis,* Ilias knew he had no choice but to submit, willy-nilly, knowing that in time, all things pass. For a while his natural curiosity overrode his fear. He would let the winds blow and the seas tumble, and he would watch.

"He lowered his sail to prevent capsizing. He let go the tiller on which he had been idly leaning, as it was the current now dictating the course; and as the boat drifted, so did he let himself be taken, becoming simply a witness, for better or for worse.

"For worse! The ark of his mind began to feel the strain. Fearful thoughts of his annihilation seeped in and dampened his earlier buoyancy of spirit. Doubts wracked the edifice of his accustomed self-confidence. Where was his shore, now the old homeward horizon was veiled, and above what unfathomable depths was he now suspended?

"For better? What better than this home he knew within himself? The sum of all his moments, the memories that were his life? But the certainties of this old accustomed self were now foundering. Was this the end? Was there nothing more?

"Then the wave came. He hadn't seen it coming. It just appeared on his left, as if from nowhere, a great mass of water rising ever higher, greater than anything he could have imagined. And then to his right, distant but fast approaching came another vast swelling sea. As the two waves reached overhead, their curling fingers formed a gigantic canopy of paired hands set to clasp and crush him down to some deep subaquatic bosom. The little boat slid quietly into the vacancy of smooth water which now formed as a placid valley between the two mountainous seas.

"Ilias cried out. He didn't know to whom or to what, but a cry arose in him from a place so deep, so original and with such certainty. He had reached the end of himself, as he knew himself. But something remained. Something abiding. And he knew that even should the great waves destroy this appearance of Ilias and his little boat, that the origin of Ilias would remain. His cry became a cry to this origin, from a most ancient memory, through the mouth of the fearful little man in his frail boat, beneath the great flood of nature, that puny creature now full of hope and growing certainty in something beyond but not other than himself.

"And from deep inside Ilias heard the urgent response: 'Take hold of the rudder of the ship'. The order resonated within him strengthening his whole being. Whereas before Ilias had been content to surrender the course of his boat, and his life, to some other agent, now he took command as if his life depended upon it. His precious life within this ark, no longer a collection of memories, but an unending path of infinite possibilities extending beyond time itself.

"For the present, his path was a slender route between those great waves cowering overhead, for the inundation hung suspended as if in disbelief at the outrageous cry of the little man below.

"Now Ilias became aware of an oceanic presence rising behind him, greater than the two waves above, supporting him with a strong backing, like a magnificent army.

"And still within him came the command, 'Take hold of the rudder of the ship'.

"There was no longer any doubt, and as he gripped the rudder in both hands, the water behind rose higher. The two clashing waves fell aside and were subsumed in the greater sea. And Ilias surfed that sea down and down and down, guiding his little boat onwards until his world came into view again, his familiar horizon, his shoreline, his land, and with a deep sigh of relief he and his little boat came to a gentle stop. Breathless, he gulped, as one nodding off to sleep returns with a jolt to wakefulness.

"It was then that Ilias realised he was not holding the tiller of his boat, but was pulling on the line of his lobster pot.

"Safe again in his known world, Ilias reflected on that ineffable mystery within himself, a mystery with which he had only ever felt the closest, if unconscious, intimacy, and which, though hidden, he now understood to be his true identity.

"As Ilias hauled on the line of his lobster pot, he wondered. He wondered at the difference between the familiar curves of his little world – the harmonious lines of nature's forms, the diverse inclinations of wife, children, community; the flux of human relations, the erratic order of the wider state; even the bending line of the seashore, the ungraspable nearness of the horizon, the unstill waves of the sheltering sea within whose sphere great fish swam in circumnavigation – and the rest."

Here the storyteller stopped and took a glass of tea that was offered. His audience sat open eyed, reflecting on his tale. Certainly Satanaya had found the tale thought provoking.

'And what of the rest?' she wondered. 'What of the day?' and she looked above to the fading light that still veiled the stars. 'And the night? Doesn't the night hide from us all the comforting proportions of the day, while showing the immensity of the heavens? And what of that which we cannot see, buried in the infinitely small? within the specks of salt, the ocean dried on the back of my hand?'

Satanaya sensed a rising terror like a wall hiding a beauty beyond her imagination, an inexpressible beauty, ever escaping, barely beyond reach of her curiosity. Satanaya's mind rolled along like this awhile, until it seemed it broached the edge of her knowledge and she found herself contemplating an abyss.

In the face of this inexplicable vision, what did she feel? Not fear. Wonder perhaps. Or maybe both? Fear in her stomach – or was this awe, the incapacity before the ineffable? And wonder – was this also a colour of love? And between these two she felt a longing stretching before her, like the sea stretches out to the sky, and the sky stretches out...to where? She felt herself to be a question for which all this, known and unknown, was unfolding in her at every moment, not so much as answer, but as in a mirror she was recognising some ancient yet familiar identity, which was also a kind of truth. At the same time it was a vision new and continually renewed. She too was a fisher, and she longed to cast her line into the deep.

Then the storyteller took another long draught of tea, banged his drum to command attention, and completed his tale:

"The fisherman looked inside the pot. There was a lobster, a large dark thing which would fetch enough in the market to feed his family for a week. He lifted the other pots, and in each one he found a decent-sized lobster. Taking hold of the rudder, he turned his boat in the direction of home. It had been a good morning's catch."

FOURTEEN

To the Holy Mountain

Acre to Kfar Kama, Galilee

HEY APPROACHED ACRE in the late afternoon, the sun a cloth of gold over the decaying masonry of the fortifications, just another ramshackle seaside town of dusty ruins and crumbling ramparts. As the main Crusader port it was the wealthiest town in the Kingdom of Jerusalem. After Jerusalem fell to Saladin, Acre surrendered, but was retaken by Richard the Lionheart in 1191 AD. For the next hundred years it was the effective capital of the Christian kingdom and prospered as a busy entrepôt in the East Mediterranean trade between Europe and the Silk Road.

A cycle of siege and destruction by local warlords and foreign empire builders continued into the eighteenth and nineteenth centuries: Napoleon's abortive adventure in 1799; Ibrahim Pasha of Egypt, who destroyed the town thirty-two years later; Austrian, British and Ottoman troops retook the town, and Acre returned to Turkish control, a far-flung outpost of a disintegrating empire. Yet human habitation has persisted here for more than seven thousand years

'See these ancient stones,' said Mansur, 'they're like people. They go on and on, as empires come and go. The people remain, we live, we die, grow food, raise families, love, hate, kill, just continuing the cycle. We carry on, with the stones, trimmed a bit here, recut to fit the design of a newer wall. Few of us ask why. And if we do, we mostly push the thought away so fast, like a stone that doesn't fit. No wonder progress is so slow, we are always repeating our mistakes.'

Satanaya looked at her father. He was becoming more and more pensive as the journey went on, vocalising his thoughts, imparting snippets of his own inner life, as if showing a map of journeys he had made in his own soul; he wanted her to look, to see perhaps the path as he did, in the event that she too might find herself travelling in the same verdant valleys and trackless deserts of self-discovery.

'Strangely, we never look to the origin of things, always wishing to escape into a future of our own creation. We miss out on the riches that we all share, the commonwealth of spirit.' he said, echoing the old goatherd's tale of the previous evening.

Satanaya wondered about this 'commonwealth of spirit'. Was it the same as community? She didn't think her father meant this exactly. Certainly the strength of coming together in community was vital for survival, but if that community was static, if it was a closed thing, and couldn't allow influences to enter from outside, to share and benefit from this 'unknown', how could it grow? She remembered the vast wave of the unknown from the goatherd's tale. That wasn't a closed thing. Maybe it was like this spirit, a commonwealth of possibilities that everyone could share in, benefit and grow in. Life seemed to her in that moment to offer her a blank page. A vast open landscape to be filled endlessly with... with what? The very undefined presence of this strange thing called the future thrilled her with its possibilities.

They made their way through rubbish-strewn streets to the Khan al Umdan – The Inn of Pillars – a vast two-storied colonnaded court, the upper story supported by forty marble columns purloined from the ruins of Herod the Great's palace further down the coast at Caesarea. The caravanserai had seen better days. Even in its dilapidated state, its size evoked a bygone magnificence, an austere grandeur in its fortress-like seat by the harbour. It was still used, mainly by Persian refugees who had taken over part of the building: Baha'i pilgrims visiting the tomb of the sect's founder Bahá'u'lláh. Weedy tufts and saplings scrambled out of cracks high in the walls, thick grass squeezed up between the paving stones, and the ordure of animals lay uncollected in the open courtyard. A grizzle-haired gate-keeper in a battered fez lay slumped on a rough divan at the entrance, raising himself no more than was necessary to palm the accommodation fee and hand over a key to one of the rooms behind the colonnade.

The travellers unpacked and set up camp. They watered their horses at the octagonal stone pool in the centre of the enclosure. Mansur went to bathe at the celebrated Al Basha Hammam. Satanaya walked to the harbour. Looking out over the fishing boats, across the bay to Haifa, and the snow-covered slopes of Mount Carmel glowing pink in the dying light of a winter sun, she contemplated her immediate future.

She felt confused. This journey home had a sense of inevitability about it, yet it didn't seem real. She tried to imagine the future her mother wanted for her, a future she had been brought up to expect: the courtship dances, the betrothal, the wedding; she created in her mind a sort of existence: a husband, a home, a village, children. But none of these reflections rang true. And yet, gazing out to sea, to the westward sun, she felt a glimmer of light and life flowing into her. She thought of Europa, 'maybe Papa was right.' she laughed, 'To be carried off on the back of an animal and have a continent named after you. Not at all bad, even for a princess.'

From Acre they headed inland along hilly roads east in the company of European pilgrims visiting the holy places for Christmas.

With a Muslim father and a Christian mother, Satanaya had been raised between two faiths. Mansur's beliefs were informed by the universalist Adige code of Khabze, and his Sufi grandfather's way of unity, a way devoid of fanaticism and the narrow literalism of so many who claimed to follow the prophetic religions, whether of Moses, Jesus or Mohammed. Mansur's god was a god of love. His faith was encompassed in the single idea of submission to this one absolute and all inclusive reality, wherever love's paths led, even should the exterior expressions of religion dictate otherwise. For Satanaya's mother Gülay, submission was also inherent in her belief as a devotee of the Virgin Mary.

Their arrival in Nazareth with the Christians prompted Mansur to relate the story of Jesus and Mary as it appears in the Qur'an. She had heard the Christian story from her mother, and at Seydnaya: of Mary's birth, the Annunciation, and the birth of Jesus. Now her father spoke:

'Much of the Christian story of Jesus and Mary is also familiar to Moslems. Take the appearance of the Angel Gabriel to Mary, which we celebrate as *Eid al Beshara*, the Feast of the Annunciation – yes, we too have angels and Archangels – just as you see in paintings in the churches, Gabriel on one side facing Mary, the light of the Holy Spirit pouring forth between them.'

Satanaya remembered a painting in Seydnaya: Mary on one side, bowing in complete humility, and opposite her the angel, also bowing under its great wing; from above a hand appears dispensing a spiral of light in which a tiny dove is descending to a small tear in the virgin's robe in the region of her womb, from which flash tiny sparks of light. The picture had made her so happy; the balance of heaven and earth, spirit and matter, male and female, joined by the divine hand, was perfect.

'The story of Mary in our Qur'an is not so different,' said Mansur, quoting:

' "She retired from her family to a place towards the east, and took a veil to conceal herself from them; and we sent our spirit Gabriel unto her, and he appeared in the shape of a perfect man. She said, I fly for refuge unto the merciful God, that he may defend me from thee: if thou fearest him, thou wilt not approach me. He answered, Verily I am the messenger of thy Lord, and am sent to give thee a holy son. She said, How shall I have a son seeing a man hath not touched me, and I am no harlot? Gabriel replied, So shall it be: thy Lord saith, This is easy with me; and we will perform it, that we may ordain him for a sign unto men, and a mercy from us: for it is a thing which is decreed. Wherefore she conceived him; and she retired aside with him in her womb to a distant place;'" *

---

* Koran, Sale translation Page 249, Sura 19:20

'Mary must have been so frightened.' said Satanaya. 'I mean, having a baby, and not being married, and all those ignorant people and priests who would think she was a prostitute and probably would like to stone her.'

'Exactly. But when Mary brought the newborn Jesus to the Temple, the baby spoke – that seemed to convince them.' and he quoted again:

"the child said: Indeed I am the servant of God. He has given me the Scripture and appointed me a Prophet,

And made me dutiful towards my mother, and not made me arrogant, unblest.

And has made me blessed wheresoever I may be, and enjoined upon me prayer and almsgiving so long as I remain alive.

Peace on me the day I was born, and the day I die, and the day I shall be raised alive!" *

'Talking in the cradle, that would have convinced me!' she said 'But why is this so important? It seems confusing sometimes. Here are two religions, both are venerating the same prophets...more or less. And yet they seem always to be at such odds.'

'Perhaps it's because they are seen as separate religions,' said Mansur, 'each excluding the other. Which is how they have appeared, in history. One prophet after another. Yet each building upon the preceding one, with each new revelation. Remember, we are all the heirs of the spirit of Abraham – the Muslims through Sarah's maid, Hagar, who gave birth to Abraham's first son, Ishmail, when Sarah couldn't conceive – and the Jews through Sarah who gave birth to Isaac. And Jesus, as we know, was a Jew, yet he brings in all humanity. But there is something special about Jesus. He came, and went, and they say he is to come again. Only next time he won't be coming as a prophet. Not in the sense of bringing religion – that was completed with Muhammed. His 'second coming', they say, will be to open the door to a completely new possibility for humankind. What that will be, who knows? Some say he will come as the universal saint. Whatever the case, I would hope it brings us out of this madness we are caught up in... the wars, the greed and the poverty, the oppression of one class over another, one belief over another...'

'And one sex over another?' said Satanaya.

'Yes, that too. But much will have to change in people's understanding for that to happen. '

---

* Koran 19:30-33

'Change how?' .

'We need to understand what a human being is. Not just beyond all
our divisions as nations, tribes, religions. We need to understand what
divides bodies as male and female, when we are all made of the same
elements as the world around us and breathe the same air. Stop breathing, and our bodies return to earth and rot like the figs on the trees. We
must look further and find what unites us on the inside, what makes us
feel compassion towards each other, what makes us love; we need a mind
that goes beyond divisions, that unites beyond matter. They say that the
heart is that mind which unites. Then we must pay attention to knowing
with the heart. We have to start at the point where we are united as one
human being.'

Satanaya listened. Though she found the concepts difficult, she knew
if she just listened without trying to fix on the words, something came
through, meanings behind the words, giving her a taste of something true,
of something compelling her, bringing a feeling of freedom and spacious-
ness she had never known before. She saw that truth was not something to
be proved intellectually, but that it had to be felt, known and understood.
It had to be tasted, like the bouillabaisse, in her whole being.

Their route from Nazareth took them just a few miles north around
the base of Mount Tabor, a smooth and dome-shaped mountain rising
steeply almost two thousand feet with little preamble of foothill or interrupting gulleys, above the flat expanse of the Valley of Jezreel. She pondered
the occasion that had given this phenomenon such significance: the Trans-
figuration of the Christ – when the predominance of his spiritual nature
over his human nature was evidenced to three of his closest disciples, in
the presence of those most holy and venerable patriarchs, Moses and
Elijah. Satanaya's time in the convent of Seydnaya had familiarised her
with the event as described in Luke's Gospel:

> '...he took with him Peter and John and James, and went up into the
> mountain to pray. And as he was praying, the fashion of his
> countenance was altered, and his raiment became white and dazzling.
> And behold, there talked with him two men, who were Moses and
> Elijah; who appeared in glory, and spoke of his decease which he was
> about to accomplish at Jerusalem.'*

---

* *Gospel of St.Luke, 9, 28-31*

Satanaya reflected on this uncreated light, the all-consuming light of glory, at once a blessed, liberating balm but also an unbearable flame. Suddenly freedom became terrifying, and the light seemed as a fire.

Then her father, as was his wont upon viewing the sacred mountain, repeated aloud the famous Light Verse from the Koran:

'God is the Light of the heavens and the earth. The similitude of His light is as a niche wherein is a lamp. The lamp is in a glass. The glass is as it were a shining star. Kindled from a blessed tree, an olive neither of the East nor of the West, whose oil would almost glow forth of itself though no fire touched it. Light upon light. God guides unto His light whom He will. And God speaks to mankind in allegories, for God is Knower of all things.'

The fire in her heart became light again, a cool, bathing light like the light of dawn. It was a day of openings and mysteries. A few miles further and they reached the village of Kfar Kama.

FIFTEEN

Dancing in the Moonlight

Kfar Kama, Galilee, Northern Palestine

 HE WINDOW BAR dissected the small square of sky beyond into two dense rectangles of cloud which stretched across each pane as a bare canvas. Inscribed tenuously within the frame: reaching out to each other, the branches of two leafless trees, waving in from left and right, arms, hands, fingers, separated by space and divided by the window bar. Satanaya was looking out from the reception room of her parents' small stone house. The sky lightened as the cloud lifted a little and pale blue streaks began to show in the misty air where the twig fingers grasped longingly but never met.

The canvas became a portrait as a face entered the frame and paused briefly in front of the right-hand pane. Beneath a tall *kalpak* of grey Persian lamb: head, shoulders, eyes, eyebrows, a nose, a mouth, the faint beginnings of a beard, fair wisps upon upper lip and chin: a pale face, thin and reddened on high cheeks, with eyes that looked nervously, first up at the house – his own and the sky's reflection preventing him seeing the eyes beyond the window glass – and then about him in the street. It was Timur. He had come to call. Not on Satanaya, but on her mother, Gülay. His sister accompanied him.

Satanaya slipped back behind the curtain that led into the ladies quarters and waited. She heard Timur announce his arrival at the door with a loud *'Salam aleikum!'*, followed by her mother's response, *'Wa aleikum salam!* Who is there?'

'I'm Timur, son of Dzagashta.' he said, giving his father's Adige name. Satanaya heard the door open.

'Welcome, Timur.' said the middle-aged woman. 'Please come in.'

Timur and his sister removed their leather boots and entered the reception room where Gülay arranged some cushions on the felt-covered floor. Timur was careful not to sit cross legged, but knelt on one knee, an Adige custom which would allow an ever-alert warrior to rise quickly in case of danger or attack. He wrapped his big sheepskin cloak around him, keeping his eyes down, looking at the floor. His sister, a married woman a few years older than him, sat a little way off to his side. Gülay sat opposite and began the conversation in a formal way. She knew that the good form, the *'adab'*, was to speak to the young man only indirectly, hinting discreetly of the purpose of his visit. All that was necessary could be said by simple inference and code.

'Hoş geldiniz – You come with sweetness.' She greeted the boy formally in Turkish, which had become the *lingua franca* for many of the Cherkess diaspora, particularly among the young.

He responded: *'Hoş bulduk* – we have found sweetness.' then: 'May your family prosper. What news? (*ne var ne yok?* – what is and what is not?)'

She: 'There is no bad news. We hear of a young eagle in the hills of Galilee. It has not harmed the sheep. Apparently it is seeking a mate. Perhaps it is looking to build a nest here.'

He: 'Yes, another eagle has been reported recently in the area. I trust Mansur Efendi returned safely?'

She: 'God is great. The Sheykh is well and resting from the journey. It is good to have the family back together at last.

He: 'It's good to hear of their safe arrival.

She: And your father and mother are well?'

He: My parents are well and send *salams* to you all.

She: It's nesting time. So many birds pass over Galilee.

He: Perhaps the eagle seeks its mate near Mt Tabor, or comes to drink at the village spring?'

She: 'Yes, we will watch to see if they dance in the sky together. Will you drink tea?'

Timur nodded. Gülay rose and went to make tea, and the sister followed. Meanwhile Satanaya sitting behind the curtain observed the young man through a narrow gap. He looked nervous, uncomfortable even. He was good looking, quite beautiful, with the face of youth that could belong equally to boy or girl and still look right. But it really gave nothing away. Aloof perhaps, but not arrogant. Nevertheless he seemed slightly distant, as if he were somewhere else. Or wished to be. She was not disappointed in what she saw, but felt neither attraction, nor repulsion. She needed to speak to him directly if she was to discover the person behind the face.

Since ever the world has danced. In *'sacred pomp and genial feast delight and solemn dance, and hymeneal rite; with torches flaming, to the nuptial bed: the youthful dancers in a circle bound to the soft flute, and the cithern's silver sound:'* while *'matrons in a row stand in their porches and enjoy the show.'* So Homer inscribes upon the shield of Achilles the marriage dances of the ancient Hellenes.

The Kurds of the Eastern Anatolian highlands join couples in marriage with great wedding dance circles. In the mountains of Peru the young perform the Kantu, the hopping dance, twisting and turning, flapping their outstretched arms like courting cranes; while in the valleys of Manipur on India's eastern jungle fringes, boys and girls meet under moonlit skies to dance the *Thabal Chongba* – 'dancing in the moonlight', holding hands in rows of circles, leaping and dancing together to the sound of cymbals and drums, the accepted manner by which the sexes become acquainted.

The aboriginal communities of Australia sing their land into being with the circular breathing of the didgeridoo, marrying heaven and earth in their ceremonies and corroborees. Dervishes turn upon the axis of their hearts encircling and encircled by their sheykh, their fellows and their own existence. And Jesus enjoined his disciples to hold hands in a ring, while he stood within singing *'The Whole on high has part in our dancing'*, confirming that the very being of existence, in compassionate condescension, participates in the human dance, and by this means the earth is blessed.

Soon after Satanaya's return an evening of dancing was arranged by the elders at Kfar Kama. When Satanaya stepped out of her parent's house to join the communal dance she was attired as a true daughter of the Narts; a long dress of fine black velvet, open-fronted at the breast in a deep V, embroidered with rich passementerie of silk and silver thread in traditional motifs of her Shapsug tribe, edged in white silk, its narrow waist held with a broad belt of finely chased silver, and from the shoulders the sleeves extended like the drooping wings of cranes veiling her hands; beneath she wore a white silk shirt fronted with a dozen pairs of gleaming silver buckles, and under that the traditional lambskin corset; upon her head a tall ornate toque embroidered like her dress, and a fine white veil fell mist-like from its crown and over her shoulders, the whole ensemble designed to show off her fine waist, her high breast and tall, slender form.

Timur stood in all the finery of a noble Circassian warrior at the edge of the gathering circle of dancers. His cloak of dark felt, the full length wide-shouldered 'schakwe', he shrugged off nonchalantly into the hands of a young male relative waiting behind him like a pageboy. Beneath the cloak he was wearing the traditional 'cherkesska' jacket: buttoned at the waist and open below, generously cut, it flared out down to the knees in a dashing manner, well-designed for mounted combat. Above the waist, on left and right breast of the jacket were attached vertically the tubular cartridge cases for holding gunpowder and shot. Under the *cherkesska* he wore a high-collared cream silk shirt; knee-high boots of soft calf-skin encased his feet, and his head was crowned with a wide *kalpak* of silver-grey Persian lamb. In the tight-fitting belt encircling his narrow waist hung a long silver-handled dagger in a chased silver and leather scabbard.

The dancing took place upon hardened earth in the centre of the village, an open area surrounded by houses and shaded on one side by a gnarled old carob tree. Here, on rough wooden benches sat the old people of the village and the married women. On the periphery young children were playing their own dance games in imitation of their elder siblings. Unmarried girls, and young men stood about in separate groups, dressed in traditional clothing, ready to take part in the dance. An older man clapped his hands and called out to them to come and dance. The musicians began to play, a fast repetitive melody on a 'shipekshine', the slender, dagger-shaped, two-stringed Circassian violin, to the beating of a frame drum. The gathered crowd joined in, clapping in time to the brisk rhythm.

The young women entered in a line, in a slow dignified walk circling the centre of the space. The long sleeves of their robes which hid their hands waved gently as they turned in half-steps, now to this side, now to that, giving the impression of slender young birds testing their wings before flight. The boys entered the arena, one at a time, performing quick, outlandish movements with their feet while keeping their bodies erect. From time to time one would drop to a squat, then leap, spin around, and land on the same spot, tossing his head back with a flamboyant grin.

Within the dance circle Satanaya did not feel at all comfortable. She remembered her childhood, when with her friends she had copied the older girls, imitating their steps, posing with straight back, head high, haughty chin set firm, condescending look in her eyes, and trying not to laugh at the strange poses she and her friends took. She felt no amusement now as she nimbly made the short stepping movements, just an odd sense of dislocation, perhaps even alienation. Someone observing carefully would have seen the nervous look of a deer stepping from the protection of the woods at dawn to graze in the open. Perhaps for Satanaya it was more the resignation of a lamb to the slaughter, or even the confusion of a slave being appraised on the auction block – these were the images which came to mind as she faced the boys who danced with such confidence, such arrogance, such command, circling around her, quick-stepping with avid glance as if assessing a herd of prize horses before choosing which to mount. She tried to laugh it off, assuming an even haughtier expression than her would-be suitors.

Her thoughts went back to evenings at Beyt'ur-Rahma when she had mingled with intelligent and sophisticated adult company, the literati and glitterati of Beirut – where the conversation had transcended the narrow conditions and traditions of tribe and nationality. At the Beyt she had been valued as a person in her own right, and she had begun to develop a sense of her individuality. Here she felt strangely divorced from the scene around her, which felt for all the world like some primitive cattle market, where she was the cow being considered for its breeding potential – it was all she could do to stop herself running back into the house. Slowly she regained her inner composure and found a place in herself where she could take part in a detached manner, observing the scene with dispassion. The other girls, all as immaculately and ornately presented as herself, were performing as if in a dream, an hypnotic daydream, and they appeared to be enjoying themselves.

Satanaya spotted Timur. She thought he looked rather sweet. Boyish... girlish even. Fair haired, he couldn't be more than seventeen or eighteen himself. He lacked the aggressive brio with which the other boys tapped and spun their way between the girls; he danced with grace and lightness. As she watched, she saw he wasn't dancing for them at all. Yet he was smiling – perhaps it was simply for the joy of the dance. And then she understood. He wasn't performing for the admiration of any of these girls, but for the audience of onlookers – or was there someone particular in that crowd he hoped to please?

Now he was dancing around her. Their eyes met, but the look was not the usual searching and weighing up with which the other boys had checked her out, but more of a passing hello to one among many, nothing personal, certainly nothing intimate, friendly enough but at the same time actually dismissive. He was so at ease with the situation that Satanaya found herself suddenly quite riled. It could not have been worse if he had simply ignored her. She had always known that she was considered beautiful, as well as intelligent, and she had recognised the looks men gave her either as compliments to be enjoyed with a quiet smile to herself, or as unwanted attention which depending on the situation could be batted off with a laugh and a toss of her head, a withering glare or a simple disdainful turning away. But this empty gaze from Timur pricked her girlish pride and ire rose in her throat to redden further her blushing cheeks, and lightening flashed in her eyes.

The dance moved on, and another partner appeared before her, but her thoughts were still with Timur. She was upset with his indifference, but then, had he not simply been mirroring her own disinterested pose? Yet this indifference, while infuriating, had a certain attraction. Whether there was spark enough between them to jump the firebreak of their pride and posturing, time would tell.

'So, what did you think? He's handsome, isn't he?' Her mother began the moment Satanaya came inside after the dancing had finished.

Satanaya feigned puzzlement. 'They were all good looking, I thought. Which one were you thinking of in particular?'

Gülay gave her daughter a knowing smile. 'Perhaps you'll meet him at the spring tomorrow when you go to bring water.' It was an accepted tradition for young people of both sexes to meet and get to know each other at the village well.

'Or in the sky above Mount Tabor?' said Satanaya. She was not smiling.

Gülay frowned. Gülay couldn't understand her daughter's restlessness since her return. Perhaps she just needed more time to settle back into home life. Best to leave her alone, she thought. It never occurred that her daughter, rather than welcoming the opportunity to strengthen the tribal bonds in these fractious times might be in complete turmoil over this whole marriage business.

'Well, anyway, I think it would be good for us all to meet.'

Satanaya knew whom she meant. She just snorted and went off to bed.

Elsewhere in the village, another conversation was taking place. Mrs Kiliçzade, Timur's mother, was holding forth.

'My dear son, so what did you think? Beautiful, yes? And her father is an elder of the village, and the grandson of a sheykh. Though why Mansur had to marry a Christian is quite beyond me. And the girl a Christian too, it seems. Well, we'll have none of that monkery in this house. She'll have to convert, of course. We can't have our grandchildren going about with crosses round their necks and worshipping icons.'

Timur looked glum. He didn't know what to answer.

'Well, yes. She is beautiful. There's no denying that.' he ventured. 'She'll certainly have no trouble finding a husband. All the boys are talking about her. But you know I don't want to marry, not yet.'

'Nonsense.' She looked at her husband who was sitting relaxing with his pipe. It was obvious that he didn't wish to get involved. He knew his son had expressed an interest in the army and rather hoped he might join up before matrimonial matters arose. He was still young.

'Well, the boy must do what he must, dear.' said Kiliçzade, 'I agree it would be a good match, but I don't see how her being a Christian, if indeed that is the case, need come into it.'

'If she's going to come into this house, she has to become a Muslim, and that's that.'

'But my dear, you know in the Holy Koran it says there must be no compulsion in religion.'

'Of course, but it doesn't say there shouldn't be persuasion.'

Kiliçzade sighed. He knew there was no point arguing. 'Yes, dear. As you say.'

'I shall speak with Gülay Hanım and we'll arrange for you two young ones to meet.'

Timur sighed. This was not going to be easy, he thought.

The meeting was not easy. For a start, neither Satanaya, nor Timur knew that the other had no particular wish to enter into such a commitment. Each had their reasons, and although it had nothing to do with what each thought of the other – under other circumstances they might have got on quite well – the finality of what the two mothers were proposing hung over the conversation like a death sentence on their individual hopes. It was dark. It was awkward.

Timur found it hard to look directly at Satanaya. This annoyed Satanaya, who felt confused and a little angry.

'Who is this boy?' she thought, 'who does he think he is? He hasn't even the good grace to look me straight in the eye when we speak. '

'My god, she is so beautiful,' thought Timur. 'Like a Russian princess, I imagine she expects to be waited on hand and foot.'

'And yet, he seems so sweet, so gentle. Perhaps he's just shy.' Then Satanaya remembered his manner at the dance. 'No, not shy, just an arrogant son who thinks he has inherited his father's rights as a hero.'

'Yes, she's beautiful, and maybe she isn't putting on airs. That's it, she's just shy. No, I bet that's a feint. To trap the unwary. Part of her charms. Seems so innocent, but underneath she's a man-eater.' Timur also felt confused.

Satanaya poured the tea, and offered some biscuits, her first attempt at making *senioras* after her excursion to the biscuit factory in Saida. They had turned out rather well, not too hard but with a good crack on biting, and the taste was buttery and rich. She noticed Timur's mother down her biscuit in a flash and take a second. Timur's *seniora* sat in his hand like an unwanted child. This did annoy her.

'Of course, we must give the Imam plenty of warning for the wedding ceremony. And I suppose you will want Satanaya to make *'shahadah'* * said Timur's mother.

Gülay winced, and looked at Satanaya.

Satanaya was not biting. Her inclination was to groan on the inbreath with a deep note of boredom and roll her eyes, but she controlled herself, remaining silent while a shadow of a smile passed over her face.

'Well, let's take things step by step.' said Gülay, 'But aren't you two going to speak to each other?'

It was so embarrassing for both the young ones. They exchanged cautious smiles, said how nice it was to meet, briefly compared travel notes as refugees are wont. Evidently Timur wasn't particularly interested in food so they discussed horses. This was an area where all Cherkess could talk for hours on end, like the weather, and the tension dissolved into a grey watery communication.

Each came away from the meeting feeling even more confused and upset. But at the same time, each intuited that the other might be a secret ally in their wish to remain single.

---

* The Moslem confession of faith, meaning 'to bear witness', i.e. that God is One and Mohammed is His prophet.

SIXTEEN

Tryst on Mount Tabor

Kfar Kama, Palestine, 1898

HESE WERE DIFFICULT weeks for Satanaya. The dance. The meeting with Timur and his mother. Her own mother's constant remarks and hints. Still her feelings regarding the boy remained confused. She couldn't understand why, but something was not right. Yet at the same time it all seemed right. His aloofness at the dance, given its stylised form, was fitting. He was presentable, good looking and he danced well. Then meeting him – his behaviour, while distant, had not been arrogant. In fact he had even seemed shy. Many would consider him quite charming. But the questions kept coming: could she come to like him? Would she – could she – ever grow to love him?

And would he like her? She still felt surprised at his apparent indifference to her beauty. She remembered the compliments of the older men she had met in the Beyt. She knew her looks made her desirable and she resented the lack of response on his part. He wasn't giving, that was it, really. She could imagine the possibility of liking him, as a fine child can be likeable, and maybe he could become loveable, as one may become fond of and love a likeable child. But she felt not a tinge of passion for this fair-haired boy with blue eyes who danced with such joy and freedom, yet gave nothing back. It was as if she had been presented with a painting, perfectly composed and beautifully executed, but which just hadn't moved her. A matter of taste perhaps. But as yet he didn't have eyes for her. Was love also like that – something that had to be acquired or learned? This was what confused her. She had heard often enough from her parents and elders that as long as there is a seed of compatibility, love would grow in time with the right nurturing. That may be so, but she had tasted love, of a sort, and knew its taste, and so far she couldn't see a seed in this proposed relationship. Except perhaps that they both loved horses. But that was hardly a good basis for a marriage, was it?

One morning she saddled up her beautiful Arab mare, a bay she had named in Turkish, Tarçin, for the dusty red cinnamon colour of her coat. A good ride would clear her head. Gaining open country she gave Tarçin her head and let her run a good ten minutes before reining in and turning towards Mount Tabor. She wanted to gain some height, somewhere quiet to sit and think.

Mount Tabor rises steeply out of the flat Plain of Jezreel, a little west of the Sea of Galilee. It is a virtually symmetrical dome, a rocky mound isolated in geological time as the land around was washed away by erosion, On this tree-clad breast of earth and rock, topped with a cluster of ecclesiastical buildings, for more than two thousand years have lived, prayed and fought various Biblical armies, monks and hermits, crusaders and Arabs; even Napoleon Bonaparte when he invaded Syria fought his Battle of Mount Tabor in the nearby valley.

There was a coffee house in the small Bedouin village on the skirt of the mountain, where Satanaya would go to escape the irritations of her siblings. She left Tarçin in the safekeeping of the proprietor and headed uphill through the pine trees which covered the lower slopes. Half way up the mountain where there was a clear view across the land in the direction of Kfar Kama she sat down beneath a small oak tree. Although the air was cool, in her thick sheepskin coat she felt comfortable.

She relaxed, leaning back into the roots and trunk, enjoying the scene below, down over the fields to her village and beyond to where lay the Sea of Galilee, hidden behind the hills above Tiberias. Lingering thoughts from the previous night gradually faded into the background and she became calm.

In the distance rose the twin-peaked hill, the Horns of Hattin, and she remembered her father's enthralling tale of Saladin's strategy to defeat the Crusader army. How first he drew them out of Acre by attacking their fortress in Tiberias, and lured them from their stronghold in Saffuriya, a few miles north of Nazareth. It was mid-summer. The land was a burning anvil under the sun and hardly cooled at night. Saladin had established supply lines of camels bringing water from Tiberias. He then cut off the Frankish army between the springs of Tur'an and Tiberias, thus denying them water and driving them up onto the Horns of Hattin where, in spite of a number of desperate counterattacks, weakened by thirst, their situation became hopeless. Surrounded by the Arab army, it soon became a rout. When the Royal Tent of Guy de Lusignan fell, the Crusaders surrendered. From then on, the Christian adventure in the Middle East began to collapse. The Cities of the Kingdom of Jerusalem fell like dominoes – Acre, Nablus, Sidon, Beirut – and barely three months after the defeat at the Horns of Hattin, Jerusalem surrendered to Saladin. The Catholic Pope on hearing the news is reported to have died of shock.

Satanaya gazed out over the plain. Two horsemen were approaching the mountain from the direction of Kfar Kama, heading for the same small village where she had left her horse. The riders disappeared from view but a short while later she heard the sounds of people climbing the steep slope through the trees.

Satanaya didn't feel like company, whether strangers or not – and if they were the riders whom she had seen coming from Kfar Kama, chances are they would be neighbours, and probably gossips at that. She decided to keep out of sight until they had passed. She hid just in time to see two young Circassian men, dressed in long cloaks and sheepskin kalpaks emerge from the thicket below and stride towards her hiding place, then stop. She was sure she would be discovered. But they were too intent on each other to notice the crouching girl observing them through the foliage.

She recognised Timur and one of the boys who had been at the dance night.

'The view is great from here. Come on, Timur, let's sit down for a bit.'

They spread their cloaks on the dry earth and took off their kalpaks, running their hands through their hair, moist with sweat from the climb.

'So, my dear,' said Timur, once they had settled themselves comfortably, 'what can I do… I mean, what can we do? There's no reason on earth I can give my family why I shouldn't marry the girl. She's beautiful… even I can see that… almost as beautiful as…' he turned and looked fondly at his companion. 'And the other boys in the village are so jealous, they've been lusting after her since ever. And then along comes the new guy, the hero's son, and he's expected to sweep her off her feet. But I tell you, Murat, she'd be wasted on me. She is such a beauty, and you know, to let that beauty go to waste would be a sin – a sin I'm not prepared to commit, for the sake of our friendship, as much as for hers. And you know how much our friendship means to me.'

'O Timur, you say such sweet things, that's what I love about you. But then you are the most beautiful boy in the village so how can she resist you? As for me, I couldn't give a toss for her, she could have any man she wants, and welcome, as long as it's not you. I don't want to share you with anyone. But you, you were so polite. You even went to meet the mother. And when you danced with her – how you didn't trip up, I'll never know – you kept looking at me all the while.'

Satanaya's ears were burning now, and if those two had turned around at that moment they would have seen her blushing like the burning bush itself. She knew some men preferred the company of their own sex – she had seen visitors at Beyt'ur-Rahma exhibiting less subtle but obvious indications of this preference. Were these two like that? She knew men often formed close friendships, yet still found sweethearts and wives. Perhaps these two were just best friends…

'O Murat, you know how much I love you!' Timur's declaration was heartfelt. 'I couldn't bear to be parted from you. And to share myself with another? I really don't know what to do.'

'The Army – we could join up. I hear the Sultan is recruiting again and educated Circassians who can ride and shoot are being accepted for officer training. You should have no trouble, being the son of the hero of Plevna.

If they don't accept you, you could be my orderly.' This last remark elicited a sharp elbow in the ribs from Timur. 'Anyway, I'm sure if we claim to be cousins, which we must be somewhere down the line, they'll let us stay together.'

Murat's suggestion was not without foundation. Only the year before, in 1897, hostilities had broken out between Turkey and Greece when the majority Greek population in Crete had rebelled. The uprising led to brief but all-out war when Greece invaded Turkish Macedonia in March that year and the Sultan's army responded by marching into Thessaly. An armistice had only recently been declared.

'But of course, it would mean leaving all this.' Murat spoke with mock seriousness, his arm sweeping the air to indicate the vast land of the Galilee that lay before them.

Timur laughed. 'You mean ALL this?' and he too waved his arm across the sky. 'This dry desert, this land of exile? Breaking our backs as we try and break this earth.' He stopped and was silent a while, as a new thought entered his mind.

'You know, when my father tells his stories of the Adige lands, of the mountains and valleys, the constant running streams, the waterfalls, of hunting deer and wolves in the forest, the freedom of that land, why, it just makes me want to fight like he did against the Russians. Better to die fighting for freedom than to end our days here, chained to this dry earth. Of course, it will mean leaving our families… that will be hard, but we will have each other.'

Then Timur pulled Murat towards him and hugged him fiercely. Satanaya watched in fascination and covered her mouth to silence the gasp that rose in her throat. She began to cry silently as she felt the deep passion of the two young boys. Was this what was meant by brotherly love? The thought that she might become the cause of their separation was unbearable.

Satanaya held her breath; she watched through the thin green veil of leaves as the two young boys gently caressed each other's faces, running their fingers through each other's hair, just as she and Yusuf had done.

When Satanaya was much younger she had sat with her father sometimes while he led study and conversation with young men, discussing the *khabze*, the moral and spiritual code of the Cherkess. He had introduced one session, on relationships, saying, 'the identity of the loving soul is neutral, it is neither man nor woman; or perhaps even it is both, one moment feminine and receiving the love, the next moment it is male and giving.' His words came back to her now. 'The tides of the human heart flow both ways,' he continued, 'and through this heart the whole universe suspires into and out of existence, dying and reborn at every instant to give the illusion of time. In all this, love is beauty's slave and makes slaves of us all, and who are we to judge how and where beauty should choose to appear?'

The two boys pulled apart and sat for some time in silence, still holding hands in that closest bond of love and friendship. At last they got up and wandered back down through the woods, leaving Satanaya with even more to think about. She felt strangely connected to the predicament of these two young boys. She waited a good hour before returning to the coffee house and collecting Tarçin. She racked her brains over how to proceed and came to the conclusion that her father was her only hope.

Satanaya met Mansur as he was leaving the mosque in Kfar Kama just after the midday prayers.

'Papa, we must talk.' she said.

Mansur was accustomed to his daughter's determined, if somewhat abrupt way of expressing herself, once she had the bit between her teeth over some matter, and he recognised that certain look which brooked no refusal. He sighed the indulgent sigh of the long-suffering and affectionate father.

'Yes, my dear, what is it?'

She led him away out of earshot from the other men.

'There is no way on earth I can marry that boy Timur. I'm sorry but I'm not going to be handed over like a piece of meat in the market. And as for love, well, I'm definitely not in love. In fact I don't have any particular feelings whatever, except perhaps dislike for the little boy.'

This last remark although it came with a petulant sneer, hurt her to say it.

'And yes, I know what you're going to say: that love has to grow from the seed, that it takes time and nurture, and all the rest of it. Well, there is no seed, none from me, and certainly none from him that I want planted in my earth. I don't see how time would change this. And as for nurture, I know nurture from you dear papa, and from the kitchen in Seydnaya, and from Lady Gülbahar, but I feel stifled here in Kfar Kama and…and… I want to go back to Beirut and continue to learn. What is there for me here? Papa, don't you see, with Lady Gülbahar I have a chance, a real chance…'

'But my darling child, you know how difficult it is for single women alone in the world. This is why we have tribes and communities, so we can look after each other.'

'But Lady Gülbahar will look after me.' Satanaya was adamant.

'Perhaps. But your mother, she will never agree. It would break her heart.'

Satanaya burst into tears. 'And what about my heart?'

The decisive weapon, tears, would bring her father to the point of surrender. At any rate, that was Satanaya's thinking. But if she had known Mansur a little better she would have realised that a simple, calm statement of certainty would have had the same effect. However, neither strategy would have achieved the desired result with her mother. Mansur, with his firm grounding in the traditions of his people, had always acted as the peace envoy between mother and daughter, and this would be no exception.

'Of course, I shall speak with her. Don't worry, I was expecting this and I have been preparing the ground. I did warn your mother that it was unlikely that you two would make a good match, whether you got on with each other or not. Now I shall just have to find the right moment to break the news. It won't be easy as I know she has her heart set on this. But in life there are certain things that are unavoidable. None of us know our destiny until it unfolds, and how we respond is a matter of character. You have been well educated. We shall have to see what happens now.'

'And if I take matters into my own hands?'

Mansur looked at his daughter. Headstrong, wilful, he was not sure how to take this challenge.

'Let's just wait a while and see, shall we?'

Mansur feared Satanaya really would take things into her own hands, and so he took precautions. On the pretext that her horse needed to be re-shod he removed Tarçin to the farriers, that is, to Kiliçzade's compound. Satanaya was furious. She certainly had it in mind to run away. She knew she had to get back to Beirut, but said nothing and fumed in silence.

Elsewhere in Kfar Kama, a not-unrelated conversation was taking place between Timur and his father, the old war hero Dzagashta-Kiliçzade.

'So, what's it to be? Am I about to gain the most beautiful daughter-in-law or not?'

'No, father, I'm afraid not. You know it wouldn't work. Yes, she's beautiful – you'd have to be blind not to see that. And intelligent. But I'm far too young to take a wife. No, it's not on. I know both our mothers have been planning this, but I have to follow what my heart says. And besides, I have decided to join the army. And so has Murat. We are going to Constantinople to join up. Please father, let me go with your blessing.'

Kiliçzade, once a huge man, was now a true *ak sakallı dede,* a wise old 'white-beard'. Stooping slightly from the weight of a full life, he got up and embraced his son.

'Don't worry. It is better that you follow your heart in such matters. The head will catch up in time, and it will have its day. But first youth must be allowed to roam if it is to find its true home. A spell in the army, if that's what you want, although in my experience there are far safer ways to navigate this life. But then, safe has never been our way, not the Adige way. Leave your mother to me, but first I must talk to Mansur. I'm sure he'll understand, he's a just man. As for his wife, well, each of us has accepted his allotted portion...'

A few weeks later, the men and older boys of the village gathered in the courtyard of the widower Amjad's house. Wine appeared, and arak. Musicians brought out their drums and fiddles, and when sufficiency of alcohol had been consumed, the dancing began. It was assumed by the women of Kfar Kama that this was a prelude to a kidnapping, or as other traditions would have it, a men's 'stag night' prior to a wedding. The talk within the male gathering, however, was of things military. It wasn't a secret that quite a number of the young lads were thinking of joining up and this was their good-bye party.

In Adige tradition, a wedding can be a long drawn out procedure, so in the days that followed, when nothing was said by any of the parties of the presumed betrothal, the gossip splashing about among the women at the village well had nowhere to go and quickly dried up.

Meanwhile Satanaya plotted. Not that her plots came to anything. She could see no easy solution to her predicament. Her mother kept out of her way, occasionally bemoaning the fact she would lose a daughter, and had no sons to bring a young wife into their home. Life in the village continued along its accustomed paths, while beneath the surface it could not be denied that something was afoot.

SEVENTEEN

Views of a Kidnapping

ATANAYA DID NOT abandon her escape plan for want of a horse. She had some money of her own – Lady Gülbahar had provided her with a generous allowance, and she had saved up a little from her share of the tips left by wealthy patrons of the Beyt. At any rate, she had enough for a ticket on the steamer to Beirut, even if it meant travelling steerage. But first she had to liberate Tarçin. Her consternation on finding that the paddock where Kiliçzade kept the horses before shoeing was empty was only matched by her disappointment at her father's devious behaviour.

Satanaya knew intuitively that in any military campaign the judicious dissemination of misinformation can be an advantage in lulling one's opponent into a false sense of security; make one's adversary believe one thing, and then do the opposite. Thus the superior strategist maintains the element of surprise. Then following the instance of attack, a well-thought out exit plan must be in place. Of equal importance, however, was to know the opposition's plan, and here Satanaya was at a disadvantage.

Satanaya left Kiliçzade's paddock trying to figure out her next move. So, her father was one jump ahead of her. They both knew she couldn't leave without her horse. Mansur was relying on this fact to keep her in place. Well, we'll see about that, she thought. She knew she couldn't travel on foot, alone, to the coast. Even she wasn't that foolhardy. She had to find where Tarçin was hidden.

She was walking in the dusty streets of Kfar Kama, lost in thought, when a horse galloped past on her right, almost running her down, its rider firing a pistol in the air. Three shots she counted. So she did not notice, until she felt the strong arm around her waist hauling her up and over the saddle, another horse and rider come up on her left. Then, with the rider's firm heel in its flank this horse also broke into a gallop, following in the dust of the first. She was half-aware as she flew face-down and side-ways along the familiar streets and by-ways, that the villagers, rather than coming to her aid, were in fact cheering and clapping this unruly caval-cade. She tried to scream but all that came out was a stifled sob.

Satanaya had had the breath knocked out of her in the abduction, and it was some moments before she realised what was going on. It was a kidnap, the accepted form of marriage proposal in the Adige tradition. This usually takes place after a period of courting, and with tacit approval of the bride-to-be. The man would carry off his girl on horseback, and if the bride's parents didn't agree to the marriage, she would go and stay with the groom's female relatives until things were sorted out. If her family remained opposed, the wedding could go ahead anyway, but she would not return to her own family. If everyone was happy, the bride would continue to live with the in-laws and the marriage would take place with much feast-ing, dancing and singing.

Satanaya would never be a compliant wife and she was certainly not going to allow herself to be subjected to the indignity of kidnapping. It all seemed out of character after what she had witnessed on Mount Tabor, and only strengthened her determination to escape. The arm that held her down was strong and the horse was moving at full pace. She struggled vainly, finally managing to free her left arm from between her chest and the saddle. Years of lifting pans and stirring soup had given her strong arms and a firm grip. She grabbed the rider's left leg and pulling it towards her, sank her teeth into his shin just above the top of his high leather boot.

A muffled cry came from somewhere above her head, but the arm pinning her down did not weaken.

'Satanaya, stop. I'll explain in a minute. Please STOP!'

It was Timur.

Satanaya did not stop, but bit down even harder until a sharp whack on her behind made her cry out and the rider quickly removed his leg from her mouth and pulled it back out of harm's way. Then she began to scream.

In little more than a minute the two horses and their passengers reached the edge of the village, at which point Murat fired his pistol again. Carrying on a little further they turned off the road and headed into open country in the direction of Mount Tabor. Reaching a small depression in the land they rode into a grove of small oaks, olives and fig trees, and reined in their horses. The strong arm of Timur released his hostage, who slipped backwards off the horse and collapsed in a heap of fallen leaves. Here, in uncharacteristic show of emotion, she began to cry.

'Satanaya...'

It was her father's voice.

'No, not you too!' Her tears were now of disappointment. 'Where's Tarçin?'

'Satanaya, stop it. It's not what you think. Look at me.' The authority in Mansur's voice caused her to stop crying and sit up and listen. Looking around she saw that Timur's father, Kiliçzade, was also present, and standing nearby was her horse tethered beneath the trees. Now Timur spoke:

'Satanaya, we had to do it like this. Let me explain... although first I must congratulate you on the most convincing show you gave them back in town. After the way you screamed, there'll be no doubt that the kidnapping was genuine, and that we have eloped in full-on traditional Adige style. But don't worry, we don't have to get married. For now we'll let them believe we have. In fact, your father says you are going to go back to Beirut. And Murat and I are going to Constantinople, to join the Sultan's army.'

'But...' Satanaya looked at each of the men standing around her, and quickly stood up. She was furious. 'Did you have to do it like that. I could have really hurt you if I had been able to get my hand to my knife.' So saying she drew out a small dagger from the side of her boot.

'Well, you didn't do so badly with your teeth.' said Timur, pulling up his trouser leg to reveal his bloodied shin.

Kiliçzade and Mansur both burst out laughing. Satanaya caught Murat's look of alarm and sensed the boy's barely contained desire to tend his friend's wound. The consoling glance behind his weak laugh did not escape her.

'We've brought your luggage.' said Mansur. 'It's curious though, everything was already packed, as if ready for a journey. Still, it was quite a job getting all this out from under your mother's nose. I hope we haven't missed anything.'

Satanaya began to relax a little. She looked through the bags that Kiliçzade handed her. Everything seemed to be there. Takla's cookbook and her own notebook was safely stored within the old *kazan* along with the wooden spoon.

'Well,' she said, with a reluctant smile as the possibilities began to dawn, 'I suppose we've all burnt our bridges now, haven't we?'

Timur and Murat exchanged glances. Satanaya was touched by the fondness that passed between them.

'For you, yes, and good luck.' said Kiliçzade, 'Your father and I have yet to face the music at home. Still, for now, everyone will be happy enough. Later we shall explain that you wanted away for a new life; we'll let them think you did marry, in Beirut or wherever. And then news will filter back perhaps, that it didn't work out, you separated, divorced, whatever. But by then, in a year or two, no doubt there will be other dramas to occupy their minds and this will become history.'

'In the meantime, Satanaya,' said Mansur, 'there is a ticket booked for you and a horse on the Haifa steamer. Timur and Murat will see you safely to Haifa, where you have a ticket booked. And then they must head down to Jerusalem to enlist. The boat leaves early tomorrow so you have some hard riding to do. And here a little something for you, my darling daughter. Not exactly a dowry, but it should see you out of trouble for the time being.' He passed her a purse which by its weight and the dull clink of small coins, Satanaya guessed contained gold. She turned away from the men and hid the small leather pouch on her person.

Farewells were made, tears kissed off wet cheeks amidst brave laughter, and everyone remounted. Two boys and a girl galloped off into the west, wind in their hair and excitement bursting in their breasts. And two old men walked their mounts side by side back into Kfar Kama, full of trepidation as they discussed how they were to break the news to their wives. They decided to say that they had both opposed the marriage, and this had been the cause of the couple's elopement. It paid lip-service to tradition, where if neither family agreed to a proposed union, a stalemate would make elopement the only option. Later the fathers would appear to relent, and the mothers would be led to believe they had won over their husbands, so that it would be permissible on all counts for the couple to follow their supposed hearts' desires.

And so were planted the seeds, as far as anyone in Kfar Kama was concerned, for the Romance of Satanaya and Timur, tales of which were many and varied, acquiring the status of legend as years passed.

A short way down the road upon which they had made their hasty departure, Satanaya reined in her horse, calling the boys to stop.

She looked at the two lads, who were drunk with excitement from quaffing deeply the heady cup of freedom. Satanaya was more sanguine, although she felt no less the thrill of release.

'Look,' she said, 'I don't know about you, but this is a pretty serious step we are taking. I have no idea if and when I'll ever get back here. It's likely to be years if our story is going to stick. And you, once you're in the army, it will be the same. You might never return. Are you sure you want to do this?'

Timur and Murat looked at each other. It was not necessary for them to speak, their eyes told Satanaya all she needed to know. The happiness they showed was infectious.

'I guess that's it then.' She was smiling now, feeling more at ease with the situation. 'But why don't we enjoy this time together. I've always wanted to go to Jerusalem, and this may be my only chance. I know I'm meant to get the steamer tomorrow but we can change my ticket in Nazareth. Please take me along with you?'

For Satanaya, nurtured by childhood stories of wondrous events of the past, Jerusalem had always appeared as a magical, mystical place that so far existed only in her imagination. Now she had a chance to see it for real. Something else provoked her desire to meet the great city. Something ineffable, as yet unknown which somehow connected her to Jerusalem in her own soul. Perhaps a portion of this unknown might reveal itself as she travelled in its presence.

She pressed her case: 'You're not expected anywhere yet. You have papers, letters of recommendation, laissez-faires, that sort of thing, don't you? Are you game? Come on, just for a few days? It'll be fun. We'll just say you are my brothers who are escorting me. We could even pretend to be Christians if that will make it easier.'

The two boys looked at each other, a little disappointed to be saddled with a girl for longer than necessary. And then they looked at her. It was obvious she had made up her mind.

'Timur?' said Murat.

'I'm game if you are. Anyway, we're in no particular hurry…'

And that was how Satanaya came to travel to Nazareth, and further, to Jerusalem – which is called *Al Quds,* the Holy – and there make the pilgrimage to the farthest temple.

EIGHTEEN

The Pilgrims' Way

 BRIEF RAIN SHOWER fell as they pulled into Nazareth. Depositing horses and baggage in a small khan on the outskirts, the boys went to a nearby *çayhane* and were soon drinking tea with a couple of Turkish soldiers and discussing the ups and downs of life in the Ottoman army. Satanaya set off into the village.

Ever since her 'escape' from Kfar Kama, Satanaya had been experiencing a mood of expansion and exhilaration. She felt she was on the brink of a new sense of self. For weeks she had been in a cul-de-sac of uncertainty and dread, but now her future lay wide open, an unknown that would unfold by her own steps and according to her own choice. Here, as she trod the stones where prophets had walked, she became aware that this journey was not just a journey in time, to be completed at some inconceivable point as her death, but an undertaking into the depth of who she was, a journey of self discovery, with no particular end in sight. Whatever this outward travelling might reveal, for the present it was the vastness of an interior destiny that claimed her attention.

Early spring was already showing in Palestine. Bright blossoms of yellow broom poked through in abandoned corners and scarlet Persian buttercups were emerging from the damp earth. Satanaya began a bouquet. Behind a crumbling wall she plucked pale blue blooms of flax on slender stems and pretty rock rose pink and white tumbling from the mortarless gaps in the stone. Purple irises with saffron tongues completed the arrangement.

A dusty path strewn with pebbles and rubbish led to an old church her mother had often mentioned, called the 'Bashara'. This was an Aramaic name meaning 'an announcement of a joy to come', and was the word the locals used to refer to the Annunciation.

She entered the small stone building and through the empty nave, bare of seating, bereft of iconostasis, and down the half dozen steps into the barrel-arched sanctuary, where at the end of a small grotto a large flat stone indicated the location of the altar. And here she continued her meditation. Gradually her outward awareness, perceptions of heat, cold, wind and weight, even sight and sound and smell, subsided; the concrete, physical world relinquished its hold, as she submitted to a subtle yet overriding sensation: the simple conscious awareness of her existence. Her existence, yet not her existence. Yet in no way did she feel estranged in this. Immersed in calm, her thoughts left no more mark upon her mind than the wake of a drifting boat leaves upon a still lake when moved by a deeper current.

She remembered where she was, and she remembered her mother's telling of the Annunciation story. Here, within these not so solid stones, the great *Ruh*, the Holy Spirit, Gabriel the Archangel appeared in visible form as a handsome youth, to the virgin Mary. And Mary, fearing for her modesty, instantly withdrew within herself, claiming sanctuary with her innermost reality. And then, as she seeks refuge within the fortress that is her Lord, her God, and in the extreme intensity of her retreat, and her being joined again to the source of her existence, she is informed that this angelic apparition is in fact the work of this very reality, the true manifestation of her Lord. And blessed in this knowledge her soul now dilates in ease and pleasure to receive: the inspiration of the spirit, the inseminating breath which carries the creative word.

It is a mystery the magnitude of which Satanaya could glimpse but a fragment, yet she recognised something of this supreme mystery of Love, and her heart expanded to receive this knowledge. As she stood in this ruined arcade of broken tiles and jumbled mosaics she made her inner declaration to the mystery of love, that its spirit would be her guide from now on. To reach out to, to experience, to learn to know love in all its ways became her pledge to her soul.

Then she became aware of water, the sound of water, flowing. The sound seemed to come from all around her in the small chapel, but particularly beneath her feet.

Lying in a corner of the grotto she found an old earthen pot full of brittle sticks of shrubs and desiccated blooms. She went outside to look for the source of this water. Nearby was a low stone building covering the area of a water tank, with a faded wooden sign lettered in Greek: Mary's Well. Village children were playing on the steps leading up to the tank where women were filling large bulbous clay pots capable of carrying four or five gallons each. When full, they balanced these upon their heads on a twisted quoit of cloth, and gracefully descended, chatting and laughing together all the while. Seeing Satanaya's little earthen pot they giggled behind their hands, but when she explained it was for flowers for the Virgin they hushed and nodded respectfully. She left the pot in the church with the fresh bouquet as a thanksgiving.

Returning to the khan, Satanaya passed an old lady sitting by the roadside with some vegetables spread out on an old sack – a few onions, carrots, potatoes, some dried peppers and little heaps of beans, as well as fresh green leaves and herbs: parsley, dill and mint, purslane and beetroot tops, and some well-aged lemons. She had a small vegetable plot in a village near Mount Tabor and came into Nazareth whenever she had surplus to sell. Satanaya bought a few supplies for the journey ahead, enough for a generous soup or stew. The old lady's prices were already so cheap that Satanaya bargained gently, more out of politeness, to honour tradition, than to gain advantage. She paid a few piastres, and despite protests, persuaded the old lady to keep the change.

At the *çayhane*, meanwhile, Timur and Murat had been thoroughly

inducted into the mysteries of military life according to the local brotherhood of soldiers, and were full of bravado for their future life when
Satanaya rejoined them.

They departed Nazareth before dawn, joining a small caravan bound
for Jerusalem. They formed a mixed bag of travelling traders and pilgrims,
Christians, Muslims, Druzes and Jews, about twenty in number, some on
horseback, most on donkeys, and a Bedouin family, father and mother and
four children all piled atop a couple of camels, with a third beast to carry
their baggage. This motley train was escorted by some of the same soldiers
who had entertained them the previous day, for it was not unknown for
nomadic tribesmen to practice their sport of raiding caravans in the hilly
country that lay ahead.

The day of departure dawned brightly. Patches of deep blue splashed
between light clouds, then from the west rain hurried in to intercept the
travellers' path as a blustery wind swept across the Valley of Jezreel.
Showers curtained the sky, obscuring distant Mount Carmel, darkening its
forested slopes of oak and pine, bay and olive, and turning the road ahead
to mud. As Mount Tabor fell behind Satanaya looked at her two companions, so young and full of confidence, riding close together into an
unknown future. Yet despite their evident good spirits she felt a strangeness. Her discomfort came from the confusion in her sense of normal. Was
it normal for them to prefer each other rather than girls? The fabric of her
upbringing, the structure of her community and the strictures of the wider
society said no. But perhaps, she thought, being normal didn't necessarily
make things good or right or true. And when she looked at these two,
sensing the undeniable joy and sweetness they shared in each other's
company, she knew that where love was concerned, normal didn't come
into it. It was something unique and uncontainable. Love demanded
something better than normal. She still worried for them, but not about
them.

They passed the turn-off towards Endor. Here long ago resided the
eponymous Witch, the medium who on King Saul's behalf, contacted the
spirit of the prophet Samuel, and gave news of Saul's immanent destruction and defeat of his army in battle with the Philistines. Saul, whom
Samuel had anointed as first king over a united Israel, enthroned by a

mystical condescension of prophets playing on pipes, drums and lyres, was now doomed to die in ignominy having disobeyed the divine order. Thus the way was clear for David the shepherd to rise to the throne.

Satanaya felt a chill wind blow from the direction of Endor, a shivering breeze lifting and rolling the sun-curled mantle of fallen leaves below a withered bent-back oak. The party of wayfarers and pilgrims quickened their steps and moved on south.

The caravan walked and rode twenty five miles that day, up and down the muddy hills. After a wet morning the rain mostly held off. The air warmed, the ground became drier and apart from a few brief stops for convenience and sustenance, they continued beyond nightfall. Late in the evening they reached Jenin and tumbled into the little caravanserai. Everyone was tired, but tea was brewed, flat bread re-heated for a quick supper of goat's cheese and olives. The gates of the stone keep were locked against the perils of the night. Bedrolls were laid out and Satanaya fell asleep to the rasping rhythm of her fellow travellers' snores.

From the moment they had entered Nazareth, it had felt they were travelling into the past. Mount Tabor always had an ageless presence, but now with each mile it seemed they were journeying back through ever deeper layers of time. The accumulated history of the hills, the rocks, the earth and the generations of human hopes and actions weighed upon the pilgrims' souls as an ancestral inheritance, for some a burden, for others a boon.

They journeyed south through the hills of Samaria over poor tracks and roads that connected impoverished villages; crumbling dwellings of rough fieldstone and adobe, the occasional mosque or chapel. Most important were the wells, covered in domes or barrel-arched roofs. Some had been in place since the days when prophets still walked these hills and valleys. The wells were often in a bad repair, their stone structures cracked by earthquakes, patched with weeds, and saplings taking root wherever they could find purchase, steps worn to deep bows where rainwater pooled and sparrows drank. But the wells still functioned, women gathered to exchange the daily news, and men stopped to chat and look on as their tough wives hefted filled urns with heavy arms, and ragged children ran to and fro, the little ones clinging to their mother's skirts.

The daytime heat increased. South from Jenin the land was poorer than in the Galilee where the lakeside land and the plains of Jezreel afforded a reasonable living from the soil. They crossed a rugged landscape where for millennia the inhabitants had toiled to terrace the slopes for a marginal livelihood, cropping hardy olives and small fields of grain, tending herds of unruly goats and compliant sheep. At the village springs the travellers would halt to refresh themselves and their animals, hear the local gossip, which consisted mainly of complaints to any who would listen, about their neighbours, the tax-collectors, and how hard their lives were. As they penetrated further into Samaria they crossed the ancient caravan route that led from Egypt to Damascus. Occasionally a flood meadow would surprise with fertile orchards showing fruit blossom and green fields of vegetable crops. From time to time the far distant sea and the coastal strip of yellow sand were glimpsed in the west.

The journey was made in stages, each day reaching their destination as evening drew on. From Jenin they made it to Sebastieh, site of ancient Samaria, atop a steep hill along Wadi esh-Sha'ir, the Valley of Barley, where King Ahab and Queen Jezebel worshipped idols. Before the dilapidated ruin one of their company, a little Arab woman who rode a donkey, opened a tattered book in goatskin cover and quoted in gloomy tones Isaiah's prophesy: *Woe to the crown of pride, to the drunkards of Ephraim, whose glorious beauty is a fading flower, which are on the head of the fat valleys of them that are overcome with wine!* *

These ancient warnings made Satanaya feel so ignorant. And vulnerable. She thought how when her own beauty was pointed out to her, even though she didn't see this herself, still being in the innocence of self-conscious youth, she also knew in her blushing the flickerings of pride. That a flower should fade, however, did not seem such a bad thing. Seeds would form, and fall and their beauty return, or be harvested, then ground and baked as bread. She thought of Mother Superior, whose ageless fading endowed her with a kind of transparency through which shone an inner wisdom and beauty. And Lady Gülbahar's intelligent wit remained undimmed in her twilight years. Surely the seeds of their love had fallen in fertile earth. She was reassured in these thoughts, though she knew she had everything to learn, and not just about cooking.

In the adjoining village they fell into the caravanserai, exhausted but still more hungry than tired. Immediately they set up their camp kitchen

---

* Isaiah 28:1,(KJB)

– small fires set beneath metal tripods of long rods held loosely by an iron ring at the top beneath which a pot was suspended by means of a hook and chain.

It was the chickpeas which did for Satanaya that night. She knew disaster lay ahead when she saw how the little Bible-quoting Arab woman cooked the chickpeas. Not only did she not soak them long enough, but when cooking, she didn't change the water twice, as Satanaya's mother always insisted; she didn't even change the water once. She cooked them in the same water they had been soaking in, adding the tomatoes and cumin and salt straight into the pot with the peas. No matter how long they boiled, no matter that she knocked them back in the pot as they jumped about in their efforts to escape, just as Rumi, the great poet of Konya describes, they barely softened, thereby retaining all the pent-up evil of their gaseous disposition for a subsequent counter-offensive. Not wishing to draw attention to herself, Satanaya accepted with gratitude the proffered dish when the little group sat down to eat. She herself had contributed a delicious ragout of her Nazareth vegetables to the communal meal, and there was plenty of soft flat bread freshly cooked on a *sajj*, a concave metal griddle, over the fire.

The chickpeas did not go down without a fight. Satanaya woke in the middle of the night with violent stomach cramps and an urgent need to break wind. But she dared not, for fear of the consequences. Instead she crept from the room in the khan, careful not to disturb the sleepers, rolled in their quilts and felts upon the little wooden divans that lined the walls. She might not have bothered. As she felt her way slowly across the room, the walls resounded to faint whines, soft crumps and rapid fire *futfutfuts* as of a distant battle. The intestinal combat which raged that night was not mustard gas. Nevertheless it hung in mid-air as a thick cloud of methane above a swamp. It occurred to her that if someone were to light a lamp… she quickly banished the thought. She reached the door and fell outside, gasping with relief the fresh night air.

A bright moon lit her way to the well where she took a metal jug of water and hastened to the primitive latrine at the far end where the animals where stabled. There, to the gentle night-time sighs of donkeys, horses and camels, she was quickly relieved of her urgent burden, and abluted of its pollution. She returned as quietly as she had come, but turning the corner outside the stables, she was surprised in the moon-illumined yard by the sight of her two boyish companions, standing by the well entrance in deep embrace. It was too late to turn away, to pretend she hadn't seen, for in the soft light of the night her eyes had met theirs even as they pulled away from each other.

Satanaya had been disturbed in her feelings ever since her private view on Mount Tabor. Initially she had been confused. 'It's not natural' had been her reaction then. And yet, recalling the tenderness of the encounter, and sensing the deep passion that had accompanied it, she had been reminded again of her own moment with Yusuf, her own broken-down attempt at love. And the question arose for her, was this so different? The more she had considered it, in the light of her own experience, and the realisation of her powerlessness in regard to her own feelings when love had entered her heart, the more natural this love between Timur and Murat appeared to her. So much so that now, in this moment of revelation in the moonlit courtyard of the caravanserai, beside the well, she felt relieved of yet another burden, a loathsome secret became a joy expressed. She went up to the two boys, standing pale and momentarily drowned beneath the shame of a judgement that they did not own, and she wrapped her arms around them and hugged them tightly. She kissed them both on the cheeks and smiled into their eyes in such a way that each knew they were joined, all three together in a love, unspoken yet known in their hearts. Then she replaced the water vessel by the well, stepped back, and returned into the khan.

Existence is infinite and oceanic. It hides so many currents which move this way and that, some flowing above and some beneath us, some descending with news from celestial realms, some rising upwards, upon which we tie our highest aspirations, some like the earth simply receive the pain of birth, of our growing and our dying, some are whirlpools sucking us into intimacy with darknesses, some streams rush in tumultuous waves of relationships and histories tossing us through times without pity, while other waters hold us imprisoned in still pools unmoving and stagnant. But one current overrides and is the source of all movements in this ocean of being, and that is the fluency of love. And the current through which love best loves to run is the tide of compassion, whose ebb and flow at every instant bears love's will into action, bringing all potentials into its own being, completing the incomplete through knowledge of itself as no other than this existence of love.

Satanaya lay awake with these thoughts in her mind, pondering this love that flowed in all things, the love that lay behind all these small loves. Even the love of Murat and Timur was drawn from this great reservoir, this unstoppable wave sweeping through the great mansions of eras and long rivers of times. How could anyone judge the right or the wrong of this? It was what it was, and it appeared great and golden in her mind, an energy that bound everything together, and to which everything, as magnificent as stars and humble as a mouse submitted. Satanaya felt like a mouse in this immensity, but a mouse that was loved, wrapped safe in this infinite and all-embracing compassion.

NINETEEN

The Sweet Company of Nablus

T BREAKFAST the next morning, Satanaya sensed a change of mood, a lightening of the air between herself and the two boys. For the first time since their adventure began she felt accepted by them, and was not simply an inconvenient piece of baggage, the irritating adjunct to their cosy twosome. Now they were a circle of three. No mention was made of the previous night. Everything that needed to be said had been sealed by the embrace at the well.

They set out from Samaria in the half-light of dawn. Satanaya rode behind them where the narrow track allowed only for two to ride abreast, as it wound down through ancient olives trees and beneath the stone arch of a ruined aqueduct. She watched the pair as they chatted, relaxed, amiable, as close as school friends for whom the outside world existed merely as a place to pause between their private flights of fancy, a place to rest their weary bodies at night; nothing more, for their eyes and thoughts were exclusively for each other. Satanaya had been allowed entry, but not access to all levels of this intimate territory.

Yet something had changed for the better and pierced the gloom that previously had blanketed their natural cavalier spirits. Perhaps the sharing of their secret, while unspoken, yet revealed and veiled by night, had alleviated the tension of their predicament, a predicament imposed by the accepted mores of their times. Seeing them riding high above the ancient land, she knew a hard road lay ahead for them. Would it last? she mused. Would the fineness of their manner with each other, the vigour and purity of youth – could this survive the rough environment of military life? Would they even be able to remain together? – perhaps, in the way brothers were, close friends from the same village might also be allowed to stay in the same units.

Something of eternity inhabits the most transient things: the light glinting on the edges of forms; the glow in the eyes. We see but don't see it. Love alights momentarily where it will, and is startled to flee by the least hint of captivity. Yet where it sets its foot, in the dust of its imprint an echo remains forever, like a pathway of return to its source. And so the truest moments of life are touched with the imminence of their own passing, the knowledge that eventual ruin lies ahead for all the happiest blooms of life. Satanaya could not but help feel a sadness at this intimation of future sorrows even as her heart rejoiced in the present.

The day felt more like autumn than spring – sun warm without being fierce, air clear and dry. Far back in the north, ever snow-capped Mount Hermon poked its gleaming pate above the Galilean haze. The caravan moved at an easy pace, the day's goal being Nablus. Early in the march, Timur and Murat galloped off with one of the soldiers for an hour or so, returning with a larder of bloodied gamebirds hanging over their saddles. They had shot pigeon and partridge, and that evening the party would sit down to a feast.

Between a threat and a promise, near the ancient site of Shechem, Nablus nestles in a natural cleavage separating two hills – Gerizim, the mount of blessings, sacred to the Samaritans, and Ebal, the mount of curses. A city fought over and destroyed so many times over four millennia, yet always picking itself up out of the dust and trying again. It couldn't be otherwise, set at the crossroads of major trading routes since time immemorial. But Satanaya wasn't thinking of history, nor the religious arguments over whether the mountains were sacred or not. She was more interested in tasting *knafeh*, the sweet sheep's cheese pastry which the Palestinians of Nablus made famous. *Knafeh*, according to a note in Takla's cookbook, is the equal of *halawet el jibni*, a fine local delicacy of Hama in Syria – a dessert of sweet cheese in a semolina pancake scented with rose and orange blossom water and sprinkled with ground pistachios. Satanaya was determined to discover the truth of this comparison, so on arrival in Nablus, leaving Timur and Murat to deal with the accommodation, and while the rest of the party prepared the cooking fires, she went in search of the best confectioner in the town.

Searching the narrow streets for a particular *knafeh* shop called Al Aksa, recommended by the Cairene, she came upon the Church of St Photini, an Orthodox church in the south of the town built over the Well of Jacob. She knew the Gospel story of Jesus meeting the Samaritan woman at the well, how Jesus cut through millennia of historical tradition and religious prejudice by asking her – a non-Jewish female, and a Samaritan at that – to drink from *her* vessel. A woman who, as Jesus reminded her, had not only had five husbands but was now living with another man to whom she was not married. And he wanted to drink from her vessel? This was the kind of prophet Satanaya could relate to. Jesus was not veiled by the Samaritan woman's evident reputation. He saw her in her essence, and he saw her inner yearning for love. He spoke to her, heart to heart, and invited her to drink from his own vessel, a draught of the living water of the Holy Spirit. Not the usual manner of a Jewish rabbi towards women, nor any rabbi that Satanaya had ever come across. And certainly not a Samaritan woman's response, to accept an invitation from a Jewish man, to sit with him and discuss matters of body, soul and spirit.

Satanaya entered the church. She drank at the well and afterwards stood contemplating the ikon of St Photini, 'the illumined one', as the Samaritan woman had been baptised. Sanctified in beauty with gold halo and celestial robe, the saint's eyes seemed to look far beyond the gathered pilgrims. Curiously, not unsurprisingly, these eyes reminded her of Lady Gülbahar.

A bearded monk in attendance related the grim story of Photini's cruel martyrdom at the hands of Nero.

'I only hope Lady Gülbahar's end is not so grim.' thought Satanaya. Her lady, she knew, would not approve of martyrdom.

"So unnecessary." Satanaya seemed to hear the Châtelaine's words, "This human life is too valuable to let any ignoramus remove it just to please his ego. And besides, I'd be too afraid, I'd admit to anything to stop the pain."

Lady Gülbahar certainly loved life, and she had suffered in her time. But still Satanaya couldn't get the Samaritan woman out of her mind. What kind of love could have so inspired Photini that she could suffer so at the hands of the Romans, remaining faithful to the cup that Jesus offered her at the Well of Jacob? She must be something else altogether, that woman. And that love must have been something so much more than all the loves of this world. The thought was almost too much to bear, but she concluded that even the loves of this world have their place.

The thought of Lady Gülbahar reminded her of sweet things, and she continued her search for the *knafeh* shop.

The old market of Nablus is a warren of narrow arched-over streets bustling with trade – cloth sellers and tailors, farriers and blacksmiths, pots and pan sellers and tinsmiths, grain merchants selling seed and animal feed, saddlers and cobblers, all the necessaries of the agrarian market town, with mosques and churches, bath houses and restaurants, and of course the confectioners. And taking pride of place among the Nablusi sweetsellers are the *knafeh* shops. And of the purveyors of this celebrated sweet, none reaches such summits of perfection of taste than the ancient house of *Halwiyat al Aqsa* – The Aksa Sweetmaker – one establishment set in two shops facing each other at the top of a narrow lane. It is behind the an-Nasr Mosque, the site where tradition has it Jacob's sons brought him the bloodied coat of Joseph. A Byzantine church stood here until the Knights Templars arrived during the Crusades and built a round church, later transformed into a mosque when the Mamluks, the next conquering heroes came along and began to make *knafeh*, as they have done ever since.

Satanaya observed a steady stream of customers queueing at one shop to purchase a square of the rich dessert of sweetened Nablusi sheep's cheese topped with a golden crust of 'kadayif' pastry. Five yards away in the shop opposite she found the patissier at work. He was a small, round man with a red face and cream puff cheeks underlined with a well-trimmed moustache; on his head a red fez, and around his girth and covering his long white smock was a well-buttered blue apron. She watched as first he lined a large flat tray with butter which he set to heat over a charcoal fire on a brick and clay stove. Then from a large copper mixing bowl he took handfuls of chopped *kadayif* – a kind of fine shredded-wheat pasta – and sprinkled a half inch layer evenly over the melted butter. From another bowl he scooped handfuls of soft cheese which he distributed over the *kadayif*, all the while turning the tray round over the heat so the desert cooked evenly. When he judged the cheese had melted sufficiently, he removed the tray onto a metal stand, and covered it with another tray, and then flipped the two trays over, just as she had seen Clotilde flipping a tray of *Tarte Tatin*, only much bigger. The chef was well practiced and looked as though he could flip huge trays in his sleep. Given the number of trays he had to flip each day – for the line of customers diminished not at all while Satanaya watched – she thought he probably did go to sleep counting flipping *knafeh*. Then the *coup de grâce*, as he lifted the lid and ladled hot syrup over the now golden crust of the *knafeh*, and the sweet honeyed scent of rosewater, sugar and butter wafted to her nostrils. She quickly joined the queue in the shop opposite, and when her turn came and she dipped her spoon and brought to tongue the soft crisp cake of dripping melted cheese and syrup, she discovered something she had not known before: perfection does exist in this world. Her response to this realisation was to pay for a whole tray of freshly cooked *knafeh* to be brought to the caravanserai later that evening (for this confection should always be eaten fresh from the fire). It would be a special treat for her fellow pilgrims. For though all had been generous in pooling resources while on the road, the fare had been meagre at the best of times. And she could easily afford to pay from her 'pocket money' without dipping into her father's gift.

Satanaya returned to find the pigeons and partridges plucked, gutted and prepared as she'd instructed, with the breastbones and backbones carefully removed, ready to be spatchcocked and grilled over charcoal; the bones, with herbs and onion peelings, were set to boil for stock. She had decided to cook *fava*, and if there was time, some *baba ghanoush*, as well as a tasty *firik pilav* to go with the meat. By now there was no argument among the rest of the travelling troupe that she was the best cook, and all were ready to serve her needs as choppers and fetchers, sharing ingredients as well as cooking pots for the communal supper. They had bargained with local farmers and their wives as they came in from the fields to purchase sweet home-pressed olive oil, sesame paste and yoghurt, as well as the necessary lemons, onions, aubergines and fresh dill.

For the *'fava'*, Satanaya cut several onions in small dice, sweating them in the pot with a good measure of olive oil until they took on a pearly translucence as they softened, just as tight muscles soften and relax in the heat of the hammam. To this she added a few cupfuls of washed *fava* – dried and skinned broad beans, dusty yellow in colour – and poured over a few ladlefuls of the stock strained through muslin. She set the pot to simmer gently in a corner of the fire until all the ingredients had well cooked, the stock absorbed and the beans dissolved nicely. Satanaya seasoned the mix, which was now quite sloppy, with a little salt, lemon juice, more olive oil and a good handful of chopped fresh dillweed, She poured the *fava* into a cold bowl, dipped in a finger, tasted, and gave a hum of satisfaction. She was happy with the result. There were still some bits of soft but undissolved *fava* bean, but this would not detract from taste or appearance. Then she placed the bowl of *fava* in a cool dark corner by an opening in a wall where it would catch the cool night air and set by mealtime.

For the *Baba Ghanoush* she took half a dozen aubergines, piercing each with a knife as one might prick sausages to prevent them exploding, and placed them on the grill. She turned them regularly, letting them cook evenly while the skins slowly charred. The long purple pods turned black and became quite limp and shrunken-looking, here and there emitting little fumaroles of steam which cooked the flesh inside as it searched out avenues of escape. She scraped out the well-cooked flesh into a bowl and with a small knife chopped it up small without actually mashing it. To this she added a few tablespoons each of yoghurt and sesame paste, a few good splashes of olive oil and half a cup of lemon juice, a teaspoonful of ground cumin seeds, more chopped dill, and salt to taste. She folded this into a homogenous mix, not fussing if the occasional small piece of charred aubergine skin crept in, as this would enhance the desired smokey flavour. She tasted. Mmmm. A little more lemon. Perfect.

Satanaya read in Takla's Cookbook, from a pasted-in letter written in the Cairene's familiar hand:

Firik, freekeh, farik is the perfect dish for the cook 'en route'. An easy-going ingredient, and quite forgiving as its preparation allows a reasonably wide margin of error given the vagaries of foreign cooking devices and the unforeseen and unavoidable circumstances that the wayfarer will encounter. This is not surprising when one considers the origins of this dish.

From ancient times from the Oxus in the East to the Danube in the West, through lands watered by Tigris and Euphrates, and down to the Orontes and the Jordan, even to the desert-ebbing shores of the Nile, wheat, milled for bread-flour, has been the staple of civilisation. Yet, in these lands, the constant flow of tribes, back and forth in search of land on which to multiply caused havoc in the natural order whenever blew the hot winds of war. Crops of wheat, which in time should ripen into a golden harvest, would be abandoned by villagers fleeing the invading armies, and the still-green fields would be torched by the descending hordes. Returning to their charred fields when the wrath had passed, some clever cook discovered that the husks and chaff had indeed burnt, but the moist, soft grains inside the ears of wheat not only survived, but were perfectly dried and ready for the pot. The grains, which obtained a greenish tinge to their otherwise grey-brown dullness, were much smaller than fully ripened grains, and as a result required very little cooking time, which was convenient for the traveller or the refugee in flight. Such became the prestige of this burnt green wheat, that it acquired a special place in the burnt offerings of Moses who commanded his people: 'And if thou offer a meat offering of thy firstfruits unto the LORD, thou shalt offer for the meat offering of thy firstfruits green ears of corn dried by the fire, even corn beaten out of full ears.'* Apparently the Lord and Moses were also partial to young pigeons, so the two dishes are often served together.

Satanaya followed the Cairene's instructions, finely dicing some carrot

---

* Leviticus 2:14

and onion, which she softened in butter in Takla's *kazan*, to which she added a few cups of *firik*, turning it over a gentle heat. She then poured in enough stock to cover the *firik* by an inch, seasoned the pot with salt and a bay leaf, and let it simmer quietly until it was soft, occasionally adding a little extra stock. After about thirty minutes she stirred in a handful of bulgur, to lighten the dish and absorb the remaining stock, and took the *kazan* off the fire.

The pigeons and the partridge, by now well-marinated in lemon juice, olive oil and oregano, were placed above the hot embers of the fire where they sizzled away; rugs were spread and everyone gathered to eat. Piles of *khubz*, flat bread, came warm to the *sofra* and all dipped in heartily to the *baba ghanoush* and *fava*, supplemented with plenty of garlicky pickles which the soldiers had brought. Favourable hums rose from the delighted diners, and they glanced at each other in surprise.

'Where did she learn to cook like this?' muttered the old lady of the badly-cooked chickpeas.

'Goodness, she's far too young and still unmarried.' commented another.

'Not for long, I shouldn't doubt.'

The soldiers smirked soldierly smirks, but dark glances from Murat and Timur wiped the leers from their faces. The more the travellers ate, the less they spoke, and the hors d'oeuvres were soon vanquished to the last wipe of *khubz*, and a calm of satisfaction reigned beneath the flickering light of the caravanserai.

The roasted birds and the *firik* were devoured with great swatches of parsley and much delight, as well as more pickles. When all had eaten their fill, Satanaya gathered the bones and left them to simmer gently with the remaining parsley, carrots and onions for a hearty breakfast broth next morning.

As each went to their cots for the night, the chick-pea lady grumbled to some of her companions, 'That was all very well, the food that is, but she left the garlic out of the baba ghanoush.'

The women looked at each other.

'Oh, did she?' said one.

'I never noticed.' said another.

'I thought it was delicious just as it was.' said a third.

It was true, Satanaya had not used any garlic. But then she rarely did.

Aside from a personal aversion to its acrid odour on breath and skin, she had nothing against this noble plant *per se*. She had noted the Cairene's remarks that while garlic had excellent medicinal properties, many an impoverished cook covered their inability to develop taste in a dish by its over-use. Besides, she invariably found the required taste with onions, scallions, shallots or leeks.

TWENTY

Investing the City
Jerusalem I

ERUSALEM – crucible of histories and prophecies. And wars. Over what? The chance to tell one's story. But the city is the story. More precisely, the history is a rock. Now, where has this been said before? The Stone of Scone, once the pillow stone of Jacob's dream, transported by Jeremiah to become the crowning omphalos of the Scots? Uluru, the great rock of universal ambulation in central Australia? The holy rock from outer space in the cube house of the Ka'ba in Mecca ? But none more coveted, more loved, more died and killed for than the rock of Urusalem, Mount Moriah, the Temple Mount, Zion, David's City, The Noble Sanctuary, where three thousand years ago the wandering Israelites made a home for a little wooden box containing the tablets of Moses, a legal document of which statutes one commands that man should not kill man. And Urusalem became Jerusalem, the City of Peace, *Al Quds* – the Holy. Here, where a noble ram replaced Abraham's sacrifice of Isaac. Where King Solomon built a temple, which was destroyed, and rebuilt, and destroyed again. And all the while the temples of the spirit, the thrice-blessed and holy forms of the human emergence were destroyed and rebuilt and destroyed over and over, for the love of a rock. In the City of Peace, the Holy, something had got lost in the translation.

The travellers reached the city at the back end of the day after a night in a flea-ridden khan somewhere between Nablus and Ramallah. Jackals had howled in the hills all night and on the morrow heavy clouds threatened rain that did not fall.

They halted at the Damascus Gate. A bustling market was in progress below the city walls. Farewell hugs and promises of continued friendship were exchanged as the tentative unity of the little convoy was undone, each constituent parting to its respective quarter: the Jews to the south near the Wall of Lamentations; the Christians – the Armenians, Catholics, the Orthodox in their various colours – Syriac, Greek, Russian, Serbian and so on – headed for lodgings in the western part, spreading in from the Jaffa Gate; the Moslems kept close around the 'Haram al Sherif', the Noble Sanctuary, the raised platform on which sits the Dome of the Rock and the Al Aqsa Mosque.

The little party of Satanaya, Timur and Murat headed up to where some Adige people – a retired soldier and his family – kept a *funduk*, a small hostel on the Mount of Olives. They rode east keeping the high city walls on their right, past Herod's Gate, turning and descending past the Lions' Gate, with its four friendly leopards carved in stone. They crossed the Valley of Kidron and climbed up through olive groves, where goats and sheep grazed on thick spring grass and young boys moved slowly, cutting fodder as they went. As the travellers reached the summit the sun was low on the western horizon, seeping through the clouds behind the city like blood into cloth, soaking through the dark outlines of the minarets, domes, towers and temples of the fabled city. They found their billet amid a small settlement of pilgrim hotels and eateries, and were welcomed like lost sheep by their Adige hosts.

Satanaya woke just before dawn, and in the birdsong that heralds the coming of light in spring, the *beshara* of the morning entered her heart as a sweet breath. Her father had explained this word to her as 'the announcement from the Unseen of a joy to come'. It is the moment on wakening, before thought and memory have time to interfere, when an intimation of this joy is present. He would quote the old wisdom-saying that a special mercy was present for the world each day, to be received in this tentative moment of darkness, 'like the day is contained in the morning's dawn,' he would say, 'and to be captured by this moment is to be freed from a lifetime of history.' The birds completed their noisy song and all was still again. She lay drinking in the silence until the sun rose then she got up quietly and went outside to wash.

The cherry trees in the orchard surrounding the *funduk* were in blossom and the bees were humming, earnestly setting the fruit. A grapevine over the terrace had begun to sprout new leaves. 'The season for making *dolma* will soon be here.' she mused. A fresh breeze blew from the east shimmering over a sea of wheat in a nearby field and turning the silvered branches of the olive trees into a cascade of light. Winter lemons hanging in a tree by a water tank glowed a brighter yellow as Satanaya's face warmed in the sun. She then set off to discover Jerusalem.

Next door to the hostel was a six-sided domed building of old stone, surrounded by a high wall. Her hosts said this was the place of the Ascension of Christ, where forty days after Easter he had been taken up in a cloud. It was a place of pilgrimage for both Muslims and Christians. She entered through the small doorway and stood beneath the unadorned dome where a small rectangle of marble stones marked the spot of the Ascension.

Satanaya stood wondering what exactly it all meant. Logically she knew a man should not rise off the ground and out of sight, unaided by any physical support, yet apparently an event had taken place. Perhaps, she thought, there existed some unseen force, complimenting the pull of gravity but opposing that downward collapse with an attraction upwards, something that held her in balance at every moment, a supporting spirit that allowed her to move, and then to stop, to stand and kneel and lie prostrate. And perhaps, under certain conditions, to fly.

Bells rang nearby. She looked up at the light pouring in through the narrow windows some fifteen feet above. From here the walls converged, rising to form the dome in rings of pale cream and grey stone blocks. The light. It was always the light. The magic of appearing and disappearing. Perhaps this was that unseen force – the light not the darkness, the light not the heaviness. Or was the heaviness of earth and all its forms simply the light concentrated, trapped by her thoughts, shaped in her imagination, netted in the illusion of separation, weighed down in space and time, the transformation of love as desire between... between the many that yearn to be one. Surely it would be a simple thing, really, to rise upon a breath of light, dissolved, absolved, and free to fly as a vaporous cloud to the heavens. But the heavens themselves? Now that, thought Satanaya, was another thing. Perhaps heaven was simply a world of light. Or was it the light of this world without the dark? How she longed to meet that lightness.

The flickering of candles in the sandbox against the wall signalled the approach of visitors. Breaking her contemplation, she slipped out and away into a narrow lane of dusty Arab houses descending the sloping terraces of the Mount of Olives, bright with flowering mustard.

Across the valley rose the precipitous face of the Temple Mount, and crowning the sand-coloured walls of the city of Jerusalem, within the enclosure of the 'Haram al-Sherif', shone the Dome of the Rock, the cosmic lodestone of religious hearts and their dividing sword, the oyster grit of the pearl of evolution. The dark ribbed dome of weathered lead glowed dully.* It would be almost a century, and as many years of struggle, before it would receive its celestial raiment of gold from the unborn future king of an Arab nation still in waiting. She spied small groups of pilgrims crowding the area by the nearby Al Aqsa Mosque, but as she descended further the city and its people sank from view. Reaching the bottom of the hill, above a doorway in a wall, she saw a sign: 'Hortus Gethsemani' – the Garden of the Olive Press – and was drawn into a grove of ancient olive trees. Gnarled and twisted over many centuries, great trunks of indeterminate girth, ancient barrels of time-oiled memory which bowed down in dignity their branches bearing thin leaves and winter-blackened fruit.

---

* The dome was originally covered in lead until substantial restoration in 1959-62 when it was replaced with aluminium-bronze plates covered in gold leaf. In 1993 the covering was refurbished with 80 kilos of gold donated by King Hussein of Jordan.

Satanaya recalled Jesus' words from the Gospel of St Matthew; *'My Father, if it be possible, let this cup pass from me. Nevertheless, not as I will but as Thou wilt.'* Suddenly the confident excitement of the morning deserted her and she was filled with fear: fear of the deep unknown that lay before her, fear of losing the happy life she had led until now, a fear perhaps of losing herself because of this strange choice she had made. She leant against the wall and cried into her hands; she cried a kind of grief for the life that was over, the family she had left behind, and came the thought: it's not too late to turn back. But she knew there was no going back, she would never be satisfied with the kind of life that Kfar Kama held for her. She looked into the garden. The spring sunshine washed over the leaves, as shimmering glisks on rippling water. Its warmth touched her eyes and she bathed in its light. The tears stopped, her thoughts subsided and her mind cleared. At that moment a young woman entered the garden. She was heavily pregnant with two chattering young children in her train, her tiredness evident from her preoccupation with childbearing and rearing. But Satanaya also saw in her a woman's determination and acceptance of her portion, free of self-pity. And her mind went back to Nazareth, and the extraordinary burden that Mary had willingly accepted. She remembered her own pledge to the mystery of love and a new certainty settled within her. She knew now that her life would continue to unfold exactly as intended, from a source deeper than her fears; from her origin. All she had to do was to trust and keep on going.

Satanaya left the peace of the garden and joined the early morning throng making its way into the city. Crossing the Valley of Kidron, she stopped beneath the city wall. She was thinking about a question her father often discoursed upon: why these three religions, Jews, Christians, Muslims, each with its own tribes and sects, its own prayers and curses, its rituals and its blessings? Mansur had likened it to a thread – in fact three threads – turning around one another to form a single rope, and each thread made up of many finer threads, each a single individual belief more or less in accord with those around it. Together they made a single rope. It was then that she grasped it. This one rope which held all these different beliefs was not just a collection of opinions, but was bound by the spirit of a common substance, a single truth from which each individual truth or belief devolved, like a specific description; each individual thread uniquely situated to present one point of view within an indivisible whole. Everything describing one thing, each in a different way.

But still the question persisted: why can we not agree we are seeing the same thing, albeit discreetly, distinguished only by the place of vision? Why do we imagine we are each seeing a different, separate reality? Was it simply a matter of growing up? Just as children are veiled to the wider world beyond the family door, perhaps it was the same with beliefs. How long would it continue like this? Till our spirits grow, perhaps, till we leave ourselves and travel in a wider place. She looked around and pondered again the threads of the rope. Perhaps even a rope starts out life as a single, undivided thread, she thought.

A single stream of water was seeping down from a crack high up in the wall and puddling beneath a small olive tree growing by the path. Satanaya watched some sparrows approach from different directions and drink together at the water's edge. She continued her walk. She was in no hurry. The sun was getting warmer, and she wanted to get to know her surroundings. She followed the path below the steep east face of the Temple Mount, through the old Muslim cemetery and past the Golden Gate, with its massive double-arched entrance, the 'Bab al-Rahma' – the Gate of Mercy – and the 'Bab al-Tawba', the Gate of Repentance. These portals to the city had been blocked up since the time of the Crusaders. Here it was the Jews drove the 'scape-goat' from the city each year on the Feast of Yom Kippur, the Day of Atonement. A goat, loaded up with all the sins of Jerusalem to be expelled and sacrificed. Satanaya had always felt sorry for this goat. But now, looking up at the blanked-off portals, she wondered if the goat's day had finally come, and all the sins of a millennium roamed loose within the walls, desperate and confused, looking for the exit and causing mayhem in the interim. Another tradition held that the Messiah would enter here at the Second Coming. Perhaps, she wondered, it was time to break open these gates.

She continued her circumambulation, past the strangely named 'Dung Gate'. Obviously this had been a midden, the back end of the city so to speak, and she hurried on beyond the great Ayyubid Tower. At the Zion Gate, she ventured a little way into the city, to where bearded men in black coats and wide-brimmed hats trimmed in fur were passing in and out of the Moroccan quarter, suffering harassment and complaints from their Magrebi neighbours. She followed them through narrow alleys to within sight of the last remnant of their former Temple, the Wall of Lamentation.

Side by side stood Jews from as far afield as Afghanistan and America, wailing and nodding and gnashing their teeth, and waving prayer books in common lament.

Satanaya felt uncomfortable. Although dressed modestly and wearing a head scarf, everywhere she felt the eyes of suspicion and prejudice and she quickly moved back to the city's perimeter.

TWENTY-ONE

The Holy Sepulchre
Jerusalem II

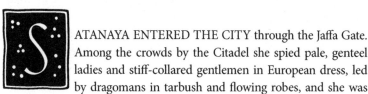 ATANAYA ENTERED THE CITY through the Jaffa Gate. Among the crowds by the Citadel she spied pale, genteel ladies and stiff-collared gentlemen in European dress, led by dragomans in tarbush and flowing robes, and she was reminded of Beirut. But humanity was here in all its guises, each diluted among the general mass so as not to pose a threat to others: a scrimple of nuns, wimples wide as cherubs wings, fluttered excitedly around their guide, a severe young priest; Franciscan friars in sackbrown robes went about important businesses swinging hardwood rosaries hooked in white cords round generous waists; the aforementioned Ashkenazi men in black sporting cheek-dangling kisscurls, a dark-robed Bohkharan rabbi in

embroidered fur hat surrounded by his young pupils – boys of fourteen or fifteen in red yarmulkas and gloriously coloured kaftans of heavy silk; there were well-fed Orthodox priests in stovepipe *kalimavkion* hats, and barefoot Russian peasants, half-starved, in patchwork rags, gazing to an inner distance as their lifetime pilgrimage reached its climax; Turkish soldiers lounged outside cafés smoking long pipes, and a proud Bedouin in a goatskin cloak marshalled his smelly herd through open ground by the Citadel as if leading a tribe of heroes.

Satanaya was pulled into this maelstrom down narrow streets paved in stones polished smooth by millennial pounding of pilgrims' soles. Arched and built over, these thoroughfares became dimly lit tunnels. Every other corner sported a sign locating events biblical and historical, commemorated forever in the present; for Satanaya it was enough to be a simple observer within this atmosphere of remembrance, unconcerned by specifics, recognising the movement of hearts, the longing which impelled this traffic of souls in endless peregrination, each offering in their own way the mite of their intentions.

And everywhere the holy souvenir sellers: hagiographic postcards, and calligraphic prayers in Arabic, Greek, Cyrillic and Hebrew, ornamental hands of Fatima, seven-branched silver menorah, blue beads against the evil eye; purveyors of wood from an endless supply of the one true cross, a shop offering 'widow's mites' for sale to pilgrims and 'genuine' coins of the 10th Legion, hammered out with rough dies in backroom workshops. And voices from the shadows as shopkeepers disgorged from within glittering caves of trinkets, crying: '*ahlan wa sahlan...* welcome, welcome, come inside just for one minute...'

'I don't have a minute,' said Satanaya to herself, 'I have all the time in the world just to wander.' So she followed the parade, while always in the side streets, behind doorways and in stairwells lurked the ever remaining guardians of the city. These keepers of the shadows for ten thousand years, handing over the watch at the close of their designated terms, like the passage of the streets, they vary little, accommodating the changing fashions of their guests, before returning whence they came.

Feeling faint, she realised that it was already early afternoon and she had left the Mount of Olives without having breakfast. She gave a coin to a water seller and drank avidly from his beaten brass cup. A small food stall was busy serving bowls of fresh warm *humus* dripping with olive oil, and chickpeas and *ful medames*, with soft pads of warm pitta bread. She paid for a bowl and sank gratefully onto a low wooden bench behind the stall where women sat.

Refreshed and fortified she returned to the flow and was carried along into the spacious courtyard of the Church of the Holy Sepulchre. She entered and found herself within a labyrinth of naves and apses, ascending domes and descending crypts, chapels and ikons gilded and glistening in candlelight; a sanctuary crowded with lay pilgrims and clergy of every Christian sect, their humble followers, their ecstatic devotees, and the harsh guardians of this hallowed house of many mansions. Tradition has it that the corpse of Jesus, crucified on the rock of Golgotha (also now within the precincts of the Church) was laid here in a cave-tomb which had been prepared for Joseph of Arimathea, a local Jerusalem council member, and from where Christ rose again after three days in the underworld.

Satanaya had always found the Christian story of the Resurrection intellectually problematic, though not impossible when considered from the point of view of the imagination. And truly she felt no opposition in her heart to the essential elements. Muslims and some Christians have it that it was not Jesus who died, but another who was crucified in his place. And neither partisan disputes his continuation in life, even to the present day, whether in an intermediate world, or as some would have it, in a cave in Yemen, or alternately, in some remote mountain fastness of Tibet. Well, Satanaya knew intrinsically that she herself had not appeared ex *nihilo*, from nowhere and for no reason, and she had no doubt that death, while a mystery, was not simply an end. Likewise she viewed the universes as a generally well-constructed and beautiful arrangement, and not without purpose. The negative states of the world could in most cases be ascribed to a falling short in humans' behaviour to one another, especially in manifestations of murder, war and other acts of oppression; or like the weather, simply the natural entropic effect of time. So she was quite happy to consider in a positive light the resurrection and life after death until either proven right, or wrong.

Caught in the teeming throng, she drifted with the stream, until on a whim she spun off into a side eddy where few people strayed – down and down again she went, descending stone steps to a deep cavern hewn from solid rock many yards below the main body of the church. And in this cool dark cave, lit only by a few oil lamps, she found a place of stillness and deep peace. Here she knew no need for thought, nor even prayer, just simple acquiescence to a will so great it included all her own little hopes and desires, without judgement or condition.

As a foetus in a womb submits willingly to birth she felt at one with this will, or whatever it was, in her own wish to emerge into its greater light. It was just a moment, but a moment which encompassed her whole future. She knew she had been given a glimpse, a key to an essential freedom, a moment of return to source. It was confirmation that whatever might appear in that illusion of future, and all that had been lost in that irretrievable past, was covered: forgiven, absolved, of all blame, fear and lasting pain. This freedom now tasted, would remain with her, even when hidden in time, as a silent companion on her journey to be recalled in times of doubt, and whenever she felt that ineffable yearning of the heart.

Then all too soon they came, the fearful mumbling grumbling pere-grine crowd, the sweating huffing panting devotees with their cries of despair, their weeping and their ecstatic ejaculations of pious imitations. But in all this Satanaya held firmly to her certainty which she knew would somehow carry her through whatever storms lay ahead.

And as passing locusts having reaped their fill, they left. An Abyssin-ian – a Copt – entered, prostrated, kissed the altar, and departed. Deep beneath the earth the air was cool and fine, and Satanaya felt inclined to remain, alone in the *sakinah* of the place. In a far corner she noticed a woman sitting quietly reading scriptures. She greeted her and asked what part of the building this was.

'This is where they found the "True Cross".' said the woman, 'There was a temple to Athena above here. Empress Helena, the mother of Con-stantine the Great, had it demolished. Then they dug down and found the cross on which Jesus was crucified.'

'It must have been pretty huge, I suppose.' Satanaya said, a little impi-ously, remembering all the little 'True Crosses' for sale in the shops above, 'You know, to have lasted so long…'

'Yes, but it was wood from a magic tree.' said the woman. 'It began with Adam…' and she launched into her tale:

'You see, Adam the first man had become ill. This was after the banish-ment from the Garden, and Cain was banished after killing his brother Abel. So Seth was sent to the gates of Paradise to see if he could get some Oil of Mercy with which to anoint his sick father. Instead Archangel

Michael gave him a cutting of a tree, perhaps from the tree that bore the Forbidden Fruit, we don't know. When Seth returned, he discovered that Adam had died, and so he planted the branch over his father's grave. It grew there until the time of Solomon. It was such a magnificent tree by then that Solomon had it cut down and built into his great house called the Forest of Lebanon. Now, when Bilqis, who is the Queen of Sheba, came to visit, she recognised the tree to be that from which the Saviour of the World would be hung up on. On this account, Solomon had the tree buried. One day the people in Jerusalem were digging a pool for washing their animals before sacrificing them in the Temple, and they came across this ancient tree. Thereafter the pool acquired a virtue: from time to time angels would descend, and stir the water, and whichever ill person got to the water first, they would be cured. From the wood of this tree they made the cross for the Crucifixion.'

Here the story took a strange twist – illogical even – nevertheless, Satanaya refrained from interrupting as the storyteller was obviously overcome by the emotion of her tale: apparently the tree had become four different trees, and the cross was constructed of a combination of palm, cypress, cedar and olive.

'And then the Cross was buried again, until Empress Helena came to Jerusalem on a mission to find it.'

The story then took another, grimmer turn, and became something of a diatribe against the Jews. For generations, she narrated, the Jews had kept secret the tree's whereabouts, fearing its discovery would diminish their influence in the land, and signal the dominance of Christianity. Empress Helena, who is considered a saint, gave an ultimatum to a Jew who knew the cross's whereabouts: life or death. The poor fellow was subsequently starved into revealing the hiding place.

'That's when they dug and found the cross.'

At this point, apparently the earth moved, sweet scents arose, and the keeper of the secret, unsurprisingly, made immediate and joyful conversion to the new religion. Now the woman began to relate the discovery of the nails, and looked set to impart a whole history of the Byzantine empire. Satanaya had had her fill. She left a few coins and excused herself, retracing her steps up the stone staircase, now noticing the Crusaders' graffiti of small crosses cut in the wall.

In the main body of the church crowds were queueing in their thousands around a tiny stone structure, the church-within-the-church that marks the agreed spot of the Holy Sepulchre. Robust Greek priests marshalled the mob with severity and reprimand as emotions overcame dignity and pilgrims fought zealously to enter the low portal and touch the sanctifying spot. Satanaya, while curious as to what lay within, satisfied herself with a thrice-circumambulation of the little building's perimeter.

Mentally she joined her own prayer to that of the masses, but her pilgrimage, she was beginning to understand now, was taking place within herself. It was the journey of the human heart, to union with a beloved whose location, while not confined to geographical space, yet still could take form, a mirror in which to become known. Nor was true yearning expressed simply through pious repetition of formal prayers, no matter how much this practice was sanctified by tradition. Outwardly, she may have performed the pilgrimage, while inwardly she longed for a love with an ache and an urgency that outstripped her powers of thought and imagination. Nevertheless, as she left the church, her whole inner being felt lightened; just as the city was illumined now by the late afternoon light penetrating the canyons of streets, silhouetting bell towers and minarets against the white glare of the lowering sun, projecting long shadows before the happy children running towards her on the golden burnished pavements, drawing to her the cool breaths of approaching evening.

The Dome of the Rock
Jerusalem III

 EXT MORNING the companions together made the final pilgrimage, to the Dome of the Rock. Through the narrow streets, elbowed by strident black-hatted Orthodox monks, zealous young students of the Torah in white skull caps, and obstinate mullahs in green turbans, Satanaya felt she was wading through flocks of lost sheep herded by so many ignorant shepherds. Oh, the Jews with their wailing, the Christians with their flailing, and the Muslims unfailingly correct in their bowing and prostrating! No, she was not going to be counted among that crowd of imitators; all those men following men. Satanaya was a Circassian woman, and with her two gay companions, she was going to meet her God wholly and completely as herself: free of expectations, returning love for love, a lover's union; on equal terms with that which has no equal, as the image reflected in the mirror has no existence other than the origin it reflects, the ineffable mystery veiled only by the unknown of her own heart. Only there, in that private place, after the annihilation of conflicting thoughts and drowning emotions, would she beat her breast, and in the secure sanctuary of union, cry out, and plead her case.

Approaching the hallowed *temenos* of the Haram al-Sherif, the Noble Sanctuary, all history fell away. Beyond three tall cypress trees, nearby the pendant little Dome of the Chain, sat the magnificent temple, bound in a cienture of glorious turquoise tiles over which calligraphy flowed like ribbons above the walls of the great octagon supporting the sombre grey-ribbed dome, a throne on high beneath the infinite blue sky. It was the most beautiful building Satanaya had ever seen.

She knew of this place as a child from her father telling the story of Mohammed's Night Journey, the *'Mir'aj'* – a sort of stairway to heaven. It had been one of her favourite stories because it took her into realms of the imagination, a world to which she felt somehow closer than the the rough world she inhabited by day. It was a world where she could travel without limits and delight in wonderful ideas and stranger places. As she entered the building it all came flooding back:

'The Prophet, God bless him and give him peace,' he would begin the story, 'was in Mecca in the holy place of the Black Stone, the sacred stone that fell from heaven in the time of Adam and Eve, and where Abraham built the first house to worship God. Just as Muhammed was falling asleep the Angel Gabriel appeared. Mohammed was so surprised that he knocked over a glass of water. And then Gabriel, (because Mohammed was almost asleep he didn't feel any pain, explained her father) Gabriel cut him open and took out his heart and washed it in wisdom and certainty, and put it back in his chest. Then the angel brought Muhammed a magical animal called Buraq, a white steed which carried him in an instant from Mecca to the holy temple in Jerusalem, for this steed could leap as far as the eye could see in a single bound, and it reached Jerusalem in just a few strides. He tethered Buraq and went into the mosque to pray.'

Satanaya's eyes would widen in wonder as she imagined riding such a horse, and her father continued:

'There Gabriel offered the Prophet a drink, asking him to choose between milk and wine. Of course, he chose milk. Probably he thought he might fall off Buraq if he drank wine. Then Gabriel took Muhammed up to the seven heavens, and in each heaven he was welcomed and prayed over by the prophet in charge. Adam, then Jesus and John the Baptist, Joseph, Idris, Aaron, and then Moses. And in the seventh heaven he found Abraham leaning against the *'Beyt al Ma'mur'*, the house around which all the heavens turn, and where 70,000 angels come and go each day, and never the same angels but always a new lot.'

And again Satanaya would marvel, unable to comprehend such a number, replenished daily.

'From there he was taken to the *Sidrat al-Muntaha* – the Lote Tree of the Extreme Limit, where the world of spirits ends – a golden tree with branches of ruby and emerald, and it takes a hundred and fifty years to go from the foot of this tree to the top...'

At this point Mansur's children would always ask how could he have travelled this all in one night, and the answer was always the same, on his Buraq of course, his magic horse.

'And the leaves of the *Sidrat al-Muntaha* are like the ears of an elephant, and so big they would cover up the whole world. And from its branches hang fruit shaped like jugs of water and the whole tree glows from top to bottom in heavenly light and the branches are covered in golden angels that no one has ever seen, just as a tree is covered with locusts glittering in the sun.

'It is so beautiful that there are no words in the world to describe it. At this point Muhammed was addressed in the Great Presence of God, who told him that his people were to say 50 prayers every day and night. So back he went. At the fifth heaven, Moses warned him that his people would never say so many prayers, so he returned and asked God to reduce them by five prayers., "Still too many," said Moses, "they'll never manage", so back up he went, time and again, until he had bargained it down to only five prayers a day, each of which would be counted as ten, because God always has more to give. And when Muhammed arrived back in Mecca he was just in time to catch the glass of water he had knocked over when Gabriel first appeared. And not a drop was spilled.'

And now here she was, in the place where the magic steed had landed a split second after leaving Mecca, drinking in the magic. The military bearing of the two young men, dressed in their tall kalpaks and Cherkess jackets with the rows of cartridges on their chests, brought to attention the Turkish guards who saluted them as they made their way into the building and performed their circumambulation around the exposed rocky outcrop in the centre of the temple.

Satanaya leant into a corner and made herself very still and very small. She had discovered something during her visit to Nazareth about the value of withdrawal in situations that needed clarification. And in the interior space that opened for her now, she again became aware of a thread. For her this was a major thread, and she wondered how no one else could see it, this single line linking all these prophets together; how each came bringing something important and worth knowing, something of true value, from Adam to Abraham to Moses to Jesus to Muhammed, each with some vital knowledge for humanity about the human reality. She saw that for most people religion was little more than a set of rules, a fixed set of rules like a uniform relevant once for a specific people at a specific time. Now she threw all these clothes to the four winds, and found herself standing there as if a naked spirit. These people who called themselves Jews, Christians, Muslims – such small thinking to imagine they could encompass this magnitude in the narrow confines of their separate histories. No, these divisions were no longer supportable; 'there is a story here,' she thought, 'that these prophets are telling, and that is the story of who I am, and no black hat rabbi, collared priest nor bearded imam can come between this and my heart. Something else is moving in me and it doesn't stop at religion with its god of separation. There is no end to the descent of the spirit.' She remembered how she had felt in Nazareth, in the Church of the Bashara, the grandeur and loving tenderness of the spirit as it expanded in her own breast, a mirror of that great annunciation of joy, a joy that is to come. Another mystery to nurture and be nurtured by in the outward life to come, the life of her future present.

The gentle tapping of a cane by the building's caretaker awakened Satanaya from her reverie. She became aware of the call to prayer from the Mosque of Al Aqsa, nearby across the paved court from the Dome of the Rock. While Murat and Timur went off to pray with the congregation of men, Satanaya quietly slipped away and out of the Haram al-Sherif.

Satanaya had one final visit to make before leaving Jerusalem. She rode

Tarçin out of the city to the little village of Ain Karim, some five miles west in hilly country covered in pine trees and flowing springs. It was for her mother really, that she went, to the birthplace of John the Baptist, where Mary met her kinswoman Elizabeth, each with a babe in the womb which moved at their approach. Here the words of the 'Magnificat' were revealed; it was her mother, Gülay, who had taught her at an early age to repeat the prayer's opening lines, *'My soul magnifies the Lord, and my spirit rejoices in God my Saviour ...'* whenever she wanted to show gratitude. It was a simple thing that had stayed with her, and walking now in the wooded glades of Ain Karim, among the irises and bright flowering mustard, with butterflies awakening in the spring sun, she felt herself come alive inside, her soul magnifying and rejoicing in this great unknown reality. Her gratitude was for all that had brought her to that point, and now her pilgrimage was completed, she felt prepared for whatever this unknown would bring.

Timur and Murat had been well received by the military authorities in Jerusalem. The Governor personally provided the son of the hero of Plevna and his friend with letters of recommendation to contacts in the Harbiye Military Academy in Constantinople and all necessary permits for travel to the city. A few days later the three vagabonds boarded a Russian cargo ship carrying returning pilgrims to Odessa via Beirut, Cyprus and Constantinople.

The parting on the quayside at Beirut was a strangely wrenching affair. During their brief adventure they had come to know one another in a way that even lovers rarely do, deeply, with trust and honesty. And although so little of words had passed between them, yet each felt accepted and joined to the other in ways that no physical union would have brought. When they had talked, it was in terms of wonderment: of the yearning to meet the unknown of their futures, and discover what each one's path in that world would bring. And that path for all three was into a world wider than their imaginations could conceive. But wonderment brought with it a kind of perplexity, and the oscillation of mind that ensues from this state. So, with wonder also came a kind of fear, an awe of the unknown such that as they made their farewells, they clung together in a long embrace, with tears and forebodings of what would happen when they let go. But the little storm passed quickly as the wonderment swung back bringing the excitement and sense of freedom that comes with embracing the unknown.

Their moment was broken by a single long blast of the ship's horn signalling immanent departure. Fond last looks were exchanged between ship and shore. As the vessel pulled away, she turned her back and gazed up at the green slopes of the Lebanon. She experienced again that strange sense of doors closing firmly behind her, and in spite of the hollow ache occasioned by the parting of friends, she recognised the thrill of a new life opening up. She tightened the girth of Tarçin's saddle and set off up the road to Beyt'ur-Rahma.

TWENTY-THREE

The Sponge of Love

Beyt'ur-Rahma, near Beirut, 1898

T THE BEYT'UR-RAHMA the almond trees had already shed their pale bloom, and young velvet-green drupes were showing on the branches. Satanaya climbed the steep path to the house beneath a magical bunting of pink, white and magenta blossoms.

Lady Gülbahar was sitting on the terrace in her pale blue and white striped dressing gown drinking her accustomed late morning coffee.

'Ah, Satanaya, you're back. Just in time, we have a major soirée this coming weekend. You'll enjoy it, they're a young crowd – poets, writers, etc.'

Had time stood still? Had it really been six months since Satanaya had ridden away with her father? The Beyt and its châtelaine seemed quite unchanged.

'Now, do come up quickly and tell me all your adventures? Did you marry the boy? …No of course not. Silly me. You wouldn't have left him quite so soon I suppose. But then… one can never tell.'

Satanaya tethered Tarçin and ran up and embraced the old lady.

'Oh Lady Gülbahar, I'm so happy to be back with you, you have no idea.'

'Was it so bad, then? Was the boy so dreadful? Was his mother a Circassian witch? Your letter didn't explain anything at all.'

'No, it was fine. Really. And the boy was actually quite charming. Just not my type. I'll explain it all in a minute. I just missed being here so much.'

Pelin appeared with fresh coffee and pastries, gave Satanaya a big hug, and just couldn't stop beaming. All she said was, 'My sister!'

Clotilde arrived and crushed her assistant passionately to her motherly bosom, leaving her covered in flour.

'Ah ma petite, enfin tu es revenue à nous, grâce à Dieu.' said the cook, tears in her eyes.

After coffee Lady Gülbahar took Satanaya's arm. 'Come, my dear, let's walk in the garden. It's particularly nice this year, and who knows how many more times we shall get to see it together.' She was looking into the distance, down the slopes to the faraway blue of St George Bay. 'Come, there are things we have to discuss.'

With walking stick in one hand, and leaning on Satanaya's arm, she led the way down the steps of the terrace.

'You see,' said Lady Gülbahar, 'I've decided to get married again.'

Satanaya stopped and looked at the aged châtelaine.

'Aha! you didn't see that coming, did you? It's the French Baron, the one who helped the Ambassador with his vines when he was setting up the vineyard. He's a very old friend of mine too, from before the Ambassador's time, but we needn't go into that, it's too long ago.

'He is quite in love with me. He always was. And I find him charming. He's a complete gentleman. We don't sleep together, that would be just too undignified at our age, don't you think? But he comes into my room each evening, sits on my bed a while and we chat, then he kisses me goodnight and goes off to his own room. It's for the company, you see. When you get old, loneliness can be a dreadful bore. For him, the winter climate here is so much better than his draughty old chateau in France. He keeps himself busy helping Gérard with the vines during the day, and I have this house to manage. So we play cards in the evening and enjoy the company of guests on weekends. You see, it's a different kind of love. We are completely at ease with each other. We love the same things. Mostly. And we share so many memories. And we each have our own opinions, so we disagree too, and our conversation is not boring.'

Lady Gülbahar looked at Satanaya and smiled, 'You're not shocked, are you?'

'No, not at all. Heavens, no. I think it's wonderful. And there'll be a wedding to prepare.' Satanaya was already dreaming of the feast.

'But there's another matter.' Lady Gülbahar continued. 'Quite a serious thing, in fact, which concerns you Satanaya. You know I have no children, and one day, soon perhaps, who knows, I shall pass on, and Le Baron… he's even older, so there's no saying when he will… *cassera sa pipe,* so to speak, though he has no pipe to break since he stopped smoking. What I mean is, neither of us have any children. Though I suppose you and little Pelin are like my children. Now, I've already adopted Pelin. How would you like us adopt you as well? Of course it would not change the fact that you still have both your parents. This arrangement would be for… let us say, the convenience of the future. If I, as the Ambassador's widow, first adopt you, then you would have far more rights in the Empire than you would as a refugee. And then, when that is sorted out, the Baron can adopt you, then you would not only be French, but also become a Baroness one day. What do you think?'

Satanaya was now stunned.

'Oh Lady Gülbahar, are you quite sure? Of course it would be wonderful, but I really don't know. So far I seem to have been quite the unreliable daughter. I know myself well enough to see I would disappoint most parents. I had better explain what happened in Kfar Kama…'

So, after Satanaya had related all that had gone on in Palestine, including the deception of the kidnap, the trip to Jerusalem, the parting with Timur and Murat and so on, and she and Lady Gülbahar had continued their conversation during a quiet lunch just for the two of them, and drunk a couple of glasses of wine and weighed up the whole situation, they both agreed this adoption thing sounded like a very good idea, and they had better get it all worked out soon because the Baron, as has been intimated, was none too nimble on his pins any more, and even putting aside broken pipes, popped clogs and mortal coils, it seemed wise to move things along.

'You see, Satanaya,' said Lady Gülbahar, 'the world is changing. Who knows how long it will last here in Beyt'ur-Rahma. You are already becoming a woman of the world. The time may come when you might have to travel beyond the shores of Lebanon, and for that you need certain things.'

The soirée was memorable, but the mundane details passed into oblivion like fireworks: a dazzling display of noisy fun and sparks of light, leaving in its wake drifting smoke, darkness and silence.

Yet something lingered in that smoke: Khalil. There was a fierce beauty behind that name; and behind his beautiful sad face, a gentleness within that defensive look of proud fear which longed to be soothed and made safe. Yet this beauty drew from deep within Satanaya a memory, and with it a terror, the terror that comes from fear of losing that precious thing, that timeless and incomprehensible feeling which presages the arrival of love in the heart.

She remembered Yusuf, and the wrenching pain of first love's parting. And though that pain had passed, still something had touched deep in her soul, cut into the fabric of her thoughts and left its imprint. She saw that this young man too wore the effects, if not scars, of the pain of love.

Khalil had arrived at the Beyt with a number of young bucks – poets and would-be world changers from down in Beirut – brash, happy chaps full of inspiration and the certitude of youth discovering themselves and their world for the first time. Some were still at college, others were writers, one was an editor of an Arab newspaper prone to being censored, if not actually closed down by the Turkish authorities for espousing nationalist views. They wanted to be modern. They were dissatisfied and wanted the world on their own terms.

Khalil was different. Not that he wasn't as arrogant in manner as his friends. Nor was he disdaining of the past nobilities and good earth of ancient wisdom in which his ideas were rooted. But the expression in his face, in his words, in the poems he read, belied a deep sadness that yearned to surface, and when Satanaya looked at him she heard this plaintive cry within her own heart. It was then she had recognised him, the boy with the long hair glimpsed from afar, descending the gangway of the ship from America, as she returned with Clotilde from her first trip to the market. It was the same look that had captured her gaze then. And although she had not realised at the time, being still held within the heavenly nimbus, the delicious afterglow from imbibing the fabled bouillabaisse, his face had remained engraved in her memory.

Their conversation at table had been fleeting, occupied as Satanaya was with helping serve up the food. Lady Gülbahar had been quite definite that her presence at these evenings was an essential part of her education. However, there was much to attend to besides exchanging witty repartee or conversing knowledgeably on subjects which as yet seemed of little concern to her. The political situation in the Middle East, in Beirut in particular, was always a hot topic, and this soirée was no exception. The Arab nationalists were represented as usual, and the arguments flowed back and forth over whether nationhood was a matter of religious consciousness, cultural identity, linguistic unity, or the expression of common political will. In this last mentioned, all were in broad agreement that any nation of Arabs would necessitate the removal of the Turkish, that is the Ottoman, overlord.

One of the bright young things, whose father owned estates in the mountains, had provided the Beyt with a couple of deer, so the feast had centred round a vast casserole of venison with wild mushrooms cooked long and slow in red wine until the meat fell away from the bones in tender hunks infused with earthy forest flavours. The dish was served with mounds of mashed potatoes and platters of red cabbage cooked with apple and raisins.

They had eaten well, and drunk even better, and the conversation had been boisterous and argumentative, in particular between the editor who had claimed any Arab nation's constitution must be rooted in the Koran, and the Maronite students who objected, saying that an Arab nation had to include the Christians of the Levant, and the Jews too for that matter, on equal terms. Khalil had broken into the argument by calling for a return to the values of the Abrahamic religions, without the oppression of forced adherence to any particular religious dogma, so that even agnostics and modern free thinkers could be at liberty to maintain their views.

'We cannot hope to bring our Arab nation into the modern era if we simply depend on the laws and mores of desert tribes. We must extend our thinking beyond tribal loyalties to an inclusive system of universal human values. In spite of our differences, we are all the inheritors of Abraham – Jews, Christians and Moslems alike.'

He said this with conviction and passion, and was about to launch into a thesis whereby he married the ancient prophetic wisdoms to the spirit of the Age of Enlightenment, and to explain his inspired vision on human rights in which all people partake of a single humanity. But the wine had taken over the conversation. Everyone was talking over each other and his words were lost on most of those present – clever intellectuals who preferred to get bogged down in a semantic morass over the meaning of 'Arab', a discussion that became ever more divisive with little chance of uniting the warring parties.

He turned to look at the young lady who had dined with them. She was clearing the table, removing empty plates and platters, replacing soiled napkins, refreshing the wine and the water carafes. He shrugged and smiled, as if to say, 'well, one tries.' Satanaya laughed, and his expression changed first to mild annoyance, then to concern, as he realised that perhaps she was not mocking him at all, but rather sympathising with his dilemma.

'So, what do you think?' he said.

'What do I think about what?'

'Well, … Do you think it matters, how we are going to live together if the Turkish yoke is removed? After all, there are those who say it's the only thing preventing us indulging in an almighty bloodbath.'

Satanaya blushed nervously and said the first words that came into her head: 'I think if we understood anything at all about love, anything at all, and practised it, it would be better for us all.'

'Exactly. Exactly exactly exactly. Thank God there is at least one sane person here who understands what I've been trying to say. One love – it's the real message of unity, our true inheritance from Abraham, like hospitality and caring for each other. Look, we haven't been properly introduced, my name is Khalil.'

'Ah, so that's why.'

'Why what?'

'This interest in the prophet Abraham. Abraham is called *al Khalil* – the one who is intimate with God – lost in love, drowned even, like a sponge soaked with water.'

Khalil was surprised to find a girl who could converse on his favourite subject. 'That's amazing, who told you that?'

'It's just something my father would say, whenever he met anyone called Abraham, or Ibrahim, or Khalil. He used to say that people called Abraham were often big people, as if they carried a lot of responsibility around with them. And he would say they could soak up love like a sponge soaks up water, because that's what God puts into all of us. But with Abraham it's just that it's specific.'

'So I'm a love sponge, am I?' Khalil laughed gaily. Then he fell silent as if remembering something, and vanished in himself with the memory to somewhere very far away.

'What's America like?' Satanaya had been wanting to hear about America all evening, and this was her chance.

'Hmmmm. America. It's big. Really big. Everything about it seems larger than life.'

'And the people?

'You know, in a way they're really just the same as us. There are Leba-nese and Syrians, as well as Jews and Irish, Italians and other Europeans. And black people of course. And there are the original Americans, the ones they call Red Indians, who are not red at all; they have been left with very little, but they remain connected to the spirit of the land. They are the true owners of America. Anyway, the Americans all argue just like we do. But there's something else, something quite different which happens to people there after a while. People believe they can do anything, and no one tells them they can't. There is so much energy, and everyone works really hard. And they think big. Bigger than you can think here. For a start, there's no one telling you that you should think like this or be like that. Not like here. Of course there are laws and all, but there's something else, so that if there was something you wanted to do, something really extraordi-nary, well, it just seems possible to do it in America.'

'Do you mean like the railways?' Satanaya had heard the Germans were building a railway to Beirut, but so far there had been little evidence of progress.

'Yes, of course, but it's more than these big projects. It's not just the country that is being opened up, but minds as well.'

Khalil paused briefly, searching for the right words. 'I don't know... imagine you were a painter, and here in Lebanon you were only given forty or so different colours to paint with, while in America there would be a hundred and forty colours, a thousand and forty, whatever; and here you could only paint a miniature, while in America you could paint a canvas as big as a house. Yes, that's it really, the possibilities seem bigger.'

'And does that go for love too? Does Khalil soak up more love in America?' Satanaya found herself looking into Khalil's eyes. They were large but not the kind of dark pools like Yusuf's. Khalil's eyes looked right back at you, as if he might enter your soul. If you wanted him to.

'Perhaps.' he answered. 'But perhaps we should discover our America right here, then there would be no need to cross the ocean.'

'Maybe the ocean is just part of it. Like Columbus daring to sail into the great unknown.' Satanaya was enjoying the way this was going.

'Ha! I would probably fall in and drown, especially if it was an ocean of love.' He was mocking himself now.

'Then who would you be? Khalil or love? The water or the sponge?'

'Ah!' Khalil enjoyed her riposte. He paused and slowly extemporised:
'If love comes
then I must go
if love comes
naught would show
but an empty shell
rocking in the swell
of the ocean floor.'

There it was again – those eyes. Satanaya knew something was com-municating, travelling, penetrating the veils between them. What was it? They were in their own world, a place of intimacy in which words were messengers carrying their souls' announcement on every breath. They were as oblivious to the rest of the party, as the party in its wine-brimmed overflow was oblivious to their own seclusion.

The magic that enveloped them was broken gradually as the guests drifted homeward, and gaps like vacancies of light showed in the festive aura of the house. A veil descended upon the inner workings of their hearts, and when Clotilde came and opened all the windows and the fresh night air flooded the room, Satanaya felt she was waking from a dream. Only then was she aware that Khalil had been holding both her hands all the while, and her knees were closely touching his. They stood up and went outside.

'I must see you again, Satanaya.' Khalil's voice was calm but with an assured insistence. 'Would you come and see me in Beirut? There are many coffee houses where we could meet, where no one would comment. I'm in college most days, but I can easily miss the classes, they don't really amount to much. Frankly, I learn more from the conversation in the coffee houses than I do from the priests.'

Satanaya looked at him, unsure whether to be concerned at his forwardness or just amused. The fact was she had enjoyed their time together in a way that was different from other occasions in male company. He was probably a little younger than she was, perhaps even more naive, for all his worldly talk. No, she wasn't concerned. She felt safe in his company, and happy, and if he continued to amuse her, all the better.

'Now I must go as well, I don't want to travel down alone. Please pass on my thanks and goodnight to Lady Gülbahar. I promise I'll be in touch.' And with that he kissed her hand and with a farewell look deep into her eyes, turned and hurried after a party of young men who were making their way down the front path, singing *gazels* to the accompaniment of oud and tambourine.

Satanaya waved them off in their horse-cart, and as they descended and the music faded, she sensed, as if a lingering perfume, the echo of a wild, inspired beauty.

TWENTY-FOUR

A Rendezvous in Beirut

ATANAYA WAS DREAMING of a doorway. She stood before it, and she knew she must enter. But as she approached she felt a quickening fear, for she knew that once through there would be no returning...

She gripped the door handle. It was an action of intention. She was full of trepidation, but a decision had been made and now there was no going back. She turned the handle, and in that moment everything vanished. The next thing she knew she was waking up, as if arriving back after a long journey, with all the weight of the experience of a long journey remaining, as a taste, a scent, but without any remembered image upon which to anchor it. It was as if she had spent years away but now had no memory at all of where she had been. It was disturbing, having experienced a whole other lifetime, with nothing to show for it but the certainty she had been away, wherever away was. She remembered the story of the Night Journey of Muhammed, and laughed to herself. 'Well, at least it is possible.' she thought, even as the sense of distant journeying began to fade. 'But I do wish I had the strength of mind to remember where I went.' There was nothing else she could think, about the dream, at any rate.

Then something else came back to her. The soirée, the night before, the meeting with the young man, and she felt that quickening fear in the pit of her stomach, the sharp, almost painful pulling right down inside, leaving her oscillating between joy and panic. It was a place she had always known existed, but never really acknowledged. She felt warm within the soft linen sheets, her face cradled in the cool of the pillows, and she remembered Khalil. Her whole body suddenly felt pleasurable and light beneath her quilted bedspread. It was Sunday. Lazy morning day, Lady Gülbahar called it. She felt delight throughout her whole being, and at that moment, as she held the image of Khalil in her mind, she had no inclination for anything else.

Seen in retrospect, her affair with Khalil was inevitable. It becomes a story. But we can only say what we see, and who is to say what might be seen beyond the eyes. The weeks passed, and rather than fading, that exquisite pain beneath her ribs sharpened as she lay awake at night, and awaited word of him by day. Then a letter came. From Khalil. Writing to say he remembered their conversation with fondness and that he wished to see her again. Would she meet him to continue their conversation? He gave his own address, and the name of a European-style hotel in Beirut, in the French quarter, where they could sit and drink coffee and talk in private without attracting undue attention.

The letter was brief and to the point. Polite, nothing more. It was signed simply, 'I remain, your sincere friend, Khalil.'

Since her return from Palestine, Satanaya had made the Friday trip to market with Clotilde a number of times, and was familiar with the various marketeers, the butchers, the vegetable sellers, and purveyors of necessary household items. This week, Clotilde was not feeling well, and asked her assistant if she would make the trip without her.

Satanaya tried not to sound too eager. 'I guess so.' she said, 'I hope they won't try and cheat me when they see you're not around.'

'No need to worry about that, I'm sure.' said Clotilde, 'I think they are rather in awe of you. I chat too much anyway. Get some artichokes, they should be at their best around now. And new green beans too, if they're not too pricey, buy a few kilos, they'll make a lovely cold olive oil dish.'

So Satanaya set off early in the morning in the horse and cart. She brought freshly cut spinach from their own garden for Mr Jemil the vegetable man to sell on their behalf. She couldn't decide whether or not to see Khalil, and while some part of her definitely brightened at the possibility of a meeting, she felt nervous at the prospect. She had written a short note which she left at Khalil's address, saying she might or might not be at the hotel at around midday. But in the end it was not necessary. As she was finishing her shopping, and was settling up with Mr Jemil, she turned to find a young man standing behind her.

'Good morning, Miss Satanaya.' he said, bowing slightly and tipping his hat. It was a flat cap, of the kind popular then among working men in the United States, and positively *de rigueur* for the returned immigrant in the Lebanon. The bright sun shone on his thick black hair, tumbling wantonly from beneath the cap onto his shoulders. Satanaya, taken by surprise in the busy market place, did not immediately recognise Khalil. In daylight, in the same ill-fitting suit in which he had stepped down the gangway off the boat from America the year before, something was familiar.

'Satanaya, it's me, Khalil. Don't you recognise me?' He was laughing, a light, easy laugh.

'Of course, I'm sorry. I didn't just expect to see you here.' She felt breathless as she took in the eager young face before her.

'Well, I found your letter about an hour ago, and figured you must be somewhere around here. I really wanted to see you but your message was a bit vague. Intriguing even.' Khalil smiled.

'I can't imagine what was intriguing. I just didn't know whether I'd have time to see you, that's all.' said Satanaya, a little too brusquely. She felt the need to bring under control the initial excitement that this sudden apparition had provoked. But it wasn't really working. She realised she was panicking, and that her heart was beating faster than usual.

'Well, shall we walk and talk, or do we meet at the hotel? Or do you want to come to my place.'

Satanaya was confused, and feeling self conscious. She became aware of Mr Jemil behind her. What must he be thinking? A young lady, unaccompanied, talking to a young man in the street. She turned around and smiled at the greengrocer.

'This chap will take my things to the cart. He's one of Lady Gülbahar's boys.' she said.

Khalil looked a little put out, but quickly grasped the situation and collected her purchases from behind the stall. Satanaya led the way through the crowd while he laboured behind with a large box stuffed with fruit and vegetables. Evidently he was not used to manual labour.

'Let's not go to the hotel,' Satanaya said, once the goods were stowed, 'I don't have much time. Perhaps we could go and have tea down on the waterfront.'

Satanaya tipped one of the young market boys to keep an eye on the horse and cart. At the harbour, they sat among fishermen at a small tea stall, at a table by the water's edge.

When they had first met, cosseted by the blanket of night, time had stretched, barriers had been fluid and few, and in the safety of the Beyt an intimacy had arisen naturally. Everything seemed different in the naked light of day, without the wine, without the music. Facing each other now a shyness came over them. Their conversation began on conventional lines but soon began to stray.

'I love the sea.' said Satanaya. She looked straight into Khalil's eyes.

Khalil accepted the look, then turned his gaze towards the water.

'Yes, it makes me feel so small.'

'But it's so pure, so vast, so blue. It's a relief just to look at it.' Satanaya too had now turned towards the water.

Khalil began to recite:

'Blue like the eyes of the Circassian girl,
My heart looks into this vastness
Will we remain pure if union beckons?
Will this sea relieve us of our burdens?'

Satanaya felt herself blushing. She looked at Khalil and tried to take the measure of his words. The breeze off the water was cool on her cheek, and the light spray made her blink. She felt helpless and adrift. Khalil was still gazing out to sea, and she saw someone just as helpless, vulnerable. Just a boy with poetry on his lips. Pretty poetry. Pretty lips.

She wanted to wrap him in her arms right there, but held back, embracing the image in her heart instead. They sat in silence a while. Satanaya spoke:

'That's beautiful. Well, I think poetry always sounds beautiful in Arabic. So you are a poet. What else do you do?'

'Oh, I write and I paint, and I drink too much and think too much. What else is there to do? I'd love to paint you one day, if you'd let me. If you'd like me to.'

She laughed. Khalil smiled. He loved that laugh. It did something to him inside. It made him feel safe, it made him give up for a while the sense of doom that seemed to follow him everywhere like a disconnected shadow always trying to catch up. And when it did, it enveloped him, and the only way he knew to put it back behind him was to drink wine and talk loudly, declaiming and arguing with his friends. What he felt now with Satanaya was something else, another kind of intoxication, and he wanted to drink it in until he became senseless.

'Well, would you?' said Khalil.

'Would I what?' Satanaya too had gone somewhere else in her thoughts. Somewhere she hardly dared admit. Somewhere dangerous.

'Let me paint you?'

'Oh, that. Yeah. Maybe. Why not?'

'I'd like to paint you right now, just as you are, with that look.'

Satanaya frowned. 'What look?' she said.

Khalil stirred his tea and left the tiny spoon in the glass. Then lifting the glass and holding the spoon away from his lip with his little finger he took a few sips.

'Well, it's hard to describe. Kind of faraway, but not vague. Something you are seeing, not on the surface but deep down. As if you were looking into the sea, and instead of just gazing dreamily into the unending deep, you were looking at yourself.'

Satanaya took a long gulp of tea.

'Aren't you hungry?'

'What?'

'Aren't you hungry? I am. All this sea air makes me ravenous. There's a great place for fish soup over there. Really, trust me, it's the best. All the fishermen eat there.'

Satanaya hadn't changed the subject consciously. She was in fact quite suddenly hungry. But the moment – for it had been that, a real moment of deep connection – had moved on.

'You really do like food, don't you?' said Khalil, a little put out at being hauled back in from the deep sea drift of his thoughts. Food was the last thing on his mind.

'At least as much as I like poetry and good conversation.'

The bouillabaisse was balm upon the nervous souls of the two young people. Tender hearts are prone to capsize in the strong winds of deep emotions, and food cooked with compassion brings life and strength to human possibilities, setting straight the course and relieving the constriction of those yearning for love. Over bowls steaming with rich aromas of seafood and herbs, Khalil and Satanaya began to relax in each other's company at last. They told each other stories from their brief lives, and in this way each learnt a little more of the other.

Khalil walked Satanaya back to the market where they parted, promising to meet again soon. As horse and cart wound up through the pine-clad hillsides Satanaya, comfortably replete from the soup, the warm sun on her back and the lingering presence of her day with Khalil, felt herself upon a threshold that needed only time to reveal the full vision of what was opening before her.

TWENTY-FIVE

An Affair Progresses

 HALIL LAY ON HIS BED and stared out of the window at the hot blue sky of the east Mediterranean. The stillness of the afternoon was broken only by the distant shouts of a street hawker spieling his wares as he barrowed his goods along the street below.

Khalil was in love. That was nothing unusual for an eighteen year old boy who had just spent hours in the presence of a beautiful young lady – it was a simple automatic response. But this was a complete distraction. His books lay on the floor where he had tossed them in frustration. Unable to concentrate, he stared out, seeing nothing, trying to remember the details of her face, the smile, the perfect lips, the black hair, those blue eyes. Were they almond-shaped eyes? he wondered. No, they were round. Large and round and they looked right into you. They saw you, they didn't waver, weren't preoccupied with some internal thought or image. So simple, but frighteningly truthful. How did she do it? Why no fear? He always looked at things from a detached position, like someone watching side-on in a private box at the theatre, separated from the crowd, able to come and go at will. He knew he held back. That was his protection. His defence. But she... her look seemed to cut away whatever came in between, peeling back the rind to get to the fruit. He felt quite naked beneath such a gaze. How would he paint her?

He suddenly sat up, grabbed paper and a soft pencil and began to draw. He worked fast, holding her image in his mind against the blue of the sea and the sky: the chin, the strong curve of her eyebrows, the straight nose, the hair, not so much curly as wavy, a long neck. Then he realised he was remembering her from the soirée. In the market she had worn a scarf over her head like a village girl. Perhaps that was why she had been unsure of meeting at the hotel. Then the eyes, those round open eyes that saw everything without surprise. Her mouth wide, her lips full – not so full as to be immodest, but full nevertheless. He found his pencil hesitating upon her lips, as if to draw them would be presumptuous. He put the sketch down on the bed. He looked at it and it looked back. It seemed to be saying something, protesting. A head without a body. 'No!' He said it out loud, and grabbing the picture he tore it up there and then. He knew it would haunt him in inappropriate ways if he left it, like a dream, a fantasy woman. Still, he couldn't help conjuring Satanaya's face again in his mind, her face against the deep blue of the sea, and he resolved to see her again as soon as possible.

In Beyt'ur-Rahma they sat at supper eating fresh artichokes with a light olive oil and lemon dressing seasoned with a little salt, sugar and Dijon mustard. Clotilde was telling Lady Gülbahar how well Satanaya had managed with the shopping.

'I wonder' said Lady Gülbahar, 'is it always necessary for you both to go down to Beirut shopping every week.' She was addressing Clotilde. 'I know you've plenty to do in the kitchen and you're very busy in the vegetable garden with all the new greens coming up – perhaps Satanaya could do the shopping on her own for now? You could still go whenever you felt like a day out, or if we had a big evening to shop for.'

'But do you think it safe for her? Beirut is a big city now, and Satanaya is still just a young girl. Can she manage among all those rough types in the market.'

'You said yourself she got the best prices out of the traders today. And she managed to find her way around Palestine and Jerusalem, among all those Arabs and Russians and Turks, not to mention the Druzes. Anyway, what does Satanaya think?'

Satanaya, who had just scraped the last artichoke leaf of its soft flesh, and was engaged in removing the furry choke covering the heart, was feigning nonchalance at the trend of the conversation. Of course she thought it a marvellous idea, but under the circumstances she felt it best to pretend to side with Clotilde at first and then, reluctantly accept that it would be good for her to get used to this new role.

'Don't worry, I always carry my Cherkess dagger, Clotilde.' she said

'*Que Dieu te protège, ma petite!* You mustn't make jokes like that!' Clotilde patted her own breast as if to calm her heart.

'No, really, I do, Clotilde, look.' and Satanaya reached down under the table, ruffled around and drew out a small but lethal looking blade.

Clotilde opened her mouth in horror, speechless.

Lady Gülbahar just laughed and said. 'Of course she does, and so do I. What Circassian lady worth her salt wouldn't carry her knife. And know how to put it to good use.' and she then produced from the belt of her dress an even smaller piece of sharpened steel, with a handle of chased silver and a big ruby on the hilt. 'I find it quite adequate for peeling fruit, don't you Satanaya?' Clotilde then burst out laughing at what she thought was a good joke on her. Satanaya and Lady Gülbahar laughed too, but for different reasons, and they returned to the important matter of the artichokes.

And so it happened that Satanaya and Khalil were able to meet on a regular basis, with Khalil acting as porter as she went from shop to shop making her purchases. They did this as efficiently as possible, and then would find a suitable place to sit and eat lunch.

At this time, with Lady Gülbahar's encouragement, Satanaya began to adjust her clothing, metamorphosing from village girl with headscarf, via Circassian maid to European lady. She did so in stages, in order not to

unduly upset the traders. Lady Gülbahar also gave her lessons in makeup, something Satanaya had always avoided since she found the local village girls' use of kohl around the eyes, from childhood onwards, somewhat startling. Satanaya had the complexion of a healthy country lass, a light tan on her naturally pale skin, so that what caught one's attention was always her large powder blue Circassian eyes.

'The fashion now is a pale look, so perhaps a little powder,' and Lady Gülbahar produced a box of small paper tissues coated in fine white powder. 'First you must use moisturiser on your face, and then the powder tissues, then a little rouge on cheeks, and then more powder.' And with a delighted Pelin helping with the maquillage, they made her up before the large mirror in the châtelaine's bedroom.

'Now a little rouge on the lips. Not painted on, just enough to give them that 'bitten' effect, and a little brown shading on your eyelids, and we're done. Not that we could make you more beautiful than you already are, my dear, just highlight your good points. A lady always makes an effort to look her best, your face is your gift to the world so don't be stingy. And you'll see, it will change the way you see yourself. You are no longer a village girl, Satanaya.'

Looking at herself in the mirror, Satanaya laughed. 'You're not trying to sell me off to your old 'Madam' are you?'

'You'll see, with the right clothes your dance card would fill immediately at any Embassy ball,' chided her mistress.

As well as the makeup, Lady Gülbahar was always coming up with little presents, a bonnet or a pretty crocheted shawl, a small purse and a lacy parasol – things to make a girl look more like a woman.

'Beirut may not be Paris, but it enjoys style, nonetheless.'

Lady Gülbahar was so enthusiastic in Satanaya's transformation that she wondered whether her mistress knew more than she was letting on. But she was enjoying the fuss, and the different sense of self that this dressing up gave her.

Whenever the two young fondlings were able to meet, they would sit by the harbour. With the city behind them, the sea, with its wide horizon and the noisy surge of waves between rocks, afforded them the illusion of a private space in which their intimacy could grow. And while on the surface their talk was of small things, deep down stronger currents were moving in them.

Khalil often spoke of America, and of the family he had left in order to complete his education in Lebanon. He missed his family, and the world he had begun to inhabit. The world of artists and poets of the New World. Satanaya shared his enthusiasm for modern literature.

'But that's not to say I don't have feelings for my Arabic language roots.' he said one day, 'In fact, I wish I could express as well in English what I feel in my soul, but I guess my soul will remain Arab.'

'Do you really think souls have nationalities?' said Satanaya.

'Of course they do. Don't you have a Cherkess soul? Don't you yearn for the freedom of the mountains and the energy of the fast flowing rivers of the Caucasus? Don't you come alive when you gallop your horse through the forest and down the valleys with the wind in your hair? My soul yearns for impossible loves, that's an Arab soul.'

'Well, if you put it like that, maybe you are right. In a way. Yes, I do yearn for those things, but I believe my heart is bigger than my soul, and my heart yearns for a love that is here and now, in the earth and sky, in real people, in flesh and blood. And more than that, something I don't have words for, but it's not impossible.'

Satanaya looked at Khalil as she said this. But her look posed a question, a question to herself – about Khalil – what was it she saw in this young boy? She felt again the desire to wrap herself in him. He seemed so vulnerable, yet he acted so bravely, as if he wanted to be a warrior. But he wasn't a warrior. Not the sort that wore a sword and went into battle to conquer the enemy, to smite heads and demand obeisance. His battle was within, and at times against the world, but inside he seemed to be fending off the demons of his not-knowing. She felt herself reaching out to him. Perhaps this was her soul too, looking to join with another, to help, to protect, to join forces.

'Maybe souls can grow,' she said, 'grow beyond the lands of their birth, grow into wherever they find themselves. Like you in America. Maybe this will come in time. Maybe you just have to love the world a bit more.'

Khalil remembered how he had opened up in that big land across the ocean. There was a truth in Satanaya's words.

'But don't you think this world is a trap?' he said. 'Look how people are, how they chase rainbows for such little things, and still they are unhappy? How they fight and kill over things that have no lasting value. Everything dies in the end.'

'You mean like religions, like nations? People certainly like to fight over these things. Perhaps it's the souls that are fighting?' said Satanaya.

Khalil hadn't been thinking of this. In fact he rather thought that religion and nation was a safeguard, a necessary order for survival, a fixed point in the chaos of life, and he said so. Satanaya disagreed.

'But look how the world changes.' she said, 'It never stays the same. The world isn't a static thing. Even in the fields, each year it's different. Different flowers come up one year to the next in the same field. Trees grow and they die. A meadow with cows in one year is growing beet the next. And then it floods and the river changes its course. This is the way of nature. Surely we should follow this example. We need to be able to change easily. In Syria there are whole towns which were abandoned when the trade routes changed.'

'In America they think they can control nature.' said Khalil, looking far away now to the horizon. 'Who knows? Perhaps they can. But you are right, nature is our teacher too. It has all the attributes of a god. Perhaps it is just that, the attributes of God. Its waters gave birth to us and the air continues to give us life, the sun nurtures us, and the soil feeds us and provides all we need to grow. Nature gives us shelter, and protects us against its attributes of might and majesty. It shows us beauty, for a day, for an hour. Its seasons give us time to learn, to know and to love. It shows us its anger; and it takes life too, violently and gently, but always inevitably. We come from it and return to it. No, they won't be able to control it because they'll never submit to knowing what it is, that we are of the same substance as nature.'

He turned to Satanaya, who was looking at him with amazement.

'Where did that come from then? You came over quite... I don't know... mystical for a while there.' she said.

'Oh no, it's just something we have been discussing in college. The immanence of the Divine, and how to avoid pantheism by seeing oneness, not as a collection, but as singularity.' said Khalil.

'Oh yes?' said Satanaya. 'Like, the god of the bread, or God as the bread? So what do they say about love.' She was trying to change the subject.

'Love the bread.' said Khalil, tearing a piece from the brioche, spreading it with butter and apricot jam and popping it in his mouth.

'I say, if you love the man, you love the God.' Then, nervous but smiling, she reached over and took Khalil's hand in hers. She had taken the initiative. In that instant something happened, a joining, a tentative mingling of souls. It was not the same as when Khalil had held her hands at the soirée, not a simple act of companionship, but something much closer. Now as Khalil felt her warm fingers entwine in his and squeeze gently, his heart began to race. And something as tangible as the hands themselves really passed between them, like a knitting of the threads of a common desire, a desire which flooded through them both, penetrating like water in a dry sponge.

They sat in silence for what seemed ages, but the converse continued, the steady lapping of the waves against the seawall taking the place of their words, the quiet rhythm of its ebb and flow carrying the gentle intimacy of their nascent love to and fro between their souls.

TWENTY-SIX

Kissing in the Rain

 ATANAYA AND KHALIL met each week in Beirut, and their intimacy grew subtly. This incremental getting to know each other increased their confidence as they trod this nascent earth together.

Without realising, they were opening a new fluency in their lives, as in a flood a riverbed is discovered where only flatland had been, a pathway on which to mingle their separate burgeoning streams. Here they found their individual passions mingling in a single broader course. Their conversation at times seemed boundless, for initially it was in words that their intimacies were exposed, before being proved in deeds. They shared their dreams, dreams that this exposure to a new world had provoked. They shared their dissatisfactions. In their young vision, so recently parted from their origin, unconditioned still by the deepest effects of birth, and as yet unbowed by the sufferings of experience and responsibilities of knowledge, they looked and saw beyond the obvious horizons.

What their society with its political and religious authorities told them was beyond reach or impossible, was already present within their vision of the human potential. They considered false the constraints imposed on life from outside, and so invalid in this new world they were creating for themselves.

Summer came slowly to the Levant that year, but when it did it came on strong. Hot winds replaced the lifegiving breezes of spring, scorching the slopes and burnishing to gold the corn in the valleys and burning the grass on the high pastures to dull brown. Only by the river banks did green remain, and in the trees the sheen of the leaves disappeared under dust. The herds of black goats moved slowly on the hillsides and the beasts of the field stood still wherever shade could be found. The birds were not seen from soon after sunrise until sunset when the cool air blew in from the sea to refresh the land again.

One Friday, Satanaya set out to market very early to avoid the worst of the heat. When all the shopping was done, the weather finally broke. A sudden fretting of the calm waters of St George's Bay, a disturbing wind along the waterfront, and the terraced trunks of palm trees began to bend and toss their fronds in a wild dance. The same gusts blew through the market, knocking about the umbrellas of the vegetable sellers and flapping the awnings of the stall holders. In the harbour the fishing boats tossed and their rigging rattled. Massive clouds moved in from nowhere and the first drops of rain began to fall, pimpling the surging skin of the sea, stinging on the roofs and spitting pockmarks in the dry dust of the roadways. The thickening atmosphere pressed with black hands of mist and rain upon the town and dark clamourings of muffled thunder poured from the mountains, while lightning chased the sky.

Satanaya was dressed for summer in her first European outfit. French design, run up by Lady Gülbahar's seamstress from the latest Paris fashions: a wide-brimmed bonnet with pretty ribbon flowers stitched on the rim; a white lace-trimmed sunshade; a long-sleeved lace blouse; and below skirts of tiered lace, petticoats down to her ankles; too much lace perhaps, but when a girl is being courted... Her slim waist and firm young bosom needed no contrived emphasis, so Lady Gülbahar had agreed the severe whalebone corset was both unnecessary and absurd in the hot climate. She herself had long since given up such painful concessions to fashion, and Satanaya too had no taste for imprisoning herself in a straitjacket.

The wind first turned her little frilly parasol quite inside out and no return. The heavy rain made short work of the homage to Paris summer couture, despite the competent needlework of the Beirut seamstresses. The starch fled, the ruffles sank, the petticoats stuck together like sheets of unfloured baclava pastry and clung to Satanaya's body like a wet plaster cast. The dainty hat pondered the situation bravely, briefly, letting the rain make rivulets among the ribbons and the bows, and having soaked its fill, simply collapsed like a disregarded soufflé. Satanaya, in her deflated ensemble, looked and felt pathetic.

Khalil was also soaked through, his wet curls dripping from beneath his sturdy flat cap, his shirt and woollen trousers drenched, but he still managed to effect a rugged piratical appearance. His eyes met hers and he began to laugh, which, with the rain still streaming down, made him even more attractive to Satanaya. But seeing the state of her own dress she was furious.

'Look, Satanaya,' said Khalil, 'why don't we go to my rooms so you can change and let these dry off. The storm won't last.'

Satanaya hesitated momentarily. So far she had resisted Khalil's invitations to visit his rooms. Now, with the storm, the streets were empty, and veiled under the dark sky and steady rain she embraced her incognito as a foreigner in a foreign town

'Yes, why not. I'll catch my death if I stand around in these wet things.'

Khalil lived in a small apartment above a shop, a few blocks back from the sea, in the Christian quarter. His room-mate, a fellow student, was at college, he assured Satanaya, and would be out until the evening. The apartment was reached by a staircase at the side of the building. The landlord ran the hardware shop beneath and usually sat out in the street, but the weather had driven him inside and would be unaware of her coming and going.

It was a small apartment, with one room for kitchen, eating and living, and another where the two students slept and studied. Once inside, the import of the situation descended on them. Khalil felt embarrassed, and whatever previous imaginations he might have entertained about bringing a woman to his room, in the cold wet light of the afternoon, his bravado, such as it was, drained from him. In truth, he was a callow lad. Satanaya, on the other hand, was intrigued to be in a young man's domain. She wandered round the room, examining the sketches pinned up on the walls, illustrations of the town, boats in the harbour, fishermen and marketeers at their stalls.

'These are lovely,' said Satanaya, 'did you do them?'

Khalil smiled shyly.

'So, where can I take these off these wet things?' said Satanaya, starting to undo her shoelaces.

Then he grasped the situation. Satanaya was shivering.

'You're cold. Let me get you a towel.' He went into the bedroom and brought out a towel and some trousers and a thick shirt.

'Here, put these on, they might not fit you, but you'll be warm.' He nodded towards the bedroom door. 'I'll light the stove and make some tea.'

Khalil turned his back and stripped off his own wet shirt and hung it over a chair. He began to dry his hair with a towel. Satanaya stood watching him for a moment. She noticed how pale his skin was, how small he looked, just a boy. Then she went into the bedroom.

The fire was alight when she returned, and the kettle was on. Satanaya hung up her wet clothes wherever she could around the room while Khalil made tea. It was the first time they had been alone together in this way. She in his clothes, he just in a pair of trousers, sitting side by side on the floor in front of the fire. Outside, the rain poured down. Khalil got up and fetched a blanket which he placed over Satanaya's shoulders and she spread it around him so that the two were wrapped together in its wool. She looked at him shyly, smiling. He returned the smile and took her hand.

When they kissed, their lips were trembling with cold and shyness, and their eyes were closed. The rain continued to batter upon the roof, drowning out the world, drowning them within their gentle passion. In the darkness of her closed eyes, beneath the veil of the storm, Satanaya let the waters wash over her as she surrendered to the rising warmth of their bodies together. Khalil wavered between belief and disbelief: belief in the eternity that this moment was bringing, in which all his doubts were banished; and disbelief in himself, that he could sustain this moment and its happiness.

Satanaya had no doubts. Her only thought, as the warmth became a heat within her, was just how much passion could she sustain without complete abandonment. She opened her eyes and beheld the soft lashes of this lover. Long dark lashes in pale olive brown skin and dark brows. His mouth was soft and open. The tip of his tongue undecided, timid, between her lips. She closed her eyes again and let herself breathe with his breathing, parting her lips a little more and, sinking into a deeper space, opening herself wide within her being so that this other, this person, this boy with his long hair and his pale, bare skin who seemed no different than herself seen a mirror, mingled his breath and his being with hers. Perhaps this moment only lasted a matter of seconds, but for lovers, a moment within the orbit of the beloved is an instant of eternity.

The silence brought them back to earth, like dancers when the music stops. They disengaged slowly, their lips clinging to the last. The blanket slipped to the floor, and they blinking as sleep-awakening babes into each other's eyes. The tea, in little glasses placed by the fire, was still hot. And sweet.

The rain had stopped. The song of small birds emerged from the orchard at the back of the building, and somewhere a cockerel was crowing in this second dawn. Through the window, pale clouds emptied of rain could be seen running high above the sea, moving south in a brisk wind. The sun was breaking through on the western horizon and on the trees the leaves rinsed clean of dust shimmered and sparkled darkly. They sipped their tea. Khalil broke the silence, awkwardly at first. Or so it seemed to him as he tried to put into words something he felt so deeply.

'I don't know how to say this…' he began.

Satanaya smiled. She felt happy, and had no need for words, but she knew Khalil needed to speak, as his way of understanding his own feelings.

'I've fallen in love with you, Satanaya.' he said, 'I want to tell you so much… but…'

He was faltering, feeling frustrated at not being able to find the words, the beautiful words, that always came to him when he was alone.

'Maybe that's it.' she said, 'Maybe there aren't words. Maybe that's the point. Perhaps it's simply in the breath?'

They sat looking at each other. Khalil moved close to kiss her again, but Satanaya pushed his lips away gently with her finger.

'No, this is better.' she said, holding his face a few inches away and gazing into his eyes, still close enough to sense his breath mixing with hers, smelling his clean warm skin, drinking in the dark longing in his eyes. She broke the spell by giving him a big hug and whispering in his ear, 'I think perhaps I'm in love too.'

Satanaya's clothes were now dry, and though the starch had gone, a good shake brought some life back into the ruffles of the skirt and blouse. The hat, though, was pretty much ruined. As she bent down to put on her shoes, she noticed beneath the bed, hidden almost by the drape of the bedcovers, a pile of sketches. She pulled them out and glanced through them. There were all sorts of pencil and charcoal drawings, of hands, legs and arms, of figures, clothed and unclothed, men and women, strangely sexless beings shaded in their intimate details, but all holding in their eyes this look of longing, looking aloft as if searching for something just out of sight. Then she found drawings of herself, simple portraits, smiling, always smiling, but looking into a distance, not so much with longing, but as if towards an object recognised but still far off. They weren't bad, she thought, not bad at all, especially as they had been drawn from memory. She replaced them and finished dressing.

While Khalil distracted the shopkeeper, she slipped out of the building and made her way back to the market, to where her horse and cart were waiting under the watchful eye of Mr Jemil the green grocer.

She drove back to the Beyt, her mind in something of a pleasant whirl. She had said she was in love, that was certain. But with whom? Who was this person she had shared herself with in such an intimate way? Who was it she was really in love with? This boy of beautiful words and portraits of longing – she needed to know him better.

They continued to meet, in the market; they continued to kiss, in the clandestine privacy of his room, and each time the depth and extent of their intimacy grew. As the boundaries of their desires extended, Satanaya became concerned. She knew she couldn't trust herself to remain forever in this elevated plateau of high emotion and sincere feelings of love, without the fine balance of their noble aspirations being tipped over by the deeper passions of their souls and bodies into a more complete union. She knew she would have to take this next step sometime. Khalil was so well behaved, pushing gently, but never insisting, and always accepting her refraining hand when the limit had been reached.

Yet she knew that if she was ever to reach the hard skin of this earth, to feel the full footfall of her physical presence in contact with the totality of her environment, to be truly human, then this descent to the last rung of birth, to complete her sense of 'I', she needed to make some commitment, some further submission to life; for otherwise she would simply float across this world like an untethered balloon, touching, bumping the ground as it skimmed over the world without ever truly landing; in proximity, certainly, but not yet united with this her earthly origin, with her body. And though her body was clearly aching for his, she had yet to agree this to herself. Satanaya decided it was high time she spoke to Lady Gülbahar.

TWENTY-SEVEN

Advices and Responses

ADY GÜLBAHAR'S long journeying in the world of human relationships had led her down many a curious path and passing destination: from early liaisons within a range of houses of ill-repute, some humble and some classy; to dalliances down avenues of seclusion, with furtive trysts and hasty escapes; to excursions in elegance upon the grand boulevards and plush mansions of high society with the Turkish Ambassador. Satanaya was no longer bewildered by the variety of scenarios of her patronne's past adventures. Yet still it took courage to reveal to Lady Gülbahar the matter of her own clandestine relationship with the young Khalil. She woke early, knowing the best way of having a private chat was to bring the châtelaine her morning cup of coffee. She knocked on the bedroom door and a voice from within called out 'Enter!'

Lady Gülbahar was already sitting up in bed, her pince-nez perched on the end of her nose, reading an old copy of The Times.

'It says here,' she said, translating aloud from the newspaper, 'that *"The Standard Oil Company paid the largest dividend ever distributed, disbursing to shareholders a total of twenty million dollars ($20,000,000) in cash and broke a record of a stock dividend paid by the Pullman car company."* You will see, my dear, this century is going to be the century of oil. Mark my words, the age of steam will be eclipsed. And all this just when our friend Gottlieb has died. So young, you know, he was only sixty-five, and he didn't live to see the full benefit of his invention.'

Satanaya was puzzled. Who was this Gottlieb, that he should be so young at sixty-five? And what did he invent?

'Oh my dear, you are still so innocent.' said Lady Gülbahar, putting down her paper and eyeglasses, and accepting the small cup of Turkish coffee. 'Herr Daimler – Gottlieb that is – he invented the petrol engine. With Mr Benz of course, but Gottlieb invented petrol. You might say between the two of them they invented the automobile.'

Satanaya looked even more puzzled.

'Oh, it was a fad of the Turkish Ambassador. He loved inventions and followed the progress of the automobile very closely, so naturally I took an interest. And then we met Gottlieb on a visit to Europe. The Ambassador wanted to buy one of his machines himself, but I persuaded him that for the roads round here horses were so much better, especially in the mud and rain.' She paused and looked closely at Satanaya. 'Now, what is it dear? I can see you are holding something inside that wants out. Come and tell all to your Auntie Gülbahar.'

This irrelevant preamble of her mistress had put Satanaya at her ease, and she began her tale of Khalil, how they had talked at the soirée, and their subsequent meetings in the city.

'Ah, so you've made a little love-nest, then?' said Lady Gülbahar, giving Satanaya a mischievous smile. Satanaya blushed. 'Oh, to be young again, free as a bird to hop from tree to tree... These days it is all we can do to remain on one branch and not fall off.'

'No!' said Satanaya, 'We are serious. We are in love. That's what I want to talk to you about. In any case, I didn't want you to think I was deceiving you, spending all that time in Beirut when I should have been back here helping Clotilde.'

'Tsk tsk. Don't worry about Clotilde, she manages fine. So, at what stage is this… mmm… love affair? Has it… errr… reached a conclusion? Have you slept with him?'

Satanaya reddened further. 'No, no…n..n..not yet… not exactly… but…'

This was very sudden. Satanaya had intended to broach the subject gradually, building up to the point bit by bit. Admitting these intimacies to another person was not easy. But Lady Gülbahar wasn't one to be bothered with such niceties.

'Look, lovely Satanaya, not a lot escapes your old auntie. And I'm afraid, like it or not, I do have my little spies in the market. I mean, fancy calling that nice young man Khalil your kitchen boy! Mr Jemil saw through that one straight away. And as for Khalil's landlord, he was laughing fit to burst when he told us of your 'secret' rendezvous that rainy day. But don't worry, nothing will get back to Khalil's college – not from us anyway – those priests are the ones you have to look out for. It might be better if in future you carried on your affair out of town. Here perhaps, or in one of our shepherd's huts up in the summer pastures. They're not in use at present as we sold most of our animals in spring – Abu Aswad the stock-man predicted it would be a dry year. So, tell me, just how far have you two gone?'

With some difficulty, in spite of Lady Gülbahar's uninhibited manner in discussing intimate matters, Satanaya explained that they had gone just about as far as possible without… well, here she stumbled, she couldn't bring herself to say it so Lady Gülbahar helped her again:

'Without penetration? Yes, a good point to stop and take stock. Well, you have come to the right place, and if I may say so, at the right time. So far you have behaved with admirable self-control, which cannot have been easy, for either of you. In the heat of the moment, many a slip…but let's not go there yet. The question is, do you want to? Both of you?. If not, then, well, having come so far, it's probably better you stop seeing each other right now, otherwise it will cause problems. Of course, there are other ways of easing the tension, but they are ultimately unsatisfactory at this stage in your relationship, and somehow miss the point. You say you love each other, so either it remains internal, a possibility, or you go the whole nine yards, so to speak. When two people are in love, and there are no impediments, then making love with our bodies is a real form of union, a real expression of love. But only you can decide for yourselves. What do you want, Satanaya? What do you both want?'

'Yes, we want to… to make love.' There, she had said it. 'In fact he wants to marry me. But, you know, after all that business in Kfar Kama, I don't know that I'm ready for that. Does it have to be marriage?'.

'Well, many people would insist on marriage, and for very good reasons. Commitment. Children. Social partnerships of families. And of course there are religious considerations which many adhere to, though I think that you are both past that stage. In fact, it would only complicate matters in your case. What about children?'

This was the area that Satanaya felt quite certain about. She had nothing against the little creatures; on the contrary, remembering her own childhood she had a natural affinity with the very young. Up to a point. What she felt now was the need to experience fully the freedom she had felt since leaving home. Her travels in Palestine had given her a taste for the wider world, and she wanted a lot more of it before she could consider settling down. She had been born into a changing world, and saw her future stretching beyond the obvious, to horizons distant and as yet unknown. Even this time with Khalil she saw more as a series of unique events, singular moments in an evanescent world rather than an inevitable continuum. Children were not in the equation.

'No, I think not.'

'Then,' said Lady Gülbahar, reading between the thoughts that were so evidently pouring into Satanaya's mind, 'You definitely do not want to get pregnant. So here we need to make sure you understand clearly certain things.

'You are in love. Wonderful, long may it last. You are both so beautiful. I should be jealous of your youth…but I have had my time. Instead, I can enjoy watching yours. Now, let's look at this. For some people, the union which we call making love happens simply with the breath and the eyes; for some it's just the vision of beauty through the eyes, and for some just being in each other's presence is enough to bring about this union. For others still, the mere mention or thought of the beloved brings with it a scent sufficient to annihilate themselves in love… But you are going deeper. The great sheykh of Damascus, Ibn 'Arabi – and who would know better, for he was foremost among lovers – wrote that the greatest union in this world is when two people make love, knowing who it is who makes love, and to whom. He was a mystic, for whom beauty, which is the sole object of love, is an absolute, appearing in every form; so beauty makes love to beauty. It is the key to the treasure, and the treasure itself. If we can discover that, if our loving can be of that kind, then the delights…ah!' and here Lady Gülbahar allowed herself a moment of reverie in which she seemed to quite disappear from herself.

'Now, back to the sex. Really, it would be best for you to keep this to those few days after your period finishes, unless of course you want to get pregnant; it is better that way – more pleasurable by far if you treat it like a wonderful feast – and good for him too, it teaches him self-control, most important in a man… and then of course, in the between times, a great deal of pleasure can be had without penetration – ah, yes, that word again – and that teaches him patience, and you.'

Lady Satanaya then described methods of prophylaxis she had learnt as a young prostitute in the Beirut brothel, before her freedom was secured by the legendary tycoon-turned-goatherd, Daud al Arwadi. These involved sponges soaked in lemon juice, or cotton wool covered in a paste of ground acacia bark, dates and honey to be used as vaginal pessaries. Also mentioned were various herbal concoctions said to be efficacious in bringing about terminations.

'Above all, keep yourselves clean, especially afterwards. In the end the pleasures of the body are temporal, but love is eternal.'

'What was it like for you, Lady Gülbahar?' said Satanaya, 'I mean, the first time.'

'The first time… what you've got to understand, Satanaya, when I came to the brothel I was a virgin, and little more than a child. But I was beautiful, and the Madam had made me realise how valuable I was. So, this had advantages, in that my 'first time price' was very high. You know how men are about things, like breaking in a fine horse and being the first to ride. I was well prepared, and given a little, just a little, opium before it happened. It relaxes you, you see, and everything feels good. But not so much that one falls asleep, as you have work to do, you have to perform. So I was trained in how to give pleasure, to do things to make the man feel good too, to smile in a particular way, to pretend to be feeling the same pleasure.'

'What was he like? The man, I mean? Was he okay?'

Lady Gülbahar laughed. 'Well, actually he wasn't bad looking. And luckily he was not rough. He had some experience, and he wasn't one of those who really prefer boys, so nothing too weird. It was over quite quickly. I think I excited him a bit too much. Then of course he wanted to do it again, and he was relaxed and because of the opium I wasn't sore, though I really wanted to sleep. After that it just became routine, like any job really. I was lucky with the Madam, she wouldn't take any nonsense with the clients, and we were allowed to refuse anyone who didn't behave well. But some girls did have bad experiences, drunk men, violent men. A brothel is a strange world, but it is also like being in a family. And ours was a good family. But still, we all lived in the hope of being rescued by a handsome prince, as I was eventually by Daud. It's a Cinderella life, and you know, you don't have to live in a brothel to experience that. I know of some girls who left their husbands because of the way they were being treated, and joined us. They preferred the brothel life even to that.'

'So, some were there by choice?'

'We were all there by choice. Even if our choice seemed without alternative.' Lady Gülbahar rubbed her eyes and looked through the window, down over the hills to the distant sea, remembering a time long ago.

'What do you mean, "seemed"? I don't understand.' Satanaya was sitting on the edge of the bed and looking intently at her mistress.

'Look, I was living in slavery in a Beirut brothel. I performed acts there that were odious to me because I thought at first I had no choice. But I never agreed in my heart to these actions. I built an inner fortress in myself that nothing could touch, no one could penetrate. This is what it means to be Circassian. It's a way of being. That is our *khabze*. Our honour is paramount. I prayed that I would be released from this prison. I built a future in my mind, an escape plan was shown to me, and I took it. When someone shows you love, no matter how strange it may seem, it is a way to take. And when Daud showed up I took this way. He was different. He was kind, he was fun, and he always treated me as a lady, even there in the whorehouse. He reminded me of who I was, and when I showed myself to him, when I let him in where I had never let anyone before, he treated me accordingly and returned the favour. He bought off the Madam, and gave me this villa, and asked nothing in return. We became lovers, and then friends. It was a relationship of equals, a true friendship.'

'But what of all the others, all those who live there and suffer. Do they

have a choice?' said Satanaya

'I don't know. Perhaps they do, but the alternative is hard and maybe their choice is to remain. It's a mystery, surely. But you, you have a choice, and now you seem to be taking it.'

'Yes I suppose I do.'

They fell silent. Then both simultaneously reached for their coffee and sipped the now cold, sweet brew.

Not long after, when the moon was on the wane, Satanaya rode out after supper and met Khalil on the road beyond the Beyt. They dismounted and embraced, and walked together, leading their horses. Satanaya had made the arrangements, and informed Khalil of the new trysting place, without mentioning her conversation with Lady Gülbahar. The half-light of the gloaming took her and Khalil into a different world. A world of lovers, and secrets too subtle for the rough light of day. They reached the shepherd's hut an hour later, at the end of a valley where a spring gave water even in the dry periods, and cypress and cedars grew on the hillsides. The hut had been prepared by Satanaya earlier that day, with clean bedding, a supply of bread and cheese, fruit and a bottle of special cuvée from the Beyt's vineyard.

Excitement mixed with nervousness, passion flowed with tender love, like two anxious deer they fretted and petted and fell to their embracing with a shy self-consciousness that was relieved finally when Satanaya produced the sponge and lemons. Then they both burst out laughing, and began to relax and not take things too seriously. This was just as well, for as any cook will know, the first attempt to make a sponge cake invariably results in a soggy mess of eggy flour or a charred crust of sugary ash.

They slept a while, and then, sometime in the early hours as light crept in through the open doorway, Khalil opened his eyes and looked at the beautiful girl cradled in his arms. As he began to stroke her hair, her face, her body, he found himself as much aroused by the sheer beauty of form which he perceived in the soft curves of her naked limbs, as he was by touch of her warm skin against his own. The colours of her body showed a palate he would forever after try to imitate with the tints and pigments of his paint box; the pale apricot of her cheeks, tones of pink and orange and red, a colour all its own; the watery violet and rose shades beneath her eyes, and her breasts a white deep as polished ivory. He closed his eyes and was transported by the sweetness of her breath, mingling with her perfume of musks – both black and white – ambergris, vanilla and rose, a special mix that Lady Gülbahar had recommended as 'sweet but not overpowering, warm but not hot, romantic but not to the point of obsession.'

Satanaya felt safe, and when they made love again, she responded to Khalil in a way that ensured a more satisfactory outcome to his endeavours, which were no less, and no less timely than her own renewed ardour towards him. As they lay entwined in the dawn light she understood that she had acquired some part of this element earth, which entered like an anchor and held her still in the water of her being.

It had always been there in potential, but where before she had felt an emptiness, an unfilled need, she now found a completion. At last she felt fully planted in this earth we call the world. And after the wonderful light-filled lightness of being that had come with their union, as the dust of their passion settled over the coming days and weeks, with it also came a feeling of gravity. For desire once awakened exerts a pull, the pull of the larger body for the lesser, and God help her if she didn't now feel her smallness, her insignificance, in the face of the earth; and with this pull came a distinct and different sense of separateness, something she now experienced for the first time, a self apart, distinct from all around her. She began to yearn again for that closeness of bodily union. Her desire was awakened and its pull was strong and the only place this passion could be satisfied was with Khalil.

Khalil wrote to Satanaya a few days later, with a sketch of her leaning against the doorway of the shepherd's hut. This time the sketch did not end at her neck. The accompanying note was very romantic. It began "I sought the face where beauty's light appeared, and drowned in beauty's light" and continued in like manner, ending "Where beauty walks, where e're I look I only see your face."

If Satanaya hadn't been so enraptured by her recent experience she might have laughed at this purple prose. As it was it simply awakened the memory of that night, as a particular scent evokes a past event.

The lovers met throughout the summer, stolen nights of passion in the shepherd's hut, and on market days, sober and intense conversations at the harbour side. And when apart, Khalil buried himself in his painting and composing heart-rending letters and poems of yearning. Satanaya chopped

her onions and occasionally wept a few tears of longing into the pots of
stews, which added a certain saltiness to the table at Beyt'ur-Rahma. But
mostly she basked in the warmth of this newfound energy, an energy of
earth and womanhood, which renewed each time she gave herself into
Khalil's embrace.

TWENTY-EIGHT

Coming and Going in Beirut

HE ANCIENT CITIES of the Eastern Mediterranean, forever blessed with the fertility that arrives with rain and sun in generous measure, made pleasant with cooling breezes wafting over the opal sea, and serviced with natural harbours, forests of timber for shipbuilding, mountains holding back the desiccating heat and sand of the desert then drawing in and receiving the rainclouds' gathering tumult from above the sea, falling waters to be returned in well-fed streams carrying the harvest of silt from tree-clad valleys of oak and cedar, bringing this richness to the coastal plain and depositing it as a fecundity to make possible a paradise for the refuge of humankind. And just as the fruits of this hallowed earth prospered and multiplied in groves and orchards of mulberry and pomegranate, citrus and vine, so the untilled soil of human souls was inspired by the rain of intelligent spirit, to take the letters engraved in the hearts of the prophets and seers, the poets and storytellers, and with pens of iron and burnt wood and quills of birds begin to inscribe, in sand, upon rock, on the skins of animals and eventually on the processed pith and pulp of plant material their vision of an unspeakable beauty, so awesome that in the smallness of their afeared minds they shunned this grand meaning of themselves, relegating it to the realm of suns and moons and fixed stars, and were not satisfied with this distancing until they had completely separated their god from their own souls.

Beirut along with the other cities that line this edge of the world, Arwad, Tripoli, Byblos, Tyre and Sidon, was born out of this necessary imperative that is *word*, becoming one end of the frame of a loom in time and space, holding the warp-threads which stretched from the interior cities of Aleppo, Damascus, Jerusalem, and through which the shuttle-tongued weft of nascent civilisations cried, announcing their birth in stories and histories, poems and prophecies which sprang forth to water the parched hearts of the desert people.

From the time of the Ottoman conquest of the Middle East by Sultan Selim I in the early 16th century, Lebanon had proven a difficult province to govern, and often times Constantinople left local administration in the hands of Druzes and Maronite Christian chiefs. But in 1860 serious conflict broke out between Druze and Christian, first near Beirut, and then in Damascus, where more than 10,000 Christians were massacred, with connivance of the Ottoman occupying forces. Here the exiled Algerian mystic and freedom fighter, Emir Abdel Kader, personally gave sanctuary to many Christians fleeing the slaughter, and is said to have faced off a riotous mob intent on murder. Such events, which had grown out of an oppressive feudal system operated throughout Lebanon by both Maronites and Druze overlords upon the peasant populations, led to a military intervention by France. There followed a flood of Christian refugees into an area of Beirut which the French administered, and over the next fifty years an exodus took place of more than a quarter of a million Lebanese into Egypt, Europe and the New World.

Beirut consolidated economically and became a city of *fin de siècle* vibrancy and oriental charm helped both by the protection of France and by its burgeoning silk industry. Mid-19th century town plans show Beirut surrounded by acre upon acre of mulberry groves. Mount Lebanon became a hub of silk production for export to the fashion centres of Europe, shipping via Marseille, and Beirut overtook Acre as the most important port in the East Mediterranean. Modern buildings were constructed in the French architectural style, with broad avenues replacing narrow crowded lanes in the well-to-do areas, and two universities were founded, one American and one French.

The city and the land where Satanaya and Khalil watered each other's hearts with passion had become a bridge between the ancient and the modern, a truly cosmopolitan city. Yet it was a stew of a city, where every possible ingredient has been placed, not always in a combination that makes for good taste and harmony of palate, but a stew nonetheless. A hotchpotch, a mixture, a salmagundi, but not necessarily a cornucopia. Still, apart from periodic disruptions among the tribes in the Haran, Beirut now enjoyed a degree of peace and prosperity.

But all the while in their long and blissfully hot summer, Satanaya was aware of a sadness like an impenetrable wall in the depth of her lover's heart, its melancholy shadow dispelled only in the light of their closeness and rapture, but which returned in all their partings.

Gradually Khalil unfolded the story of his early life, of his hapless father dogged by bad luck and worse decisions, who brought the family to penury and ill-repute such that his mother had no choice but to abandon her husband. In truth it was a fleeing through love of safety for her family. Cutting her losses she gathered her brood and emigrated to America, joining the great Levantine diaspora. In America Khalil, the bright one, the one with imagination and subtlety of thought, continued his studies while his elder brother took factory work and his mother and sisters went hawking household goods and linens from door to door in their new land. Khalil prospered. His drawing was getting noticed, he was being introduced in artistic and literary circles, the beautiful Lebanese boy with the intense, sad eyes and shyly direct manner.

Now, he told Satanaya, he was not learning, not progressing in the direction he would like. While he needed to stay in Lebanon to perfect his Arabic in the soil of his birth, still he yearned to stretch his wings in the fresh air of America.

Summer's heat gave way to autumn reflection. But a reflective surface mirrors changes. Satanaya lay in the long grass above the Beyt, at ease in herself. Floating. Held in a wonderful present, her whole body delighting in the balmy timelessness of the season. Not a worry in the world. No guilt, just gratitude.

A hoopoe alighted upon the stone wall at the meadow's edge, looking for something it did not find, and then flew off. Satanaya followed its flight until it went too high and disappeared from sight.

Khalil's letter was brief, fraught in temper, and unclear. He wrote that he had received word from America that his sister was ill. His mother needed him to return. He was torn, but he knew where his duty lay. He was booking the first available passage home. He would come and see her tonight.

Satanaya knew this wasn't the whole story. When they had talked of America, Khalil had enthused for hours over the possibilities that awaited them both, if only they could marry and go together. They would open a restaurant; she would cook and he would paint the customers. But Satanaya was certain her immediate future lay with Lady Gülbahar. It had all seemed perfectly simple. She had good employment and was being thoroughly educated in the European tradition at so many levels. The soirées had introduced her to a world she had never dreamed possible, a world in which she felt certain she would make her own way one day. But Khalil had his own dream.

She read the letter again. She refused to accept its contents, resisting the inevitable, trying to push away the descending cloud of fear and despair. She imagined new, more satisfactory scenarios to give her hope. He should wait, another letter would come telling Khalil the emergency was over and his sister was recovering. Or the family would return to Beirut. Her mind was out of control. She had to see Khalil. She no longer cared who might see them together. Anyway, if he was leaving Beirut, then he was leaving college, and what the priests thought was of no matter. She left a note for Clotilde, saddled up Tarçin and rode in haste to Beirut. Khalil wasn't in his rooms. His landlord said he had gone out early that morning and hadn't returned. She headed towards his school, but as she passed by the port she saw him coming from one of the shipping offices.

'Khalil, what's going on?' Satanaya was in tears and trying to hold back from embracing him publicly in the street. She desperately wanted to cling to him, to make sure he was still there, solid, warm, her home.

'Come back to my rooms, we'll sort this out.'

But what was there to sort out? Khalil was leaving by ship for Marseille in three days time. Then taking the train north to Le Havre to board a transatlantic steamer. He had no choice, he said. It was simple, his mother needed him. His mother whose husband – his father – had spurned any responsibility for the family, needed her son. There was no question of his not coming to his sister in her illness, which might well be fatal.

Fear and despair hung over them both, and they tried to push it away with frantic, fervid lovemaking. They counted the days, the hours, until in the end they were dry of tears, worn out by their emotions but unsleeping. Khalil drank more and more wine to deaden the pain, but it only deadened his better feelings. Satanaya couldn't eat. She clung to Khalil in bed, eyes closed, trying to regain that timeless union, beyond the division of continents and parting seas. She had no strength to resist this dark submerging tide. Nor could she bring herself to see him off on the quay. She had enough sense not to be so cruel to herself and to him. She helped him pack his few things, they made love one last time, and with a final tearful look into those sad brown Lebanese eyes, she left. The proud Circassian girl rode out of Beirut, up into the hills beyond the Beyt, high up above the shepherd's hut to that cleft in the mountain called the Cave of the Womb. There she sat, head buried in her knees pulled up to her chest while the little coaster drifted out of Beirut harbour, and making steam under a thin trail of grey smoke, disappeared into the western sea. Then she wept.

The inhabitants of Chez Gülbahar knew from Khalil's landlord the disaster that had struck. As Satanaya passed them in the corridors of the house that evening their eyes spoke their sympathy. Even Lady Gülbahar, who had little time for negative emotions gave her a warm hug, full of a life's learnt compassion, and let her go to her room where she cried herself to sleep. She lay on the bed for three days. Little Pelin brought her meals and valerian tea, which mostly went untouched. She emerged on the third day, but she was in no way resurrected. She continued to inhabit the tomb of her disconsolation.

Satanaya felt numb and disconnected, as though her sensibilities were wrapped in cotton wool. From time to time she would burst into tears as the memory of her loss stabbed her in her stomach, as her little heart broke up bit by bit, until there really was nothing left but a hole, an emptiness below her breast that nothing could fill. She felt the pain of her loss as a lover feels the death of her beloved. It was the pain that comes when two joined bodies are torn asunder. For in the physical act of love we create deep ties of emotion which are a kind of grafting at the level of the psyche, and subtle arterial connections are formed between souls, which when pulled apart cause pain and bleeding no less real than if the arteries of our physical hearts have been grafted together then severed. She walked endlessly in the hills where she found relief in falling prostrate on the ground and letting the earth soak up her tears as the blood of her sorrow flowed from her aching soul.

His letters came as bittersweet arrows to her heart. First from Smyrna. In an outpouring of high-minded aspiration Khalil attempted to reconcile his suffering by identifying it with the passion of his personal Christ. This did not help Satanaya one bit, who had no wish to be the victim cast aside on her lover's own road to Calvary. Much less would she be the dutiful bereaved mother, some sad reflection of a sainted *pietà*. The next letter came from Naples. Khalil had calmed down somewhat, but while still anxious over his family's situation, he gave little thought to the girl he left behind. Eventually he wrote before embarking from Le Havre after spending a week in Paris. Evidently the distractions of the gay city had relieved him of concern for Satanaya, as well as his sister. Florid descriptions of meeting the fashionable artists in Montmartre, of drinking absinthe in the cafes of the Left Bank, and mingling with the louche society in Pigalle left nothing to her imagination. His repeated invitation to join him in America was half-hearted, it was as if he had asked her to a party, giving no date, nor address to *respondez s'il vous plait*.

Rocked between hope and despair, she slept little. She cried a lot and didn't hide her tears. She took long rides in the hills, but most often she walked, weeping freely in the open air, clinging to the trunks of trees for comfort, or lying upon the earth to gain some sense of bodily belonging, like a child crying upon her mother.

In the end it was Lady Gülbahar who helped her out of the slough of despond, taking her to task one morning during breakfast. Satanaya was sitting in silence, staring blankly at a piece of toast on her plate. She had put butter on her knife when a thought, some memory, a fantasy perhaps of her lost love returning, possessed her and made her forget completely where she was.

'Would you kindly pass the toast, Satanaya?' said Lady Gülbahar. Satanaya continued to sit unmoving, as if in a trance. Lady Gülbahar repeated her request. Still no response.

'Enough!' Lady Gülbahar smashed her coffee cup down in its saucer with such force that the coffee spilt all over the table. Then she took her napkin and threw it at Satanaya. Satanaya jumped, having no idea what was going on.

'If you can't at least have the good manners to pretend to take part in the conversation, you might as well go and eat your breakfast in the kitchen!'

Satanaya's face flushed a deep crimson. She had never heard her mistress raise her voice like this. She was at a loss as to how to respond. She was angry, not at Lady Gülbahar herself, but at being caught out in such a state. In fact, she had been angry a long while but was unable to admit it, and it was with Khalil she really felt angry, and now it burst out:

'But why did he have to go, just like that? As if it didn't matter what was between us? And now he's completely forgotten me?'

'Oh Satanaya, you think you are so important, you think your little affair so important.' Lady Gülbahar did not water down her admonition. 'You are behaving like a spoilt child that has had its sweets taken away. Can't you be grateful for what you had. And what you still have! You said you didn't want to be tied down. Look at Pelin, does she mope about, mourning the loss of her family? Do you ever see her complain? Now look at yourself.'

Satanaya blushed even more. She knew her mistress was right and she felt ashamed. All the same her pride had been hurt, and for that she burned. She knew she must apologise, but she could only mumble through welling tears, 'I'll clear the plates away.'

Picking up a few things she rose from the table and rushed out. In the hallway she stopped and leant upon the sideboard, weeping. She felt an arm around her shoulder. It was Pelin, who just smiled at her and hugged her, then took the plates from her hands and together they went down to the kitchen.

Lady Gülbahar and Clotilde were obviously in cahoots, for from then on the cook took Satanaya to task as never before. Gone were the lazy chats over the shelling of broad beans, the gossip over the cleaning of the rice.

And no longer the leisurely rides down to market with endless cups of tea. Instead Satanaya was put on preparing food for the farm workers and other menial tasks. And when it came to washing-up, everyone remained at table enjoying fruit and coffee while she sweated over the sink.

When love becomes poison, hard work is the antidote and time the best doctor to ensure the patient's return to health. Gradually Satanaya found the safest place was in surrender. She learnt to untie the knotted threads of their sweet hours of love, casting off memories which burned her as a fever; and when she ran out of tears she learnt to abandon her sadness. She returned to the starting place, making soups: broths, bean soups, lentil soup, chowders and creamed vegetables, building up to sturdy borscht and meaty potages, and widening her remit with subtle onion and herb soups, gradually bringing taste back into her life, and with it a little colour.

TWENTY-NINE

The Chickpea in the Pot

 ATANAYA EVENTUALLY found the strength to put aside her sadness and busy herself with matters in hand. With this slow severance, a weight lifted, and one day it was gone. She had prayed deep to the very borders of her soul, to that mysterious self within. And in that surrender, she found herself embraced in a profound solace.

Now, walking among the meadow flowers beyond the house, on a perfect morning of warm sun, a gentle breeze on her cheeks, she realised her prayer was answered.

She was free of Khalil. Gone were the knots and the pain of memory. She felt nothing but ease. In an instant she knew what it was to be free of the objects of love, no matter how beautiful. Beauty was something else, from which she could never be separated. Looking at the meadow, she glimpsed what she had been created for in an illuminating flash which filled her surroundings and restored her soul. An instant of beauty which came as a kind of salvation delivered through the forms in which love moved.

Her heart had been broken, destroyed even, by partial loves. But something quite different was taking its place, a heart of certainty, lifting her up to a secure place. She looked at the world around her, and began to weep; not out of sadness this time, but in gratitude and relief, that all this beauty could be for her. And if for her, then for all. And she wept for the sadness of the world, for its pain, for its loss of loves, for its fears, but mostly for its own heart-breaking longing to be free; and she wept tears of compassionate love. Something had unlocked inside her. In her vision the world became whole again, and her tears turned into tears of joy.

For some reason Satanaya found herself thinking of the *kazan*, the old burnt cooking pot that she had dragged around with her ever since leaving Seydnaya.

'I must get it re-tinned. I must cook something again in Takla's *kazan*.'

She almost shouted it to herself. Suddenly the *kazan* had become very important to her. She rushed to her room and took the fire-blackened vessel from the cupboard. She removed the cookbook and the wooden spoon and various bits and pieces she had brought with her from Kfar Kama. She took the pot outside and gave it a good clean.

Hidden away behind the port and the market in Beirut were a number of small streets, each dedicated to a different trade – metal workers, coppersmiths, tinkers and silversmiths, as well as furriers and tanners, saddlers and cobblers, tailors and haberdashers.

Outside the shop of Moses Shadinyan rose dozens of *kazans* in towering pagodas of copper and brass, each set one atop the other in diminishing size, from huge cauldrons fit for a Janissary field kitchen to more modest pieces such as Satanaya carried.

Moses Shadinyan was an Armenian tinsmith and considered the best, not just for the quality of his craft, which was unequalled in Beirut, but on account of the stories he could tell. He had learnt his trade in the central Anatolian city of Konya and spent his younger days wandering through

Ottoman lands as an itinerant tinker. As old age came upon him, he settled in Beirut where he was respected in the community as much for his wisdom and compassion as for his skill with pots. People called him a Sufi, but he held no particular form of belief to the exclusion of another, giving requisite value to each and all, and he was kind to all comers whatever their beliefs.

Satanaya entered the little shop, its shelves crowded with new and as yet untinned brass and copper pots, bowls, water jugs and coffee makers of all sizes. An elderly man sat in the rear at a dark wooden workbench.

Giving the customary salutation, 'salam aleikum', she presented her rather wounded *kazan* for his appraisal.

'Aleikum salam.' he responded. 'Well, what have we here!'

The eyes of the old tinsmith widened as he took the pot in his hands. He slowly turned it round, inspecting it carefully. Finally he put it down on the bench and looked at Satanaya.

'I don't believe it.' he said, frowning. 'How on earth did you come by this?'

Satanaya was not expecting to be interrogated for something so commonplace as a simple *kazan*. Did he think she had stolen it?

'Why do you ask?' she said.

'I'm sorry, but you see, this is no ordinary *kazan*. Surely you must know that? It is a very ancient piece, made by a rather special coppersmith in my hometown, in Konya. This coppersmith made *kazans* for a very special cook... maybe you have heard of Shams Ateşbaz Wali, the saintly cook of Mevlana Rumi? But how...? this is a very rare piece.'

'It's a long story,' said Satanaya, 'It came to me by way of the Lady Takla, who was the cook at the convent of Seydnaya. She was given it by an Egyptian *bey* – the Cairene, they called him– although I believe his family may have come from Montenegro or Albania originally, in the days of Mohammed Ali Pasha, the Governor of Egypt.'

'Ah, then that explains it.' said Moses Shadinyan, who immediately deduced the provenance of the pot. 'Yes, that makes complete sense. Mohammed Ali's grandfather was born in Konya.'

'What do you mean?'

The tinsmith smiled mysteriously and taking a piece of fine wire wool he gently scoured the lower edge of the blackened pot to reveal some writing engraved around its base.

'See what it says here, in Persian:

"z'an ke be lazzat na roy ad lahm-o post
chun na-roy-ad, che godaz– 'ishq-e dost?
– *Without pleasure, flesh and skin do not grow;*
and unless they grow, what shall the love of the Friend consume?"

'It's from the famous story of the chickpea in the pot, part of Rumi's
great poem, the Mathnawi. Surely you know it? No? Then come back here
and have some coffee and while I get my furnace up to heat I'll tell you the
story.'

He led Satanaya behind a leather curtain into his workshop. It was a
dark place lit only by the light through the open back door and the fiery
glow from a small forge in the corner. Moses Shadinyan put some more
charcoal on the little furnace, and began to prepare the coffee. He put two
heaped spoons of finely ground coffee from a wooden box into a little
cezve, added sugar and water, and placed it near the heat.

'Rumi was the master of deducing the simple from the complex, and
revealing the complex in the simple.' he said. 'The story of the chickpea
comes right at the heart of his huge poem, the Mathnawi. It is full of tales
about the relationship between human beings and their the hidden reality
which he portrays as an exchange between lover and beloved, who are
ultimately identical. And it has more than twenty five thousand lines.'

Then Moses Shadinyan began to quote from memory:

'Behold the chickpea,
boiling in the pot
jumping up and trying to escape
crying out, "It's hot hot hot!
What is this jape?
I thought you loved me,
that's why you bought me,
was it not?"

'But the cook, with her spoon
just whacks the chickpea down,
"Now just behave yourself, you clown
and cook for me nice and light.
I'm not doing this from spite,

but to bring out your true worth,
to let a little heaven leaven your stiff earth.
You were green in the garden, drinking cool water,
but that was only to make you fit for this hot water."'

Here the tinsmith paused and lifted the *cezve* from the fire, tapped it gently on the edge of the hearth, returned it momentarily to the heat, twice, and then poured the coffee, making sure each cup received a little of the *köpük*, the foamy crema on the top. The dark aromas cut through the ancient tar and woodsmoke reek of the gloomy workshop. He passed a cup to Satanaya, sitting on a rough bench beneath a shelf piled with a jumble of of old pots awaiting mending and re-tinning. He returned to his seat and sipped his coffee before continuing:

'Rumi then explains that all comes from Mercy, the quality by which the universes come into being – as if a great breath was blown upon the potential of existence releasing this constriction and giving form to the infinite possibilities hidden and unexpressed in the great unknown. We struggle to know ourselves and the universe. When love comes along, out of the window goes all our knowledge and we enter a different life. And so the lines on the pot:

"Without pleasure, flesh and skin do not grow; and unless they grow, what shall the love of the Friend consume?"'

'We have a word in Persian – *puhte* – it means thoroughly cooked, mature. And another word comes from this – *puhtegan* – meaning wise people, people skilled in the knowledge of sacred truth; that is, the saints. They have been thoroughly cooked, like the chickpea, their egos burnt up by love, consumed like the old tin in your pot. They are restored to life in a new skin from the Friend.

'Now, about your pot… it has a long history. They say that the holder of such a pot, to become a real cook, must become like the chickpea in the poem; he – or she – must also go from the state of the raw, then be cooked, and then completely burnt… in the fire of love.'

The tinsmith then went to work. He dipped the *kazan* in a weak solution of muriatic acid and scoured it, both inside and out with a folded piece of rough canvas, dipping it again in the acid solution, then rinsing it in water.

He pumped on a foot bellows until the hearth began to glow. Tin melts at 450 degrees Fahrenheit, one degree lower than the burning point of paper, but the old Armenian knew his trade and had no need of a thermometer to tell him the temperature.

Gripping the *kazan* in a pair of long-handled steel tongs, he presented it to the subdued flames of the hearth, resting it on the edge and rotating it to heat it evenly. All the while he pumped the bellows, exciting flames from the charcoal and sending sparks flying into the air. Judging the moment, he tossed into the pot some powdered sal ammoniac, then turned it briefly upside down over the coals.

'This is the flux which allows the tin to bond with the copper,' he shouted above the roar of the bellows.

With a heavy wad of cotton he wiped the flux around the inside of the pot, tipping in scraps of tin left over from a previous job. He then stirred in fresh tin from a bright new stick and let it melt and perform its alchemy with the copper and sal ammoniac flux. All the while he deftly turned the old *kazan* above the heat, a few inches at a time, while noxious fumes poured out of its dark interior and escaped through the open door.

Now he worked furiously, wiping the inside of the *kazan* with his cotton wad, liberally tossing in extra flux while constantly turning it in the flames. Caught in the light of the fire, the inside surface of the newly tinned pot gleamed brightly. Wipe, turn, heat, flux, on it went, the tin thickening with each rotation. Then, after just a couple of minutes, Moses Shadinyan removed the *kazan* from the heat, tipped out the excess molten tin into the left-overs tray, and giving it a final wipe around the rim, set it on a shelf behind him.

'We'll let it cool down while we finish our coffee, and then polish the outside, just enough to remove the soot and bring up the fine patina.'

This he did upon a treadle lathe to which he attached a course metal polishing buff. Pedalling away, he set the contraption spinning. The buff made a searing sound as it scraped off layers of hardened soot and burnt-on cooking oil. Then the buff was changed for a softer polisher, and adding a little tallow, he polished again until a fine sheen emerged upon the dark verdigris of the ancient *kazan*.

'There you are, my dear.' said Moses Shadinyan, handing back her now gloriously burnished pot, 'So, what will you cook in it?'

Satanaya had no doubts. She held it up and looked inside and saw her own face reflected in its bright silvery base. 'I guess it will have to be chickpeas.'

They made their farewells, and as Satanaya rode off, the old Armenian tinsmith called after her, 'and when you get to Konya, please give greetings to Shamsuddin Ateşbaz Wali from Moses Shadinyan.'

That night Satanaya leafed through Takla's cookbook until she came to a section dealing with chickpeas.

"The chickpea is a native of these lands and has nourished us well since first we cultivated the earth. The younger and fresher they are, the more willingly they submit to cooking; they shed their skins without reluctance and soften easily to make the creamiest humus. Old chickpeas need long boiling to soften their hardened interiors, in which case the addition of bicarbonate of soda to the soaking or cooking will expedite this process; and much rubbing against each other between the cook's two hands to loosen their thick skins and much pounding with pestle to break them down into a paste suitable for the table."

Since visiting Moses Shadinyan, although Satanaya continued to correspond with Khalil, her feelings had changed. She knew their ways had parted. One day she received a letter telling her of his new patron, an older lady who was keen to promote his paintings. She replied, formally ending their relationship and wishing him well. It was a relief.

For the next few years Satanaya became the chickpea, boiling away in the pot of her kitchen, being rubbed by the two hands of Providence: one caressing, the other chastising. But Satanaya was a young chickpea. Time spent in the kitchen was balanced by study. Lady Gülbahar set her books to read, in French, and gradually in English too, as well as poetry in Persian and Arabic. Sometimes of an evening, they would sit together and recite the old Nart tales remembered from childhood, each filling in where the other had forgotten, so that between them they would complete a story.

For now, the only romance that Satanaya experienced was in the pages of books. As for love, that showed in unexpected ways. She noticed how Clotilde conducted herself in the kitchen, the manner the French woman possessed and was possessed by the action in producing a meal. In Clotilde she saw the unity of the process, from the moment the menu was set, the gathering of the ingredients, the basic preparations, the cooking, tasting, adjusting to a finer degree of taste, bit by bit until the result matched the intention; and then the moment when it was revealed at table, complete;

and each time a unique expression, no matter how often they had prepared that dish, and always beautiful.

It was the same with the poetry she read, the music of the words revealing ever subtler nuances as her appreciation grew. Likewise in her outdoor ramblings, she saw the variability of landscape – the seasons and their weathers unravelling meanings – so that this moody world became a mirror to her own feelings.

More than anything, she looked; and in looking she saw; she listened, and listening she heard; she touched, and touching she felt. Her world became a face, a person even, with whom she could communicate as with a friend. It spoke at times as a lover, at times as beloved, now it carressed and now chastised, narrowed and widened, brought her close and became distant; and again so often she was the little chickpea, beaten with the spoon and complaining too. But waking each morning, and stretching in the air of the Beyt'ur-Rahma, she felt grateful for this home in which she grew. And she wondered, like the chickpea, when and whether she would ever be suitable for the table. She was young, and still imagined that life would reach a point of arrival, a place where its results could be seen. What she couldn't see in her energetic impatience was that in each moment she was reaching a point of arrival, with its inherent result, and that each moment also carried a point of departure. There was simply no time to stop. And in that no-time, her life unfolded with an amicable sense of endlessness.

THIRTY

A Marriage of Spices,
Herbs and Other Angels

 ATANAYA READ from the section on wedding feasts in Takla's cookbook. It was a pasted-in letter in the Cairene's handwriting, with some marginalia, practical notes and references to recipes, added by Takla herself.

'Think of your spices as your paintbox. When you make a painting, you do not use just one colour, unless you are simply emphasising the pure form of the subject, as in an ink drawing or charcoal sketch, or as in our case, sprigs of rosemary inserted into a gigot d'agneau rôti, to sharpen the taste of the fat to something less heavy and marry its aroma to the meat.

The full picture requires the full palate, so that the desired effect is presented by a subtle combination of colours, applied in proportion and

giving appropriate balance of light, shade, depth, so that, if God wills,
the spirit of the representation may shine through and vivify the
picture.

　　So it is when spicing your food. Less is best, for spices are the
accent, not the language; and the gradual building, like the artists'
layers of paint, will raise the simplest of ingredients to sublime heights
of eloquence of taste if the leaven of love guided by knowledge is free to
enter through the hands, heart and vision of the cook.

　　The point is not to make the dish taste of the spice, but to bring out
and enhance the best expression, with the desired inflexion of the taste
inherent in the particular dish. So, in seasoning for kibbeh, or dolma or
köfte, for instance, the various combinations of spices, cinnamon,
allspice etc., become as a network of hidden agents relaying a multitude
of aspects as information to the Sultan of Taste, which is not as some
would have it, the tongue, which is the Sultan's wife, but the nose.

　　With perfumes, it is the blending and combining of the single
essences – the attars of rose, verbeine, ambergris, sandalwood, the
various musks and other distillates which, when warmed by the
lifeblood flowing beneath the skin etc., rise in new apparel, and which
when inhaled upon the breath excite the lovers' passion to ever new
heights of ecstasy in their union. Perfumes are there to bring out the
scent of the well-beloved, the best of scents. Only in a secondary use are
scents there to mask the odour of the bodily clay. When the beloved
bathes in rosewater, it is not so we smell a rose, but that the perfume
illumines that in her which corresponds to the rose. So, in that instant,
we may say, 'my love is scented 'like' a red, red rose', not that she is a
rose. If she was a rose, then poor would be the fellow who takes such a
beloved in his arms, for he would awake bloodied in a bed of thorns,
with petals dashed and fading scent (though this is not unknown!).
Better the beloved who is sans pareil. Similarly with spices: the
cinnamon and nutmeg bathing the gigot of lamb, crusting its buttered
skin as it roasts slowly in the oven – only a fool would ingest these spices
alone in preference to that to which they beckon, the tender, succulent
meat, its juices running freely.

　　And all this, the spices and the herbs savoured, the images
described in bedazzling tints and shades of paint, perfumes sweetening
bodies joined in conjugal acts, all these are merely metaphors, threads

of imagination to lead us to a door – the door from our mundane
existence…to what? To the question itself, the question that both veils
and reveals the image of our true longing, the reality of our love's desire.'

Whatever else, thought Satanaya, the feast must be beautiful. She put down the book and composed herself for the task in hand. It had been intended as a small affair, the late wedding of Lady Gülbahar and the French Baron, but somehow word had spread. Perhaps due to the declining years of the happy couple, their equally aged European friends, suspecting that this event might well be the last chance to meet this side of the inevitable departure, had journeyed from their chateaux, schlösser, palazzi and palacios, via the great imperial capitals to a pre-arranged rendezvous in Marseilles, from where they boarded the steamer for the Levant. When the vessel docked in Beirut, after an easy passage on mild seas spent mainly playing bridge, catching up and swapping memories, there emerged from 1st Class cabins and staterooms a merry party made up of ageing school chums of the Baron and aquaintances of late Turkish Ambassador, who had a nose for a good feast, and a few confirmed batchelors who still doted fondly on their memories of the Lady herself from earlier halcyon times. There were locals too, regulars from the soirées: poets, writers and musicians, mostly budding nationalists, as well as resident Ottoman pashas and French officials in Mount Lebanon.

With so many guests expected, the wedding preparations were undertaken as a military campaign. Satanaya smiled and shrugged, wondering if she would be waiting until her eighties before she married. Clotilde laughed, remembering her own country wedding. And Pelin's eyes lit up with complete excitement. Lady Gülbahar had bouquets of flowers delivered to the guests' hotel in the German quarter. Her venerable fiancé the Baron, accompanied by Gérard the winemaker, who now doubled as his butler and drinking companion, made a rare trip into the city, bringing cases of good wine to greet the visitors personally.

Now Satanaya had to concentrate. It was to be, appropriately, a feast where east meets west. First the meat:

The lamb –not young lamb, but ewe lambs left to fatten over the winter and slaughtered now in the late springtime, when the meat would still be tender, but more flavoursome and able to take the stronger spice mix that Satanaya had in mind. She took leg and shoulder, boned, trimmed of most of the thick fat, cut into generous pieces 'at least as big as a hen's egg', which she marinated overnight in a mix of sun-dried tomato and paprika pastes, olive oil, pureed onion, pomegranate molasses and a *baharat* of paprika, cummin, coriander, allspice, with ginger and chili flakes.

The chicken too was boned, each bird into eight or ten pieces, and marinated for an hour in lemon juice, then overnight in a mixture of mustard, tomato sauce, thick yogurt, pureed onion, melted butter, pomegranate syrup, oregano and a milder spice mix similar to the lamb but in different proportions, with the addition of turmeric, and without chili and paprika.

The pieces of lamb, basted in oil, and the chicken pieces with added breadcrumbs and butter, would be roasted in a hot oven. Separate stocks were made of the bones and carcasses of each meat, to flavour two different pilafs which would surround the meat.

The pilafs themselves were the golden settings in which the jewels of meat were placed. For the lamb, robust Baldo rice cooked in rich stock, coloured yellow with *haspir* – safflower stamens – and sparkling with tiny bird's eye currants, browned pine-kernels and with a hint of cinnamon. For the chicken, delicately perfumed long grain rice from Hindustan, the fragrant 'basmati' grown in the snowmelt of the five rivers, the Punjab, first turned gently in much butter over a low heat then cooked in saffron-infused chicken stock, seasoned with cardamom seeds, with a suggestion of garam masala and rosewater, with pale sultanas and a colourful dice of petits pois, carrots, celery and onion, the whole dish to be showered with roasted flaked almonds and gold leaf as it left the kitchen.

To sustain the guests through the wedding service, and allow them to enjoy the generous libations of champagne pouring forth from the cellars of the Beyt'ur-Rahma, Clotilde prepared a vast array of *amuse-guele* to serve as they assembled in the early afternoon: little puff pastries spread with creamed wild mushrooms, wild asparagus or purslane in mild sheep's cheese; thin slices of grilled veal kidney on a canapé soaked in a buttery *jus* flavoured with truffles and masala wine; and crumbly sambusak pastries with savoury fillings.

A munificence of Middle Eastern mezes – *humus* of course, and smoky *baba ghanoush*, crisp kibbeh, tangy tabouleh, roasted peppers, fresh fried anchovies and battered prawns, would precede the main courses.

In the yard behind the kitchen the local baker had built a series of wood-fired clay ovens, reminiscent in miniature of domed retreat cells surrounding a dervish *tekke*. Here the meat would be roasted and fresh bread baked throughout the day.

Under the châtelaine's direction Pelin was tasked with arranging the decorations. She engaged the local tailors and dressmakers to sew their cloth scraps and offcuts into penants which she attached to lengths of gardeners' twine provided by Gérard. As the wedding day approached, strings of gaudy bunting appeared in the trees lining the final hundred yards leading to the Beyt, and continued up through the front garden, around the house and up the gentle slope of the meadow at the rear where the celebration itself would take place. Japanese paper lanterns would illuminate the paths after nightfall. With the flower arrangements Pelin had taken special care to bring about a natural look, nothing fussy or formal but lots of meadow grasses and wild flowers mingled with hollyhocks and lilies. Little vases containing forget-me-nots, pimpernel and wild thyme were suspended at eye-level on ribbons in unexpected places. And everywhere a lot of roses.

The quartermaster in the Turkish army barracks in Beirut, given the nod by the Governor himself, had provided the Beyt with a magnificent Imperial military tent, a relic from the days when the Sultan himself came on campaign with his army, and now used on rare occasions for entertaining foreign dignitaries. It needed a cart drawn by four oxen to bring it up the steep way. A platoon of the military band, the *mehteran*, erected it, and later provided some of the music for the ceremony. Three central poles, each with its own sleeve of gold-embroidered crimson cloth raised a vast cupola of crimson and blue canvas a full six yards above the ground; every square inch of the tent's interior was patterned with floral applique and geometric patterns in imitation of a palatial throne-room. It had a conical roof at one end above a small raised platform where the marriage would be celebrated. The whole affair was more than twenty five yards long and ten yards wide – fifteen when the sides were raised with small poles to form awnings, allowing free movement all around. Boarding had been laid on the ground beneath and covered with magnificent tribal rugs from the collection of the late Turkish ambassador.

A distant cousin on the distaff side of the Baron's family, the Ritter Ernst von Marx of Bad Homburg, although unable to attend the festivities himself due to hosting Kaiser Wilhelm and Crown Prince Edward of Great Britain on the same day, had nonetheless sent along his pastry cook to prepare the wedding cake. This woman, whom the Ritter had poached from the Hotel Sacher in Vienna, prepared that establishment's renowned chocolate torte according to the original recipe.

Another old friend and confectioner, the Swiss philanthropist and proto-psychologist, Eliza, known as 'The Pfiffli', took the Orient Express from Zurich to Constantinople where she boarded a steamer for Beirut. She had scoured the chocolatiers and *Süsswarenläden* of her city collecting an extravagant assortment of ingredients, and in the days preceding the wedding she created a plethora of multihued sweetmeat delights which were placed with Pelin's little scented bouquets, in shaded locations around the garden.

Morning dawned misty, presaging a clear and sunny day. It was all hands on deck as last minute details were attended with mounting thrill. Satanaya's dishes now needed little but placing upon the stove or in the ovens, and so she was able to assist Pelin in dressing the bride.

'It has to be green.' Lady Gülbahar declared, when discussing the bridal apparel. 'Green like the fountain of youth! Ha ha!'

Spurning the tightly corsetted fashions of the time, the big hats and leg-of-mutton sleeves and cascades of lace of La Belle Epoque, the dame had gone for the Circassian look, without the pinched waist. And so, out of a sandalwood trunk came pill-box hat with wisp veil, full-length embroidered silk coat with sleeves like wings, long shifts, with chased silver belt and bejeweled dagger. The ensemble was completed with a triple-string of pearls, a gift from Daud the Arwadi many years before.

'Oh, I do hope *le Baron* doesn't make off with you on a horse!' cried Pelin, whose pretty head was full of wild imaginings following Satanaya's description of her departure from Kfar Kama.

'Ha, I'd like to see that! Or maybe not, he'd be bound to fall off.' said Lady Gülbahar

The wedding had been solemnised earlier in the week before a notary at the French Consulate in Beirut. A special ceremony had been devised for the celebration at the Beyt. The celebrant was Moses Shadinyan, who unbeknown to all but Lady Gülbahar, was a sheikh of the Mevlevi Order in the local dervish lodge. It had been hoped for a joint celebration, with the Armenian tinsmith joined by the centenarian Mother Superior of Seydnaya, but it was pilgrimage season and the good nun's duties lay in her own house. She did send a brief homily, however, which Satanaya read out.

Mother Superior's Speech

'Let us speak of love and marriage, in the light of this global event today.

'Marriage is an order of union, and union here concerns two individuals, one of the east and one of the west; of two human beings, apparently distinct, unique, singular even, affirming their essential oneness at the level of truth, beauty and love, their origin and their destination.

'But, we are not here simply to celebrate the union of two tribes, for this recognition of the essential oneness of love cannot be limited simply to this couple alone. For these two torrents of love, bursting forth from the wellsprings of their individual hearts today, may be likened to parallel streams which after long journeys of life in this world, in an act of joyous self-sacrifice, now overflow their banks, to meet and mingle in a greater flood, enhancing love at every turn with the experience of years, and accepting still further tributaries to join and grow as a river, a river which will not be satisfied by forming its own private lake, but must expand to engulf its margins and attain the ocean of love itself. Thus today we are invited to a celebration of love. For we are all emergences from this ocean of love, we are moved by love, and we return to love, for we are the beautiful human places where love has appeared.

'Let us drink, not simply to the Baron and our dear Lady Gülbahar, but to Love itself – that we too may become intoxicated – and drunk into consciousness on that finer wine – so that whichever way that river turns, we too may drown again in Love's ocean without a shore.'

Candles were lit, vows and rings exchanged, and the party began in earnest.

The wines provided by the French Baron were the best of the best: the champagne which preceded the wedding feast included (for family only) his last remaining bottles of the famous Veuve Cliquot 1811, the *Cuvée de la Comète*, a truly stellar vintage whose *foaming whirls as white as Cleopatra's melted pearls* were equal to the lustrous strands adorning Lady Gülbahar's neck; the claret, Chateau Haut Brion 1874, an exceptional year weatherwise which produced a wine of remarkable quality, soft on the palate with an enchanting bouquet of ripe cherries with a lingering suggestion of tobacco, and in the mouth its time-softened tannins deepening into undertones of sandalwood and leather. The Burgundy was a Chambertin of exquisite fineness, introducing itself with a nosegay of violets and sweet-peas, yet proving robust of body and lingering of spirit. And then it was back to champagne which flowed from magnums all night as the musicians played and the guests danced and danced until they flopped and dropped. Savouries and icecreams were served throughout the night, as the party continued until dawn.

It is no exageration to say that the wedding of Lady Gülbahar and the French Baron was imbued with the sweet scents and good tastes with which love enlivens the humdrum of mundane existence. Perhaps too the mature vintage of the matrimonial couple lent a lightness to the whole event, for when two lives already lived to the full come together in late union, the superabundant grace of their years blesses all.

THIRTY-ONE

The Eagle and the Dove

O, WHO WAS THIS Daud fellow?' asked Satanaya one evening while saying goodnight to her mistress.

Lady Gülbahar was sitting up in bed taking a last cup of coffee before turning out the lamp. Satanaya liked to visit her mistress at this time, when everyone else had gone off for the night. She would sit at the foot of the lady's enormous bed and they would chat a while. Satanaya would ask her about her past life in the Circassian lands before the flight, and how she came to fall into the hands of the Beirut pimps. Whenever Lady Gülbahar had mentioned this fellow Daud, it was always with a fond glint, a wistful, almost glazed look in her eye.

She smiled and sighed, sipped her coffee, and leaning back among the pile of pillows began to speak:

225

'Ah, Daud… Daud the Arwadi. Now, there was a real lover… a real charmer, and a gentleman… and something of a rogue with the ladies… before his… what shall we call it?… before his 'conversion', that is. Afterwards he only had eyes for his little Takla. And someone he called Shams. I was never sure exactly who, or what, Shams was; some kind of a dervish, or a shaman, an *ahi* perhaps. Whatever. The stories he told would make your eyes pop. Truly, he got into some scrapes. But Daud was kind and gentle, and above all generous and a real friend. Look around you – this villa and the land – he bought it all for me when he rescued me from the brothel.

'With Daud it was all for the sake of love – he never seemed to want much if anything for himself – he seemed to enjoy being able to help a poor Circassian girl like myself get back on her feet after all the trouble I had ended up in. And I was able to help him a little too – after he'd lost everything to the bandits and was on the run. But as I was saying, before all that we had a lot of fun. He'd visit Beirut every few months on business and always spend a few days with me, sometimes longer. He'd take me out to the theatre – we'd dine in the French hotels in Beirut. Such wonderful times, fabulous dinners with champagne and icecream. And we dressed so well – he'd have me fitted out like a real French lady, all in lace and buttons and bows, and take me to parties in the embassies. He'd even dance in public with me – can you imagine! A young girl, an ex-prostitute, evidently his mistress or a courtesan really, but he didn't care.

'He loved his business. He was a ship owner and was very rich then, but he didn't care about money. Afterwards we'd come back here in a smart landau and make love – all night sometimes if he was leaving the next day. He showed me what love was about, the giving and receiving of pleasure, and helped me to put behind me all the awful experiences of my former life.

'And his stories! Oh my, he had so many stories to tell of the wild times he had in the ports up and down the Mediterranean – tales which generally involved his righting some wrong inflicted by a villain upon some poor family whose beautiful daughter was in danger of having her reputation besmirched by said villain.

'More often than not his adventures would involve hasty departure from a lady's bedroom to avoid her being implicated in some sordid affair, always leaving via the window, never the door, or hiding under a bed 'til the coast was clear; and chases over rooftops and scaling walls. You never knew whether to believe his stories, but it didn't matter. It was the way he told them, with such enthusiasm, as though the whole future of the world depended on him and the lady in question escaping all blame of impropriety. And you wanted them to be true because this was your hero-lover putting the world to rights.

'Later – after the 'conversion' that is – the stories changed. His tales were no longer about him at all, but seemed to come from some ancient place, as though he was reading stories from an old book – like parables, but not religious, just very human stories. Which was strange because more often than not they involved animals – animals which spoke and had feelings like humans.'

'What kind of animals?' asked Satanaya. She was intrigued and though it was late she wanted to hear more.

'Well, there was this goat. I think it was a goat. Maybe that was Shams. Oh dear, I don't remember, it was all so long ago now. There was a story about an eagle and a dove. I remember that one very well because it was the story he told at our wedding – when I married the Turkish Ambassador. And the little maid I had then, she who sorted out that insufferable oaf Haywani, who wanted to kill Daud – well, she was completely infatuated with Daud who had also saved her from the brothel – this maid had an extraordinary memory and remembered the story word for word, and we wrote it out together. I keep it right here, a little memento of Daud and my marriage to the Ambassador.'

Lady Gülbahar turned to the bedside table and took from the drawer a sheaf of papers. Propping her pince-nez upon her nose she began to read: 'The Eagle and the Dove...' and then a strange thing, she closed her eyes and told the story word for word from beginning to end without once looking at the papers. Gülbahar had never consciously memorised the story, but now she was repeating the words as if hearing them said again somewhere deep in a distant vault of her mind:

'Among the mightiest kings there are kings of peace. Among peacemakers there are warriors of stealth. There was once in days gone by an eagle. A proud and magnificent creature who by his might and majesty held the throne in the kingdom of the birds. His wing was strong and his eye was keen, and his beak was the terror of all who beheld him. No shy bird was he, soaring above peaks and beyond the

*clouds and thunderstorms, he tracked from on high the river valleys
from source to sea, encompassed desert wildernesses with the ease and
haughtiness of true command. The puny towers of men he disdained,
taunting their feeble arrows by dipping in and out of range, while
feeding at will on lamb or kid as the season provided.Now, this eagle
had it all. His eagle wife was a fierce lady, his equal in all respects and
more, for each spring she provided him with healthy chicks which
fledged as strong young birds. One year, however, his world turned
upside down. While the eagle was ranging for prey miles from home, a
hunter spied the nest. He shot the eagle wife, then climbed up and
netted the unfledged eaglets, taking them away in a sack. When trained
they'd fetch a handsome price from a desert prince.*

*The echoing boom of the hunter's gun rolled thunderous down
canyons for miles and miles until it reached the eagle, who sensed the
danger and turned back from his own hunt. Scouring the distant cliffs
he saw his eagle wife sprawled lifeless on a ledge below the now empty
nest. His eagle eye clouded over in rage, and sorrow's arrow pierced the
core of his eagle soul. With heart rent he cried aloud and flew up and
up high into the thinning air. He let the thermals carry him, blindly
surrendering to the winds of fate until eventually this king of birds
reached beyond the circle of breathable air. Still further and further he
flew until even his profound and hopeless sadness succumbed to the
mortal need to breathe and he could rise no further. He was losing
consciousness, but what did it matter whether he lived or died when all
he had ever loved was gone.Now, his wings still outstretched and
numbed in frozen flight, the great bird began to fall, helicoptering in
slow descending vortex. As he fell, the warmer currents began to melt
the stiffness of his wings, and blood returned to his eagle brain. His
heart began to beat and thick oxygen flowed in his lungs once more.
And as the eagle spiralled gently towards the earth, he did not crash,
but rather glided lower and lower until he landed with a thump on a
ledge of stone. There the eagle lay, the wind knocked out of him, for a
long while. When finally he came to, he found himself face to face with
a terrified ringdove upon whose nest he had just intruded. Poking out
beneath her breast feathers were two ragged looking chicks, scrawny,
thin and also terrified. Now, one could imagine that the eagle would
have accepted the scene before him as a generous table laid by*

Providence itself. But in his recent painful experience, his desperate flight of self-abandonment and careless fall, something had become disconnected in his eagle sensibilities. Instead of seeing a tasty morsel waiting to be plucked, what appeared before him now he beheld in the light of compassion born out of his own pain, as his old world died. His vision was an epiphany of beauty itself, a helpless thing, a frightened thing, a thing to be loved and protected.

The dove, that gentle appearance of all that is lovingly feminine and worthy of love, was not only frightened and in shock at this terrifying arrival on her doorstep, but alas she was sick. Her mate, if you could call him that, was a pure white tumbler, a handsome rake of a domesticated pigeon from the town nearby, who had, as it were, tumbled by, tumbled upon her and tumbled off again just as quickly to God knows where, and had left her with two waifs to feed, and she now suffering from a fractured wing after fighting off an attack by a couple of jackdaws who had tried to raid her nest, and with no husband to defend her, and no way even of collecting the grain the pilgrims scattered in the courtyard of the Great Mosque.'

And,' the she-dove moaned inwardly, 'now this great dumb brute of an eagle just sitting there, I suppose trying to decide which of us to eat first – my poor chicks as little amuse-gueules, or me the main course followed by a little savoury. Well, he won't get much satisfaction out of me, I'm all wasted thin anyway. Well, I suppose I mustn't give in without a fight. O bother this life! What did I do to deserve this?'

But the eagle just looked at her, and looked at her and looked at her. It was the first time he had been this close to another kind of bird that had not ended up as his dinner. He was transfixed by this vision of beauty. The eagle interpreted the dove's helplessness as the sublime quality of one whose appearance is fleeting; of a passenger of spirit who longs to return home. He felt that if so much as a single thought should disturb the tablet of his mind this tenuous image wafting to him such sweet scents of beauty, provoking deep love longings in his heart, would vanish, as a reflection on a lake vanishes at the merest sough of wind. He held his breath and gazed in awe.

This she-dove, although she was ill, had a magic breath. What do we mean by magic breath? Her breath was sweeter and more pure than the dawn when it breaks at the world's end, where the unseen meets the

seen, where light emerges from the night, and day is born. Clean and
sweet and pure because this dove, despite life's tribulations, was faithful
to her true self, which was goodness itself. And the magic of her breath
was that it could change all that came in contact with it. Like a fragrant
perfume entering a dull room brings light, and the colours shine again.'

At this point in the story Lady Gülbahar sighed. Her eyes, like
Satanaya's, remained shut. Fleeting images of beauty and scents of love
descended upon their hearts. She paused a little before continuing in a
firm tone:

'All nourishment comes out of the earth, and it is a worm. Let me
explain... There is a worm, a tiny worm of many colours which passes
from the earth's heart through to all living creatures, up through the
rock of mountains and through the waters, through the tilled fields and
the forest's bed of leaves, through all the plants and animals, the flying
insects and the crawling things, the birds and fish and the human
people, and from each to each it passes, collecting and joining each
thing to that heart of earth. And when it reaches the wind it passes to
breath and fire and light and spirit, on and on it never stops its
wriggling until it has encompassed the whole of the universes.

The worm of nourishment passed on the breath of the dove to the
eagle, and from it passed all the knowledge of the mother dove, of
nourishment and care and fear for her young. And the dove wasn't
even aware of this tiny multicoloured little worm so small yet so potent
which carried earth's secrets encoded like a beaded thread thinner than
a tiny spider's web upon her breath.

The knowledges of this worm include the knowledges peculiar to
doves. The eagle, whose eagle heart was empty of all his previous
knowledge, received in total the being of the dove's heart upon his own.
Instinctively he understood the situation and knew he must act. This
poor lady before him was in deep distress, and it was his duty, as a dove
(as he now knew himself to be) to come to the aid of this poor mother
dove and her chicks. He immediately lifted his wings, flopped from the
ledge and took flight for the city. As he swooped down upon the court of
the Great Mosque in Damascus in the late afternoon, the pigeons
which fed from the grain laid out there scattered in a rush of wings,
and the air was filled with the screams of frightened pilgrims who

gathered up their children and fled within the colonnade. The eagle who thought he was a dove calmly filled his beak brimful with grains of wheat from the marble paving and flew back to succour the she-dove.

'O my God, wouldn't you just know it. Here comes that brute again!' the she-dove groaned, wearily preparing herself for the inevitable. But after another clumsy landing on the narrow ledge, the eagle spilled from his beak the golden grains before the amazed eyes of his newfound sweetheart.

The dove began to nibble. She knew immediately that this was the grain from the courtyard of the Great Mosque, good grain from Egypt no doubt, light and easily digestible. She chewed up some more and fed it to her chicks before turning to the eagle.

'Mmm. well, I suppose you want to fatten us up first do you? Perhaps you have forgotten, but we usually take water with our grain.'

'Oh dear. Yes, I'm sorry. I forgot.' The eagle was covered with shame before the beautiful bird dressed in iridescent feathers of mauve and mushroom-grey with the dark ring around her neck and cinnamon flecks across her back. 'I'll get some straight away.'

So off he flew, to where the Barada River spreads out into the Meadow Lakes. The women gathering herbs along the bank screamed with fright and ran to save their babies as he swooped down low and scooped up a good beakful of water. He brought this supply safely back to the ledge where he poured it carefully in a small depression in the rock. The pretty lady dove still suspicious eyed the eagle as she sucked up some water and fed her chicks.

'You are a strange one.' she said. 'But what about some worms, how do you expect these little ones to grow without worms.'

Out of the deep compendium of dove-knowledge so recently laid upon his heart arose a vision in which birds pecked in the furrows of newly ploughed fields. Off he went again, to where farmers were turning the earth preparing to plant the new season's crops. Crows and sparrows fled at his approach, and it was easy picking the little wriggly things from the earth. He returned and emptied his beak of half a dozen fat worms before her. This time it was the dove who was amazed.

'Well, I never. Here, why don't you have a couple, there's more than enough for us here.'

The eagle smiled inwardly at this small and unexpected kindness.

He hadn't realised just how delicious a worm could be until now, offered to him from this beautiful creature. In a very short time the eagle had become the perfect father and husband for the she-dove, his eagleness subsumed in newfound doveness. He fed her and the chicks devotedly, until her wing had healed and the chicks had grown and fledged and flown off to fend for themselves.

It was time, thought the she-dove, for this strange bird to move out. For a start, she needed to get a new brood going, and there was no way she was going to mate with that great hulking monster, even if he was the gentlest bird she had ever known. And anyway, all her friends had shunned her since he'd been on the scene, and now she was feeling better she was beginning to miss the girly chat. So she decided to broach the subject of the eagle's true identity.

'Tell me,' she asked the eagle one day, 'has it ever occured to you how different we two are from each other. I mean, you a great big beaky clawed thing, and me just a tiny wee pidge of a girl. Don't you think it's time you went off and found yourself a wife? One your own size, that is?'

Such a situation had never occured to the love-traumatised eagle. His identity was simply a mirror to the needs of his beloved and he had no thoughts at all about himself.

'I... I... I really don't know...' the eagle stammered. A strange feeling welled up in him.

'Now see here,' said the she-dove, 'It's high time you took a look at yourself. You're not a dove you know. I mean, ok, you can eat grain and worms and all that, and you're really kind of peaceful, like doves are meant to be, but you need to find yourself a big eagle wife...you know... Get it together. Find an eyrie. Raise a couple of chicks. All that stuff. You'd make a really great dad, just look how you cared for me these past weeks. And for a start, haven't you seen yourself in a mirror? YOU'RE NOT A DOVE.'

To be quite truthful, all the eagle had seen since his fall to the dove's ledge, was the image of the little ring dove with her dark red eyes and her delicate pink legs. Waking, sleeping, on the wing, even dipping his head at the water's edge it was not his own image reflected that the eagle had seen. Burnt into his heart from the moment he had first set eyes on her was the face of the little dove. The eagle looked at her hopelessly.

'Oh dear.' said the dove, as an inkling of the situation dawned, 'this is going to take some careful working out.' She thought for a bit. 'Look, I've an idea. Come with me down to the water and I'll show you something.'

Together they flew off to a secluded corner of the Meadow Lakes, and at the water's edge she said, 'Now, look into the water. What do you see?'

The Eagle peered down upon the glassy surface. First he saw the reflection of the dove. Then next to her, the great bronze feathered beast that he was. Only, he didn't see it like that. He didn't recognise himself at all in the picture. He thought as any dove would, seeing a great monster standing behind his beloved about to pounce. He turned around sharply to face the brute. Nothing there. He looked this way and that. Just the rustling reeds and the deep blue and empty sky above.

'No! no no no.' said the dove exasperated. 'Look again. It's you. That is you. YOU ARE AN EAGLE.'

Slowly the worm of discriminative knowledge insinuated itself between his heart and his beloved dove. He looked. He saw the reflection. He stepped back. It stepped back. He stepped forward. It stepped forward with him. Up, down, left, right, as he performed this strange pas de deux with himself, the differentiating threads embroidered the surface of his seamless heart and imparted the essential determinations, names, qualities and their relationships specific to eagleness. Now he connected with the image. It was him. He was it. But where was the dove? Where was his beloved? It was ok. She was still there. On the bank of the lake. In the watery reflection. And, strangely, in his heart too. Only there was something else. This eagle fellow – he was certainly out there, in the reflection. But now he looked at his own claws, turned his head and looked at his own broad wings, pecked his beak into his deep breast and felt his thick strong feathers. For the first time since his fall he became aware of himself in the exterior. But when he looked inside, no eagle. Just this feeling of love, and a vision of formless beauty.

Well, the eagle stood on the water's edge for a very, very long time. Day passed, night passed. The dove remained nearby, just in case. Then, in the morning, things began to happen. Flying high above on

*broad-spanned wings a she-eagle appeared. Circling lower and lower,
she became more and more curious, and came to land a few feet away
from the eagle and the dove. The dove took her leave, and the two
eagles faced each other. It didn't take long for the magic worm of
knowledge to pass upon the she-eagle's breath to the eagle. Immediately
his world expanded to include the height of his true inheritance. And it
didn't take long for the eagle's own magic breath of love to do its work
in the she-eagle. Beauty took wing again in the eagles' forms, and
together they flew off to find a new eyrie. For the rest of their long lives
together, this pair of eagles never hunted birds, and nor did their
children, nor their children's children. So, if you ever see an eagle out on
the plain, scratching around in the earth, pulling up worms or
gathering the fallen grains of corn, chances are it is a descendant of the
eagle that thought it was a dove.'*

Satanaya, who had been listening intently to the story opened her eyes
to see that her mistress was already asleep with a soft smile on her face. She
tidied the papers away, took the pince-nez from Lady Gülbahar's nose and
placed them on the night table. She blew out the lamp and quietly left the
room.

THIRTY-TWO

A Valediction Forbidding Mourning

HEN DEATH CAME to the Beyt, it first left its calling card. Two mild winters followed the wedding. Then late in the year a chill descended. Snow fell unseasonally early on the ancient cedars of northern Lebanon, and spread south to coat Mount Lebanon in the following days. The Baron had been pottering about in the winery with Gérard, doing a little tidying up after the vintage had been barrelled. He caught a chill, nothing much but enough to keep him in bed for a few days. Afterwards he kept complaining of being tired. Nothing new, but the tiredness persisted. His appetite diminished, and as winter set in he remained indoors. He spent his days writing in his study with a fire burning continually, a blanket over his knees, a cashmere shawl upon his shoulders, and his favourite beret on his head. Lady Gülbahar

235

encouraged him to come for walks, but he resisted. Then, on New Year's
Eve, warmed by wine and good cheer, he ventured outside to watch the
fireworks display. The next morning he woke with a streaming nose, and a
dizzyness when he tried to get out of bed. He lingered on like this for a
couple of months, as winter wore itself out. He no longer enjoyed food, and
the once formidable frame of the French Baron became gaunt and thin.

One morning Satanaya entered his study with a cup of tea, to find him
being helped through the French windows into the garden by Gérard.

Satanaya put the tea down on the desk. The journal where the Baron
recorded his observations on the vineyard and the vintages, a task he had
neglected since the previous harvest, lay open before her. The ink was still
wet where he had been writing. She found herself drawn to read the shaky
script:

*'Would I have acted differently?' he had written, 'Could I have? And
how? Is this, who I am now, the result of my own actions? Did I write
my own destiny? Or did fate drag me willy nilly to this end? Or am I
simply the field of the action, the floor of the winery, the barrel or the
bottle? All I have done is to accept or deny, the vintner sorting through
the crop, tossing out the mildewed grapes, separating the ripest, the ones
with the best bloom of must, from the less developed. Did I choose? And
is a right choice even a choice at all, or is it only a knowledgeable
submitting to the necessary? The wine is the real actor, the wine still in
the soil, in the grape, that has not even come to ferment, never mind
the barrel or bottle. It tells me what it wants. But do I hear? Do I listen?
I cannot blame my ears if the message is not received. But it no longer
matters. It's done. What matters is what I have built into – the bridge I
am about to cross – will it be familiar or foreign? Is it a return to my
homeland or does it lead to exile? Does it even reach the far shore? That
is what counts. Memories are our footprints and they will fade, yet the
path remains. All the while I thought I was the one making the game,
playing the lover. But have I been able to receive love? Have I, like these
fields, let my own heart be ploughed. Has my wine matured in all these
years? Well, soon enough, soon enough I too shall join the earth. Then I
guess we shall see how well I shall fare in the terroir that awaits.'*

Satanaya found the two of them in the vineyard. The Baron sat there
in a wicker chair sucking in the warmth of the early spring sun and gazing

at the neat braids of vines leading up the slopes. Gérard stood nearby. Satanaya waited a little way off.

When the Baron spoke his voice was clear but barely audible, as if coming from a great distance:

'Has it all been worthwhile?'

At first she thought he was just speaking to himself, but the old man was looking at his manager.

'Gérard, what do you think? It has been worthwhile, hasn't it?'

Gérard turned and looked back into the faded grey eyes of the old Baron. What he saw brought tears to his own eyes and he looked away.

'Of course, of course, we wouldn't have it any other way.'

Less than a week later the Baron gave up the ghost. He was buried in the French cemetery in Beirut, according to the Latin rites, and later his bones were returned to join those of his ancestors in the crypt of the family's chapel in their chateau on a Médoc hillside.

Lady Gülbahar changed after this. It was as if she knew her turn was coming and wanted to ensure that all things were arranged that should be arranged. One day, in late spring, a few weeks after the forty day rememoration for the Baron, she called Satanaya to her room.

'Well, my dear, time marches on and we must deal with certain matters.' She then opened a large document box and took out a sheaf of official-looking papers.

'Now, we know my time may come any day...'

'Oh no, my lady, you look fine. Is something the matter?'

'No, Satanaya, everything's fine. But let's face facts. I am well over ninety, and frankly, since the Baron left I've been thinking, what's to keep me here? But before I go, I really do need to put things in order.'

'Go? where?'

'Oh, I don't know, perhaps a little hermit cell in the convent in Seydnaya.'

'What! you can't be serious.'

'Or, perhaps I should take a cruise. You know, that's being recommended as a cure for mourning widows nowadays. Perhaps I would meet some nice young man...'

Satanaya looked puzzled.

'Silly you!' said Lady Gülbahar, 'Of course I'm not leaving, Satanaya, unless it's in a coffin, and then only up the hill to be by the Turkish Ambassador. He was my favourite husband, you know. I can't really count Daud, that was different. No, I shall die and that's that... When? I have no idea. But I have no intention of leaving things undone. Now, look at these.'

Lady Gülbahar pushed the papers towards Satanaya. On top was a large scroll, in Arabic, with a French translation – it was the Baron's will, in which certain financial provisions had been made for his widow. A codicil confirmed that a small villa in the mountains behind Nice had been left to his adopted daughter Satanaya, now a French citizen. Then there were official adoption papers for her, nationalisation documents and such like, as well as property deeds and instructions for the bank giving Satanaya and the other staff various stipends from the Baron's estate.

'You know I have decided to leave most of my property here to a foundation for the benefit of abandoned and rescued women. Clotilde and Gérard will stay and manage the farm and vineyard, with a pension, and a cottage is set aside for them for as long as they choose to remain. Pelin will be in charge of the foundation, she has the strength and resolution needed to see such a project into being. In another age she'd have made a great mother superior.'

'Now, what about you, Satanaya?' Lady Gülbahar shuffled through the pile of papers until she found her own will. 'You'll see I have left you shares with an income to keep you comfortably. You may stay here, if you wish, but somehow I don't see you hanging around for long after I've gone. In fact, I've taken the liberty of writing to various contacts of mine, here and in a number of hotels abroad, and...' ruffling through the papers she pulled out a bunch of letters tied in ribbon, 'look, this is from the owner of Shepheards in Cairo, and this from the owners of the Grand Hotel de Londres, and another from the Pera Palace Hotel, both in Constantinople, and there's an invitation from the Mazloumian brothers who are modernising their hotel in Aleppo. And here, look, the Kamenitz Hotel in Jerusalem responded positively. In addition I have written introductions to a number of good families in Constantinople who may require the services of a governess. I think your education here should fit you well for such a position, which would give you entry into another level of society altogether. And of course, there are many of le Baron's friends who would make you at home in Europe, should you ever decide...' Here Lady Gülbahar paused briefly giving Satanaya a firm look over her pince-nez to get her full attention.

'Now, you could live quite well on your inheritance without having to do much at all. You could have the life every pretty young girl dreams of. But that isn't the point. You told me yourself you have a job to do. The first thing is to become a cook. You've come a long way on that path, but it isn't over. Perhaps it's just beginning, because becoming a cook is the same as becoming yourself, and that, my dear, is a path without an end. So, whatever happens, work at this, whether for money or not isn't important. What's important is that you cook, that way you will grow.'

Satanaya left with a bundle of documents and her head in a whirl. She had often wondered where her life might lead, once her mistress had passed on, but it had always seemed a very distant thing, a book on a shelf out of reach, to be read eventually, but not today. A little later the imminence of the situation hit. She broke down in tears and ran back to Lady Gülbahar, embraced her, sobbing and begging her not to leave her yet. So intense was Satanaya's outburst, that the venerable châtelaine, not usually one to indulge in uninhibited displays, herself began to cry, and then, laughing through her tears, hugged Satanaya closely and comforted her as a mother would an upset child.

'Oh, I am so lucky to have daughters like you and Pelin. God is great, and me such a terrible old woman! There's time yet, there are still things to do, but you must get used to the idea. You've come a long way, Satanaya, and have a lot further to go. But you'll want to leave here one day. It will be easier once I've gone, that I promise you. Now, go and fix us some coffee and something to eat, all this weeping has given me such an appetite.'

Spring gave way to summer, and the pattern of life at Beyt'ur-Rahma settled down into a quiet routine. The soirées were rare events now, although occasionally, at Lady Gülbahar's insistence, Satanaya would organise a little party of younger folk, student friends from Khalil's time, musicians and poets, to join with visiting young Europeans who had been given introductions to the grande dame by their parents or grandparents. Lady Gülbahar and the Beyt had become something of an institution, a kind of hidden national treasure that the true cognoscenti of the east sought out on their tours.

During one of these evenings a couple of young staff officers of the

Ottoman army, fresh from Constantinople, somehow found their way up
to the Beyt. Captain Ali was an easy going and friendly fellow, in a well-
tailored uniform. His companion, Captain Mustafa, was fair-haired and
good looking, and wore simple regulation issue. He seemed awkward, and
masked his discomfort by donning an ill-fitting air of disdain. The latter's
only contribution to the general conversation was to mutter dismissive
comments in poor French when one of the eager young Arab nationalists
tried to provoke a response from the soldiers by jokingly calling for the
Turks to leave Lebanon.

'But, my, isn't that Turk good looking!' Lady Gülbahar whispered an
aside to Satanaya, who could not but agree, though she laughed at his
grumpy demeanour. She couldn't help noticing his piercing blue eyes,
deep, and thoughtful. His stiff edgy bearing made her believe he wanted to
be somewhere else, somewhere… somewhere quite in the future. It was a
look that mirrored something in her own mind.

Captain Mustafa for his part had noticed Satanaya the moment they
had arrived, but partly out of shyness, and partly because it was not in his
nature to compete for a favour which he felt he deserved anyway, he had
unconsciously avoided her. And when later in the evening his companion,
the ever-romantic Captain Ali nudged him and nodded towards her, while
reciting an impromptu couplet,

'Circassian maid who's caught the moonlight for your face,
Come, quench the sunfire of my heart in your embrace,'

Mustafa gave his friend a resigned smile and said, 'Go on then, say that to
her face and see where it gets you. I dare you!' and he went off to refill his
glass.

Purple, coalescence of life's incarnadine with infinite blue yonder; the
night sky before dawn. On such a holy morning Lady Gülbahar surrendered to spirit's strength and took her leave. The smell of sweet violets
pervaded the air when Pelin entered the bedroom just after daybreak. The
lace on the open windows billowed in the fresh breeze rising from the
waters of the Bay of St George.

Satanaya had visited the châtelaine late the previous night, and sat
beside her in the candle light. They had talked of pleasant things, the
Baron's jokes which nobody understood but at which everyone laughed –

it was just the way he told them; the Ambassador's happiness after a thankless early marriage, developing the vineyard of the Beyt; the intensity of Pelin's trust and trustworthiness, and the homely warmth and hospitality of Clotilde and Gérard.

'But you know, Satanaya.' Lady Gülbahar had confided, 'All this will come to an end. I saw it at the wedding, when all the Baron's friends were here, it was a swan song for our generation – for our era perhaps. This world is changing. It's too perfect, but perfect for so few of us. It can't continue. You've heard the nationalists, they want Lebanon for themselves, and you've seen the Jews are beginning to return to their holy land. The trouble is, it's no longer just theirs. Not the nationalists, neither the Jews, nor the Arabs, and certainly not the French or the Turks. You must get away soon. Oh, Clotilde and Gérard will probably move back to France eventually, you know the Baron left them a small holding in Bordeaux, good vines, and a winery. And Pelin, she's seen the other side of life often enough, I feel if anyone can weather the coming storms and survive, it will be her. But you, Satanaya, you must make a future that can't be turned upon the fates of others. I think you know this, that is why you must go on, out from here. "When the spirit moves," Daud once said, "no one hears. It's more silent than the wind. But if you see the leaves turn, turn with them and then go wherever your heart tells you." '

At that moment a breeze lifted up from the sea and shivered through the branches of the mulberry tree in which dark ripe fruit were beginning to fall.

'Ah, how the times are changing. It used to be so gay, this life, so full of light, but now it seems only dark times lie ahead.' Lady Gülbahar sighed and looked towards the dark corner of the room.

'Don't say that, Ma'am, you'll make us all sad.' said Satanaya.

'But it's true, my dear. Times were when the world turned on the values of a small, select group, people who held power with responsibility. They saw the importance of the beautiful things in the world, like the Baccarat crystal or Hereke rugs, Chinese porcelain, furniture from England. Powerful people who also valued those who brought beauty into the world with their words or music, their paintings and fine craft and jewellry. And food of course. But the things you cannot eat, they also nourish and sustain something in us, drawing light into the souls of those who appreciate their beauty.'

Lady Gülbahar looked at her hand resting on the counterpane, her large amethyst ring shedding purple and gold from its multitude of facets, joining and dividing the single light of the candle's flame. Her look hardened.

'We cultivated refinement of taste. It was a way to be, but it had to be learned. And not confused with fashion, though there is good taste in fashion, as well as bad. Fashion changes, as do individual tastes, but THE taste, the good taste we seek after, the ability to recognise the truth in whatever form it appears, and to discern its degrees, to know the bad from the good, the better, and the best, this is a subtle thing. It is not about possession, but about appreciation, and praising the good. When people only see the outward riches of our lives, and miss the inner wealth that all possess, they see nothing, and are left with nothing. You'll see, they'll destroy all this and be left with nothing.'

There was something strange in old lady's voice now, something which spoke of finality, like a voice of prophecy. Satanaya was troubled and didn't know what had come over her mistress. Then Lady Gülbahar turned to her, and all darkness had gone from her eyes and the kind, familiar light had returned.

'So, sweet Satanaya, may your road be easy.' She had closed her eyes, but opened them again as Satanaya rose to blow out the lamp.

'No, leave it burning.' Lady Gülbahar looked at her and smiled, 'Stay with me a while, I need a daughter's company tonight.'

Satanaya sat back down, and eventually in the relaxed calm of the night, she fell asleep in the armchair. She dreamt she was smelling the scent of sweet violets. It was Pelin's cry that woke her in the dawn. Satanaya looked across at her dear mistress. There was a smile on her face, left there as her last word, the final signature of her life, for the body was cold. The lamp had burnt out as she slept.

The funeral was scheduled for the afternoon of the morrow. Visitors streamed up from Beirut all day and through the evening. A pale pinewood coffin was brought and left outside her window. That night a strong gust of wind caused a shower of well ripe mulberries to fall upon the lid, coating it in their purple dye. Too late to replace, Satanaya mashed up the fruit and spread the colour evenly over the coffin. Lady Gülbahar would be borne in purple into the next world.

After the interment, when the funeral supper was well underway,

Satanaya slipped away. She saddled up Tarçin and rode high into the hills above the Beyt. There she looked down onto the distant sea, a silver sheet beneath the lowering sun. She cried again, not out of sadness, nor of fear, but in response to a deeper emotion, for the love of what had been and now gone, and for the sheer joy rising in her as she recognised a spirit greeting her from a greater universe; she knew then for certain that all her memories of her mistress, all her words, advice, stories and that mischievous smile, would remain in her heart as a guide wherever her life now led; and she knew that Lady Gülbahar's soul, its very meaning, once bound and concentrated in that lively body, finally slowed to a halt by the weight of time and now released upon the wind, inhabited every breath she breathed.

THIRTY-THREE

Lentil Soup at Domenico's

Beirut/Damascus, 1907

HEN DURING ONE OF THE LAST soirées before she passed away, the venerable châtelaine of the House of Mercy had remarked to Satanaya on the good looks of the young Turkish staff officer, and Satanaya had agreed with her mistress, that was by no means the whole story. Not until the guests had departed, and Satanaya lay awake recalling the events of that evening, did she remember where she had seen this Captain Mustafa before.

It happened like this: in the years following Khalil's departure, from time to time Lady Gülbahar would send Satanaya on what could only be described as 'work experience' trips, or more accurately, 'locums' – sorties out into the world of society where she could gain further experience by putting into practice her burgeoning talents as both cook and hostess. It was Lady Gülbahar's great concern that Satanaya did not simply sit back on her inheritance, substantial though it would be, but that she should make something of her life. And for that she needed to be in the world gaining experience and developing relationships of every kind beyond the protective walls of the Beyt. It might be that one of the Lady's friends in Beirut was giving a party and needed expert help with the catering; an Ambassadorial do for a visiting dignitary required French cuisine, or Russian, or Ottoman; or perhaps a hotel, on the eve of hosting the wedding of a local magnate's daughter, had been let down by its staff.

Clotilde would often accompany Satanaya on these expeditions, which had the nature of military campaigns, everything worked out in advance, transporting equipment and produce in the faithful old cart and if necessary setting up a field kitchen. Satanaya would bring evening dress and make-up: because beautiful young people bring life and ornament to any gathering, Satanaya herself was quite sought after by many a hostess. One suspects the call for help was sometimes merely an excuse to have the lovely girl present at the party. After the food had been prepared Satanaya was expected to mingle with the guests, be vivacious and sparkle like the diamond pendant pearl earings by Van Cleef and Arpels which Lady Gülbahar sometimes let her wear. Satanaya never disappointed in this respect, and it could be guaranteed that at any party she attended she would be found surrounded by all the most eligible batchelors, and viewed with wistful nostalgia by the older married men.

But the time she was sent to Damascus to help out in Domenico's restaurant when their cook was taken ill was different. Domenico was an old friend of Gérard's. They had met on board the boat which brought Gérard to the Middle East. Domenico came to work on the Hejaz railway, but missed the pasta his mama used to make. When he had saved enough money he brought his family over from Sicily. They set up a little trattoria in the Christian quarter of Damascus where they served the foreign workers who were building the railway to link the Levant with Constantinople.

Domenico's restaurant was always busy and when the cook was taken ill, he needed someone to hold the fort with him and his wife Beatrice until he recovered. So Satanaya took the new railway from Beirut to Damascus. For a few weeks she rolled out the dough of whole egg and durum wheat flour; she cut in strips kilometres of tagliatelle and spaghetti, pinched the waists of an infinity of fafalle, and stuffed endless quilts of tortellini and ravioli. She also introduced Domenico's wife Beatrice to recipes from the Beyt. These included her own stew of aubergine, peppers and red onions baked in olive oil, with puree of sun-dried peppers and tomatoes, cummin, cinnamon, allspice and oregano, served with yoghurt and rice. She also persuaded them to try her kibbeh stuffing for their ravioli. But it was her lentil soup, that steaming potage of homely good taste made with butter and grated vegetables, the same that had welcomed her to Seydnaya so many years ago, which the hungry workers returned for again and again.

It was the lentil soup that also inspired Captain Mustafa with thoughts of home, compelling him to request the cook's presence in order to compliment him in person. Satanaya had observed him through the hatch from the kitchen. She did not see the young Turkish staff officer who would eventually attend a soirée at Beyt'ur-Rahma and whose destiny would later determine for a while her own, for he came out of uniform, wearing the rough outfit of a foreign labourer – flat woollen cap, heavy woosted jacket and trousers and a collarless shirt. Nevertheless she instantly felt a strange feeling in her stomach, a nervousness that she could not interpret, whether it was of revulsion or attraction. Perhaps it was both. Unquestionably there was an element of attraction. He was handsome, of medium height and fair haired, with a look of uncompromising certainty in his blue-grey eyes. The evident coolness of this look, however, was encompassed within an aura of warmth and self-confidence which she found unusual in one so young. But he looked dangerous.

'Very dangerous.' she thought to herself, 'like a hunter, a bird of prey. Would I be just another dove whose heart he would rip out and devour?'

The cafe was full that night. Everyone was drinking wine. A small band of musicians – accordion, fiddle and mandolin – began to play. They would all be dancing soon. It would be an opportunity to meet this Turk if she wished. The Italians were so sociable, especially here in a foreign land, and nothing would be thought amiss of her carousing with them. She was tempted, but something, she didn't know what, told her that she would have to deal with such a fellow on her terms, and the time wasn't propitious. The ill cook had recovered and it was Satanaya's last night in Damascus. She saw Domenico go over and clear the officer's plate away, and then lean over to listen above the hubbub of the cafe as Mustafa asked him something, waving a hand towards the kitchen.

She panicked. 'Beatrice, I think that Turk wants to speak to me. I can't. I don't know why, but I can't. Tell Domenico I had to go. The service is finished anyway. Please apologise for me, say I have a headache, that I'm tired, whatever. I'll drop in tomorrow to say goodbye but I must go now.'

At times, when something completely new appears within the orbit of our world, there may occur a jarring, a discomfort in the soul, provoking a negative response; or this unrecognised arrival may prompt in us a demand to adjust our thinking. So we create boundaries which, in time, through education, love or simple habituation, may disappear of their own accord.

Perhaps it was like this when first Satanaya came across Mustafa. Like in art, when first appears a revolutionary departure from an accepted norm, it may feel awkward, as if warping our accustomed ideas of beauty. El Greco, Goya, Carravagio – these artists might not spring to mind when first embarking on the study of art. For many they demand an abrupt shift of perspective, a standing outside of our comfort zone. Rather, we may recognise more easily the warmth and motherly curves of Reubens, the strength and humanity of Michaelangelo, the wisdom and compassion of Leonardo. Then when we feel sure of ourselves, we may be prepared to step into the shadowy recesses of doubt and unknowing, and admit of those darker passions which move us beyond the borders of established conventions to create worlds unexpected and new.

Was this what she saw in Mustafa that first time? Was it this that made her step back into herself, pause and catch her breath before it led her to a place from where she might never return? For certainly she felt a discomfort, a shifting, as if his whole being said 'I dare you'. And her only response was 'no, not now'. What was it about him that provoked this? Perhaps, even in his raw state of youth, there was a glint of a deeply hidden potential. Raw humanity is not simply uncut stone, for spirit needs only time and circumstance to shape and polish the facets of the ark of its expression. Perhaps Satanaya saw something of the emergent shape, part-formed, unwieldy, an embryonic vehicle still in the trial of birth, and she was both attracted and repelled. She was fascinated and her retreat was in awe. Was he enemy or friend? Lover or killer? Whatever, she had known this was not the time to initiate a relationship charged with risk, and had quietly left the cafe.

Now, lying in bed, relaxing at last after a long day both in the kitchen and playing the genial hostess, it came back to her. That uncut block of rough youth whom she had taken for a simple labourer, the one who had frightened her yearning soul by his strangeness that night in Damascus nearly two years before, was the same man transformed now by dress and environment into a smart young Turkish captain. But no less strange for that. Aloof and shy at the same time, with those eyes that took in everything. Had she not been busy with her duties, and less absorbed by her own state she might also have felt those eyes surveying her, taking in her own striking beauty, her own air of independence.

THIRTY-FOUR

Satanaya Sets Her Compass

Lebanon, Autumn 1908

 SATELLITE HELD IN ORBIT by earthly attraction circles awhile its place of origin. Building up a velocity of intent it awaits the propitious moment, when, gathering strength from this homeward pull, it receives a self-generated impulse which propels it out and away, beyond the expected spiral of return, and begins a journey of discovery in unknown worlds

Just so did Satanaya in the trajectory of her departure and future peregrinations in the world conform to an established, though broadly hidden, order and intention to travel from her known estate to that more ancient, as yet unseen origin within herself.

After Lady Gülbahar's funeral, Satanaya had ridden up behind the Beyt, where finally she could express her grief, alone above the sea and beneath the sky, crying until her tears became tears of joy as she realised the spirit of her friend and mentor remained with her, invisible to her eyes yet no less present to the eye of her heart.

Satanaya rode on up to the shepherd's hut. She had made it her place of retreat in the years since Khalil had left. Here she kept a stone jar – a small larder storing olives, goat cheese, *firik* and dried apricots. And here she rested in quiet meditation, reflecting on her time with Lady Gülbahar, wondering where her own path led now her guide had gone to God. Darkness fell. She lit the small stove and cooked up some *firik*, which she ate with goat's cheese. Then, wrapping herself up in a thick quilt, she lay down on the bed of goatskins and fell asleep, exhausted from the past two days.

That night Lady Gülbahar appeared to her in a dream, radiant and looking more alive than ever. They were together in a strange city of wide avenues of shops and mosques. They came to a large medrese – a cloister of domed cells surrounding three sides of a courtyard with an ornate fountain in the centre. A large building formed the fourth side, with some larger domes, and a conical fluted drum covered in turquoise-green tiles towered over one corner.

Lady Gülbahar approached the building. On the threshold she turned and said, 'See you later.' Satanaya asked Lady Gülbahar where she was going, and Lady Gülbahar said, 'I'm going to visit a friend of the friend.' and disappeared inside. Above the doorway were the words, 'Do not look for our grave in the earth, for we are buried in the hearts of the wise.' As Satanaya tried to follow, she woke up.

It was enough that Lady Gülbahar had come to her in a *mubashirah*, a dream of good news, to reassure her of her well-being, but after a few days she began to wonder what else the dream might mean. Who was this friend she was visiting? And for that matter, of whom was this friend the friend? She found it quite puzzling. And this city? Was it real or imagined?

In the weeks following the funeral, she forgot about the dream. There were letters to be written, to some of the most illustrious addresses in Europe and the Middle East, informing them of the sad demise of the châtelaine

– Pelin dealt with most of this; lawyers were consulted over Lady Gülbahar's will, with papers and deeds to be signed and exchanged – which involved Pelin, Satanaya, Gérard and Clotilde, as well as some of the retained farm workers who had been left small parcels of land; and then there was the Fortieth Day rememoration ceremony to be organised. It would have been a vast affair had not Lady Gülbahar specified that in view of the age of many of her friends, it should be kept low key, with just the staff of the Beyt and a few remaining survivors of enduring friendship from Beirut.

One morning Satanaya was sitting in the kitchen watching a pot of chickpeas bubbling away on the stove. Suddenly one of the peas shot out of the pot and bounced off her forehead. The sting of the steaming pea made her jump and something woke up in Satanaya. She looked around at her own *kazan*, sitting away on a shelf, clean but unused. She saw again the engraved writing in Persian and remembered the story of the chickpea, and her dream came back to her.

'If anyone should know its meaning,' she thought, 'it would be Moses Shadinyan.' So after lunch she rode down into Beirut.

When Satanaya told him the dream, Moses Shadinyan laughed out loud.

'You want me to interpret it? Well, this is easy. I always said our dear Lady Gülbahar kept the best of company. Your mistress was in Konya visiting Mevlana Jelaluddin Rumi. He is known as *'hakk dost'*, the friend of the Real, the friend of God, who is *the* Friend. You know she was quite devoted to Rumi and loved to hear his poems read aloud. But maybe there was another message in the dream besides her coming to say hello to you from the other side.'

'What do you mean?'

'I have no idea. Perhaps it was an invitation. You will have to work that out for yourself.'

Satanaya returned to the Beyt. For months she continued to work away, cooking lunch for the farm workers with Clotilde, helping out with the bottling and storing of various crops of fruit and vegetables at they ripened. But it was obvious that things were changing. There were a few soirées, but it wasn't the same. The Beyt without Lady Gülbahar was like a ship whose captain has gone ashore. Certainly there were officers capable of managing the vessel, maintaining it in port and for short sea voyages, but no one had that bigness yet to steer the place the way she did.

One day, as the pomegranates hung heavy amid gilded leaves, and chaffinches and long-tailed tits climbed among the fig trees, nibbling the last of the sun-dried fruit, Satanaya remembered Lady Gülbahar's telling her how times were changing, and she must go and make a future for herself, just as Daud had told the Lady, 'if you see the leaves turn, go where your heart tells you.'

The idea had been growing ever since her visit to Moses Shadinyan and now she made up her mind. She decided to travel to Anatolia, to visit the tomb of Mevlana Rumi in Konya.

She put her affairs in order as best as she could. She organised travel passes with the French consul in Beirut. Remembering Lady Gülbahar's comments about the future of oil, she had already invested much of her inheritance in shares in Standard Oil Company as well as the Anglo-Persian Oil Company. She also kept significant funds on deposit in the Ottoman Bank for which she carried letters of credit. She acquired stout travelling clothes and sewed most carefully a variety of gold coins into the collars, cuffs and waistbands of these, in such a way that they could not easily be felt by roving hands. Some coins she even disguised as cloth-covered buttons. She also packed the revolver which had belonged to the Baron, his MAS 11mm service revolver which still lay in the drawer of his desk with a box of ammunition. She had seen the Baron dispatch a wild boar with it once when they were riding together in the hills. The beast had thought itself cornered as they disturbed it in a thicket, and had attacked them wildy. But the Baron, despite his age, maintained a good aim and fired from his rearing mount, downing the beast in one.

'Just in case I come across any unruly bores in the wilds of Anatolia,' she thought to herself as she fashioned a discreet holster to wear beneath her clothes, 'After all, a Circassian girl travelling on her own must be able to look after herself.'

She was only partly joking, for she knew that travelling alone as a woman in Ottoman lands, Muslim lands, especially in the back country, could be dangerous. Even in Palestine, accompanied by her Circassian 'fiancé', her unveiled appearance had sometimes raised eyebrows. So she would go in the guise of a European traveller. She had considered acquiring a dragoman and some servants, but as she intended her journey to be one of self-discovery – as much an inner pilgrimage as simply a journey from A to B, she eschewed such extra baggage.

Travelling by train would have been easier had there been a direct route to Konya, but as the rail link to the Levant had not been completed through Adana, she would first have had to travel by sea to Constantinople or Smyrna. She was not yet ready to visit the Great City, although that was her ultimate destination. Besides, news spoke of political unrest in the capital, and the European papers were predicting that the Young Turks would try and oust the Sultan before long.

On the day of departure, she saddled Tarçin before dawn and rode down to the harbour. She had booked a single cabin, and stabling for Tarçin, on a liner returning from Alexandria and Haifa. The vessel would call first at Famagusta in Cyprus before heading along the Turkish coast to Constantinople and Salonica. Her plan was to disembark in Mersin, and make her way overland along the coast to Silifke and from there travel north over the Taurus Mountains to Konya.

Pelin, Gérard and Clotilde came down to the quay in mid-morning for the farewell party. They brought a picnic lunch of cold partridge, which they ate with a bottle of the Beyt's great vintage, named 'L'Ambassadeur' in honour of the late diplomat.

The mood was sombre. 'There have been too many good-byes lately, please let this be just an *au-revoir*' pleaded Clotilde, who was forever sobbing and mopping her eyes.

Gérard just sat there sipping the wine and sighing. No one knew whether the old vintner's tears were due to Satanaya's departure, or for the indescribable feelings of pleasure this great wine evoked. Most likely it was both.

Pelin and Satanaya had stayed up talking half the night and were both too worn out emotionally to feel sad. Now they chatted away merrily about nothing at all as if simply parting for a few days.

In mid-afternoon a blast of the ship's horn signalled visitors to leave the ship. The little party bade farewell at the gangplank. They blew parting kisses from the quay as the mooring lines were dropped and the vessel made its way out beyond the mole and into the Bay of St George. They waved until the ship turned towards the open sea and Satanaya went below to her cabin where she opened her heart and wept.

She fell asleep exhausted. When she woke she felt empty. All those extraordinary years in the House of Mercy seemed suddenly unreal, a room so close but no longer open to her. But wasn't it also the House of the Womb? Was that why she felt so naked and vulnerable, like a newborn? And although her new life beckoned, for now she remained in an isthmus in time. She felt numb, and somewhat afraid. Nevertheless she made herself leave the cabin.

Up on deck night had fallen and the First Class passengers were milling around in the balmy November air, awaiting the dinner gong. Somewhere in the crowd she could hear a man speaking in the Cherkess language. It made her heart jump. She looked around and saw a group of young Turkish army officers. They were handsome dark-browed warriors with fine moustaches and tall kalpaks of Persian lambskin upon their heads, evidently returning from duties in Palestine and Syria. Satanaya was quite taken with excitement at the sight of these figures speaking her language and she remembered her family and her days in Kfar Kama. Perhaps they knew of Timur and Murat? She had to find out. Standing by the rail, gazing out to sea where a crescent moon low on the horizon gave glinting highlights to the gentle swell, she edged closer to the group. The one speaking was from Rihaniyya, another of the Cherkess villages in Palestine. He had visited Kfar Kama and she remembered seeing him at one of the dances before she had left. She had to meet them, perhaps they had news of her family.

The gong sounded and she lost sight of the soldier as the tide of people pulled her into the dining room. As she looked around, a steward approached and nodding to the table where the ship's captain was greeting passengers, said: 'The Captain would be honoured if you would grace his table with your presence, Mam'selle.'

She immediately recognised Commodore Fogarty, an occasional but much loved visitor to the Beyt on the infrequent occasions that his sailing schedule allowed him to escape. He was a descendant of one of those Irish adventurers who made revolution in South America in the days of Bolivar and San Martin. He loved his drink, but only ashore, and he was always the life of the party with his singing and stories at the table in the Beyt. The warm tones of his gentle brogue floated towards her.

'My darling Satanaya, what a great pleasure it is to see you. Come, my dear, you must sit at my right hand and tell me all the news. I heard the dear lady passed away, it broke my heart you know, never was a kinder woman in all the world, to be sure.'

So, it seemed that Satanaya was going to be well attended for the duration of the voyage. Across the dining room the ears of one young Circassian officer pricked up at the mention of that name, Satanaya. He glanced over in her direction with both surprise and recognition. Satanaya, caught between the two, waved a polite greeting to the younger man, wondering who he was, and took her seat at the Captain's table. 'Yes,' she thought to herself, 'this beginning bodes well for my adventure.'

THIRTY-FIVE

Aphrodite Bites

Famagusta, Cyprus, Autumn 1908

HE OVERNIGHT CROSSING from Beirut to Famagusta was a transition between worlds. Satanaya had woken before dawn and now stood on the open deck at the stern of the ship, watching the stars fade into the new day, a feint glow showing in the eastern sky somewhere over the mountains of Lebanon and the hills of Palestine. As the ship approached the coast of Cyprus she heard the sound of a dawn riser from among the crew performing his devotions on the deck below.

He was reciting a prayer which her father used to say at daybreak:

'*Allahumma ajal fi qalbi nuran – O God, make light in my heart*' it began, and she felt a stirring deep inside, as though her own breast were expanding with this same light.

The voice continued: '*Light in my seeing, light in my hearing, light on my right, light on my left, light above me, light below me, light before me, light behind me...*'

About her the dawn gave way to brilliant sunshine as morning broke upon Aphrodite's island.

'*And make Thou for me light... light in my tongue... in my sinews... in my flesh... in my blood... in my body... in my soul... and magnify for me Light. O God bestow upon me light.*'

The supplicant fell silent. Satanaya breathed the fresh sea air and bathed in the awakening light over the land. Her world became illuminated as if for the first time and she felt reborn. A short while later the ship berthed in the newly completed harbour at Famagusta, built by the British Administration.

Cyprus had undergone changes of late, having been occupied and administered by the British since 1878. In a secret deal during the Berlin Congress that year, the Ottoman Sultan had ceded control of the island in exchange for British protection of his empire from further Russian aggression following the Seige of Plevna and the subsequent investment of Constantinople. For Britain, having a base in Cyprus helped safeguard its route to India via the Suez Canal.

Satanaya was desperate to escape the attentions of some European passengers who were determined the tall blue-eyed Circassian beauty would accompany them on their tour of the sites. She was about to go ashore and explore Famagusta on her own when a waft of bergamot cologne and a tap on the shoulder made her turn. It was the Cherkess officer from the previous night, a tall young man with dark hair, darker brown eyes and a neat moustache. He was dressed in topcoat and fez, and introduced himself in the Adige language:

'Permit me, but I think we may have met before, or at least, in passing. In Kfar Kama, at the dances. My name is Anwar and I'm a Captain in the Sultan's Army. Forgive this outfit, but ever since the British took control, it's better for Turkish military to go in mufti. Are you headed into the town?

On your own?'

Satanaya was a little upset to be discovered at her first attempt to have an adventure.

'And what if I am!' she said, rather coldly, 'Are you telling me I'm not allowed out in the street here without a chaperone?'

He laughed. 'No, no, you misunderstand, I merely thought you might like some company. And to speak Adige. I know I would.'

Satanaya calmed down. She looked at the young man who seemed genuinely friendly, and she too wanted to speak to him in her own language. It would be good to have company while exploring, so she decided to apologise and play the meek defenseless woman, just a little bit, so as not to make him feel bad.

'I'm sorry.' she said, 'You must think me so rude. I'm afraid I'm a bit wound up. You see, it's my first trip alone, and to be truthful, I am a bit nervous. I really would appreciate it if you would escort me today. But let's be quick, before the English ladies capture me – the ones at the Captain's table last night want to take me on their tour and I just couldn't bear it.'

They descended the gangway to the quayside.

'Why don't we start right here.' said Captain Anwar, pointing to the great defensive walls of the old citadel of Famagusta which rose up before them.

'We studied the great seige of Famagusta in the Military Academy – how the Sultan's army laid seige to the city for over a year before the Venetians surrendered in 1571. They gradually destroyed the towers and blasted holes in the walls – they're thirty yards thick in places. The Venetians had blocked one of the breaches with a huge spiked wheel. Then a fellow called Canbulat Bey came and rode his horse right over the wheel and crashed on top, breaking it. The rest of our army followed. But of course, Canbulat and his horse were killed in the process. His tomb is now a *makam* (a place of spiritual help), and the locals bring their children here and pray that they may become as brave as Canbulat...'

'Gosh, how interesting.'

Satanaya looked at the officer and smiled. She wasn't really interested in the history but she enjoyed his enthusiasm.

They entered the city through the Sea Gate and down narrow dusty streets of old houses and shops which gave onto a large open market square. Opposite stood what appeared from outside to be a great Gothic cathedral. Originally the Cathedral of Saint Nicholas, the conquering Turks attached a minaret with muezzin's balcony to one of the battle-damaged spires and renamed it Aya Sofia Camii – The Mosque of the Holy Wisdom.

Satanaya covered her head and they entered. They walked a few feet into the left hand aisle and stopped: a spacious interior filled with light, free of the dark wood of pews; round pillars lined outer aisles of the nave, with tall arched windows rising higher and higher to the finely ribbed arches of the ceiling; the heavy gilt, the rood screen and carved tombs stripped out, all the painted iconography gone, just whitewashed walls and bare stone glowing pale and sandy like the desert, with pellucid diamond panes filling the window spaces where once was pictorial stained glass; and in place of an echoing cold stone floor, the comfort of soft wool carpets red and blue beneath their feet.

'Now, look up.' said Captain Anwar. 'What do you see?'

In the ceiling high above their heads, Satanaya could make out a circular depression, a couple of feet in diameter. She looked at him expectantly, but he said nothing. They continued inside.

No altar, just a simple wooden platform midway down the ninety metre aisle. They walked its length to the end and came upon a simple calligraphy, a Koranic verse: '...His Throne is extended over Heaven and Earth, and the preservation of both is no burden to Him...' – the verse which is followed by those oft-forgotten lines of tolerance, '... let there be no violence in religion'. As they retraced their steps a rose window high above the entrance glowed down on them. Tucked into the right transept was the qibla, the niche indicating the direction of Mecca, set at an oblique angle from the line of the nave, the surrounding space spread with an assortment of prayer rugs, a candle and some tesbihs, and a small bookcase.

As they returned, Captain Anwar stopped again, a little before the door.

'Now, look up again, what do you see?'

Satanaya looked up at the ceiling and smiled. Where she had seen a circle, now there appeared to be a heart. She blushed.

'Clever.' was all she said, as she tried to fathom the workings of this optical illusion.

They sat down at the back of the church-become-mosque near where a low window had been opened in the wall.

'You know, when the Arab armies conquered Damascus,' said Captain Anwar, 'part of the Church of St John the Baptist was set aside for Christian worship, and another part for Muslims.'

'Times change. You'd need to build a wall between them now.' said Satanaya. 'You seem to know an awful lot for a young Circassian from the badlands of Rihanniya.'

'Oh, I'm not from there originally. Knowing an awful lot, as you put it, comes from having too illustrious forebears. My father was on the staff of the famous general, Çerkez Abdi Pasha. Apparently we're distantly related. So, I was given a pretty full-on education in Constantinople, particularly in Muslim and Imperial history. I was visiting Palestine with a recruitment party, scouting for suitable officer material from the resettled Cherkess. I saw your friend Timur, by the way, the one you were meant to marry. He made it into the officer training in Harbiye. He was in the year above me.'

'What do you mean, I was 'meant to marry'?' Satanaya was ruffled at this sudden reference to the past. 'And how on earth do you know anything at all about me?'

'Satanaya, you are famous in the officers' mess. There were rumours that you turned down one of the most eligible Circassian batchelors but eventually succumbed to his charms.'

She smiled and looked down at the ground, 'I see,' she said, 'Well, yes, I guess we were both very young. How is he? Have you seen him recently?'

'He's getting on very well. His friend Murat is with him as his orderly – Murat didn't make it into the officer school but they've been kept together.'

From somewhere high above them, not bells, but the muezzin's clarion call to the midday prayer echoed down.

'Come on, I'm sure you're bored with history. How about a little lunch?'

'And I know just the place.' said Satanaya, 'Captain Fogarty recommended it. Back near the Sea Gate, just outside the walls.'

They retraced their steps towards the harbour, enjoying the kind of light-hearted companionship that comes in those rare interludes in life when all responsibilities are suspended: fine weather, a sea voyage to a Mediterranean island and two young people with nothing better to do than stroll in the sunshine and get to know each other.

Kebabji Kel Efendi – 'The Bald Kebab Seller' was a lean-to affair housing a few tables and a counter where drinks and food were prepared. Outside was a small, domed '*fırın*' – a wood-fired clay oven – and more tables. Trade was brisk and soon they were tucking into hefty shanks of lamb, tender meat falling off the bone, cooked together with onions and roast potatoes; a rough shepherd's salad of tomatoes, cucumbers, onion and peppers, and some wholesome nutty country bread. Satanaya was keen to see how the patron Kel Efendi, who was indeed quite bald, cooked the lamb, and he was happy to oblige a fellow cook. He opened the iron door set in the front of the *fırın* and pulled out a massive tray of roasted meat and another tray of potatoes.

'Its very simple. Just put the meat in the tray with a couple of glasses of water and some salt, cover it well and leave to cook for three hours.'

Satanaya smiled to herself, she knew it was never quite a simple as that. Kel Efendi doubtless had magic fingers and honey in his heart to be able to produce this delicious repast with such ease.

They continued their idle meander throughout the afternoon. As they passed an old dungeon by the ruined Venetian palace, Captain Anwar told Satanaya about Namık Kemal.* This writer was an early proponent of Turkish nationalism who was exiled by Sultan Aziz and spent time in the very same dungeon nearly thirty years earlier, at the time of the Young Ottoman movement. Captain Anwar had similar political leanings himself, and hinted to her that only a fully democratic government would redeem the Empire from its status as the Sick Man of Europe.

'As long as the State is in the hands of the Sultan and his old men, nothing is likely to change.'

'That's revolutionary talk, Captain Anwar. You'd better watch out or you might get locked up in there yourself.' Satanaya joked, looking back at the tumbledown stone building with its iron barred window and boarded-up door.

Anwar gave her a long, worried look. 'No, you misunderstand. I am a loyal servant of the Sultan. It's just that when you look around and see the success of nations like Britain with their modern military forces and mechanised industry, and ruling so efficiently right here on this little island, I wonder if we couldn't take on board some of their ways.'

Before leaving Beirut, the tinsmith dervish Moses Shadinyan had

---

* Namık Kemal (1840-1888), Ottoman writer, nationalist and political activist.

mentioned the *tekke* of the Mevlevi Dervishes, just outside Famagusta's walls. Exiting the old city by the Limisso Gate, crossing the stone bridge over the deep rock-cut moat, now dry, they followed a long avenue to some low buildings set back among a grove of eucalyptus and plane trees. Two ancient dervishes were looking after the tekke, the rest having left for Damascus or Constantinople when the British had taken control of the island. Satanaya passed on greetings from Moses, who was well remembered by the old men.

While one old dervish served them tea, the other told them the story of another political exile, Osman Fazli, a Sufi sheykh who lived during a time of great upheaval in the empire at the end of the 17th century.

'Osman Fazli, may God give him satisfaction,' he began, 'was a very respected religious leader in the Ottoman court, and a true mystic of the way of non-existence. He had the Sultan's ear, and was never afraid to speak his mind before the powerful men who led the empire. He was always taking the government to task for breaking treaties with neighbouring states. He predicted disasters would befall the Ottoman lands due to their iniquitous behaviour, and so it came to pass. Osman Fazli was banished a number of times for criticising state policy, particularly the practice of requisitioning public property to support the constant wars. In the end he was arrested on the orders of the Grand Vizier and exiled to Cyprus.

'Not long afterwards, the Grand Vizier was killed along with a great number of Ottoman troops fighting the Austrians near Belgrade. Following the defeat, the ghost of the Grand Vizier appeared in chains before Osman Fazli here in Famagusta. Osman Fazlı asked the apparition why he had exiled him so unjustly, and the Grand Vizier just bowed his head in shame, before being led away by his phantom gaolers. Osman Fazli himself died shortly afterwards, and is buried here. Come.'

With this sombre tale ringing in her head, Satanaya entered a little room adjacent to the tekke. The simple brick sarcophagus covered in green cloth, the unadorned walls and bare floor of the small domed cell, spoke to her of the ultimate anonymity of this life. The air in the room was suffused with a purple-dark and cedary perfume, an ancient scent like something out of dreams.

The old dervish opened the shutters at the head of the tomb and daylight flooded in.

'That this place should remain at all,' he said, 'is sign enough that the spirits of truth and human courage influence us long after their turbulent histories have passed.'

It was late afternoon. It had been a full day and Satanaya had much to digest besides the lamb. She and Anwar walked back to the harbour, each wrapped in their own thoughts, their boots crunching the fallen leaves of the plane trees lining the road. Beyond in the orchards which stretched out all around Famagusta, the fruit on the trees was turning from dark green to orange and lemon respectively.

Satanaya was thinking of the journey ahead. So far the trip had been such a pleasant interlude. Now she began to feel afraid for herself. The next day the ship would reach Mersin, and she would be on her own. She really hadn't thought this through at all. Typically she had just thrown herself upon the wind, trusting in Providence to show her the way, which it usually did. But that didn't prevent her feeling a deep sense of trepidation.

Eventually Anwar broke the silence. 'It will be sad to say goodbye tomorrow in Mersin, I've enjoyed being with you today so much. I wish I was going all the way to Constantinople so we could get to know each other better.'

'What do you mean? I'm leaving the ship in Mersin. I thought you were going to Constantinople.' said Satanaya.

'But…why are you going to Mersin?'

'I'm not, I'm going to Konya.'

'By train I suppose.'

Satanaya now began to feel a little embarrassed at having to explain her plans.

'Well, no, actually. I was planning to go down the coast to Silifke and then head up through the mountains.'

'On your own?'

'There you go again! Why not on my own?'

'Well, it's just rather a long way, and, you know, a woman all alone in the wild lands of the Çukurova.'

Satanaya lifted her head, stared straight in front and said defiantly, 'I'm Circassian,' as if that was enough to frighten all the devils, dragons and mountebanks of the road into meek submission.

'Yes, of course, I forgot.' Anwar smiled.

'And why are you getting off in Mersin?'

'Well, actually, I… we… that is, my company, my lads – you must have seen them on board – travelling steerage of course – we've been posted to Konya. But first – you won't believe this – we have to travel up through Mut and Karaman. You know, kind of show a presence, let the local leaders know the Sultan's writ still runs large, even down here. These mountain people are a bit of a law unto themselves, so every now and then our masters like to send us young ones into the provinces, to settle disputes, let them know who's really in charge. We have to, you see – the Sultan depends on the villages to supply soldiers, and with all the troubles in the Empire at the moment, it's necessary more than ever.'

'So you'll be travelling down to Silifke?'

'Yes, of course.'

'And then up through the mountains to Konya?'

'Yes, perhaps we might bump into each other on the way?'

'Yes, it's possible.' said Satanaya.

'I hope so.' said Captain Anwar.

Satanaya also hoped so, but she was too proud, and perhaps too shy, to say so.

THIRTY-SIX

Between Water and Clay

Mersin, Southern Anatolia, Autumn 1908

 HE AMERICAN CIVIL WAR which was intended to end slavery in the United States was a boon to the cotton industry of the Ottoman Empire. While the war raged, the cotton fields of the Confederate States lay unworked for years. The rapidly expanding textile factories of the European industrial revolution were forced to look elsewhere to satisfy their ravenous appetite for raw material. Significant beneficiaries of this demand were the merchants and traders in the small Turkish port of Mersin and the cotton growers in the Çukurova Plain.

The Çukurova stretches back behind Mersin, east and north for up to sixty miles between the Mediterranean Sea and the Toros Mountains. It holds some of the richest agricultural land in the world. With a sub-tropical climate and soil made fertile from rich alluvial deposits from the Ceyhan, the Seyhan and the Tarsus – rivers the ancients knew as Piramus, Sarus and Cydnus – the Çukurova, as well as its endless cotton fields and orange groves, is an all year round vegetable garden for the markets of the cooler north. Mersin wasn't a great port, but its long jetties allowed regular passenger services to berth alongside the dozen or so tramp steamers that called each week to take on cargoes of baled cotton, grain and livestock.

Although late autumn, the breeze off the Mediterranean felt warm upon her face, almost tropical, as Satanaya bade farewell to Captain Fogarty. The English ladies expressed some wonder and not a little horror at the departure of the Circassian maid into the wilds of Anatolia. She saddled up Tarçin and strapped on her bags. Accompanied by Captain Anwar, with all of his horses and all of his men, and a small number of traders and returning *hadjis*, she led her horse along the busy jetty.

Satanaya was dressed in the fine tweeds of a European lady's riding outfit, the only difference being, as she had no intention of riding sidesaddle, she was wearing breeches. Admittedly these were voluminous breeches – such as would easily be mistaken for skirts, what nowadays might be termed culottes – but breeches none the less, allowing her to straddle her mount as would any Cherkess woman worth her salt.

Official formalities had been dealt with on board before disembarkation. She now rode past the customs house and the numerous go-downs where cargoes in bales and boxes and sacks awaited loading, and into town along a wide avenue lined with palm trees. Mersin was unpretentious and industrious, and evidently thriving on its newfound trading links with Europe. Satanaya felt the fresh wind of adventure in the smells and sights and sounds of this bustling town. She took in the fresh produce markets with their pyramids of lemons, oranges and bergamots, enormous cabbages, leeks and carrots half a metre long, and mounds of fresh parsley, as well as the cheese merchants and honey sellers, and the vendors of *şalgam*, a local drink made from fermented pickled carrot and turnip juice.

She passed a busy foodstall where market workers and shoppers sat around a couple of charcoal braziers bearing two large *kazans*. One pot held rice and the other a light stock in which steamed some thin, pale sausage-like things called *bumbar dolması*. The word *bumbar* was what Lady Gülbahar called the tubes of cloth she used to stop the drafts under doors on cold January nights at the Beyt.

The stall was a family affair run by Yörüks, the pastoral nomads of Anatolia. The cook-wife was a small, perfectly formed ball of Yörük motherhood, dressed in the colourful cotton prints favoured by these mountain herders, and her head swathed in an embroidered scarf fringed in tiny silver coins. She cut off a short finger of *bumbar dolması* and offered it to Satanaya who found it spicy and juicy, light and delicious, in spite of its unprepossessing appearance. The sausage was a local speciality made from sheep's intestine stuffed with rice, herbs and red pepper flakes. Ever ready to try new dishes, Satanaya sat down to a plate of rice and bumbar, and a glass of sour-tasting *şalgam*.

The bumbar stall fronted a dark goat hair tent, its open flaps revealing piles of colourful tribal rugs. Behind the tent a couple of camels were tethered. A gaggle of brightly dressed toddlers played around some older children who were preparing vegetables. Inside the tent, men were smoking waterpipes, chatting and drinking tea. A young lad, perhaps fifteen years old, sat with them, listening attentively. The men sported extravagant moustaches and black tasseled headscarves, with bandoliers across their shoulders and bright sashes round their waists. Tall leather boots and swords had been discarded just inside the tent. Something in the closeness of the group, a kind of tribal solidarity, a confidence, reminded her of her own Cherkess roots. The men appeared fierce, martial and protective of their status; and the women too carried themselves with a quiet air of strength and independence. Satanaya felt a kinship with them, and their spirit of hospitality. She soon found herself chatting with the Yörük lady cook, about sausages and their various stuffings. The family kept goats and sheep which they herded in the hills of the Göksu Valley up behind Silifke, where she would soon be travelling. The Yörük made cheeses and wove rugs, and brought their flocks down to the coast in the winter months to sell produce and trade animals. They loved their animals, their horses especially, and they loved to dance. The Yörük lady was called Mihrimar. She was concerned that Satanaya intended to travel alone, and gave her some hints for the route she had chosen.

'If you have any trouble, or need help, just mention my husband's name, Ali *Efe*, and his wife Mihrimar. Ali is the leader, the efe, of our group, and he answers to me.' she turned behind her and called out, 'Isn't that right Ali?'. One of the moustaches flexed as the lips smiled. 'Of course, *canım*, always.'

Mihrimar gave Satanaya a parting gift of an enormous piece of very mature goat cheese wrapped in a couple of rounds of *lavash*, the local flat bread.

Kargıpınarı lies south-west of Mersin nearly twenty miles along the coast and halfway to Silifke. Mihrimar had assured Satanaya that she would have no trouble finding accommodation there among the settled Turkmen nomads, especially if she mentioned Ali Efe and Mihrimar as an introduction. The coastal way being flat, Satanaya thought it not unreasonable that four or five hours of steady riding would bring her to her destination. But she had failed to appreciate that those twenty miles were punctuated with as many rivers, now in flood due to the autumn rains. At each stream she had to find and negotiate the best crossing place. By mid-afternoon she reckoned she had made ten or twelve miles at most. Still a way to go when the rain came. Rain when it comes to southern Anatolia comes with tropical abundance. The dirt road quickly turned to quagmire, the fields flooded, and progress became painfully slow. She wondered if there might be other places to stop before Kargıpınarı, but now the road was empty of travellers whom she could ask.

The heavy afternoon gloom sank into night, and with no visible moon Satanaya could no longer see the road. She dismounted and led Tarçın on foot, splashing and tripping in the water-filled ruts. At one point she wandered off the path a little. Suddenly the soft ground gave way underfoot, and she slipped and rolled down a muddy bank, coming to a stop just inches from a rain-filled irrigation ditch. A raft of ducks, disturbed by this incursion of their space, paddled off in a furious splash of quacks and wingbeats.

She groped her way back up the bank, feeling alternately despondent and angry, wondering how on earth she had let herself get into this situation, and how she was going to get out of it. She knew her impetuosity had got the better of her good sense. She had not planned for the unexpected. How could she? But she knew that rain, like mercy, should never be unexpected. It is only the timing, and the quarter from which it arrives that is unpredictable. Her privileged time under Gülbahar's wing had lulled her into believing her wits alone would enable her to deal with whatever life could throw at her. But life is fond of the curved ball, and we need to be blindsided from time to time in order to discover our true earth. And Satanaya, at this moment, was discovering sweet humility in a most literal way.

Having just saved herself from immanent drowning in a puddle, as she reached the top of the bank and felt around for Tarçin's bridle, she slipped again and fell flat in the mud. Her lovely tweed culottes, which had for the most part kept dry beneath her rubberised poncho, were now thoroughly soaked in water and clay.

'This is where I start to cry.' she heard herself saying, as she sat there in the mud thinking things could not get any worse.

But they could. As she stood up and steadied herself, preparing to remount, she felt an arm on her shoulder. And then another around her waist. A hand closed upon her mouth and a man's voice, garlic-filled breath through a bristling beard, hissed in her ear.

'Not so quickly my darling.' it said.

Satanaya struggled but the man was strong, and no matter that she twisted about and kicked his shins, she was no match for her assailant. Every ghastly thought about her attacker's intentions entered her head. After her initial reaction of terror, fear, panic – hardly familiar sensations in Satanaya's life so far – she gave in. She had no chance of fighting him off as the situation stood. She knew she must stay calm and conserve her strength.

Her assailant obviously thought he had subdued his prey, and holding her by the neck in a grip of iron, he led her and Tarçin a few hundred yards back down the road and off up a track to a small hut, a kind of farm building or stable, smelling of animals and wet straw. He pushed open the door and threw Satanaya down upon the earth floor. An oil lamp burned in an alcove in the wall, and from its meagre light Satanaya got her first glimpse of the man. His appearance did nothing to reassure her: built like a bear, in thick wool pantaloons, a heavy jacket over a filthy cambric shirt, and a dark turban which he now threw off to reveal his roughly shaven head. The dark beard glistened wet with rain, but his eye – his one eye for the other socket was empty beneath a livid scar – seemed dull, as if he was drugged, or flooded with lust.

'That's a fine horse you've brought me, dear. But first things first. Now, are you going to come nice and easy, or shall we have a little sport.'

The man leered in a way that made Satanaya realise she may not have been the first victim waylaid by this ogre. She backed into the corner. The man laughed and rushed at her, but she stepped sideways in time and he fell against the wall. She fumbled beneath her garments and extracted her holstered firearm, pointed it at him and pulled the hammer back until it clicked into the firing position.

'Stop!' she shouted.

She was unsure of the protocol for fending off would-be rapists. She did not want to kill the man, but if it became necessary, she wouldn't hesitate. Her immediate inclination was to fire at the point where his legs joined, but she decided to settle first for a warning shot on the ground between his feet. Satanaya was not too familiar with small arms. She hadn't bargained for the sensitivity of the trigger when the gun was cocked, nor the recoil when discharged. Unfortunately for the target, he had begun to move towards her. The result was a more severe first warning than she intended. The muzzle of the pistol lifted as the cartridge detonated, and she did indeed score a bull's eye, at the intersection of her antagonist's thighs. He fell back crying out and clutching at his own pestle, its fervour reduced thanks to Satanaya's wicked sharp shooting.

'Time to leave.' Satanaya announced to no one in particular, but first she shot at the light in the oil lamp. This didn't have the desired effect, for while it smashed the lamp, the oil splashed down the wall and upon the man lying beneath. The wick, however, remained alight setting fire to the filthy cambric shirt of the spatchcocked bandit. Despite his injury, the bandit jumped up and ran outside into the rain where he rolled around in the mud until the fire was out. Then he just lay there, greeting and gurning as one might expect. Satanaya felt pity, but she couldn't bring herself to put him out of his misery as she might have a rabid dog or scotched snake, nor could she risk coming to his aid.

Now it really was time to leave. But something stopped her, and for a moment she laughed. She thought of Captain Anwar, and his suggestion that they might meet on the way, and what he would think if he came across her now, what must she look like. Tarçin was patiently waiting in the rain. She led him back to where she thought was the road. Nothing for it but to continue. After all, the man might have brothers.

She re-mounted. A horse, after all, has four legs, she rationalised, and

Tarçin hasn't slipped yet. Then the shock of what had just occurred hit her. And suddenly she felt alone as she had never felt before. And afraid. She began to cry, and curse herself for her stupid pride in thinking she could take on the world just like that, and that the world would submit to her. She felt very small and unprotected. She was wet through, too cold to feel hungry, and she yearned for something familiar to bring her back to her self. She thought of her parents and family, and the tears came again. She thought of the Beyt'ur-Rahma, and couldn't fathom what had made her leave. She remembered Moses Shadinyan and the story of the chickpeas boiling in the pot, and Lady Gülbahar's dream about visiting the Friend of friend. Something happened then. Was it, she wondered, the memory of Lady Gülbahar's death, and the sense of her Lady's soul continuing in a bigger life? Or perhaps simply an acceptance that as a chickpea, her destiny was to boil until sufficiently soft for the table. Whatever it was, something from that deep mine of resilience, that had brought her this far, surfaced within her. The fear and sadness faded, and a resoluteness came to lift her from uncertainty and despond. And as the rain mixed with her tears Captain Anwar's face came to mind, and in that instant she desperately wanted to be with him.

The rain eased off, and finally ceased. High above the lonely horse and rider, the clouds parted and bright stars glinted. With the way ahead visible now, they rode on quickly for a couple of hours.

Satanaya heard dogs barking somewhere up ahead. 'Perhaps a village.' she thought. Then she heard music, someone was playing a *saz*, and voices were singing along. Then the sounds began to fade, which was curious, as she had seen no buildings, nor roads crossing her way. She backtracked a little and worked out that the sounds were coming from a clearing some way off to the side of the road. Through the misty darkness she could just make out some palely-lit shapes maybe a hundred yards away. She approached, calling out a greeting periodically, until someone answered. The singing gradually subsided, and was replaced by the growling of dogs. Then two men approached, carrying lanterns. They were dressed like the Yörüks she had met in Mersin.

'*Salam aleykum.*' Satanaya gave the universal greeting, which the men returned, adding '*Hoş geldiniz* – Welcome!'

One of the men took the horse's bridle, while the other stood at Satanaya's left stirrup and helped her dismount. She took her saddle bags and they led her across the muddy space

'You will eat with us.'

'Thank you.'

'Come inside.'

Inside was a large domed tent – a yurt – full to bursting with men and women sitting around a central brazier. They pulled the flap back and ushered her in. Then the men stepped back in surprise, as they realised that their guest was a woman. No one seemed to know what to say. Satanaya took the initiative,

'Mihrimah and Ali Efe said you would give me assistance.'

'Ah, Mihrimah *Hanım.*' said a chorus of voices accompanied by muffled laughter. 'Yes, of course.' It was apparent that Mihrimah had a certain reputation.

The ice broken, a couple of brightly-clad ladies of the Mihrimah variety took Satanaya in hand, through a back door into a large satellite tent with a central brazier. More women were sitting around a '*saç*', a domed iron griddle, rolling out and cooking large rounds of flat *lavaş* bread.

The door was closed while Satanaya changed into fresh clothes, and the Yörük ladies hung up her wet things to dry. They sat her down with a bowl of steaming hot sheep's milk, and freshly cooked *lavaş* to dip in it. Afterwards she offered the cheese which Mihrimah had given her, but they just laughed and ladled into her bowl some lamb stew from a pot by the fire.

Through the doorway in the main tent the music had begun again. She saw a man stand up, and in the confined space begin to dance a *Zeybek*. Arms outstretched like hawkish wings, as if hovering above his prey, he made his way in delicate slow stepping movements around the tent while the rest of the men sang a deep, rolling melody to the insistent ringing accompaniment of the long-necked lute, the saz.

Her Yörük hosts were most solicitous in caring for their guest, and did not bother her with questions. They showed interest whenever she spoke, but it was enough for them that she was going to Konya to visit the famous saint Mevlana Rumi, and also that she travelled under the aegis of their tribal leader, Ali Efe. And of course the indomitable Mihrimah. She lay there by the fire, rolled up in a *yorgun*, a thick hand-stitched quilt stuffed with raw cotton, and fell asleep to the trilling of a nightjar and the intermittent barking of dogs.

Satanaya woke in the early morning to the braying of a donkey and the bleating of goats. Stepping outside she became aware of the extent of this transient settlement. A couple of dozen yurts and black goat-hair tents were spread loosely over perhaps an acre of land, with horses, camels and donkeys tethered among them and a lot of chickens running around. The dogs, big sandy-coloured beasts with black faces, which had prowled throughout the night guarding the herd, now lay about sleeping. Stretching beyond the camp was a heaving sea of black, brown and white – the woollen backs of a thousand goats and sheep. Mist rose from their sun-warmed fleeces. It would be a fine day.

THIRTY-SEVEN

Of Girls, Girdles
and the Grit of St Thecla

Southern Anatolia, late autumn, 1908

 ATANAYA TRAVELLED with the Yörük as far as Silifke. Here the group had arranged winter pasture for their flocks with local landowners – some settled Yörük who had given up the nomad life.

One evening as they sat around the brazier a Yörük arrived from Mersin with a tale of a one-eyed Kurdish shepherd he had encountered along the way. This shepherd claimed he had been attacked by a wild boar, and in the ensuing affray the tusky hog had relieved him of the two valued witnesses to his manhood, narrowly missing the vital member itself, but leaving him no better than a eunuch. The men laughed heartily at this tale, the women giggled behind their scarves. Satanaya had earlier confided her adventure to some of the Yörük women, and was now the recipient of knowing glances from her confederates.

During the journey she learned of the nomads' tough life, especially the lot of the womenfolk. They were fascinated to hear Satanaya's own tale of how she escaped marriage by kidnapping, and congratulated her on her bravery in the recent attack. Satanaya didn't feel brave at all, just a little foolish and helpless as she was discovering the world also has sharp edges which can cut the unwary.

'We have kidnapping – *kaçırma* – for marriage here too.' said Derya, a young Yörük mother who sat feeding her infant while the ladies prepared the evening meal. 'But it's no fun for us. It really is a kidnap, and you know what that means for a girl.' She said no more but looked down resignedly at the little face squashed against her breast. It was evident she had not been a willing partner in this affair. Satanaya understood that the word *kaçırma* could also mean rape.

'Usually our weddings are arranged within the family.' said Elif, an older lady with the hardy lined face of experience. 'You see, it is expected that we marry our father's brother's son. So we marry our cousins. It's to keep the assets together, strengthen the family bonds. It's for the economy. The boy's family, the father that is, has to provide the bride price, which can be as much as a couple of year's income from the flocks. But the girl then becomes a part of the labour force of the boy's father. With extra hands he can increase his herds. It's all carefully worked out.'

'But it doesn't seem to allow for love.' said Satanaya.

The ladies giggled and all eyes were on Elif, whose blush showed even through her dark weatherworn face.

'Yes, well, there is another kind of bethrothal that happens,' said Elif, 'though it's usually considered kidnapping – *kaçırma* – by all but the couple themselves. We would say elopement – *kaçma*. But it has its consequences. You see, tribe is very important, and family even more so. We all need to belong socially. It is hard to break outside the bond of blood, you know, and almost as hard to live outside the tribe. But often there is a way back in, and it's usually through the women. My aunt, my mother's sister, took me in when I eloped with a boy from another group of tents. We were barely related at all, we just happened to meet at one of the big yearly markets.

You know how it is, we knew we were meant for each other. But afterwards no one wanted to have anything to do with us, let alone pay a bride price. My aunt was different, she loved me too much to let me suffer and we joined her tents. Her husband's tents, that is – Efe Ali. Mihrimah is my aunt, though we're the same age. She's a real Yörük princess, if ever there was.'

It was evident to Satanaya that the tribal system by which the Yörük lived, like the traditions of her own culture, had some validity in so far as it preserved the economic integrity of the family and group against those elements which threatened its survival. But in the changing world where she found herself travelling, where economies were more and more inter-connected by trade, she wondered whether this way of life could survive in its present form. The Circassian nation was now scattered across the globe. Palestine and Syria were seeing emigration to the Americas on a large scale. From reading the news in Lady Gülbahar's European papers she had seen how the Jews were on the march out of Russia. Revolution was in the air. And here, in this backwater of south-east Turkey, some Yörük had begun to settle down, buying land and becoming interdependent within a group far larger than these several dozen tents, a group which connected and effected through its agricultural production the trading patterns of Europe and America. Would the time come, she wondered, when even the maidens of the black tents would venture forth as she had, and take the high road to self-determination?

And would the time come, when she too would meet someone, and know intuitively that they were meant for each other? She had felt that with Yusuf, and hoped so with Khalil, but evidently it wasn't so. Could it ever be? Was she aiming too high in her expectations. Yet she knew also she yearned for more, for a love that went beyond even the stars, so there was nowhere in the universe where she didn't feel safe, at home, and at one. But right now after her recent experience all she felt was the need for the warm earth of a human love.

South of Silifke the Yörük encamped for the winter. Elif told Satanaya of a nearby tomb she wanted to visit, of a saintly lady whom she held in high regard, called Thecla. This saint, who had lived long ago, was a particular favourite among women who had problems with their marriages.

'When we eloped, my husband and I came here and asked Thecla for help. It was her spiritual influence that brought Mihrimah to our rescue and sort things out with our families.' said Elif.

Satanaya knew the story of Thecla, for this saint also has a tomb at Maaloula, across the hills from the convent of Seydnaya in Syria. There she is venerated as Mar Takla. Thecla was born in Iconium (Konya) at the beginning of the Christian era. She was sitting at home one day when through the window came the voice of an itinerant preaching a new religion. He was a rather intense but charismatic man named Paul, lately escaped from Damascus and Antioch. Thecla was eighteen at the time and engaged to be married. She became completely enthralled by Paul's words. For three days she sat there listening as Paul spoke of this new life, the life of the spirit, in which all worldly desires and acquisition are put aside in favour of the inner life devoted to the One God.

The upshot was that Thecla, like Satanaya, refused the marriage, abandoned both her mother and her fiancé and ran off with Paul and his raggle-taggle band of Christians. She was pursued on all fronts, not just by her mother and fiancé, for Thecla was a great beauty and a high-born young lady of Iconium. Roman society had expectations and the populace would not condone such behaviour. However, even the persuasive methods prevalent within the Roman Empire at the time were no match for Divine intervention. An attempt to burn her at the stake failed when a cloud-burst extinguished her bonfire, and an earthquake devoured some of the crowd. They tried to feed her to lions and bears, but a female lion ate the bear, and the lioness and the male lion ate each other. Other beasts approached her but she prayed and was clothed in the Burning Splendours. Assuming death was nigh, she pronounced her own baptism and dived into a nearby pit of water. The pit contained sharks but her holy aura of fire frazzled the fish, even as the Governer bemoaned the immanent loss of such a beauty. Next she was tied between bulls to whose testicles ropes had been attached. When red hot irons were applied to the bulls' nether parts, the animals went wild, but the fire burnt Thecla's cords and she escaped.

Thecla had now gained the sympathy of the crowd, as much for her beauty – she was continually paraded naked throughout these trials – as for the miraculous interventions. Eventually, rather than have to send back embarrassing reports to Rome, the Governor set her free to carry out her work and she left for Seleucia, which is Silifke.

Yet even here, after a long life preaching and healing the sick, jealousies arose. Some local healers accused her of spoiling their business, saying she was a virgin devoted to the goddess Diana, with powers of healing far more effective than their own. They arranged for her to be raped in order to reduce her powers. Thecla lived in a cave outside Silifke, and when the hired thugs arrived to do the dirty deed, she prayed and the rock wall of the cave opened up. A voice commanded her to enter. She went to safety and the rock immediately closed after her. She was ninety years old.

Satanaya had some sympathy for this fierce lady, for her efforts to determine her own life as well as her narrow escape from rape. She wondered though, about all this emphasis on virginity and continence whereby this new religion could effectively suppress human physical union? Were the sexual mores of the time so permissive that sex needed banning in order to re-establish the primacy of spirit over matter? On the other hand, could someone like Paul, so evidently immersed in the pre-eminence of love, could he really deny the physical expression of love between humans made in the image of love's originator? Satanaya was not convinced. On the contrary, she saw this as yet another example of men controlling the choices of women. She didn't blame St Paul, but she did doubt that everything said in his name was said by him.

Perhaps contemporary male chroniclers found it necessary to promote celibacy to counteract the fervent expressions of devotion among the womenfolk of Anatolia for this fellow Paul, who, they said, appeared full of grace, sometimes as a man, at other times with the face of an angel.

'Probably he was irresistable,' thought Satanaya, 'so they decided on behalf of us poor women, to make sure it all stayed above the girdle.'

Nevertheless, as she and Elif crossed the rough ground up a small hill and over to the ruined church that fronted the cave, Satanaya felt an affinity with Thecla. She was grateful for her steadfast example in facing and surviving her trials – trials such as she, Satanaya, feared she would fail dismally. She and Elif squeezed past a busy crowd of picnicking ladies and went behind the ruins to the cave entrance.

As they stood in silence beneath an arch of ancient stones, contemplating the presence of this valuable woman, so distant in time, yet so close to their hearts, Satanaya found herself thinking of her journey. The Yörük were on the move, coming down from the mountains, all along the coast. She would no doubt meet them again on the road to Mut and Karaman, and eventually Konya, as they drove their flocks to winter pastures. She knew now she would be welcome wherever their paths crossed. That is, if other possibilities didn't emerge; possibilities which she dared not think about, yet nonetheless had come to mind since departing Mersin. She prayed for help within this presence of sisterhood so apparent in Thecla's cave, and was left with a strong sense that there was no barrier, moral or otherwise, between the upper and lower regions of her girdle unless she wished there to be one. The choice was hers alone.

THIRTY-EIGHT

Crossing the Great Divide

South-east Anatolia, 1908

ATANAYA CAME ACROSS Captain Anwar sitting by a fountain beneath the spreading canopy of an ancient sycamore tree. The platoon was watering its mounts at a trough where a spring gushed from the hillside. While Satanaya had made her troubled way from Mersin, Captain Anwar had billeted his men in barracks for a couple of days before setting out. Now more than a week later their paths had converged on the road out of Silifke.

She demurred briefly when the captain invited her to accompany the platoon for the ride that day, although her heart had not hesitated. The time spent with Anwar in Famagusta had reawakened something in Sata-naya, something she had not felt for so long, not since those early days at the Beyt. It was the knowledge that, in spite of all the anxieties and growing pains which sharpen life's journey, places of mental respite and moments of pure joy did exist. It was this respite she had yearned for following her narrow escape from the one-eyed villain. And it was this joy and its atten-dant relaxation she now felt in the company of that young officer as they rode side by side along the verdant banks of the Göksu River. Flocks of goldfinches were mopping up in the gardens overflowing with late autumn fruit: golden globes of persimmons filled to bursting with near-liquid ripe-ness, yellow-fingered hands of bananas lifted in supplication hung in clustered tiers, and pomegranates split open on the branch, oozing blood-red pearls.

The morning wore on, and Satanaya's feeling of physical ease increased, as tendrils of desire like lazy sparks danced between her and the young man, weaving sweet threads and binding them, veiling them from the world within their own universe. It was love-making of a kind, an easy falling one into the other, the gentle touching with words, the caress of looks, so that a warmth flowed between them as rising tide submerges low-lying islands, joining them in its deepening embrace. When the sergeant rode up to ask if the troop shouldn't halt for a brew of tea, he was com-pelled to wait in silence a full five minutes until Anwar noticed him.

The road ascended from the coast in twists and turns, tracking the edge of a steep, narrow-throated canyon, keeping in sight for the most part the pale turquoise river flowing below. It is the 'Göksu', the 'Sky-Water' river, named perhaps for the opaque, milky-blue colour of its water. To Satanaya it seemed a reflection of the sky as it rushed by beneath them.

'As above, so below,' were her thoughts. 'Look, the sky in the water.' she said.

'It makes a change from water in the sky.' said Anwar, and they laughed together.

The orchards and plantations of the lower slopes, with their rich green grass and autumn colours of ochre, gold and scarlet gave way to vineyards and olive groves, and the darker verdure of mountain scrub. Towards the middle of the afternoon they crested the canyon. Beyond, the valley flat-tened out. Yet still the river retained its opaline hue, from the chalk in the water. It was good wine growing country, facing south, the chalky soil giving good drainage to make a suitable 'terroir' for the vines. Wild grape varieties grow in the forests of the Taurus Mountains which local traditions hold to be the birthplace of winemaking.*

Anwar halted the platoon near a small village and sent the sergeant and a couple of men to purchase provisions for supper, and also to buy wine, the population being Christian. Meanwhile they pitched camp within the natural moat of a sharp bend of the river, leaving only one side open to attack. Not that an attack was expected, but, as St Thecla's trials witnessed, these mountains are home to a wide range of wild beasts, including bears and hyaenas. Even rare Anatolian leopard are seen from time to time. On Anwar's orders a spare tent was erected for Satanaya by the riverside, opening away from the camp and flanked by Anwar's own tent and the kitchen stores. Soldiers had foraged for firewood during the journey, and the campfire was well lit and water coming to the boil for tea when the sergeant's team returned with half a dozen live chickens, a sack of bread, cheese, a pile of vegetables, and a couple of demijohns of local red wine. Satanaya offered to arrange the meal, and the soldiers, none of whom were in fact cooks, shyly let her take command of the mess arrangements.

She knew what she would cook without having to think about it. The birds were quickly dispatched, plucked, singed and drawn, and then jointed into eight or ten pieces. With a generous slosh of olive oil heated in her *kazan*, she tossed some roughly chopped onions and let them sizzle away, stirring regularly with that trusty wooden spoon. Smearing the chicken in a mix of tomato paste and hot pepper paste with a good dash of cummin, she seared these with the onions before pouring in a good pint of the rich local wine, and some water to cover. Into the pot went sliced carrots and leeks. After simmering this for half an hour she added potatoes and a bouquet of fresh thyme that she had gathered en route. She tasted the liquid, seasoned it with some salt and a little sugar, and left the stew to bubble away gently in the *kazan*, as the high peaks to the north turned rosy in the reflected glow of dusk.

After performing the sunset prayers, the troop all tucked into a solid hors d'oevres of local white cheese, olives and bread, and with Anwar's blessing, the demijohns of wine did the rounds.

---

* Recent studies designate both the Taurus Mountains and the Caucasus to be the origins of wine production.

Dinner was roundly applauded. The poor young soldiers hadn't eaten so well since parting from the bosoms of their families. They wiped out their bowls with bread, and the bones, gnawed clean, were put on to boil for a breakfast soup. Anwar and Satanaya sat close in the half-darkness, bathing in the warmth of the fire, the wine, and their own growing intimacy. The wine ran out as the inebriation of the troops reached the point of good-hearted companionship, without overflowing into the excesses of tomfoolery and argument. And the sergeant, who was a sympathetic concierge in all matters of food and wine and what might slip betwixt, gave the order to retire. There were few lights to extinguish, but the glow of the open hearth illumined the camp sufficient for the men to negotiate their happy path to slumber.

Not so Anwar and Satanaya, who remained by the fireside until the ring of tents rang with the snores of sleeping soldiers. Guards had been stationed far off on the landward side of the camp, and they too were soon snoozing in the vinous embrace of their bivouac beneath their cape of stars.

There was no need to speak. Everything was understood already. Two people, unattached, attracted to each in the best ways. Love is no respecter of time. They both knew this was an affair out of time, just as the journey itself was taking place outwith the normal realm of their lives. Nothing was permanent here but the moment itself, and a single moment of love bears the imprint of its eternal nature. Anwar looked into Satanaya's eyes glistening in the firelight, pale and liquid like the Göksu, and beauty's own passion rose in him. Satanaya accepted Anwar's gaze as one receives that longed-for gift; the present, still unseen, yet already enjoyed in love's own yearning for what it wants so much. What followed was simply the natural climax, the nocturnal enactment of a union already blessed in the day. Again, beyond the eyes, came the sweet mingling of breath, the kiss and the kissing; and then Satanaya took Anwar by the hand and led him to the river's edge, where they kissed some more before entering her tent, and there unwrapped, they took full pleasure in each other's gifts.

Anwar slipped away before dawn, leaving her wrapped in the warmth of her thick *yorgun* (a present from her Yörük sisters) and in the lingering scent of her lover and the rapture his gift had brought. She rose for a bracing wash in the Göksu before reveille sounded and the rough voices of waking men announced the morning.

If there were knowing looks, or nods and winks, among the soldiers that day, they were well hidden from their commanding officer and his erstwhile consort. Perhaps they were just too shy, or had been a little too drunk, and now too hungover to have realised what was passing between our two lovers. Perhaps it was simply the solace of satisfaction all round, but the mood of the troop as it set out upon the road was particularly buoyant.

Mut is a market town some fifty miles north of Silifke. From here Anwar reported by telegraph to his superior officer in Constantinople the uneventful progress of his patrol. A huge gathering of Yörük was taking place on the outskirts of the town, and Satanaya was drawn to renew her aquaintance with these independent nomads who so reminded her of her own roots. A fair was taking place. In spite of such alliances being in most cases a foregone conclusion, potential brides were being paraded by their female relations; and would-be zeybeks, the young men they call the *kızan*, in tall boots, head scarves and bright waist sashes were trying to impress the girls with their haughty moves and swagger, brandishing pistols and vicious-looking yataghans, as they danced boldly in little circles.

Everywhere the handiwork of the nomads was on display: banded kilim sacks, *'çuval'*, woven in subtle bands of pastil earth colours, embroidered *'cicim'* rugs, ornate saddlebags; and hefty shepherds cloaks of thick white felt, so stiff they serve as a vertical tent, a sheltering cave for the lone herder upon a rain-swept steppe.

Back at camp dinner that night was half a sheep donated by a close relative of Ali Efe to Satanaya and her militia escort after hearing the story of her journey. She was doing her bit for Anwar's mission to keep the peace among the mountain people, and her stock rose further in the eyes of the troops. She stewed the mutton with onions, carrots, tomatoes and local apricots, seasoned with cinnamon and a little paprika, served with green beans and *iç pilav* – rice, chopped liver and currants, with a hint of cinnamon and cooked in the fat of the fat-tailed sheep. And she didn't forget the demijohns of Mut's finest vintage, after which the troops sang a few mournful songs of heroism and death before trooping off to bed, leaving Anwar and Satanaya to enjoy the night alone.

After Mut, the little troop climbed further through a wide corridor of mountains of white stone. Like venerable hermits withdrawn to the heights, ancient cypresses and pines with thick stunted trunks, gnarled and black, stood sentinel over the valleys. Caves pockmarked the rockface all around, remnants of the time when Christians fled persecution to these high places, now left to wolves, bears and wild goats.

The journey continued in this fashion, the days riding under crystal clear skies with few sounds other than the footfall of the horses, the chatter of small birds among the rocks and the gentle rush of water whenever the way led close to the river. The soldiers included among their number some wily sharpshooters, hunters who one day brought in a dozen brace of pigeon, which Satanaya prepared as she had in Nablus, spit roasted with *firik*. And another time it was venison, cooked slowly with wild mushrooms. The evenings resounded with campfire songs after the consumption of the inevitable demijohns of red wine. The great Anatolia steppe unfolded in seemingly endless high pastures, the *'yayla'* where the Yörük brought their flocks in summer. The air was becoming cooler, the mornings crisp, but nights shared doubled the lovers' warmth.

THIRTY-NINE

Threading Mountain Passes of the Heart

Taurus Mountains, Southern Anatolia, 1908

ISTORY IS SUCH a strange thing,' said Anwar, almost to himself, as they approached a bridge across the Göksu. They had entered the Sertavul Pass, which rises to nearly five and a half thousand feet, the route through the mountains between Mut and Karaman.

'What do you mean?' said Satanaya. The two were riding side by side as they had done since the first day.

'Well, I was thinking. If one man hadn't decided to cross the river here through the water, instead of taking the bridge, we might never have met.'

'Go on?' said Satanaya, sensing a history lesson in the offing.

'Well, there was this King, Frederick Barbarossa of Germany. He was bringing a huge army down through Turkey. At the time Byzantine Christian Emperors ruled Constantinople, while Turks held much of the hinterland of Anatolia. King Barbarossa had hacked his way round Europe, more or less uniting the German states in the process, and had got himself crowned by the Pope as Holy Roman Emperor. Now he raised a Crusade of tens of thousands of Germans and hacked on down through Konya, en route to join King Richard the Lionheart and Phillip of France in taking back Jerusalem for the Christians. So, he's managed to get this far, and because the bridge is so crowded with all his troops crossing, he decides to ride his horse through the water. You can imagine him, impatient to get to the Holy Land and do his bit against Saladin and the Moslem army.'

Anwar pointed down to the rushing stream below the bridge.

'Look how strong the current is here. Barbarossa's horse was swept away beneath him. He was wearing armour but there was no way he could fight the current. He drowned, and his army just went into shock. The Turks attacked and the German army completely went to pieces. Only a handful from the original army reached Palestine. The Third Crusade failed. And Jerusalem remains in Muslim hands to this day.'

'So, when exactly did this happen?' asked Satanaya.

'About seven hundred years ago.'

'And you're telling me that in seven hundred years things couldn't arrange themselves so that we would meet – maybe somewhere else, maybe with different names, different parents, who knows? I think where love is concerned, there are no real borders, in time or in place. But that's just an opinion.'

'Yes, but don't you see how extraordinary it is, that one man's decision – we could call it his impatience, a mistake even – determined a series of events that resulted in the whole world changing.'

'But the world is always changing. If it wasn't this it would be that. You could say that all that happened, happened so we could be here together at this moment. I think that's just as significant.'

'So, are you saying that the Crusade was lost so that you and I could be here together? That the necessity of our meeting caused Barbarossa's death?'

Satanaya smiled, 'But isn't that just what you said to start with? If

Freddy hadn't gone into the water, we might never have met?'

'Yes, but…' Then Anwar saw the loop, and laughed.

'The point is, surely, that we meet, whatever else happens. Either way, love is its own cause.' said Satanaya.

As they continued climbing the steep rocky track up the pass, Satanaya broached a subject that had been nagging her ever since she had begun travelling with Anwar.

'Did you ever come across a certain staff officer, a Captain Mustafa.'

Here Satanaya described the stern young officer with the steely blue eyes and the intense look whom she had first come across some years before in a restaurant in Damascus and who later had visited the Beyt with his jovial companion Ali.

'Do you mean Staff Captain Mustafa from Salonica?' said Anwar

'Yes, I suppose so. Is there another?'

'No, not like the one you describe. He's one of a kind. Yes, I've seen him a couple of times. He's real soldier's soldier.'

'How do you mean?'

'You've got to understand, being in the army – the Imperial Ottoman Army – well, it's not easy. The way the Empire is going, you have to be pretty devoted to stay true to your vocation. The pay, if and when it comes, is lousy. The conditions often worse than basic. And I'm just talking as an officer. For the ranks it's far worse. And of course there's always the risk of getting killed or wounded – I guess that sort of comes with the territory, being a soldier and all that. It's easy for me, I have my family's wealth and influence to fall back on, and as long as I keep my head down, I'll get promoted in due course. These days there's a lot of discontent, which leads inevitably to corruption. But Mustafa, he's quite above all that.'

'Tell me how?'

'Well, when he was at Staff College, he did get into trouble. There was always a lot of talk, revolutionary talk. Unhappiness with the way the army is run by old soldiers who have no idea of modern warfare. And this often led to political discussions, you know, just among ourselves, how we would like to see the country run if we had a hand in it. Mostly it was just sounding off against authority. But for Mustafa and some others, apparently, it went further. After he graduated, he joined a group which met in secret for political discussions. There was an informer, and Mustafa and his friends were arrested. He spent a couple of months in prison, but some high ranking officers in the College were sympathetic to his way of thinking, and looked out for him, so he got away with being banished for a couple of years to Damascus.'

'That's where I saw him – he came into Domenico's restaurant in civilian clothes. And again at the Beyt, later on. Then he really didn't look happy.' said Satanaya.

'He certainly wasn't happy with the way the army was behaving there. In fact in Syria he got quite a reputation for himself, not accepting bribes, settling disputes justly between the Druzes and the Circassians, as well as arguing with his superiors. But this exile didn't stop him. He managed to set up a secret society with like-minded young officers throughout Palestine and Syria. He even travelled incognito back to Salonica where the real revolutionary action was happening. And he got back to Palestine without the authorities catching on. He even started a magazine.'

'So, he was a kind of Scarlet Pimpernel!' Satanaya had read the recently published fiction of the English baronet's exploits in revolutionary France, and was excited by the vision of Mustafa the handsome hero slipping unnoticed across borders, secret meetings, distributing revolutionary manifestos, and returning nonchalantly to drink raki with his superiors.

'Perhaps,' said Anwar, 'but he was unlikely to rescue the aristocracy. Nor did he leave flowers as a calling card.'

'So, is he one of these 'Young Turks' we keep hearing about? Does he want to bring down the Sultan?'

'He keeps his cards close to his chest. If you ask me, at present he's more intent on a successful military career. Yes, he's concerned about the state of the empire, and he's a member of the movement they call the Committee, but he doesn't get on with many of the leaders. Mustafa has little time for Major Enver, or that Talaat, the Committee's hard man. And the leaders are quite jealous of their positions and are using their influence to keep him away from the centre of power.'

'And do they have power? Is there really going to be a revolution?' Satanaya was fascinated to hear of these goings on in the corridors of power.

'Oh, Satanaya, you ask so many questions. You really will get me into trouble. Let's just enjoy life as it presents itself, here in the moment. Look around you. Have you anything to complain about? Come on, I'll race you.'

Anwar spurred on his mount, but Tarçin was already moving, and easily carried the lighter Satanaya ahead of the soldier. Five hundred yards later they reached a saddle between two hills where they reined in their mounts and waited for the platoon to catch up.

'So what's the difference between Mustafa, and someone like Enver?' Satanaya wanted to hear more about this other Captain.

'Between you and me, it's a matter of destiny. Who has the destiny. Enver obviously is going places, but it seems personal, as if he's intent on personal glory. He's a romantic. Intelligent, yes, and brave. But perhaps foolhardy too. And very ambitious.'

'And Mustafa? Isn't he ambitious? Does he have destiny?'

'I don't know, really, I don't.' said Anwar. 'I've met him a few times, and he talks well. For him it's all about the country, the *'vatan'* – you know, homeland, fatherland. He's a true patriot. Is he brave? I'm sure he's not a coward, but he's not foolhardy either. He's quite calculating. More a wolf than a fox. But definitely a leader. I don't think he considers his own position so much as his aim, which is to serve the *'vatan'*. He would measure his success by the success of his country. If that's his destiny, then, yes, he has a destiny, but it's not personal.'

'The Mustafa I saw in Beirut' said Satanaya, 'looked like a man whose destiny was thwarted. He looked frustrated, impatient. He didn't seem to have much in the way of 'joie de vivre'.'

'That was probably the result of his being kept away from the action. At the moment he's a lone wolf. He needs to be leader of the pack, but at present there's no vacancy. He did get his promotion eventually and his desired posting. To Salonica, where things are beginning to happen.'

'We heard about the unrest there and in the capital – that people were demanding that the Sultan bring back the Constitution.'

'Yes, and the Sultan gave in to the Committee. They had the army in Macedonia behind them.'

'Was Mustafa involved?'

'Yes, but much in the background. Major Enver was the hero of the day, lapping up the cheers from the crowds.'

'And Mustafa?'

'Oh, his usual reaction – did the rounds of the bars, drank a lot of raki and sounded off among his army friends, which didn't endear him any with the Committee. He complained that the Committee hadn't any real political strategy. So they packed him off to the provinces, to Tripoli I think, to spread the good news of the Constitution.'

'So, exiled again.' said Satanaya.

'So it seems. But he's conscientious. He'll make good use of his time. We haven't seen the last of him.'

Satanaya pondered this last remark. Obviously Anwar had seen something in Mustafa too. She hoped he was right. Everything she heard now about Mustafa intrigued her, as it had since she had seen him through the kitchen door of Domenico's that night in Damascus. She knew she was attracted. But it was an attraction which she couldn't understand. There were difficulties. The danger she had sensed in her first encounter from a distance – was she worried for her own safety, her emotional comfort, or was it the depth of her awe in an unknown destiny? It was a strange, intellectual attraction, a being drawn towards something she felt she had to know – his energy, his very being, his intelligence, seemed to pull her into his aura, even without his physical presence. It was irresistable, yet seemed inevitable.

At the top of Sertavul Pass a brief flurry of snowflakes enveloped the travellers. The road descended and the sun returned, and a new vista unfolded before them: sunbaked fields of wheat stubble stretching away into the distance over the steppe; the bread basket, where humans have been cultivating crops for ten thousand years.

Their last night together was like the first. Neither Anwar nor Satanaya had expected anything of the other from this precious interlude; timeless, yet with a beginning and an end, beautiful, but as with all beauty, fleeting and fleeing, ever ungraspable. Perhaps that ungraspableness is its secret, the tantalising, the flight, to and from, that stirs up in the air of our being this strange draught we call love, a draught which like air itself, we can never hold to ourselves, but simply allow it to soak into us. They loved as equals, like rain to earth, and sea to sky, with just the mountain passes to conjugate their mass, and neither could say who was which to whom. Man, woman, above, below, all things relative one to another. And when the two vanishes at the moment of union, once becomes forever.

Satanaya left Anwar and his troop in Karaman. She had dreamt that night of her mother, who was introducing her to a venerable lady of evident nobility, saying to her daughter, 'And while we are in Karaman…' at which point she woke up.

The lovers made farewell love before dawn, sweetening with longing the bitterness of parting. The soldiers as a body cried tears of protestation at her leaving, for they too had partaken of this affair, vicariously, supping each night from the loving cup of Takla's *kazan*, and tasting in her stews that overflow of joy which stirred the hand of Satanaya.

FORTY

Mader-i-Mevlana

Karaman, Autumn 1908

HE MILITARY OUTPOST in Karaman was a simple compound abutting a ruined castle, which stood upon an
ancient hill or *'höyük'*. These mounds appear throughout
the Middle East evidencing the locations of agrarian settle-
ments from earliest times. Here a small garrison was based and here
Satanaya and Anwar parted.

She did not look back, but the scent of bergamot and lemon from their
final embrace followed her into the dusty streets of the old capital of the
Karaman Beys.* She knew not to dwell on the past, but briefly her heart

---

* The Karamanid dynasty – one of the Turkish principalities ruling central Anatolia from 13th
   to late 14th Century during the decline of the Seljukid Sultanate, eventually defeated by the rival
   Osmanli (Ottoman) Turks.

soared between blissful nostalgia and painful longing. It had been an affair out of time, but its sweetness remained as a comfort like warmth in stone after the sun has set. Now the weather was turning cold. It was November. Here the temperature at night can fall below minus twenty centigrade through into February, while the skies remain a deep and clear cobalt above the wide horizon of the steppe. Satanaya had donned the many layered garb of a Yörük woman in an effort not to attract unwarranted attention, but her pale tall figure seen alongside the nut-brown faces of the sturdy round women whom she passed in the streets marked her out as a stranger. Her nomad friends had recommended a suitable caravanserai where she stabled her horse and left her baggage while she explored Karaman.

The narrow lanes were lined with squat timber-framed houses of wattle and daub, for the most part coloured with the brown earth of the steppe, the drabness of the buildings mitigated by flourishing vegetable gardens, trees in turning leaf and vines still in fruit. Grander civic build-ings, medreses and mosques stood out in pale stone, the minarets banded with sharp splashes of turquoise tiles. The conical-roofed tomb of a Karaman Bey was crowned with the huge woven twig basket of a storks' nest. The owners had flown south long since, while tenant sparrows con-tinued to lodge in its lower spaces. Everywhere were little markets and street stalls. Satanaya bought a bunch of purple grapes and some creamy goat cheese to eat as she walked.

In an open square in the centre of the town a blind beggar sat on the ground outside an ancient medrese, playing on his battered *keman* – a small bowed string instrument like a violin. The melody was unfamiliar to Satanaya. It seemed to emerge directly from within the soul of the beggar himself, drifting to her as smoke from an unseen fire. The music was more akin to a voice than notes played on an instrument; a voice that spoke with the tongue of longing. Then, from the melody, the words arrived as he sang this plaintive song:

> *My mind is torn apart with this desire*
> *To know what's love and what is rapture's fire?*
> *It knows no longer what the greater marvel be:*
> *Severence from Him or union? Please tell me.*

> *In the sacred dance Love's minstrel sings:*

'Servanthood's a prison, lordship a burden brings.

'What's Love then but the ocean of non-being.
Wherein the intellect cannot be seen.
The servant and the lord are two known sides
in which in secret loverhood resides' *

As she listened to the words of the *kemancı*, Satanaya realised that something in her had changed. Even with the ghosts of sweet longing hovering seductively at the periphery of her mind, the brief sojourn with Anwar had left her feeling strangely free. Despite the depth of passion she had enjoyed with Khalil, some small fear had always inhibited her. Ever since it had remained like a brake, strong at first, and later as a simple holding back of her emotions, unnoticed in the general pleasure of life, but still strangely present.

She felt free of this now and had been able to love Anwar freely, and he had loved her in the same way. It wasn't simply the satisfying of a bodily passion, though what had passed between them was completed by the physical act. No, the union they had enjoyed hinted of something deeper, something as yet beyond her ken, as though she had been both spectator and participant in an event so wide, so beautiful... And then she remembered something Lady Gülbahar had said very early on – that the true lover loves beauty itself, not simply the beautiful form, for the form will always pass, leaving lovers pining for something that never existed, while the true lover is taken beyond herself to beauty, if beauty wills.

Satanaya knew this was something she would have to work on. But for now, the longing itself still carried the scent of that beauty, that unimaginable beauty which invested Anwar with its own subtle lights during that week, just for her. And even here she found herself pulled up short in her thinking. For her? For whom? Wasn't she too, for Anwar, also a beautiful thing, where the escapable fact of beauty had been glimpsed... by beauty itself?

The wind blew across the square, hurrying along the fallen leaves of the plane trees. The wind continued and the leaves could not follow, but fell into corners, caught in the edges of buildings. The wind continued up and over the domes of the mosque and medrese opposite, over the hammam

---

* Rumi, Mathnawi III 4717 – 4724, adapted.

and the roofs of the town, unseen towards the mountains. And thence, who knows? Perhaps it returns whence it came, to non-existence. Perhaps that too is where the notes of all the violins and flutes and drums, played upon the hands of beggars and heard by tramps and pilgrims, then return.

She dropped a coin in the beggar's bowl. He stopped playing and thanked her. Then he pointed across the square. The sign on the hammam said 'Ladies Day'. Even without the beggar's prompting Satanaya knew this sign was for her. After two weeks of tramping, despite brisk morning ablutions in the Göksu, and liberal splashings of Anwar's cologne, she was in dire need of the deep cleansing of the steam bath.

The hammam was the best tonic for a vagabond girl lost in love. She entered the stone portals, beneath the calligraphic motto declaring, '*Sıhattler Olsun*', 'Let There be Health'. She disrobed in a cubicle, wrapped herself in a towel and joined the throng of female bodies in the steam; bodies of all shapes and sizes, ages and shades, but predominantly middle-aged and bountifully overflowing in fleshy proof of the hearty Anatolian diet of lamb fat and cereals. And aside from the lady hammam attendants, all were completely naked. Any initial shyness Satanaya may have felt disappeared in the general bonhommie, or perhaps *bonnefemmie*, of the jolly company and welcoming blandishments to remove her towel as they admired her ivory skin and deep black hair and cheerfully demanded her to tell her story. Once they discovered she was a cook, acceptance became total, for there is no subject more guaranteed to provoke lively conversation among a gathering of central Anatolian womenfolk than that of the preparation of food. As the talk turned on the merits of cooking in the fat of the fat-tailed sheep as opposed to butter, and the need to deal with the sharp hairs on bamya – ladies fingers – by first singeing, then rubbing them in the palms of the hands before cooking in water with lemon juice to prevent their becoming slimy, and progressed to a description of a mysterious cure for kidney stones involving lemon juice and a small calcification extracted from the kofana fish of the Marmara Sea, all the while the naked sisterhood of the order of the bath of Karaman turned around Satanaya, stroking her hair, pinching her gently, complimenting her on her height, the alabaster glow of her skin and commenting that although her breasts were really quite small, in relation to their own great chests of motherhood, they were sure to fill out once children came. And where were the children? Was she married?

'No ring, of course not.' said one.

'But engaged?' asked another.

'He is in Constantinople, where I must go eventually.'

'Of course. And now?'

'to Konya, to Mevlana, the Master Jelaluddin Rumi.'

'Ah! then first you are going to visit Mader-i-Mevlana, yes? To ask for children, yes?'

'Mader-i-Mevlana?'

'Yes, Mevlana's mother, her tomb, here in Karaman. Right outside this hammam in the Ak Tekke Mosque.'

And then it dawned, why she had been drawn to Karaman: the dream of her mother. First the mother, then the son. A Christic arrangement. Not surprising, the whole area of central Anatolia had been populated by early Christians, Greeks and Armenians, through the Byzantine period, and in spite of seven hundred years of dominance by the Ottoman caliphs, a strong presence persisted. Under the Beys of Karaman, Greek was still spoken so widely here – Rumi himself wrote poems in Greek – that an order was given in 1277, only four years after Rumi's death, decreeing that in all dealings, public or private, people must speak Turkish.

'So tell me about this mother of Rumi.'

The circle turned to look at a small lady who was sitting quietly at the edge of the group.

'Shehzade, come and tell our guest about Mevlana's mother.' said one of the women, and to Satanaya. 'Shehzade's Persian, and her father is a Sheykh.'

It was obvious the Persian lady was held in some esteem by the gathering who now fell silent.

'Mevlana was born far in the east, north of Afghanistan, almost as far away as China.' Shehzade began. 'His father was Bahaeddin Veled, a great scholar and *sufi*, and his mother was a princess, the daughter of the governor of Balkh, the Emir Rükneddin. Her name was Mu'mina Hatun, the Lady Mu'mina. One day Bahaeddin received a strong intuition to leave Balkh with his family and travel west, to escape from the danger of the Mongol hordes who were spreading south. So Mu'mina gathered her children – Jelaluddin was only seven years old at the time – and organised the family into a caravan with many of their relatives and off they set. They travelled for years. First they went across Persia, then down into Arabia. Here, like Abraham and those who came after him, they circumambulated the black stone in the cube house at Mecca. They continued travelling, into Anatolia and eventually arrived in Karaman. The Karaman Bey invited the family to stay, on account of Bahaeddin's reputation as a preacher, and he had a medrese built here, for him, Lady Mu'mina and their family. By now her son Jelaluddin was fifteen years old.

'But Lady Mu'mina was exhausted. She had given birth so many times, she had been uprooted from her own family and had been forced to abandon her nice home in Balkh, then dragged half across Asia by her husband, with the Mongols on their heels. Two years after arriving in Karaman, she died. She is buried just across the way, in the Ak Tekke Mosque.'

Shehzade paused and gestured to the assembled women. 'We all have a mother and are mothers ourselves,' she said, 'but here in Karaman, we are also the children of Mu'mina Hatun. She looks after us all.'

Shehzade then addressed Satanaya: 'You'll see. Go and make *'ziyaret'* and pray for her protection and *himmah* – spiritual love and blessing – for your journey, she'll look after you too. After all, her son is Mevlana, and he is a friend of the Friend. It's always good to have friends in high places.'

Satanaya remembered Lady Gülbahar's dream, and her words *'I'm going to visit a friend of the friend.'* The story was over and the Persian lady sat back. Satanaya looked with amazement at the faces that surrounded her, spellbound and naked as babies.

Although Satanaya had already washed, now came the turn of the masseuse, Jalila, a tall Kurdish woman with not an ounce of fat to show on her muscular body. Without a word Jalila lay Satanaya upon a marble slab covered with a rough cloth. Taking a coarse hempen glove she started by scrubbing Satanaya from head to foot, removing all the layers of dead skin, and rinsed her at one of the stone basins lining the wall of the hot room. Back on the slab Jalila turned the raw-skinned Satanaya on her back. Lathering up a large bag of the finest, softest cloth, the attendant washed her ever so gently, all over again. The cloth bag billowed and ballooned in soapy bubbles as it glided like silk across her body, giving her the sensation of floating in great sudsy waves of warm milk. Wet and warm from the tips of her toes, Satanaya gave herself up to this luxurious ablution, and wondered, 'Is this what it feels like inside the womb?'

Then began the massage proper. The silent Jalila's strong fingers pressed deep into the now relaxed muscles of Satanaya's calves and thighs, kneading gently, firmly; 'like a lump of soft risen dough' she thought as the lady went to work on her tummy. After reducing Satanaya's neck, shoulders and back into pleasurable submission, Jalila rinsed her again and left her to dry herself in the cubicle. After she had rested awhile Satanaya came back into the 'warm room' where the Anatolian ladies now gathered, wrapped head to food in cotton towels, drinking tea and ayran, nibbling biscuits and chatting away nineteen to the dozen.

Satanaya sat next to Shehzade, and found herself relating her dream of Lady Gülbahar visiting the friend of the friend, and what Moses Shadinyan had said, about Rumi being *hakk dost* – the friend of God.

Shehzade's eyes lit up. 'Where are you staying in Karaman?'

'In the caravanserai.'

'No, not in that dreadful place! Really, it's full of fleas. You will stay tonight with me, and when you get to Konya, you will stay with my sister Shireen.'

Later, as Satanaya left the hammam with Shezade she noticed the calligraphy above the doorway: *'Nasipse gelir, Bağdat'tan Yemen'den; Nasip değilse ne gelir elden'* – 'If it is your allotted portion, it will come to you, whether or not it comes from Bagdad or Yemen'.

She remembered Frederick Barbarossa, and wondered about her own destiny. From what quarter would she find her portion? Perhaps it was already there, in every step she took, she just had to be confident that in this process everything arrives at the allotted time. One foot after the other, and so the destination is reached. Impatience might appear to interrupt things, like Barbarossa, who it seems mislaid his portion in the anxious waters of the Göksu River, and never looked over Jordan. Or was it simply his allotted span?

a mother to a son
a son to a mother
sweet scents pass
between worlds
not so far apart

The fact is, Mu'mina Hatun, the Mother of Mevlana, does indeed look after Karaman. To this day, it is virtually without crime. The policemen patrol the town, with little to do but direct pedestrians across the street, even when vehicles are absent, so they amuse themselves by drinking tea with visiting travellers. They claim they would rather be in Smyrna or Constantinople, with criminals to chase. But would they?

Together with Shehzade, Satanaya made her visit to the tomb of Mader-i-Mevlana, and was welcomed like a daughter. She thought about Mevlana, losing his mother at such an early age. The loss of one's mother, it is said, is the greatest of losses, for there is no one to whom a person owes a greater debt, nor one more loved in her essence, than she through whose agency one is borne into this world. For in the moment of conception comes a shaft of the divine, whether one knows it or not. How can one console the person who loses their mother, other than by the extending hand of that same mercy, the *rahma* that invests with life the *rahim* of the womb. Although Satanaya had not yet lost her mother to the next world, yet she was lost to her now in her travels. Here, in the great hall of tombs where lay the remains of Rumi's mother, alongside his elder brother and other companions who had journeyed so long and hard to deliver into Anatolia the great mystical poet-in-waiting, the young Rumi, here Satanaya felt the mother's hand of mercy passing her on to her son.

FORTY-ONE

From Yayla to Yayla Soup

Konya, 1908

WISE MAN came to Konya from a foreign land, bringing many companions.

Someone asked: 'You must love Rumi very much, to come from so far away.'

'Ah, no, it is not as you think,' he replied, 'Please understand. I love what Rumi loves. And what Rumi loves, loves him.'

As Satanaya left Karaman, passing the military compound by the castle ruins she felt a little sad. A cloud covered the sun. The air was chill. Pulled between past and future, between known and unknown, with a nervousness rising in her throat, and from below the deep umbilical tug of longing for home, she knew she must find her centre – a home within herself independent of external circumstance. She yearned to discover in herself that same sense of completeness that love gave her, wherever she found herself. 'It is strange,' she thought, 'how in the distances of my journey, I find myself always longing for closeness.'

On the road again, beyond the plateau of Karaman, the great plain of Konya stretched northwards; the green sproutings of winter wheat were beginning to show. Below the dark mountain Karadağ looming to the west, distant shepherds in felt cloaks grazed their flocks of sandy-fleeced sheep upon fields of stubble while their huge Kangal dogs dozed nearby in the sun. She was three days travelling from Karaman, in a caravan of Yörük traders bringing rugs and food produce to sell in Konya. As they drew near the city, more and more land was under cultivation; little market gardens surrounded villages with generous shady trees, golden leaves glinting sharp as metal in the winter sunlight. While men guided ploughs behind horses tilling the rich soil, bundles of women bent low in rows along the furrowed earth, planting onions, cutting cabbages, lifting turnips. Everyone busy with the land. The harvest was in, sheaves standing in stooks or gathered and lying on the hard earth of the threshing floor; everywhere golden grain heaped in piles as the storehouses filled up for winter, and at the mill the graunching of stone on stone as grain was ground to flour. Woodsmoke drifting in the dusk above the houses carrying the smell of baking bread from domed clay ovens as it had done for ten thousand years in this great manger of humanity. The caravan entered Konya as night came on. The temperature dropped and snow began to fall, lightly but persistently, until within an hour the whole city lay beneath a coverlet of white. Then the clouds drifted away unveiling the risen moon steely and full.

Shehzade's younger sibling was not a quiet retiring lady like her elder sister. Even the Yörük women with whom Satanaya travelled from Karaman knew Shireen Hanoum, for she regularly shopped in the Konya market, tasting their cheeses carefully before buying. She had a good eye for fine weaving, they said. She knew quality and when she saw something she liked, she haggled enthusiastically, but not meanly.

Shehzade had provided Satanaya with her sister's address and a note of introduction. Shireen Hanoum was well known in the town, and Satanaya had no trouble finding her house. It was in a lane behind the main street which runs between the ancient Alaettin Mosque and the Mevlevihane, the *tekke* – the dervish convent – which houses the tomb of Mevlana Rumi.

She ascended the steps of the covered porch, knocked, then stepped back into the street and called out a greeting. Shortly afterwards the door opened and a woman appeared bearing a lamp. Satanaya held out the note.

'Hello, I'm Satanaya. Your sister Shezhade in Karaman said I should call on you. She said you would help me find accommodation.'

'Ah Satanaya! Yes, we've been expecting you. She also sent a message by telegraph. How is my big sister?'

'Oh, she's fine and sends her greetings.'

Shireen took the note and smiled. Then noticing Tarçin, she called out: 'Hasan, Hasan!' This was not to anyone in particular, but within a few seconds a small man stumbled out from the house next door, holding a lamp in one hand while struggling to wrap a cloak over his shoulders with the other.

'Hasan, please would you stable the young lady's horse and bring in her bags.' Then to Satanaya, 'Come dear, let's get you inside out of this weather.'

Unlike the simple cob and thatch dwellings in the surrounding area, Shireen Hanoum's house was a substantial wooden building, a *konak*, with a tiled roof and fretted woodwork framing the windows and porch. The door from the street led into a large hallway with a staircase opposite, and rooms opening off to left and right. Beyond, further doors led onto a yard which the konak surrounded on three sides. As they changed into house slippers, Satanaya could just make out through the far windows Hasan enter the yard with Tarçin. Her luggage appeared in the hall shortly afterwards.

'First your room, and then we can talk over supper.' said Shireen and led the way up the wide wooden staircase. At the end of a long corridor she opened the door onto a small room with a low divan bed against one wall. 'It's a pretty room,' thought Satanaya. The pale plastered walls were decorated with murals, and the ceiling of painted wood was laid out in a geometric pattern.

Satanaya opened the window and gazed out through the *kafes* upon the roofs of the city, with its minarets and cupolas and conical domes of the Seljuk mausoleums – '*kumbets*' – poking above the humble flat-topped dwellings, now transformed from their muddy dun colour to a glowing sheet of silver in the frozen moonlight. There, barely a hundred yards distant, rising in a mantle of turquoise green tiles now flecked in snowy ermine rose the conical and fluted drum which she had seen in her dream.

Shireen pointed: 'That is where Mevlana is.' she said, 'Well, his tomb at least. There is a poem above the entrance which says: "Do not look for our graves in the earth, for we are buried in the hearts of the wise."'

Satanaya was stunned. These were the very words she had seen in her dream, above the portal through which Lady Gülbahar disappeared. Here was further confirmation of the dream's veracity.

'Don't worry,' said Shireen, 'we still visit saints' tombs to honour the covenant of help that they represent. Their tombs are like doorways between worlds, where by common agreement their presences are concentrated. It is a matter of tact, '*edep*'. We knock on the door and ask for help. Now, let's close the window so we don't let all the warmth out.'

Downstairs a low table had been set for two. A servant dressed in the baggy *şalvar* trousers, shawl and headscarf of the village women brought a soup tureen and a platter of fresh bread.

'Ah, Nevin *teyze* *, please meet our guest Satanaya. Now what have we here?'

Shireen lifted the lid of the tureen and a puff of steam wafted the sweet dark scent of dried mint into the room. She leaned into the steam and sniffed appreciatively.

'Ah, *yayla çorbası*.' she said, 'just the thing for such a snowy night!' and began to ladle out the tangy soup which is a true comfort food of the Anatolian steppe, made from meat stock, yogurt, and mint, thickened with flour, butter and eggs.†

All the while, Satanaya had been mostly silent, intrigued by the way she had been received, as though expected, as though she was part of the family. She wanted to ask so many questions, but felt a little in awe of this evidently capable lady of the house.

---

* literally 'auntie' - a familiar but respectful address to an older woman.
† see Appendix I, Recipes.

It was as if Shireen read her thoughts:

'Now don't be surprised, my dear. Of course we knew you were coming, even before Shehzade's note. Or, at least we were half-expecting you. My brother-in-law (yes, we have another sister, Shahnaz) is related to a mutual aquaintance – Mr Moses Shadinyan. So we knew you were on your way. It was so clever of you to drop in on Karaman, as that gave us a little time to prepare for your arrival. Now drink up your soup before it gets cold, there's more to follow.'

Satanaya went to bed that night, replete with soup, pilaf and halva, and the gratitude of the wayfarer who after much strenuous effort and hard travelling knows she has arrived at a safe haven and no mere transit point. Konya was, she knew, a major way station on her journey which as yet had no fixed destination. In fact, so far most of the places on her travels had been beginnings, not endings. Konya was certainly a new beginning, of that she was certain, but was it a stopping place? What would unfold for her here must surely clarify in some way the misty questions that prompted her setting forth. Time would tell, but now she was too tired to worry. As she sank into the comfortable mattress and the soft feather pillows, marvelling at the connection between Shireen and Moses Shadinyan, sleep overtook her in mid-thought.

FORTY-TWO

Ziyaret – Visiting the Saints

Konya, Central Anatolia, December 1908

ATANAYA WOKE EARLY beneath the thick quilt and lay for ages in the dark silence, listening for sounds that the household was up and about. She was happy to enjoy the warmth and delay the inevitable stepping out into the bracing cold of morning and a whole new world. Eventually she pushed back the bedding, crossed the rug-covered boards to the window and looked out. All was still. Not a breath of wind stirred the frozen branches of the trees, bejewelled with hoar frost. Barely a sound carried through the hushed blanket of white. Woodsmoke draped the town in a diaphonous cloud as the fires' uplifting draught cooled. The weather had kept most people indoors later than usual. The sunlight shone with an intense brightness on the turquoise tiles of the Mevlevihane, but as yet gave little heat to the sky, which was a rich azure at the horizon, deepening to lapis blue overhead.

Satanaya rose and had a good scrub in the konak's small hammam, washing away the dust of the road, in preparation for the *ziyaret* – the visits to the saints' tombs – which they would make that day.*

Many pilgrims visiting the saints of Konya are drawn first to visit the tomb of Mevlana Rumi, reckoning that due to his eminence this *ziyaret* takes precedence. And Satanaya also had assumed that they would first visit Rumi. But Shireen explained over breakfast that there was a particular protocol to be followed, recognising the heritage which Rumi represented.

'*Ziyaret* is more than a simple act of pious veneration at the tomb of a master or saint,' she said. 'Rumi did not appear willy-nilly here in Anatolia, write his wonderful poems, dance his dervish spin and leave us floundering. Although from a certain perspective that's how it looks: a whirlwind out of Asia, setting the world on fire with love. But – and this is important to understand – Rumi is also part of a process in the world, a process that goes back as far as humans, and I mean the intelligent species we call Man, inhabited this earth.

'We read Rumi's poems and gain enormous benefit in our quest to know ourselves. There is great mercy in this, and his words lift our spirits. Hearts lighten and our minds may open a little. Like us, Rumi travelled this human path, but his poems arrive on the shoulders of a great education. Therefore, before we visit Rumi, we honour this heritage by first visiting two people who, after his parents, had the greatest impact in his life and work: two pre-eminent mystics, true transmitters of the wisdoms which are humanity's true inheritance.

'The first of these was Sadruddin Konevi, a contemporary of Rumi. Sadruddin was the disciple and chief transmitter of the works of his step-

---

* *Ziyaret* is the seeker's way of acknowledging those who have trod the path before them, who through perseverance and grace have arrived at the goal of self-knowledge and perfection of soul; who have reached union with the origin, which, according to inclination, is named Spirit or God, Beauty, Love, the Absolute One, or simply the unnameble mystery. These completed people, having conquered death, are considered a source of help and guidance to us poor veiled ones, rambling and stumbling along the road of life. And, on account of their closeness to truth, they are greeted with respect and humility.

father, Muhyiddin Ibn 'Arabi, the great spiritual master from Andalusia
who is buried in Damascus. Sadruddin became Rumi's teacher, though
some dispute this out of a kind of misplaced jealousy, wanting to put one
superior to the other. In their manner these two, Rumi and Sadruddin,
appeared to be polar opposites, perhaps the result of their roles: the one
being the emissary of love, the other representing Ibn 'Arabi's inheritance
of knowledge. But in their interiors we can be sure they were essentially in
agreement. Sadruddin dreamt one day that he was massaging Rumi's feet.
Responding to Sadruddin's evident surprise, Rumi said to him, "Don't
worry, sometimes it is you massaging my feet, and at other times, I am
massaging yours. This is not strange where there is unity." So, in spite of
what some people say, it is likely that the wisdom flowed both ways.

'Then there is Shams of Tabriz. He entered Rumi's life like a comet,
burning up his world as he knew it. He was a mysterious wandering
dervish, a true quarryman, who with the steel of love cracked open the
great buried treasure in Rumi's heart which spilled forth the poems of his
famous Mathnawi and the Divans we read today.'

'But without this input of Ibn 'Arabi, who is called the Axis of Knowledge, could Rumi have become the Axis of Love? Taken together they
nourish and temper this bi-polar oscillation we call life, and move us with
it. We are all spinning tops, bumping along each on our individual axes,
reacting and interacting with everyone and everything. We fight, we love
and we learn. True stillness only comes when our centre meets the centre
of it all, when we begin to turn in the axis of existence itself. They call that
the beginning which has no end.'

Awaiting Shireen and Satanaya in the yard of the konak after breakfast was
a small horse-drawn cart, an 'araba', with Hasan at the reins and quilts for
their laps. They set off in the opposite direction from the Mevlevihane, up
the main avenue of Konya, around the hill of the ancient mosque of Alaettin and along the Meram road past the railway station. The compacted
snow crunched gently beneath the horse's hooves, muting the sound of the
araba's iron-rimmed wheels. The stillness of the morning persisted, its
winter coverlet investing the city with a silent wonder, transforming the
dusty hovels of mud walls and soot-stained stone to magical snow palaces
strung with diamonds and hung with pendants of pearly ice. On the way

Shireen explained further:

'We visit Sadruddin Konevi first of all. His father was a close friend of Ibn 'Arabi, and when he died, Ibn 'Arabi married Sadruddin's widowed mother. So Sadruddin came under the Sheykh's tutelage. Ibn 'Arabi was no easy task master but Sadruddin was a willing pupil. One night the boy was found asleep at his books. From then on, Sadruddin was made to study holding the end of a rope thrown over a beam, the other end tied to a stack of books above his head. If he nodded off, the books would fall on his head.'

Satanaya knew of Ibn 'Arabi from her father, who often quoted and commented on his book called *'Fusus al-Hikam'* – 'The Seals of Wisdom'. Sadruddin had written a famous commentary on this great mystical treatise.

'If we really want to understand Rumi in the best way,' said Shireen, 'you should first study Ibn 'Arabi. After all, if you want beautiful flowers, first you must plant your seeds in good soil, dig deep and water well.'

Sadruddin's grave was in the garden of the mosque in a street of humble adobe houses a little way out the city centre. The building was locked, so Shireen collected the key from the imam who lived nearby. Steps down led into the mosque and the adjoining garden-graveyard. It was over six hundred years since Sadruddin had passed away, and the site had sunk more than a metre below the surrounding street. A simple tomb, it was open to the sky within a colonnaded square enclosure of low marble walls of geometrically carved fretwork. Above, open arches supported a conical wooden frame in the traditional shape of the Seljuk stone *'kumbets'*. In the centre was a simple tomb with a single rose in bloom showing blood red above the snow.

Satanaya stood drinking in the atmosphere. The peace of the place gradually overpowered the usual chatter of her mind. Then something happened. What exactly, she had no idea, but as her thoughts fell away, and she surrendered to the stillness of the moment, something inside her, like a weight, or a cloud, a kind of binding of knots, something she had not even been aware of, untangled, lifted, and dissolved. And she was held awhile as if outside of time. She awoke to herself with a freshness that she had not felt since she didn't know when. She opened her eyes. Shireen was waiting in the street, talking with the imam.

'I think he likes you.' Shireen said, smiling, as they got back into the *araba*.

'What do you mean?'

'Just look at yourself. You are shining. It can have that effect.'

Satanaya didn't say anything. She knew something subtle had happened. There was no need to speak, so she just smiled.

Returning down the long avenue towards the Mevlevihane, Hasan turned the *araba* left into a side street and pulled up outside a small mosque which held the tomb of Shams of Tabriz.

'Shams of Tabriz was truly a singular person.' said Shireen, introducing this second great influence on Rumi. 'He appeared in Konya when Rumi was already well established as a preacher and teacher. Rumi was thirty-seven years old, and Shams was sixty. They say he was a wild looking dervish, who stole Rumi's heart, and broke it. But that is just a romantic tale. He may well have been unorthodox in his manner, and he certainly stole Rumi away. Rumi abandoned his teaching duties and they went into retreat together for weeks and weeks. After this Rumi had no time for anyone but Shams. His pupils were so jealous, they complained continually and after a couple of years drove Shams away. Rumi was distraught and sent his son to Syria to search for him and bring him back.

'Still the pupils couldn't understand the hold which Shams seemed to have over their master. In some ways it is still a mystery, but in fact it is quite simple. Something in this meeting with Shams awoke Rumi's heart, it didn't break it – that came later – but something in Shams opened Rumi to the divine passion in which the words of philosophy and rational explanation became inadequate, superfluous. They said Rumi threw all his books into the river, but perhaps this was just metaphorical. Of course, this new Rumi didn't fit in with the accepted manner of a respected scholar and doctor of religion. Rumi began listening to music. He began to dance. And in an ecstatic state he would recite divinely inspired poems. People didn't understand what was happening to their teacher. Again they drove Shams away and this time he didn't return. Some say his students murdered him, while others say he died in Iran much later. Whatever was the case, the result was the extraordinary outpouring of Rumi's Mathnawi, more than twenty-four thousand couplets speaking of the travails of love, of separation and of union, told on a cosmic scale but with a human voice full of compassion.'

'So, is Shams' body in this tomb, then?' asked Satanaya.

'I have absolutely no idea.' said Shireen, 'If we are to believe the stories, then probably not. But does it matter? In the world he inhabits, his presence has become universal. That this is his tomb is simply a matter of agreement. A place where we can focus our attention, and be heard. But remember that saying: look not in the graves in the earth, for we are buried in the hearts of the wise. The heart is the gateway to this other earth where all sorts of treasures are buried. If we want to approach Shams, we must first open the heart.'

They entered the mosque and before them in a kind of side chapel stood a huge sarcophagus. It was draped with a dark green silk coverlet embroidered in gold. At its head was placed a tall white felt cap wrapped in the broad folds of a large green turban. A group of ladies in black were sitting at the foot of the tomb, telling beads and sighing from time to time.

'Persians.' whispered Shireen, indicating the women with a slight roll of the eyes, 'We can be very emotional.'

They stood a while paying their respects in quiet receptivity. Satanaya was somewhat overwhelmed by the intensity of the atmosphere, the mutterings and sighs of the Persian women, the magnificent tomb shimmering in the candlelight. She wondered about this character who had blown in one day with the dust of Asia, and just as suddenly was gone. She felt her heart expanding like the sail of a small boat in an ocean disturbed by a strong wind, threatening to blow her away. She searched inside herself for something to cling to, and the image of her father came to mind. She held on to this as to a solid rock. The impending storm abated, but she had felt its power.

In the little park outside the mosque of Shams, under the plane trees all glittering pale yellow and brown in their cloaks of unshed leaves, Satanaya said to Shireen.

'Wow, he is so different. It's almost as if… well…'

'Well, what?'

'Almost as if he wasn't even human, more a kind of god.'

'Ah, you tasted of the might and majesty. Well, Shams is not a god. But then, he's not other than *the* God. God is all of this – Shams, you, me, all of it – and sometimes this 'God' chooses to show Itself in one particular colour in preference to another. What you witnessed is simply that It chose to show Itself to you in might and majesty. They say true beauty never manifests without majesty. Don't worry, you'll get used to it, God willing.'

They set off for the final visit.

Afterwards Satanaya tried to remember. What had begun at Sadruddin's tomb, and furthered at Shams', continued here. Now, as if her little body had been too small to contain her heart, she felt herself expanding, opening, to allow that heart to grow. Momentarily it seemed she had lost her will, or at least that by which she maintained control, of herself, of her movements, and to some extent of her mind. It wasn't that she lost her mind, or was under some kind of spell, but rather it was like when a swimmer who is caught in a strong current, takes the path of least resistance and lets the water carry her where it will.

It began at the gate, that gate in the wall which enclosed the many domed cells and rooms of the dervish house, the *tekke*, cloistered round the courtyard with the covered fountain, before the entrance to the Mevlevihane itself, the mausoleum with its turquoise-tiled dervish hat, the place in her dream where Lady Gülbahar went to meet the friend of the Friend. Then came the crowd of pilgrims: faces, people, in every conceivable hue and dress, this tide of human flotsam carrying her through into the white carpeted sanctuary of ancient tombs and abiding peace, the tombs of the companions who had accompanied Rumi and his family on their long journey from Khorasan, and the tombs of his children, and children of his children, the generations of sheykhs and *dedes*, until like a castaway reaching the safety of a welcoming shore, Satanaya grasped the silver grille in front of Rumi's tomb itself.

Satanaya stood before the magnificent catafalque, with its dark cover of silver threaded embroidery, at its foot the looming tombstone of his father, Bahaeddin, and alongside similarly bedded in peace, his son Sultan Waled. Behind rose a wall decorated with calligraphy, prayers incribed in gold on red, blue and green, beneath an arch painted with vines and trees and paradisical blooms framing a window paned in lozenges of lilac and turquoise glass.

Satanaya closed her eyes and prayed. Her prayer was beyond thought, beyond any normal critical faculty. She found herself simply in a state of pure request. She prayed with her whole being, knowing that her supplication was heard. And what came back to her was her own voice repeating lines a prayer which became circular as the rest of the words were cut off.

'Almighty God aside from whom there is nothing else, please teach me that the sole purpose of love is beauty...' and these last eleven words repeated again and again.

'Please teach me that the sole purpose of love is beauty...' became a rosary round which her whole being began to revolve, over and over and over. And in that undelineated time, in that space that was beyond measure, she knew that she was the object of a yearning so much greater than anything she had ever felt. And that yearning, that deep longing, came from somewhere so profoundly anchored in her own being that she felt it as a promise of... of what? Of something that would always be seeking her as she sought it. A promise of joy. She would happily have stood there forever.

The sound of metal clinking on metal eventually penetrated her hearing. She opened her eyes and looked up, the circle of her prayer broken. Across from her stood a young boy, his hands outstretched in supplication, and every pilgrim passing by was dropping coins into his hands. They exchanged a glance of recognition. A knowing smile – knowing what she couldn't say. Then the swirling current of pilgrims caught her up again and on she passed until she was cast up on the shore of her erstwhile host's breast as she collided gently into the arms of Shireen waiting outside.

FORTY-THREE

Shireen Hanoum and the Bad Sheykh

Konya, winter 1908/1909

ERTAINLY SATANAYA HAD been the subject of a wide variety of states, mental and emotional, of her own making, during her visits to Mevlana, Shams and Sadruddin. But there was something else, something she had not experienced before in such a strong way. It was as if a door had opened, a door into an unknown place in her own being. A big place. A vast place. She had tasted something of this vastness and wanted more. She felt certain that Konya held a key to this taste. So, not wishing to outstay the customary three days of hospitality afforded the traveller in the Middle East, at breakfast the following day Satanaya told Shireen that she hoped to stay in the city and was going to look for accomodation.

'That won't be necessary.' said Shireen, 'We have plenty of room here. After all, it seems you have made friends with the friends of the Friend, and their friends are my friends. In any case, I shall be needing all the help I can get in a few weeks as we prepare for the Rumi's Nuptial Night Celebrations in December.'*

Satanaya was thrilled. She had been made so welcome by Shireen ever since her first night in Konya, and now she was being invited to stay.

'Are you sure? Really? I don't quite know what to say. Thank you, that would be wonderful. I can help cook and clean, I'm quite used to hard work, you know, and entertaining – in Beirut we had endless weekend guests and parties.' said Satanaya.

'Then that's settled. And don't think it's all work. We love to waste time, too, you'll see.' said Shireen.

Over the coming days and weeks, Satanaya settled into the regular rhythm of life in Shireen's konak. The year was entering the darkest days of winter. Snow lay two feet deep upon the ground and daytime temperatures rarely rose above freezing. Excursions like their initial *ziyaret* were the exception.

Although Hasan and his sister Nevin were *de facto* Shireen's servants, they lived in their own little cottage next door bringing up their two much younger brothers, as well as looking after their widowed mother.

Nevin prepared the main meal each day, as well as doing the laundry. Hassan looked after the services of the konak, ordering the coal and firewood for the kitchen and hammam. The huge iron stove in the main hall was kept going night and day so the house was always warm. As well as his ostler duties – looking after Shireen's horse and cart – he also dealt with repairs and maintenance.

Satanaya was given no particular rôle, but in time, without realising it, she became fully involved in the routine of the house. The days found her laying the table for meals, preparing tea for the regular though never excessive number of visitors and occasional staying guests, and helping out in the kitchen. There was always something to be done in the kitchen, and she

---

* The night that Rumi died in 1273 AD is celebrated as his Nuptial Night – the night he entered union with his real beloved. It is commemorated on 17 December in the modern calendar.

was keen to discover the secrets of Anatolian cuisine from Nevin.

But in such a small household, there was plenty of time for other occupations. Shireen welcomed Satanaya's company, and lent a ready ear to her new companion's stories of Lebanon and Palestine, her adventures and misadventures. At the same time, Shireen took it upon herself to teach Satanaya Farsi, the language of the Persians, with Rumi's Mathnawi as her textbook.

Satanaya quickly developed an avid interest in all things to do with Rumi, and especially the Mevlevis, the dervish order formed following his death. These dervishes lived in the dervish house, the Mevlevihane, and elsewhere in Konya. In time throughout the Ottoman lands, from Damascus to Sarajevo, Mevlevi 'tekkes' sprang up – institutions where dervishes gathered to perform the sacred ceremony of the Sema – literally, 'listening'. In the Sema, the dervishes would turn round and round, revolving on one foot, repeating prayers, invoking the name of God; Satanaya knew a little of this from her father. She had also read accounts by European travellers describing such events. According to these outsiders, apparently writing from an 'objective' point of view, the dervishes would enter into a trance, vanishing from the constraints of the world around them in an ecstatic union with their spiritual beloved. Fantastic, she thought, but who was she to argue.

Nevertheless, Satanaya was fascinated by this, and it was difficult to avoid such imaginative conjectures regarding these dervishes. Every day in the streets of Konya she would come across strange characters in tall conical felt hats and long cloaks, with deep, otherwordly looks upon their faces, looks which never condescended to gaze upon the common herd; and their leaders, awesome looking sheykhs in felt hats turban-wrapped in green ribbons. There were other dervish types, she discovered over time; the Kalendars who dressed outlandishly in animal skins and carried calabashes and spears; Bektashis who were followers of the saint Haji Bektash, an early promoter of education for women, and whose adherents had been the mainstay of the Sultan's armies over the centuries; Qadiris, named for the great saint of Bagdhad, Abdul Qadir Gilani, with their magnificent ceremony of invocation or zikr, and Rifai dervishes, who pierce their stomachs with kebab spears which when pulled out leave no marks in the skin; many mysterious and mystical tribes with endless offshoots and branches. But the Mevlevis of Konya considered themselves as the aristocracy, an early descendant of Rumi having also married into the Ottoman royal family, and their hereditary title 'Chelebi' being synonymous with 'gentleman'. And it is the Head Sheykh of the Mevlevi order who at the investiture of every Ottoman sultan girds the candidate with the Sword of the Empire's founder, Osman.

The dervish orders had grown out of the chivalric brotherhoods formed during the early years of the spread of Islam. Yet, to Satanaya, it seemed such a male thing. All these men pointing the lances of their so important questing, striving to pierce the imagined membrane dividing known from the unknown, perhaps never realising that all that exists remains ever unknown, glimpsed in its moment of unveiling and then vanishing, revealing... nothing. Nothing but that *no thing*. It was that *no thing* that interested Satanaya; that repose that comes when the trying ceases; that vastness that remains after the vanishing. And where, she asked herself, in all this jostling of male spiritual rankings, were the women? After the experience of her visits to the tombs, and her readings of Rumi with Shireen, she began to wonder if she couldn't find herself a sheykh, a teacher who could put all this extraordinary dervish world into perspective, so that she too could take flight upon a spiritual path, and not merely traipse the road of her earthly female destiny randomly as it seemed she had been doing up until now. She needed to question Shireen on this matter.

Shireen herself was not an orthodox religious person. In fact, Satanaya often wondered if Shireen was even a muslim at all. She did not cover her face like so many Persian women, just wore a light shawl of white muslin over her luxurious dark locks, and wound loosely round her neck and shoulders. Satanaya wasn't even sure if Shireen performed the prescribed five prayers a day – she certainly didn't go to the mosque. She did however retreat to her room at least once a day, with the door closed. If the door was ajar, then Satanaya could disturb her, but not if it was closed. It was always closed first thing in the morning, but strangely not during the night. What went on in there intrigued her, but she knew it would be quite rude to ask. Perhaps she was only taking a nap.

Shireen was not married. She might have been in her forties. It was hard to tell. That she was not married Satanaya thought curious as she found her hostess to be quite beautiful. Not conventionally beautiful nor with sensual appeal, she just seemed to have been made with everything in the right proportion. She had the slender oval face and almond eyes one sees in miniature paintings from the books of Persian poetry, and her figure was as lissom and her bearing as upright as a cypress. Her manner modest and contained, she held herself quietly close as the branches of the cypress tree lie close to its trunk. Yet she was certainly not shy or retiring, for she spoke easily, and her delivery was deliberate and certain; even when questioning, her words were concise, as though she had already looked at the point in question from every possible angle, and now expected to see her suppositions confirmed or not. In this way she discovered other's secrets, by assuming, with a word here and a suggestion there, that something had happened and all she was doing was opening out the branches a little to see if anything was missing, to illuminate the blank spaces. Not for herself, but for the benefit of the person she was talking to.

One day, keeping themselves warm sitting by the big stove and peeling potatoes with a bowl between them, Satanaya plucked up the courage to ask Shireen about herself. She knew that her father was some sort of sheykh or equivalent, and that she had siblings and relations dotted about Anatolia and Persia.

'Did you ever want to get married, Shireen?' said Satanaya.

Shireen looked up and studied her companion very carefully. She put down her knife and the potato.

'Well now, there's a question. I wonder what you are really asking?'

'It's just that you seem so content, living here on your own. No children. I just wondered, you know. Were you ever in love?'

'Ah. So that's it. You want to know if it's possible to be happy without love. That's easy. Of course not. But then, there is love…and there is love. And again, there is love.'

Shireen looked down into the muddy potato water and smiled to herself.

'Yes, I was in love once. I was so deeply in love. It was more than just the boy. I was at that age – I'm sure you know – when the heart begins to open… I had become a pupil of this Sheykh, a very popular man who would hold sessions in his house with many students, both men and women. He was very eloquent, quite poetical and he would talk as though inspired by love itself; about divine love, spiritual love, human love. He had a very strong charisma that made you feel loved and inspired in his presence, so that you thought anything was possible. He played on his *rebab* and sang hymns – poems of Rumi and Hafiz which he set to music. He had a beautiful wife whom we all fell in love with. The whole atmosphere of his gatherings was quite giddy at times and we would come away as if floating on air. There was a boy in the group whom I couldn't help noticing. And he would return my glances, in a sweet, gentle way. One day he came and sat by me during one of the sheykh's sessions. We introduced ourselves, and of course, with such a strong sense of love in the air, and we being so young, is it any wonder that we fell in love? You know, it was so beautiful, forbidden of course, and we arranged to meet secretly. But we never did anything, we were quite chaste, as we believed very strongly in the rules of our society and religion. We had been brought up to exercise self-control over our passions, so it wasn't such a difficult thing. For me at least. And he was very well-behaved. We drank each other's love in the only way we knew, with shy words and deep looks into each other's eyes. We weren't thinking of marriage or anything. We were happy just to drift together in this deep current of friendship. We always sat together, ate together after the sessions, wrote letters and poems to each other. And dreamed. That was enough for us then.

'But it didn't last. One day – I only discovered this later – the sheykh told the boy that I had been promised in marriage to another, and that it would be better for him not to attend the sessions as his relationship with me was not appropriate. The boy came from a village outside Konya, so from one day to the next I didn't see him any more. We never even got to say goodbye. The sheykh was very kind, or so it seemed, and paid special attention to me after that, saying that I would soon get over him. The truth is, I was heartbroken, not just in the sense you read about – you know, the pain of separated lovers. Of course there was that. But I couldn't understand how a relationship could be cut off just like that. It was like breaking a beautiful object. I still loved him, but I knew the love didn't depend on him being there. I still love him, and probably always will.

'After the boy left, the sheykh began to act more affectionately towards me, and, well, to cut a long story short, I realised that he had fallen for me. It was quite a shock, as I certainly had no romantic feelings towards him and wondered how on earth he could have believed that I might want to become his wife. His second wife, that is. He hinted as much. It was difficult. You know the tradition that one should trust one's sheykh as if he were God Almighty? Well, that might work in some cases, but I don't think

that would have done for me. In the end I made the decision that it is better
to trust one's heart even if it goes against what one's sheykh says. After all,
even if the sheykh is right, for some of us, however, and I include you here
Satanaya, it is better to trust one's inner voice. Even if your heart is open to
being misled, you may benefit by your mistake, and learn to discriminate
your own state. The religious people, the *tarika* people, they would likely
say this is heresy, but I prefer to follow the way of those real sheykhs, like
Ibn 'Arabi who says "I follow the religion of love. Whichever way its mounts
take, that is my religion and my faith."

'So I followed my heart, and I told my father who immediately forbade
me to go to the sheykh's sessions any more. In the end the sheykh left the
area. We discovered later that I was not the first one he had attempted to
seduce. You know about this thing they call the 'one night marriage', Satanaya? Where you get married one day, and divorced in the morning? It's
something men have worked out to cover their affairs and stay within the
religious law. It's a con of course, but they seem to get away with it. Well,
this sheykh was one of those one-night lovers. Not a real sheykh at all. As
my father said, a sheykh is one who has self-control. This man had little.'

'Oh, but Shireen, that's so sad. So cruel.' Satanaya was in tears, thinking
of her own dear Yusuf as she heard the tale.

'No, not at all. It was an extraordinary lesson. I just went back to the
books about love, and everywhere I read how the real lover must have her
heart broken over and over until it becomes capable of the kind of love that
goes further than mere things and appearances. My love for the boy, that
exists forever. So, I learnt early on to distinguish between the person loved,
and the form of the person loved. From then on I began to see that person
in all sorts of places one wouldn't expect. Even in the things we think of as
hard or ugly. It was always the same person.'

Satanaya interrupted her: 'You mean the beauty in the person? But it
is always so different, didn't you want to experience it in *all* its ways?'

Shireen laughed, 'In all its ways? My dear Satanaya, even the Empress
of Byzantium couldn't have it in all its ways. But let's be serious, excess in
something isn't always quality. I thirst not for love, which is everywhere,
but for that unquenchable longing that animates the love in my heart.

'Later on I did have a real love affair. I was so captivated by the form,
the physical presence of the person that I forgot who it really was I loved,
and by whom I loved. We had to meet in secret, of course. It was what the

French call 'une affaire passionelle', and could never have lasted. Stormy, torrid, deep, and he wanted so much to marry. But I became afraid I would lose that freedom that love can bring, love itself. I was afraid I would become a prisoner of the messenger of love, and so I gave it up. Not love, but the idea of marriage. Sometimes even in love one can be so cruel. No, I never married, but I discovered what it is to consummate in love. And yes, it is the most beautiful consummation in this world. But then there are other worlds too, and this one, as they say, is the lowest of the low. There are ladders that must be climbed in our lives if we wish to rise out of the mud. And as for living alone with no children, I have nieces and nephews, and for now I have you for company, don't I? That's plenty for me.'

Satanaya wasn't sure how to answer this. Surely, she thought to herself, a ladder with the bottom rungs missing would be a seriously deficient ladder. Yet Shireen had admitted that she too had trod those early steps, and now no longer felt the need nor wish to return to them. Satanaya was happy that the lower rungs remained on her ladder, no matter how high she climbed, just in case.

FORTY-FOUR

Sema

Konya, December 1908

HE SNOW REMAINED throughout December. The thin sun warmed the air a little during the day and the cartwheels and horse's hooves churned the main avenues of the town to a muddy slush underfoot. When the sun set the ground froze over in pits and ruts beneath a chilly star-filled heaven.

As the date of Rumi's Nuptial Night approached, people from far and wide began to arrive in Konya for the celebration known locally as 'Shab-i-Aruz', literally, 'wedding night'. Shireen's konak filled to overflowing with ladies and gentlemen from Shiraz, her brothers and sisters and their wives

322

and husbands, and every room was packed for a whole week with excited chattering in Farsi, singing of hymns, recitations of the poetry of Rumi and Hafiz, as well as their own compositions. Reed flutes – *neys* – were unwrapped and ouds and drums sounded and music filled the house. In the kitchen Satanaya was in her element alongside a bevy of matrons sweating and arguing over the best way to prepare the pilavs that were constantly emerging, scented with rosewater and crowned with buttery sheets of crisped rice from the bottom of the pot, to feed the hungry appetites of the konak's guests.

On the Nuptial Night itself, the city was all lit up for the festivities. Wherever there was a dervish there was bound to be something going on: *zikrs* – the remembrance of God through group invocation of the Divine Names – were performed in Konya's mosques. And in dervish lodges everywhere the *'semazens'* – those dervishes who performed the ritual dance of turning – took to the floor in time-honoured fashion in their tombstone hats of pale brown felt, discarding their black cloaks to signify the parting from worldly attachments, unfolding from this dark chryssalis and taking imaginal flight in whirling folds of floating skirts and outstretched arms, a human-cosmic isthmus receiving the descent of heavenly mercies and transmitting them to earthbound souls below.

It was on this night that Satanaya became aware of Shireen's position in Konya society. The quiet Persian lady living alone in her konak emerged from her room in a full length dress with wide skirts over shalwar kemiz, a close-fitting bodice with long sleeves and buttoned to the neck, all in the most beautiful Benares brocades of purple and black silk embroidered with gold thread, with diamond and pearl earings, a scarf of the same material as the dress, well-wrapped up in full length mink coat and ermine-lined hat for journeying into the cold December night. Her eyes were subtly lined with dark kohl, and the faintest blush of rouge lit her cheeks and lips.

'Oh my God!' Satanaya exclaimed, 'Shireen Hanoum, you are stunning. You look like a Russian princess.'

'Well, it is a wedding party, after all.' said Shireen, reddening slightly but smiling with pleasure, 'We do want to look our best.'

Not wishing to be outdone, Satanaya ran to her room and put on her own best Circassian outfit, the one she had worn at the dances, with fur hat and fur-lined cloak, and rejoined her host.

'So, where exactly are we going?' asked Satanaya, as they stepped outside.

'Ah, just you wait and see.' And Shireen led the way with some of the houseguests in her train, in the direction of the Mevlevihane. At the gate a tall dervish recognised the Hanoum and welcomed her party into the courtyard, now swept clean of snow and laid with acres of carpets, with braziers glowing in the corners. Inside the Mevlevihane, the group was seated in places of honour within the 'semahane', the large hall where the special ceremony of the Sema of the Shab-i-Aruz was to take place. Through a wide arch in one wall Satanaya could make out the silver grille and fabulous tomb of Mevlana in the adjoining hall.

For the next hour people trickled in and found their places, with much greeting and embracing between acquaintances. Satanaya was impressed by how many elegant and important-looking people came and greeted Shireen, bowing and kissing her hand, just as she saw people kissing the hands of some of the turbanned sheykhs in the audience.

As the musicians took their seats on a raised platform opposite Satanaya, silence gradually descended within the hall. A heavy thump upon a drum signalled the musical overture of the evening as a deep-voiced choir of Anatolian dervishes began chanting the haunting hymns of the ancient Mevlevi litany.

The dervishes who were to dance, the 'semazen', entered in single file, led by the Semazenbaşı, the Dance Master; each one bowed then walked slowly into the hall, heedful, like martyrs approaching death, deliberate as warriors at the dawn of battle, and took their places around the periphery. The sheykh entered last, a small man with a wise nose and age-lined face. He bowed at the waist, and the dervishes bowed in answer. He then made his way across the open space to a red sheepskin placed a few yards in front of where Satanaya was sitting.

By now the whole circumference of the floorspace was lined with kneeling figures in black cloaks. The music continued and hymns were sung, lauding Mevlana, his son Sultan Veled, and Shams of Tabriz. At the mention of each name, the assembly bowed their heads and the dervishes prostrated, as the phrase 'Haqq dost' – Friend of Truth, was repeated as a chorus.

With a sudden crash of drum and cymbals the music stopped. Ritual prayers were chanted. Then came a deep, extended sound, like the wailing of the beloved crying for its lost lover, an echo from the soul's origin, the syllable of its longing for return, the sound of its real and absolute identity: 'Huuuuu...'*

The dervishes prostrated as a single body, slapping their hands to the floor. The thunderous clap vibrated through the room, disappearing into the earth, pulling everything and everyone with it. Satanaya felt herself involuntarily exhaling in unison, and for an instant it seemed all existence was consumed in that sound 'Huuuuu...'

The dervishes rose, shedding the black cloaks, the symbols of their separation. The musicians played a funereal march and the dervishes began the Sultan Veled Walk, moving with slow, measured steps around the room. Upon arriving before the sheykh, each stopped, arms folded upon across his chest, and greeted him with the bow of peace. And he, their shepherd at the gate of that heavenly pasture, pressed the imprimatur of a kiss upon each one's tombstone hat releasing the dervish from any lingering sense of earthly gravity.

The dancers took flight. White butterflies unfolding in transcendent light as they began to turn, arms outstretched, head tilted as they gazed between thumb and forefinger of their right hand raised in supplication, the left dropped in condescension towards the floor. Right foot turning over left, round and round in slow deliberate motion, a vortex restoring light from an infinite source to a benighted world.

For Satanaya, caught up in the mystique of the moment, she could no longer tell if the dervishes' feet still touched the earth as their whirling skirts floated out around their white legs, and their feet swished across the floor, held by a tenuous gravity, as a skater's feet whispering over ice is anchored only with the adhesion of a molecular thread of water.

The turning of two dozen dervishes, around and around upon the floor, could make the viewer dizzy; or, if one gathered the meaning inherent in their dance, the audience too might enter a little into this subtle atmosphere. The dance represents the turning of the planets and the stars upon the cosmic axis. It is said that this axis is love, and each of us a planet, turning within the aura of the sun of truth. But that is only a way of saying

---

* The word in Arabic, *hu* : (هو) meaning he, she or it, referring to the Absolute Essence of Existence.

what is in the end, unsaying. The dervish, as he turns, is repeating the sacred names of his origin, and reconnecting by love to reality itself.

Satanaya heard the sound 'Allahu' upon the breath of the dervishes as they passed close by. 'Al-lah hu, Al-lah hu, Al-lah hu…' the name 'god', but not that deity so misconstrued in our ignorance of our origin as to mean a separate existent or a distant power, controlling and demanding our unreasoned obeisance.

When the dervish says 'al-lah' he (or she, for the dervish is beyond gender, as we may come to see), is remembering by name that which collects all the names of existents, resolving the contraries, in one name; so by saying 'al-lah' the dervish affirms the absolute unity of the forms which express the singular unmanifest essence.

The dervish says 'huuuu…', naming that essence, and by that all the forms are wrapped up and returned to their origin as ideas in the mind of mind. So as he turns, with every turn, the dervish counts time, saying 'hu-allah-hu-allah' quietly on the breath.

Satanaya watched spellbound as the *semazens* spun in unison around the floor, orbiting the Sheykh who proceeded upon his own circular path. The dance master, a tall black-cloaked dervish, with white beard and snow-white felt hat, moved among them like some cosmic regulator, herding the occasional dervish-errant who wandered unawares too close towards the edge of the floor. So, while some of these whirling planetary beings appeared to shift in retrograde to the general circuit, the ensemble as a whole moved in a fluid equilibrium, frictionless, never static, never simply a repetition of learned steps. She studied the faces of the men, some old, some young, all gazing at some fixed point, but whether on some far horizon, or upon some inner compass, she could not tell. Whatever their focus, they rested in it, concentrated yet effortless, not lost in ecstasy, but in dignified submission to the order of the universe.

The dancers turned, stopped and returned to the circumference; sat, rested, rose and passing the lock-key of the sheykh, received the blessed nod and turned again. Three times they went, pausing after each period of turning with hands crossed upon their breast and bowing their heads, their skirts falling as folding wings upon their legs. During the fourth and final movement, the orchestra fell silent, leaving only the tinkling of the dulcimer as the little hammers fell upon the strings like drops of water, and the soft swish of the dancers' skirts and their leather slippers turning upon the polished wooden floor.

The dervishes continued to spin, poised in perfect stillness upon the point of their own axis. Satanaya held her breath. For a moment she thought they too had stopped breathing; but gently, like the cooing of doves, arose from the floor a murmuring sound repeating within the swirl of skirts, 'huuuu…huuuu…huuuu…'

Now the sheykh rose from his position upon the red sheepskin and with his right hand upon his chest, holding the hem of his cloak, he slowly moved through the room, turning among the dervishes, processing as a shepherding sun among his planets. Satanaya remembered little after that, and if asked to describe what she had seen, it was this final movement within the stillness that came to mind, like someone meeting her from some very ancient place, so distant, yet so near.

The evening ended with further litanies and then all the dervishes filed off the floor. Shireen tapped Satanaya on the shoulder:

'Mubarak – congratulations, Satanaya! your first Nuptial Night. May you have many more! Now let's pay our respects to Mevlana, and then we'll go home and have something to eat.'

Back at the konak people began to arrive from various other zikrs and sema performances which were taking place around Konya. Very soon all the rooms on the ground floor were packed with friends and acquaintances sharing the joyous mood of the evening. A supper prepared earlier by Nevin and the Persian cousins appeared – dishes of pilav with pistachios and raisins perfumed with fragrance of orange flowers, honey-soaked pastries filled with almonds and walnuts; fruit drinks and endless coffee in tiny cups were passed around. Someone recited poetry, another began to sing, musicians took up instruments, and all the nostalgic romance of a soirée in the eastern mode was realised. Time passed and it was well after midnight before a few weary souls began to drift away to bed or to their homes. But in one room things were just beginning to warm up. The sheykh who had led the dervishes in the Sema appeared at about three in the morning, and with perhaps twenty or thirty people, men and women, and a few dozing children, began to sing hymns – ilahi. Then the zikr began, gently, just where they sat, first the regular intoning of the Muslim credo 'la illaha ilallah' which after ten or fifteen minutes morphed into *'hu…al-lah…hu…al-lah',* with a simple rhythmical accompaniment on a frame drum, its thin metal chains ringing faint shrills at each beat.

This invocation had been going on for a while when Satanaya noticed Shireen stand up and move into the centre of the room. People shuffled back, giving her space, and slowly she began to turn about on the spot, hands crossed upon her chest, a diminutive figure, the black and purple silk of her dress catching the light of the lamps, and as she turned, her skirts splayed out and her arms rose just as had the dervishes earlier in the evening. Satanaya thought of some pictures she had seen once in a large botanical book belonging to the French Baron, of a black tulip. In the first picture, an unopened bloom on a stem, a slender ebony statue of closed petals; and in the second, the flower had opened revealing its heart of bright yellow radiating striations. And Shireen just turned and turned with the weightless ease and stillness of a small cloud around which a vast empty sky prostrates, evanescent yet timeless. Her face did not have the dreamy, at times sepulchral quality of the dervishes seen earlier. Her face glowed with a quiet, unspeakable joy, as a child's face before the beauty of life.

And when finally Shireen Hanoum came to a stop, and the silk fan of her skirt sank to rest over her shalwar, and the last tintinnabulations faded from the ring-chains rattling in the rim of the frame drum, Satanaya had determined to try this whirling business herself. Back in her bedroom, and notwithstanding those extra visitors who were already bunked down and fast asleep on the surrounding divans, she attempted a few whirls. But she immediately lost her balance and collapsed upon the floor.

FORTY-FIVE

Finding the Centre

Konya, early 1909

ELL ME, SATANAYA,' said Shireen at breakfast, a day or so after all the Persians had departed, 'Why is it that ever since Rumi's Nuptial Night I am seeing butterflies dancing above your head?'

The truth was that although the konak had settled back into its accustomed calm, within the mind of Satanaya the dervishes still glided round and round in happy circumambulation.

Satanaya looked up, and blushed as she caught Shireen's little joke.

'Shireen Hanoum, I just can't get them out of my mind. The whole thing was so...I don't know...wonderful of course, but also a bit confusing. What I really want to know is, how come you were doing *sema*? I thought only men could be whirling dervishes.'

Shireen laughed. 'Why, I taught myself. It's not so difficult – the movement, that is. What goes on inside is another matter. A matter of the heart, really. And that can't be taught, it has to be learnt by taste.'

'But how did you do it? I heard that the dervishes use a nail in the floor between their big toes, and they just turn and turn around the nail. It all sounds rather painful.'

'You saw them the other night. The men, well, they do like to be so organised, you know. And they do all that stuff with the nail in the floor, and the 1001 days apprenticeship in the kitchen. I suppose boys need that kind of discipline, something to keep them in order. And they do so love their uniforms, and going about in their little groups. But you know, I'm sure Rumi didn't spend hours turning round and round a nail. I imagine he just got up and danced. Saw Shams doing it and thought he'd have a go himself. Anyway, men never like us women getting in on their act. You'd think they invented dancing. They just put their order on it. They love to make things definite. I like to think it wasn't an apple that seduced Adam, but he saw Eve dancing and, well, the rest is history. He invented the serpent story to cover himself, which he needed to by then, I'm sure.'

'And you know,' Shireen continued, 'there are some people who won't even let *sema* be called a dance. They dress it up as ritual, as sacred religious movement. But for the lover – and I dare say for the Beloved too – it is always the dance, an expression of joy, the beautiful coupling of spirit and body.'

'Another thing, Shireen.' said Satanaya, 'What exactly is this trance, this ecstasy, they talk about? They say the dervish goes into a trance when he spins, and experiences a beautiful trancendent ecstasy.'

'Ha! that's another foolishness.' Shireen's voice took on a very no-nonsense tone. 'How could he possible go into a trance – he'd just spin until he fell over. No, he is superaware all the time he is out on the floor. That's the hard part of it. He submits to the order of the dance, that's true; but reaching that stillness where he can just turn, and be the axis round which his world turns, that is a most subtle thing. When he reaches that stage, as he turns, he knows who he is and he knows where he is, because he is in his centre. That part is a mystery, each person's secret. Ecstasy? What do we mean by it?'

'But why is it only men who can be Mevlevis?' said Satanaya. 'Do we women forever have to be second-class human beings?' Satanaya was remembering the freedom with which she had entered into the social life of the Beyt and Beirut, albeit as the privileged adopted daughter of the enlightened Lady Gülbahar.

'Oh, it wasn't always like this. In Rumi's day, men and women did *sema* together. Sometimes it was a spontaneous affair. And there have been female sheykhs, even up to this day, but they do their ceremonies separately from the men. Some of the great spiritual people among the Mevlevis have been women. But things were different in the early days, in the Seljuk period. Much more freedom for women, a tradition that comes from the Turkish, rather than the Arab side of our culture. The women in real Turkish society were on a much more equal footing with men. Sadly the walls have closed in since those more enlightened times.'

'It seems sometimes that the religion encloses the human spirit, rather than freeing it.' said Satanaya.

'Perhaps that is so. I'm sure things will change one day. The Mevlevi sheykh says there are big changes coming for humanity. But how and when, who knows? For now I am content to dance in my room. I don't need permission, nor an audience when I am alone with my beloved.'

Satanaya remembered the look on Shireen's face when she had whirled so gracefully, so joyfully in her dark silks, a woman complete in her own universe, and she determined that she too would learn to dance like a woman, for her beloved, whoever, whatever that was.

'So, how do you know the Sheykh so well?' and then it dawned on her. 'Was it your father?'

'Oh, did I not say? Yes. He's coming to tea today, so you can ask him all the questions you like.'

'Look at the dear child, she has no corners, no edges. She's like a wine that has escaped the bottle, pure essence. Perhaps she's *Uwaysi*. She's like you, Shireen, but more so. No, we could never contain such a plant in our garden, not in our glass house with its strong fertilisers and composts. She'd very soon wilt and fade away. She's so close to nature, she's a wild-flower, a beautiful wildflower. Look, her stem is strong, she doesn't need the walls of the tekke to protect her, or to be held up by a sheykh to survive the winds of life. But she needs something, I'll grant you. God willing whatever it is will come to her.' and he repeated the lines: *'And God gives wisdom to whom He will, and great good is to whom it is given.'* *

The Mevlevi Sheykh, Shireen's father, smiled at Satanaya and accepted the *kalbura bastı* biscuit which she offered. He was considering the question which Satanaya had asked: whether she could become a dervish, even if she wasn't allowed to whirl with the men. He continued:

'And another thing, what would she do for a thousand and one days in the kitchens of the tekke? She already cooks better than our own *aşcıbaşı*.'†
The Sheykh took a piece of the syrup-soaked cake on his fork and popped it into his mouth. He turned to Satanaya.

'Mmmm, where on earth did you learn to make these?'

'At Seydnaya, in Syria.' Satanaya said, 'it's a convent…'

'Yes, yes, I know. And how is Mother Superior these days?'

'I really don't know, it's been so long. But probably she's fine. She always is.'

'Yes, yes, quite so. I must go and visit on my next trip to Damascus. And Shadinyan Efendi? Is he still working so hard in his little shop?'

'Yes, he's very well too.'

'You see, daughter,' he addressed Shireen, 'she has already had the best education, *maşallah*. And may it continue so.'

After the Sheykh had gone, Satanaya asked Shireen, 'What is this Uwaysi your father mentioned?'

'Ah, Uways.' Shireen sighed at the mention of his name, as if a rare scent had entered her heart.

'Uways al Karani was a poor camel-herd from the Yemen, a great Sufi who was very devoted to his mother. He received his education in spiritual matters directly, from the source within himself. He lived in the time of our Prophet Muhammed, on him be peace, although they never met each other. One time he came to visit Muhammed, but Muhammed was away.

---

* Koran II:269
† The chief cook, the dervish in charge of the Mevlevi kitchen, second only to the Sheykh, and responsible for the training of initiates.

Ayesha invited Uways to wait but he had promised his blind and aged mother he would not delay his return. When Muhammed arrived home, he heard about the visit. Such was his respect for Uways that he took hold of his wife and said to her 'Let me look into the eyes that have looked into the eyes of Uways al Karani.' The term Uwaysi is sometimes used for those who, like him, come to know themselves without intermediary of sheykh or religion. Sometimes Muhammed would turn towards the south and say, "I feel the sweet scent of the All-Merciful from the direction of Yemen", so you have some idea of the high esteem in which he is held.'

'But why did your father say that about me? I'm the last person to be spoken of in the same breath as such a one.' said Satanaya, rather over-whelmed by the import of the story.

'Oh, Satanaya, can't you see? It's not about you. It's something my father speaks about sometimes. About the changes that are coming. He says that there is a convergence of knowledge happening in the world, and that the political and religious order as we know it is already breaking down. People are beginning to question whether these empires and mon-archies can exist as absolutes in a world where people are asking for democracy. Look at what is happening in the capital: the ones they call the Young Turks, Captain Enver and others in the army have forced Sultan Abdul Hamid to bring back the Constitution and allow Parliament to reopen after thirty years. There is even talk of abolishing the Sultanate. You won't hear this talk in Konya – we're far too conservative to go against the status quo – but the sheykhs in Constantinople and Salonica give us all the news.'

'Yes, we heard things in Lebanon too. But what has this got to do with religious matters?'

'The time is coming, father says, when people will no longer look for guidance in the established forms of religion, and this will be a dangerous time. There will be a period when the world will abandon this old idea of God as a separate Being which controls the universe, an idea current among the masses of people, and which the imams in the mosques, as well as the rabbis and priests seem very fond of perpetuating. Then a kind of vacuum of knowledge will exist in the world, a real agnosticism, and for many it will be an age of atheism. There will always be people who will want a spiritual meaning to their lives, but who don't want to be preached at, but who want to find out, to know, for themselves. Father believes that this love to know ourselves is in us all, and will push us through this phase. As more and more people come to look inside themselves and recognise that we are all of a single origin, and single identity – what the Sufis call 'tawhid', the unification or union with reality – then this way will become the norm. It is really in our nature to want to know. That's what he meant by calling you *Uwaysi:* you want to find out for yourself directly. '

'But how will this come about?' said Satanaya. 'There seems to be such a huge gap between these ideas and the old world. Even in Beirut, it was like two separate universes occupying the same space, worlds carrying on within each other, neither acknowledging the other – except in matters of commerce, of course.'

'Father believes the printing press is going to be a great weapon in the struggle for change.' said Shireen. 'It is making available generally the knowledge and information that could only be accessed previously through the mosque or through the priests. And people are publishing their individual thoughts and ideas. They call it a revolution. Perhaps it's just beginning, but it can only grow. And there are all the other inventions making the world smaller – the telegraph, the steamship and railways, and of course the motor car, although we don't have many here in Turkey yet. They say we could go all the way to Constantinople in a day or two if there was a better road. The world really is shrinking.'

'But your father is a Sheykh, how does he reconcile his position with these ideas. It must be difficult.'

'Of course as Sheykh he upholds the status quo, but in private he says quite different things. He sees Mevlana as one of the beacons of this new world order, because people will always need something to satisfy their spiritual yearning.'

'But isn't the Mevlevi order a kind of religion too?' said Satanaya.

'I dare say it is like that for many. It won't be an easy time – people are slow to accept change – we are comfortable in what we are used to, it makes for an easy life. But so much of what Mevlana says goes far beyond the religions of his own time. And of our time. My father believes nothing is more important than the survival and spread of the ideas of Rumi in people's hearts, that's where it really has a life. For now, that is carried with the *tarikas*, the dervish orders, but it won't always be like that.'

'Yeah, by men, for men.' Satanaya groaned. Then changing the subject, she asked: 'So tell me then, how do I do this 'turn'?'

'Haha! I heard you fall over in your room the other night. Well, what did that show you?' said Shireen.

'That I was tired. And a little drunk on the wine of love, perhaps.'

'Perhaps. OK, here's a thing: first you need to be in your centre. You need to find your centre and learn to stay in it, no matter what else happens. Even if you are tired. Even if you are drunk on love, or on anything else for that matter. You mustn't let anything pull you away from your centre. That is the first thing – and the last. It's like Uways al Karani said, when he was asked about concentration in prayer: you should be so attuned that if an arrow were to hit you, you wouldn't even notice it. If you can find your centre, and stay in it, whatever else is happening, then nothing will be able to push you over. You'll be like a spinning top – you know, a gyroscope: it has its own centre of gravity, you can push it over, tip it on its side, on its head, it just adjusts to the new situation and stays spinning because it keeps its centre. It can even spin sideways on a wall.'

'So how do I find my centre? Where is it exactly?'

'That's for you to discover. Where are you when you are in love, tell me that ?'

'Well, I'm kind of... well, no place really. I just feel whole, all of myself, I suppose. Not really inside or outside if you know what I mean. It's all the same, it's all one thing. If I had to find a place, I suppose it is here in the centre, the centre of my chest, my heart. And yet, I'm still seeing with eyes.'

'And is that where you are when you pray?' asked Shireen

Satanaya was silent for a while, as she thought about Shireen's question.

'I'm not sure about praying. Perhaps when I'm feeling really wretched and crying and asking for help, yes, maybe. I suppose then, I pray after a fashion. And I am kind of gathered up into myself too, into a whole... of sorts.'

'And what about when you are really busy in the kitchen, too busy even to think, but still you get the job done, where are you then? Or when you see someone about to be run over in the street? You don't stop to watch, do you? You act. You shout, you pull them out of danger.'

Satanaya was getting the picture. It wasn't about the mind. Well, not the thinking part anyway. None of the examples Shireen gave had anything to do with thinking. In fact, thinking seemed to be quite the opposite of being in one's centre. She knew it well from being really busy in the kitchen, when she was totally involved, she didn't have to think, she knew instantly the state of things, how that piece of meat in the oven was doing, when those potatoes needed to come off the boil, when to move the vegetables to a cooler part of the oven. A different kind of knowing took over. It was simple, intuitive, she didn't think, she just responded from some place of inner knowing.

'So, I guess I should just go away and turn until it comes, or not.'

'Don't worry, it will come, but don't try too hard. It's for the pleasure of it, after all.'

After sitting quietly for a while in her room, Satanaya stood up, her arms folded across her chest as she had seen Shireen and the dervishes do. She stood there for a long time, not daring to move. Wanting to move, but not daring. Just waiting, as if for some word or sign. For ages she waited, standing very still, until all her thoughts had calmed down and she no longer worried whether she would be able to turn or not. Then she placed her right foot over her left, and pivoted her body around slowly on the ball of her left foot, about a half circle. She continued like this a while, then slowly let her arms unfold. This made it easier, although it also made her turn more quickly and after a while she stopped. She knew she hadn't really been centred, she had been concentrating too hard, and she felt just a little giddy. But gradually, as she practiced over the next few weeks, she began to relax, and she stopped being self-conscious about what she was doing, until she really was able to turn comfortably without thinking and without getting dizzy.

And when it did happen, the thing that happened, it was the easiest thing in the world. It was obvious really, and yet so subtle she didn't even realise at first, that it was happening, until afterwards. Or, at least until she became aware that she had been turning away while completely still. It was as if she herself was no longer moving. And everything, the room, the walls, the whole world, turned around her, and she was still, absolutely at rest, in her centre. Then the self-consious thought that 'I am in my centre' intruded, and the spell was broken. But for a while at least, she knew. She had been somewhere she had never been before, somewhere so still, so in complete harmony both in herself and in the world, they were as one thing. And, strangely, there was more, a place she couldn't describe except she knew it was there, an unseen source of nourishment, where possibilities were waiting to unfold and make themselves known to her.

FORTY-SIX
Yeşil Efendi

Konya, 1909

‘S O, YOU FOUND A CENTRE.’ said Shireen. ‘I say *a* centre, because there are many centres. The centre you found has an inside; and there is a centre within that inside, which leads to another centre, and so on like nesting Russian dolls. Or perhaps in your case, Circassian dolls. You just have to keep on looking, keep on turning. There is even a centre which is everywhere. And a centre without a circumference. But this is a start, I suppose.’

Satanaya was recounting her experience of finding her centre: the whole world turning around her, and she the axis, the still point at the

338

centre of her universe, even as her body spun round in her room. Shireen's remarks were aimed at deflating a little of her young companion's exhuberance for what was simply a state, among many states to be encountered along the way, and as such, ephemeral and not to be held onto; a state, as distinct from a station, which is a place of establishment and persisting arrival. However, Satanaya was too taken by her state to recognise the irony in Shireen's remarks.'

'It was wonderful, really, Shireen. Everything was… just… perfect.'

'Yes, as I said, there are many centres to reach before you truly reach yourself.' And that was all Shireen would say on the subject.

And so Satanaya persevered with her practice, turning every day, until she found an ease where thoughts no longer impinged and she could turn and turn with ease. And sometimes grace was there as well. Then, when she returned to herself she felt she had been blessed by something quite extraordinary. Satanaya was experiencing the world of states, and finding great pleasure in this. She may well have continued spinning around till the end of time had not something occurred which changed forever the inner landscape of her world.

She had been living with Shireen for almost a year. Her original intention had been to travel to Constantinople in stages, and eventually into Europe. She had imagined the purpose of her journeying would reveal itself of its own accord, and that it must in some way involve cooking food. For the present, however, it was the events of the Nuptial Night – the *sema* and the *zikr* – and studying Rumi's poems and stories, and her turning practice, which fed her enthusiasm.

One day while cleaning her room prior to practicing *sema*, her eyes fell upon the lines of Persian scipt engraved around the base of Takla's old *kazan*. She realised that she could now understand them herself, and there, staring her in the face, were the words,

> 'Without pleasure, flesh and skin do not grow;
> and unless they grow, what shall the love of the Friend consume?'

In her mind she saw the face of the old tinsmith Moses Shadinyan, and remembered his parting request to give greetings to Shamsuddin Ateshbaz Wali. How could she have forgotten? But who was this Ateshbaz fellow anyway? She presumed he was dead, if he had been Rumi's cook, so that

meant finding the tomb, making another *ziyaret*. She must find out and
deliver the *salam* – the greeting of peace – from Shadinyan. But first a little
turning.

She stood as accustomed in the centre of her room, folded her arms,
stilled her mind and began to turn. But it wasn't happening. Her feet
seemed stuck to the floor. Her body felt heavy. She couldn't find her centre
at all. She tried again. Nothing. She didn't feel ill or anything, but something had pushed her out of her centre and wasn't letting her get back in.
She sat down on the bed and picked up the *kazan*. She immediately felt
better, so she stood up to try again. Same thing: heavy, leaden feet and no
balance. She realised the *kazan* was telling her something, that she had to
deliver the message to Shamsuddin Ateshbaz Wali or she'd never be able to
turn. She would ask Shireen where to find him.

Shireen's door was firmly shut. Satanaya dared not disturb her, so she
set out for the Mevlevihane. Someone there would know Ateshbaz Wali,
she was sure. A group of young dervishes were hanging around the gate.
She approached them and asked, but they were embarrassed to be
addressed by this beautiful unveiled woman. They pleaded ignorance,
being either unable or unwilling to help. She entered beneath the fluted
green tiled dome of the mauseleum, which had been built by the Georgian
princess Gürcü Khatun, and stood before the tomb of Rumi. There she
gave greetings, prayed a *fatiha** and asked to be guided to Ateshbaz Wali.

As she left the building, she approached another dervish, an older
man, and asked him where she might find the tomb of the mysterious
cook. Although he knew the name, again, he could not say where the tomb
was.

'Let's go and speak to the *araba* drivers, they know Konya very well,
they make deliveries for people all over the town.' he said, and led Satanaya
outside.

They turned left and into a street behind the Selimiye Mosque opposite, towards the Kadınlar Pazarı, the women's market. They approached a
group of carts whose drivers were drinking tea and warming their hands
around a small stove in the open air. They stood up as the dervish
approached. The dervish passed on Satanaya's request. They all rolled their
eyes upwards and with a 'tut' of their tongues, tossed back their heads in a

---

* '*Surat-ul-fatiha*' – The Opening – the first chapter of the Koran.

reverse nod which in Anatolia signifies the negative.

'Perhaps he knows,' said one of the drivers, pointing out an old man further down the street. He went over to him, exchanged a few words and then came back.

'He wants to know if it's the young lady who is asking. He says he'll take her there if she wants.'

Satanaya thanked the driver and the dervish and went over to the old man. He was a strange looking fellow, quite short, stocky, and dressed in what looked like old sacks made up into trousers, and an old coat made of thick felt. On his head he wore a ragged sheepskin kalpak, and where the moths had left some wool she guessed its colour may once have been green now faded into a sort of greenish-yellow. The man was of an indeterminate age, anywhere between forty and a hundred and forty years, of ruddy complexion with a few tufts of badly trimmed beard to match his hat. But he was smiling, and as she had drawn a blank in her quest up until then, she decided she had nothing to lose.

'Ateshbaz Wali? Can you tell me where?' Satanaya said in Turkish. She wasn't at all sure what language he spoke, if he even spoke at all. He just nodded vigorously and set off down the street, beckoning her to follow.

'Wait, wait! Where are we going? Is it far? Should I get my horse?' she cried out after him. But he didn't stop. He just turned and laughing beckoned her on. She had no choice but to follow. For nearly an hour it continued like this, by which time they had passed the Mevlevihane twice, traversed endless alleys of dusty and squalid houses, before emerging below the Alaettin Mosque. He stopped before a beautiful arched doorway, adjacent a tumbledown pile of brown rubble and minced blue tiles which surrounded a raw truncated stump of masonry. Here, by the remains of the recently collapsed spire of the Ince Minare – 'Slender Minaret' – Mosque, Satanaya decided she'd had enough.

'How much further?' she asked, impatiently.

The little man, who up until then had appeared quite jolly, to the point where Satanaya was beginning to think that he was a bit soft in the head, or that perhaps she had been following a *madhub*, a holy madman, turned around with a look of furious intensity, and exclaimed:

You were green in the garden, drinking cool water,
but that was only to make you fit for this hot water.'

She remembered the words Moses Shadinyan had quoted from Rumi's story, of the chickpeas bubbling in the pot and getting bashed down by the cook.

'Well? Do you want to come to Ateshbaz Wali or not?' he continued.

Satanaya felt simultaneously cross and ashamed. Cross, because for once she found herself quite out of her comfort zone. Here was a man, by all appearances a complete tramp, a beggar even, who seemed on the one hand to be making fun of her, and yet by that quote from Rumi, intimated that he knew more about her situation than she had even realised herself. Ashamed and embarrassed, for his words had pricked her pride. Satanaya was at a crossroads. Standing below the ancient Alaettin Hill, site of human settlement since more than five thousand years, her eyes came to rest on the exquisite portal of the ruined mosque before her. Its entwined ribbon of carved calligraphy spells out the famous *Sura Ya Sin,* known as the Heart of the Koran, traditionally recited for the dead, and the *Sura al-Nasr,* the Chapter of Assistance, presaging Muhammed's death. The entrance rises to twice the height of the double doors, the whole facade a restrained riot of incription and decorative sculptings. She was overwhelmed. She stared at her feet, turned and gazing at the calligraphy, made out the lines: *'ask pardon of Him for He is inclined to forgive.'* She looked at the madman before her. Only he wasn't a madman any more, he was the most sane looking person she had ever seen. Shining through the ragged clothes and the tufty green hat, was a real human being, more real than anyone she had ever come across. And he seemed resolutely normal.

'I'm sorry,' she said, 'yes, I really do want to see Ateshbaz Wali, if you'll take me.'

He gave her that look again, intense, but now without the fury. A look – was it of sufferance? pity? compassion? Whatever, it shocked her into the present moment, it removed her past, dissolving the accumulated states of memory. She saw herself alone before this simple ragged man standing in the shadow of this grand portal among the ruins, with its majestic words flowing in the stone like light. She felt the wide surrounding plain shrinking before her; the earth now a mere pebble beneath her feet and the cobalt sky a vast unknowing waiting to be joined. She was alone, but not alone. For nothing was separate anymore. There was no longer a separate 'out there' to harm her, to seduce her, to hold her back. She felt herself reducing into the intimacy of a state of oneness.

With what awareness remained, Satanaya returned the man's look. Looking made her feel safe. She knew he was seeing her as she was, and in this conspiracy there sewed a thread of trust. Here was something she needed more, much more even, than the *sema*. It was no longer a matter of finding a centre, for the centre was everywhere. This was another kind of turning altogether.

'Well, let's go then.' he said.

Shamsuddin Ateshbaz Wali was buried in Meram, a few miles outside of Konya, as it was then. As the town expanded in the latter half of the 20th century Meram became a suburb within the greater metropolis. But at the time of Satanaya's visit, it was still known as 'Yeşil Meram' – Green Meram, on account of the orchards and gardens full of fruit and vegetables, and the verdant river banks and roadsides lined with acacias and terebinth trees. Its lushness came with the water that flowed down from the western mountains, rivers now mostly diverted into distant dams and catchments supplying the needs of the modern city, leaving shrivelled streams and dry riverbeds.

And as they walked the long walk out to the village of Meram, the man in the green kalpak told Satanaya the story of Ateshbaz Wali.

'Ateshbaz is not his original name. It's his *'makhlus'*, his sobriquet, one of those names people acquire on account of some incident or accident that marks them out in a particular way. He began life as Shamsuddin Yusuf ibn Izzeddin. He was born in Balkh, in Khorasan. Like Rumi's family, he travelled west to escape the Mongols. Perhaps he went in the same caravan, for he was in Karaman when the Seljuk sultan, Alaettin Kaykubad, invited Rumi's father to come and live in Konya. We don't know his date of birth, but he is said to have lived until he was nearly a hundred years old. He died in 1285, so he could have been as much as fifteen years older than Rumi. After Rumi's father died, he became a pupil of Rumi, who was very fond of him, and he became Rumi's personal cook. He lived in the *dergah* (dervish house) where he cooked for the dervishes. He was a very keen student and hated to miss any of the teaching sessions of his Master. One day he was about to cook Rumi's supper when he discovered there was no firewood. It was too late to go and buy more fuel and have the meal ready on time. He was completely distraught and went to Rumi shamefacedly to tell him the situation, and to ask him what he should do.

"'Why don't you put your feet into the fireplace and cook the food that way," Rumi said to him. Rumi was teasing of course, but Yusuf ibn Izzeddin took his master at his word, and put his feet into the fireplace under the pot. Yusuf ibn Izzeddin's state was of such fervent devotion that fire came out of his toes, and the meal was cooked in this way. When Rumi heard of this, and finding no other explanation than that it was a miracle, he wagged his finger at Yusuf ibn Izzeddin pretending to reprimand him, but actually joking: "Oh, so you are now *ateshbaz* (one who plays with fire), eh!"'

It was early afternoon now, and the spring sun was drying out the muddy road. A magical light filtered through the new leaves in the surrounding orchards. In the distance, poking up behind the mud walls of a small farm steading, was the conical red stone roof of a Seljuk tomb. They approached a tiny wooden gateway in the wall, above which was a small stone plaque carved in the Ottoman script. The green kalpak man – as yet Satanaya hadn't even dared ask him his name – banged on the door and called out. 'Selam aleykum, ben kadeşinim,' announcing to whoever was within that their brother was outside.

'Aleykum selam. Ya Azizi!' came a voice from the other side of the door, and a few seconds later the rattle of a lock and chain. Then appeared a tiny thing, bent-backed over her walking stick, the face beneath her scarf not so much wrinkled as engraved as a rock is by time, leaving the two clear pools of her eyes as fresh as day. She was clearly happy to see her brother.

'I have a visitor for Ateshbaz. This is Satanaya. Satanaya, this is my sister, Gül Hanım.'

Gül, meaning rose. Not a surprise, thought Satanaya, seeing the profusion of roses growing in the yard, climbing over the little balcony that formed the entrance into the lady's simple adobe home, rose bushes planted in the well which surrounded the pink stone türbe, and more roses covering the south-facing wall at the back of the yard. Everywhere roses.

'Oh, you should have warned me. I haven't swept the yard yet, or dusted in the tomb.'

The yard was deserted but for the old lady. The tomb building sat in the sunken well area, with access gained down four or five steps. Another small flight of open stone steps led halfway up the side of the little mausoleum to a low doorway.

The green kalpak man, whom Satanaya now assumed was called Aziz, gestured her forward. She made her way carefully down into the well and then up the stone stairs.

'Mind your head!' called out the lady Gül, as Satanaya stooped to enter the doorway. It was very low, with a raised threshold, so only by bowing deeply could she pass within.

The room was barely wide enough for the green cloth-covered sarcophagus that took up a third of the space. She was becoming accustomed to these places of *ziyaret* since she had been on her travels, but the sparseness, the simplicity of this vault told her something of the man buried here. *'Faites simple!'* had been Clotilde's watchword when they cooked for the workers in the Beyt. And now in this humble cook's abode Satanaya felt the echo of these words once more. The cuisine of a 12th century dervish house in Seljuk Turkey was likely to be simple. Perhaps, she thought, that was it. A simple, single taste. Was that the key? To find that one substance, to know the taste of that original ingredient and then marry it to whatever came to hand, whether food or love, however the nourishment appeared. But that ingredient was herself. Satanaya. But who was Satanaya? Who was she really. It was all very well living in the comfortable konak with Shireen, meeting sheykhs and revelling in marvellous conversation, reading Persian and whirling around in her room – but where had it got her? Where was it leading. 'Faites simple.' It came again – keep it simple. She looked around. On the wall above the tomb was a framed calligraphy. She read:

'Whoever attains the state of true meditation
That person is educated by everything.'

Satanaya held that thought. The true state of meditation – it could only be talking about union – the vanishing of the so-persistent self-reference point of ego, and the remaining of the consciousness of being. But there seemed to be so many unions, so many states of love. When would she ever reach a place of stability? Where was the simplicity?

She turned and looked again at the doorway – its abject state witness to the need to bend, to bow, to prostrate before the magnitude of the idea of union – this realisation was in itself a relief, a diminishing of that in herself which seemed to block up the stream of life which wanted to flow in her. She fell to her knees, and then full flat to the floor; she wanted the earth consume her, to take her to its bosom, just as it had taken the sweet man they called Ateshbaz, who played with fire and cooked the saint's dinner with the flames which came out of his toes, to be so buried in the substance of the earth, that when anyone called out her name, it would be the earth who answered on her behalf, in the trees and the flowers, the mountains and the valleys, with the voice of the wind. She yearned for a non-existence that would free herself of herself, and let the love she felt moving between earth and the heavens flow in her as water runs in a parched riverbed after the rain has come. And then she began to weep, not out of sadness, but simply from the relief that comes when life begins to flow anew. She wept until she felt as light as air. Until her breath was clear and her heart unburdened. Now she was ready to greet the saint, which she did with the respect and gratitude of a trainee to a master, and as her heart expanded she knew the greeting was returned with the joy of one cook to another. She gave *selams* on behalf of Moses Shadinyan and then she went outside to join Aziz and Gül Hanum.

Tea had been prepared and while they drank, Gül asked Satanaya if she had taken any salt from the tomb.

'I'm sorry, but what salt?'

'The salt in the pot by the tomb. Everybody takes a bit of salt for their kitchen, so that the *himmah* (spiritual blessing) of Ateshbaz goes into their own cooking."

Satanaya was surprised at how light on her feet Gül Hanım was, as she scampered up into the tomb, and returned with a handful of salt wrapped in a twist of paper.

'And the dervishes also put it between their toes when they're learning to turn. You know, that nail in the floor can make the foot quite sore. In fact, it's good for all kinds of infections.'

They sat drinking tea in the sharp winter sun. Satanaya was silent while the two siblings discussed the effect of the weather on Gül Hanım's vegetable patch, and the laying habits of her chickens and geese, until the time came for her to return to Konya.

FORTY-SEVEN

Meram Life

Meram, near Konya, 1909

HAT ON EARTH makes you think I might want pupils? First of all, I'm not a teacher. I'm not a sheykh. If you want a sheykh, there are plenty around here, dozens in fact. Why pick on me? And secondly, were I in that game – which I assure you I'm not – why do you imagine I would want to take you? And if – and here I am speaking entirely hypothetically – if I were to take a student, and that student was you, what in the name of all that is holy makes you think you could bear my company? Why, you wouldn't last three days – less probably – before you ran back to Konya. You wouldn't find it easy at all.'

Satanaya had no answers to these questions. So instead, she asked, would he take her on as his assistant, his servant, whatever.

'Please, Mr Azizi? I would be very useful.'

He laughed uproariously.

'And what is it you imagine you would be assisting me in? You know what I do, don't you? I collect old rubbish, things people turn out of their houses, worn out, broken things. Have you been turned out of your nice konak? Has Shireen tired of her housemate? Maybe you've been misbehaving with the soldiers in town and you are now worn out? Would you like me to collect you like a broken pot? And as for calling me Azizi, isn't it a bit soon for such intimacies?'

He laughed again, and gave her a particularly leery look, intended to shock, or at the very least put her off. Satanaya was a little uncertain at this response, but she had expected a rebuff and was not put off.

The man in the green kalpak, Satanaya now realised, was not in fact called Azizi, meaning 'precious one'. It was just a familiar endearment his sister used. From now on she would simply address him as Efendi, or 'Yeşil Efendi' – Mr Green – on account of his headgear. He didn't seem to care one way or the other.

'I could cook for you.' she persisted. 'We could get a cart and use my horse to pull it, so you wouldn't always be having to carry all that junk.'

They were standing outside the mud and timber hovel where Yeşil Efendi lived, in the corner of a field not far from Ateshbaz Wali's tomb. He had been pointing out the distant hill of Alaettin Mosque as a landmark for Satanaya to find her way back into Konya.

'Cook for me, eh?' Yeşil Efendi now changed his tack. He looked serious. 'Well, that's something I suppose. And the horse and cart thing – definitely worth considering.' Then he narrowed his eyes and viewed Satanaya with a look of deep suspicion. 'Aah, but I know your sort, once you're back in town in your comfortable konak, you'll soon change your mind. Off you go now. We'll see. I'll let you know in three days time.'

What had prompted Satanaya's request, she had no idea. Neither could she explain to Shireeen when she arrived back at the konak. Shireen was intrigued. Who was this man in a green kalpak? No matter how Satanaya described him, she couldn't place him among the regular tramps or the rag-a-bone men that trundled carts around the streets of Konya. And when three days later Satanaya packed a bag, and set off with Tarçin pulling one of her old carts, Shireen was none the wiser.

Satanaya spent two years with Yeşil Efendi. Each morning they would hitch up Tarçin and set off. Where they went, no one could rightly say, but each day they managed to find enough bits of junk, cast off furniture and old pots and rags, which when cleaned up, found ready buyers in the various street markets in and around Konya. This provided sufficient funds for their needs. Simple needs. No more the lavish banquets and hearty workers lunches of the Beyt, nor the surfeit of sweet things that spread the tea tables of Shireen's konak. Now it was basic fare, like bulghur or broken rice and beans, bread and vegetable greens stewed with onions, and just occasionally a little meat, usually finely chopped lamb made into köfte, or bones to fortify a soup. Every few days a pot of milk would appear silently outside the door. Satanaya assumed it came from Gül Hanım, from her cow, though she never saw who left it. The empty pots placed outside the door at night vanished unseen just as they had arrived.

Sometimes, if they had a little sugar, Satanaya made rice pudding, stirring the Konya *kazan* slowly over a low heat until the milk thickened, otherwise she made yoghurt. *'Faites simple'* became the order of her days, and as life became less complicated, something in her changed. Her expectations fell away, and she found pleasure in taking care of the bare essentials of existence in full awareness of what she was doing, so that nothing was missed or glossed over. To the outsider it might have seemed little ever happened. And they would be right, for Satanaya was undergoing a kind of reduction, a removal of the unnecessary accretions that coloured her identity, and thus her actions. In time, Satanaya found that her own wants, whether physical, or social, were reduced to the minimum.

And the longer she lived in the little hovel, a plank in a corner of the kitchen as her bunk, a well from which to draw water, the field for a privy and a regularly grumpy housemate who made no attempt to ameliorate their relationship with a cheery good morning (although on rare occasions he did begrudge her a compliment on her cooking), the longer she spent in green Meram in the company of Yeşil Efendi, the clearer became the lines she had seen in the tomb of Ateşbaz Wali:

'Whoever attains the state of true meditation
That person is educated by everything.'

Life became a continuous meditation, each moment presenting a lesson. A lesson in giving full value to the essentials, like waking up, breathing, feeding Tarçin, heating water for washing, fixing breakfast, cleaning the house. Nothing was excluded in this practice of awareness. And Yeşil Efendi missed nothing. If something was forgotten, he would notice it and he would scold her. Initially these scoldings left her running off in tears, until she remembered his challenge, that she wouldn't be able to bear his company. Then later she would redden and get angry at this treatment. She would even swear at him and accuse him of wanting a slave, which just made him laugh:

'No, not a slave, but we want someone who is willing, willing to see what we see. Not *how* we see, but *what*. The *how* is your own, the uniqueness of the vision only you have been given. But *what* we see… if only you would leave yourself, but you refuse to see it.'

Satanaya had passed the stage when she might have run away, but his jibes still hurt. One day, while washing the dishes, her pride smarting from a recent reproof, he came up behind her and said very quietly, wearily, but in a voice of pure compassion:

'Why are you so stubborn?'

Her first impulse, as always, was to retreat into the protective shell of her childlike self, the self-righteous 'I' against the world, as her so-strong identity came under threat. But something in his voice held her. She heard his kindness. And the power of this love, unrecognised until now, pushed her onto a threshold. On one side her past, her beliefs and her self-importance. And beyond, an opening to an unknown freedom. Only, to cross this threshold demanded a surrender, a death even, of her hitherto accustomed sense of identity, her likes and dislikes, her petty preferences, her knowledge. In the face of this vast unknown she now realised that not only did she know nothing, neither did she possess anything, not even her self. Even her own desires found no tangible object. A different want, as unstoppable as the ocean tide, was making itself known in her, the desire of this freedom itself to meet her; and it met and joined her own longing where the words of Yeşil Efendi had touched her, upon the threshold of her heart.

It was a beginning, a shift in her normal consciousness, and afterwards things began to change. But her resolution needed testing. Another rebellious outburst over her treatment some weeks later saw her banished on a stormy day to take a cartload of junk to the market where she was to remain until everything was sold. She fumed, but set off in the rain, and on the long ride into town she cursed Yeşil Efendi, warm in his little hovel, while she was left to do the dirty work. In time she calmed down, and remembered that desire for freedom. She knew she could leave Meram whenever she wanted. But she knew that wasn't the point. As she brooded, she remembered something her father used to say to his students, something she had always thought sounded nice, but until now she had never really felt its weight. About mercy and compassion, how their real meaning is not simply having pity on something, and being kind, but is to do with giving a thing its 'being'. He used to say that all of nature is compassion, that we only exist because of the mercy and compassion of the Being upon Itself.

At that moment she heard again Yeşil Efendi's words, '*Why are you so stubborn?*' She knew deep inside that she had been denying herself this mercy whenever events did not suit her. She now realised that nothing was oppressing her but her own imagining. She had taken it upon herself to serve, freely. And now she was complaining? The thought shocked her so much she stopped right where she was. Then, into howling wind she declared:

'No! Enough. I must be responsible for myself. This fight is between me and my own soul. I asked to be educated, and when I get shown a mirror, I say "No. That's not me." How pathetic am I.' And in that moment she resolved never again to see her life as being dictated from anywhere but her own desire to know herself, no matter how it appeared, and whatever it took of relinquishing blame. The emotion of the realisation overwhelmed her. She burst into tears, tears of gratitude, for this insight. And as the tears mingled with the rain, she began to weep with joy. She got rid of the junk in the market by the end of the day, and returned home, drenched, chastened, sober, but ready to start again.

From then on Satanaya began to sense this compassionate nature in her daily life; she saw this compassion breathing in everything around her, the wildlife and the trees, in the rain and wind, but mostly in the land, the dark earth supporting her and everything from beneath; and in her nights, in her sleep, in her dreams, she felt drawn closer to her own nature. She began to exhibit a wholeness in herself, and while she was unaware of it, Yeşil Efendi noticed. And although he had foresworn ever taking on students, one day after Satanaya had been with him for about a year, he handed her a small book, from a collection he kept in his room. "'*I was a hidden treasure and I loved to be known, so I created the world that I might be known*'" he quoted. 'Do you know this saying? Think about it, when you read this. That is if you still you want to learn.'

It was a book by an early Turkish mystic, Ismail Hakki of Bursa, commentating on a work by Muhyiddin Ibn 'Arabi. Satanaya opened it at random and read a little:

'Now, there is something which must be known: that a person of spiritual knowledge must understand his place of beginning and place of return, whence he came and whither he goes. This knowledge is contingent upon a journey; in fact three journeys. By journeying, here we refer to a person's spiritual journey…'*

For Satanaya the book read like a dream which on waking is impossible to describe or relate, but which seems to hold the answer to all the questions of the universe. She said this to Yeşil Efendi. He laughed in his usual uproarious fashion, as something which to him seemed completely normal, obvious even, had appeared to Satanaya as extraordinary. Then he fixed her with that piercing humbling pitying look, the kind of look that would calm a wild animal, and spoke:

'Yes, it's that simple. Reach back inside yourself. Find out who you are, that's real travelling. If any of them had the merest inkling of what they think they are understanding when they read the words of the Great Ones like Ibn 'Arabi or Rumi, they would fall down and prostrate. But no. They blithely read and discuss and paraphrase and commentate and write their poems and sing their songs and… How many of them are prepared to be big enough to be nothing, and by that nothing be suitable to receive the full weight of the Beauty.'

Yeşil Efendi had never said as much to her in all the many months she'd spent in Meram.

But Satanaya was no wild animal to be calmed. A beautiful gazelle in the dawn light grazing the grass at the edge of the forest. Wary, but not afraid. She looked straight back at him, her eyes requesting more.

He went on: 'You need to understand, why we are here. What is Man

---

* Lübb'ül Lüb – Muhyiddin Ibn 'Arabi (Turkish: Özün Özü – İsmail Hakkı Bursevi)

for ? That saying, *"I was a hidden treasure..."* – ask yourself, who is saying this, and to whom, and who wants to be known? This is speech from the origin of words, something that comes from the Divine Unknown Itself into the human heart, to us. Through the mouths of the inspired prophets and saints, it is true. But is there a difference in the end? If there is a difference, it is a matter of degree. You too are the one who wants to know. You, Satanaya, you would love to know your hidden treasure, wouldn't you? So you too are the place where this treasure desires to know and be known. You are the place of creation itself, where pure being wraps itself in this form we call you, and knows itself as you. And you? What's in it for you? Nothing, absolutely nothing but the witnessing of that. And what greater honour, what greater pleasure could there be?'

It continued like this for the next six months, Yeşil Efendi handing Satanaya one of the books from his collection, perhaps the 'Flashes' of the Persian mystical poet Jami, or 'Universal Man' by Jili from Baghdad, or Al-Niffari's 'Mawaqif' describing the stations on the spiritual journey. But most often he would direct her to passages from the works of Rumi or Ibn Arabi.

And when she had read and reread a particular text, he would let her ask questions. He would invariably respond by questioning her, so in the end it was Satanaya who was forced to dig deep and draw from the well of her own soul the meanings. And if she couldn't see what was being said, he might just tell her to go away and clean the house or cook, and that he wasn't there to make things easy for her, giving answers which she would only learn by rote, answers which would be worth no more than counterfeit coin. For if something was worth knowing, he said, then effort had to be put into finding out and verifying it for herself.

The only answer he ever gave was to his own question, asked rhetorically, 'How many beings are there in existence? One! One only and unique, aside from which there is nothing else!'

And if Satanaya's response was at a level suitable to the question, from the point of view of there being only one existence, then perhaps the Yeşil Efendi would elucidate further, expanding from his own deep knowledge of matters esoteric. And if the mood was upon him, quite wondrous things would pour forth from him into Satanaya's heart. And when eventually the *'sohbet'* – the spiritual converse – would conclude, she would know she had journeyed to some extraordinary realm of high intellect and spiritual taste, where meanings were exposed like fabulous cakes in the confectioner's window, glimpsed through the mirror of the imagination perhaps, their luscious scents wafting to her through a seemingly unreachable door, leaving her longing for their sweetness. Afterwards she would remember little if any of Yeşil Efendi's words, and yet some indefinable aftertaste would remain like a light in her own being.

FORTY-EIGHT

Sweet Scents of Meram

Meram, Konya, 1911

SATANAYA AND YEŞIL EFENDI were sitting outside in the spring sunshine drinking coffee after lunch. The slender fronds of the acacia at the corner of the house, bursting in a foam of yellow bloom, shimmered in the new light and before them a sea of spring wheat heaved and glowed green and gold. As usual, the meal had been eaten in silence. Then Yeşil Efendi, stirring the calm waters of their post-prandial meditation, said, apropos nothing in particular, (as it seemed to Satanaya) that everything was good in its essence, and that essence was absolute, one and single to the many appearances of things.

'So why is there bad?' Satanaya asked. 'Where does evil come from?'

'Well, first tell me what you think 'good' is.' said Yeşil Efendi.

'Good is… you know… beauty… things that benefit us, that nourish us. Life, perhaps. Love? Helping someone who needs help, that's good, isn't it? I don't know… wholeness perhaps – like, when I feel complete in myself…' Satanaya looked out across the field. 'The earth, with the wheat growing in it, that's good, surely? It feeds us, it's full of life from the sun and the rain, and look how beautifully it dances in the wind.'

'Oh, very nice, very nice. Satanaya likes the wind making the green grass dance. Perhaps each plant is a dervish turning round the sun. Good God, Satanaya, why must you always stop at the reflections? First find the original.' Yeşil Efendi grinned and Satanaya wasn't at all sure that he wasn't making fun of her. A period of pensive silence followed.

'And 'bad'? What is 'bad'? What is wicked, what is evil?' he asked her.

Satanaya looked at him. Now he was serious. He wasn't making fun of her.

'Look, Satanaya, this is one of the biggest questions in life, and also perhaps the simplest. Take it back to the one, the single unique absolute existence. This world, this relative existence, it is just that, relative. If there wasn't what appears to be bad, evil, lacking the thing which makes something good, then how could we come to know the good, the absolute good?'

'So you mean we cannot expect perfection, the perfect good, here in this life?' Satanaya looked disappointed.

'Some say that the real perfection includes the possiblity of imperfection, and that this life is trial.'

'That sounds so grim.'

'Not at all. This is the whole point – it is here in mortality, the world of beginnings and endings, that we can come to know, by understanding the nature of the contraries in relative existence, to join the opposites, to collect all the points of the circumference and and return them to the centre, to the original point of no dimension.'

Satanaya was puzzled, but something, about evil being the lack of something which would make it good, seemed to make sense.

'So, these negatives, evil, pain, hate etc. these are simply lacks, or the effect of a lack?'

'Exactly.'

'So they have no existence in themselves?'

'Quite. But we have to be careful. In this world, the effects have such a strong influence over weak minds, immature minds. That is why we say the world is both an illusion, as well as the truth. We must learn to discriminate, to recognise truth from falsehood. That only comes through educating ourselves in truth. Developing our minds to be receptive to this absolute way of seeing. For that we need to see things not just from the circumference but also from the point of no dimension. That is the whole point of these journeys.'

'You said that the essence is one in everything and absolute good, so is this how we strengthen our mind, by remembering this?'

'Yes, but who of us can say we are present with our essence, eh?' Yeşil Efendi gave her a stern look. 'That is why it is important that we work hard to know ourselves, right back through to our essential person.'

'But how?' said Satanaya. 'This seems impossible. I feel completely helpless.'

Yeşil Efendi recited a short poem:

'Before thinking, let go all thoughts.
Before speaking, leave off words.
Before acting, be non-existent,
Make all space for spirit's action.'

Satanaya looked intently at him. The breeze had fallen, the wheat ceased its dancing and the gentle rustle of acacia leaves receded into silence. She left her thoughts and listened.

'Spirit's action is in the breath, that is our connection.' he continued, 'Our breath is essentially good, for it is spirit, life from the origin, from the Divine. It is up to us, being the place where the breath enters and leaves, to nurture this, to not prevent, but to bring out its original sweetness, and not taint it with foul odour and negativity. So we cultivate sweetness in this receptacle that is us: in our words, and thoughts and actions, so that all that emanates from this place is good.'

He looked kindly at her.

'So, Satanaya, respond to ignorance with the qualities of the essence – goodness, love, praise, wholeness. Everything is good in its essence, and the essence is one to all the many appearances of things, good or wicked.'

Yeşil Efendi used the Arabic word, 'tayyib', meaning good, good scented, sweet smelling air or scent; for wicked he used 'khabith', a word which sounded to Satanaya as if he was spitting.

Then Yeşil Efendi went inside and brought out a large volume bound in heavy marbled boards. It was one of the first books printed in the Ottoman Empire after the Egyptian Khedive, Mohammed Ali, established a press at Bulaq in Cairo – a Turkish translation of Ibn Arabi's famous work, 'Fusus al-Hikam' – The Settings of the Wisdoms, with commentary by Abdullah the Bosnian. He read a little from the final chapter, dealing with love between man and woman.

'Good and bad, are two opposing adjectives. They are accidents for the breath by virtue of place... the breaths of the creatures are essentially good. They emerge from the origin by original cleanliness and beauty and sublety and yet by virtue of a wicked place there results for it a wicked form... It is equally so on the contrary for the good scented breath by virtue of the good scented place, where a good scented form results and the good scented breath becomes most good, just as sweet water through its running through a channel which is in a sweet place is sweet.' *

'But what makes the place good or wicked?' she asked.

'It is simply the nature of this world, a world of contraries. It has to be. How else could this world operate if it weren't for up and down, forwards and backwards, left and right – the dimensions by which we determine the absolute in space and time. How else would we recognise our essential nature as perfection, if we didn't discriminate the more or less perfect that we experience in our lives.'

'So what we call perfect and lacking, good and bad, are simply expressions of a vision nurtured in time and space?'

'Yes, we can't help thinking in more or less, high and low, far and near. It's how we make sense of the world.'

He paused, then went on:

'Which is why it is so important to remember this origin of the breath, so that what comes from us is not restricted by the limitations of place, nor tainted by the effects of these conditions. It is only in thought that these

*   Fusus al-Hikam by Muhyiddin Ibn 'Arabi, p.1091. English rendition by Bulent Rauf.

conditions have any reality. And thoughts, well, they come and go, like dust in the wind... when the wind stills, the dust settles, and the mirrors clear again. Then be aware of your breath, because the journey of return is on every breath.'

'Breath is the energy on which the vehicle of your return takes place, and your vehicle is the good thoughts and feelings, the *tayyib* – sweet – actions, based on ideas of perfection and wholeness. And the most *tayyib* actions are those undertaken without attribution to self. That is the real cleanliness. That is why service is of utmost importance. We must aim at non-existence of self in this journey we have undertaken, if we are to make room in our heart for our real self.'

Satanaya would spend her lifetime pondering these words of Yeşil Efendi, but that, she would come to realise, was the whole point.

Satanaya remembered one of the Cairene's notes in Takla's cookbook:

'On garlic and its use:
Garlic is a medicine, and in cooking it is used with discrimination, if at all. Garlic, by its essence, is good. Yet, for some natures, its odour is not agreeable. Garlic is a purifier, and naturally, in the process of purification, there is a separating of the pure and the impure. And the odour arising from the conflict of this separating is bad smelling, corrupting, decaying, like the human body made of organic matter, constantly in a process of decomposition; and that odour of decomposition is exuded on the breath and skin of those who ingest garlic. Which is why angels hold their noses when among the humans, abhorring the stench of decomposition in contradistinction to the accustomed odour of sanctity of their celestial abodes.'

Not long after this conversation the two friends were sitting outside drinking tea and nibbling some roasted chickpeas. Yeşil Efendi leant towards Satanaya and examined her closely, looking for something. As if assessing a painting. Appreciating.

'It's time for you to go,' he said after a while. 'You see, Satanaya, I told you there was nothing I could teach you. Everything you need to know is already in you. It just needed time and the right space to come out. Like this chickpea, it needed to cook a while.'

Satanaya froze in alarm. After all the trials she had finally arrived at a place in herself where she was happy living the simple life and serving Yeşil Efendi. Now she was being asked to leave.

'What do you mean, go? Go where?'

'To Constantinople, of course. There is work to be done there.'

Satanaya gave a curious frown. 'Work? What work? Cooking?'

'Cooking, yes, that too. You won't know what it is until it comes, but when it does, don't hold back. There are people who may be able to help you in Constantinople, a family who are related to the Cairene you mentioned, the one who is in that cookbook. Now go, before you see an old man cry.'

'Not before I cook you one last meal.' said Satanaya, herself also unable to hold back tears.

It was her favourite, the 'Celebration' chicken pilav, made as a special treat, and with a deep love. When she brought it to the table, the room filled with aromas of buttery rice cooked in stock and infused with cinnamon, cardamon and saffron. Yeşil Efendi produced a bottle of raki and some glasses and poured out two large measures which he topped up with water. They clinked the glasses of milky white spirit and drank together like a couple of battleweary comrades.

'To the future, to your future!' Yeşil Efendi proposed a toast.

'And I thought my destiny was to be here always.' Satanaya's emotions were stirred as a result of the alcohol, her first drink in a couple of years, and she fought to hold back the tears.

'Destiny. What little we know of our destinies except what is right in front of us.' Yeşil Efendi gazed into the little fire burning in the hearth in the corner of the room.

'You cannot know your destiny fully while of this world, Satanaya, that is the nature of this life here. What does the wheel of our old cart know of the landscape it travels through, let alone its destination? Little beyond its constant turning and prostrating in the dust of the road. Occasional glimpses of horizons and a veiled instant of infinity at the zenith of each rotation. First we need to know ourselves by finding our centre, choosing a spoke among all those spokes that life offers, and following it back to the hub. There, if we find stillness, a different vision of our journey may appear. And even then, our life continues to move forward, one moment bent to the earth, the next rising to glimpse the far-off sky; we follow our alloted paths until the end. An end which is not an end, but a transformation, to another sky, another world, where we may travel free and unbound, beyond the poor limits of this earth's gravity. Then perhaps we can speak of our destinies.'

They finished the bottle and cleared the table away. Satanaya wrapped herself in a quilt to sleep by the fire, but sleep wouldn't come. She went outside and looked up at the stars, with Yeşil Efendi's words drifting in her mind. The Milky Way was splashed across the darkness, like surf upon an unseen shore. Standing there she knew that was enough for now, to be present upon the edge of the unknown, and always to remember that; with the immensity of life before her, too intangible to grasp with her mind, but completely embraced by her expanding heart. She knew, even as her small fears prevented her now, that one day she would be unable to hold back from diving into this ocean. Already each conscious step of her journeying amounted to a degree of immersion, now with her feet in the water, now swimming in the shallows. A glimpse perhaps; an intimation of the ocean. She may have thought herself simply a drop, but her potential would be to realise this to the extent that eventually there would be no difference between this drop and the ocean itself.

The next day, as Satanaya harnessed Tarçin, loaded with her meagre belongings and a few precious books, they were both in tears. And though she had sworn not to look back, she turned her head every now and then, until she could no longer see the Efendi in his tattered old kalpak, waving, as he merged into the green feathery background of acacias, poplars and the weeping branches of the terebinth trees of Meram.

FORTY-NINE

Departures and Arrivals

Konya, 1911

ATANAYA RETURNED to Konya in early spring. The road from Meram was awash with the green of new leaf on willow, and the silky blossoms on the acacia trees danced golden in the breeze. As she walked with Tarçin, drinking in the warmth of the sun, she felt she was entering a completely different world. The world of Yeşil Efendi began to recede as if a veil had fallen behind her. Just as when waking from a deep and profound dream, she knew she had been somewhere real, but for now the gate had closed upon that other place.

Satanaya stayed with Shireen before leaving Konya. Her period of retreat with Yeşil Efendi had been of such unalloyed intensity that Satanaya had not been aware of the changes going on in her former world. Shireen now brought her up to date with the dramatic political developments in Constantinople that had followed on her departure two years earlier, and Satanaya took it in with mixed feelings.

'Our Sultan Abdul Hamid, our Caliph, has been deposed. It's terrible. How can they do such a thing to one appointed as God's viceregent on earth! It's this 'Committee' – the Young Turks, they call them – they led a revolt within the army and forced him to abdicate. And after all he had done in re-establishing the Parliament.'

Satanaya remembered her conversation with Captain Anwar and she thought of that mysterious Turkish officer Mustafa.

'So what happened? Where is the Sultan?'

'They just packed him off on a train to Salonica. He lives there under house arrest. And he was only allowed to take two of his wives, and a few servants.'

Satanaya was surprised to see Shireen so incensed. The pure lady's world had truly been turned upside down. It dawned on her just how important was this strange figurehead of a sultan for the conservative folk here in the hinterland of the country.

'And has he been replaced?' said Satanaya.

'Of course. Our new Sultan is Abdul Hamid's half-brother, Mehmet. They say he is a kind man, a poet and a man of literature. And he is a member of our Mevlevi Order. But he has spent the last thirty years locked up in a palace. It's cruel to bring him out now like a pet lion to perform in public. He was not brought up to rule. It is his keepers, those dreadful Committee leaders, Enver and Talat, who control him. They had him dress for his coronation in a green khaki uniform they'd had made in a Paris fashion house, and even invited the Christian bishops and Jewish rabbis to the ceremony. Our new Sultan has become a ruler only in name. Heaven help us, he doesn't even have a beard, only a moustache!'

Satanaya was at a loss as to what facial hair had to do with anything. Evidently the advent of modernism had produced a reaction in Shireen, and she wondered whether her friend was regressing into religious conservatism.

'But Shireen, Christians and Jews! Surely our dear Rumi would have approved. You yourself told me Rumi had many disciples of other faiths.'

'Of course you're right, I'm sorry,' Shireen admitted she was getting carried away. 'But these Constitutionalists, they have no respect for tradition. The country is changing, and I'm not sure if it is for the good. You know what they say, if you remove the hub, the spokes will collapse and the wheel cannot turn. The Sheykhs have been talking. There have been dreams... portents... they say difficult times are coming.'

Satanaya smiled to herself at the mention of wheels and hubs. She also felt for her friend, seeing how distraught she was. Yet here in Konya, so far these changes were mostly hypothetical, and the fears which plagued Shireen were the result of conjecture upon an unknown future.

It could not be denied that the engine of state had been steadily losing power over the centuries. A complete overhaul of the system, such as this revolution heralded, would likely have dramatic repercussions throughout the solid conservative heartlands such as Konya. But real change comes slowly in Anatolia. Simply declaring a new order, as the new parliament in Constantinople was doing, even if heard in the provinces, would not be received easily by hearts and minds trammelled within pathways honoured by centuries, even millennia of tradition. It would take time, and a coherent and agreeable form, for the spirit of this new order to find acceptance among the generality of people. Meanwhile, until this spirit gathered sufficient strength, a degree of chaos was likely, if not inevitable.

Satanaya was, however, intrigued by the events of the past two years as Shireen related them. She felt drawn towards the centre of things, even if the centre seemed to be disintegrating. And the centre, whatever its state, for Satanaya was now Constantinople.

'Oh Satanaya, you're going to the City.' Shireen sighed. 'I always thought I'd go there one day. But it is so dangerous to travel in the country now. Even the trains carry soldiers to protect them. There have been incidents – mostly in Rumeli – Bulgarians, anarchists – they shot the Sultan's envoy in Salonica, and only last summer they tried to kill the old General, Mahmud Şevket Paşa, by crashing his train into a river in Trakya. Luckily he had changed his plans and taken a different train. They blamed the Bulgarians again.'

Before her departure, Satanaya visited once more those masters of the most ancient days: Mevlana Jelaluddin Rumi, Shams of Tabriz and

Sadruddin Konevi. Then having acquired a railway ticket for herself and Tarçin (because a Circassian lady should never be without reasonable means of escape), she bade farewell to the old stones and conical tombs, the dusty streets full of turbanned sheyks and tombstone dervishes; she savoured again the drifting woodsmoke of the bakers' ovens carrying warm reminders of fresh bread, and relished the smells of roasting onion and lamb from the shops selling 'etli ekmek', enjoying perhaps for the last time those yard-long meat pastries that are as much Konya as the flocks of fat-tailed sheep and endless acres of golden wheat.

The whistle of the locomotive, a little 2-6-0, No.16 of the Société du Chemins de Fer Ottoman d'Anatolie, belted out a loud screech and clouds of steam hissed from the pistons as the heavy wheels found traction. Through the window of her carriage, Satanaya embraced Shireen for a final time as the train pulled out of the single platform of Konya station in the early evening, its destination the grand Haydarpaşa Station in Constantinople.

Embarking by rail as evening drew in, Satanaya experienced the rare excitement of being upon the threshhold of a new journey, her inner journeying confirmed in the constant changing landscape as the train moved, and an unknown world became known before her eyes. She was caught again, the child rocked in the cradle of yearning, desperately trying to stay awake, to stay conscious in the ever expanding beauty of life as day faded into night.

Poking into the western horizon, the cones of two extinct volcanoes drew the brilliant red sun into their cleavage. As the train gathered pace great strings of birds, hundreds of yards long, flocked in their thousands in the apricot sky, heading north companioning the carriages awhile, until the locomotive's speed and night's starry darkness outstripped even these flighty messengers.

Satanaya relaxed, and in that surrender of body and mind that final departure brings, her soul felt loved, caressed even. The feeling of 'about to be' that had gripped her initially was replaced by a comforting state of 'wait and see'. In the dying light she spied a lone wolf silhouetted upon a distant rise, heading west with intent; further on a shepherd on a hillside caught in the sunset glow, sentinel in his great cape of felt, a prophet with his surrounding flock of golden-fleeced sheep, and great tawny kangal dogs skulking the perimeter. Every few miles, wreathed in the smoke of evening fires, clusters of adobe buildings passed the carriage window. The land was breathing.

The journey to Constantinople was slow. Although the locomotive itself had a top speed of 50 mph, with its train of carriages and goods wagons it rarely reached a third of that velocity, and took nearly three days to reach its destination. The train stopped on demand. Sometimes, in the middle of nowhere a solitary horse-drawn araba and driver would be waiting by the railside, and a bundle of peasant farmers and families would tumble from a third class carriage, load their goods and selves on the cart and just head off over the plain. When the train came to a town, boys carrying trays of pastries, and sellers of water, tea and coffee would trail the platform calling their wares and hasty transactions would take place through carriage doors and windows. Satanaya had brought her own provisions for the journey, cheese, olives, some *gül boreği,* but she welcomed the fresh baked sweet rolls and hot tea.

The line from Konya, opened barely ten years earlier, ran through Akşehir, Afyon, Eskişehir – sleepy old Ottoman towns connected in the past by trade routes and the paths of conquering armies, now tied together by telegraphs and steel rails, places as yet unfamiliar to Satanaya, names that would rise to fame in the imminent future of the land; thence through the rugged hills and valleys of the original Ottoman heartland, the lands of Osman's Dream around Bilecik and Söğüt, and along the Sakarya River to Izmit at the eastern extremity of the Sea of Marmara, and transitting its north-east littoral before terminating at Haydarpaşa Station on the Asian shore of the Bosphorus.

Some time after Satanaya's departure, when Shireen could no longer resist the urge, she went to search out the man in the green kalpak. She made her way out to Meram and knocked on the wooden gate in the wall of the farmhouse by the turbe of Ateshbaz Wali. A little old lady came to the door, her name was Gül. Shireen enquired after Satanaya and Yeşil Efendi, but the lady called Gül appeared puzzled.

'I have no brothers. Nor sisters, for that matter. Yes, I think I recall a young Circassian woman. She came alone, I'm sure, and left. No, there's no house nearby where a rag-a-bone man lives. I would know if there were. I've lived in this house since I was born, and that's more than seventy years.'

And Shireen left Meram, more mystified than ever. She asked among the *araba* drivers, and even went to the markets where the second-hand dealers sold their wares, but no one had ever seen a rag-a-bone man with a green kalpak and a young Circassian lady whose horse pulled their cart. She asked her father if he knew anything about it.

'You say the man wore a green kalpak? And he looked like a tramp?' The Sheykh paused and seemed to be lost in thought. 'Yes, it happens like that sometimes.'

And there was nothing more to be said.

Satanaya stepped off the train onto the platform at Haydarpaşa Station and looked around. She had let herself enjoy the period of limbo that three days on the slow train afforded her. After all, the past was past, and about the future she could not comment. She spent hours simply looking out of the window, seeing the outside world pass by in glimpses of humanity, the actions and results, their efforts upon the seemingly impervious surface of the earth which supported this life. She saw in it the dissolving nature of time upon all this action, and wondered a little about what remained when all would be said and done. She quickly realised it didn't bear thinking about too much. It was out of her hands anyway. And yet, somewhere within this, within all this striving and movement of people and their things, when all regret and blame and self-congratulation were abandoned, she sensed there was aim, intention, will, hopes, and even a little certainty, in something called love burning in them. But again, all that was in future time, unseen and unrealised, yet to come, or not. Wait and see became her place of rest. Patience, she remembered, is the last of the qualities to be realised – the ultimate stopping place, where time itself is surrendered. And in that submission, there was only one place for her to be, in her centre, that place of no dimension, where her identity became inclusive, and her awareness a constantly expanding vision. She didn't have to whirl or turn around for this. If she remained still, she could see everything turning for her: turning in, towards, away, around, wherever, moved by a will that encompassed everything. And her choice? To accept or deny whatever these waves of existence presented her, according to a knowledge of taste, like the spices and the herbs, the bitter and the sweet, and the scents that everything exudes, good or bad, and discriminating, collecting and uniting in her heart, until that fire would become light.

FIFTY

Epilogue - The Portmanteau

Istanbul, 1976

UT WHAT happened after she arrived in Constantinople? Did she see those Turkish officers again? That one from the restaurant in Damascus, who came to the Beyt'ur-Rahma? Captain Mustafa? There's so little that I can find in the papers and diaries… there are huge gaps, whole years missing in her story before and during the war.'

It was the day of Lady Satanaya's the funeral. A mild day in early November and we were in Istanbul. A great niece of the lady had flown in from Paris with the casket containing her ashes. Prince Mehmet had arranged for a fisherman from the creek by the Sweet Waters of Asia to take us in his *kayık* down to where the Bosphorus enters the Sea of Marmara. Catching a quiet moment between the churning ferries and passing tankers, we dispersed the ashen remains of Lady Satanaya upon the waters. At the very moment of our pouring, a flock of shearwaters skimmed the surface and flew through the swirling dust. And that was the last we saw of our lady, dancing free in the wind, cheering, as she had wished, the souls of the unfaithful odalisques, the sisters of the silken bow-string, strangled on the Sultan's command, sacked up and sunk in the blue ocean stream off Seraglio Point.

Now we were sitting in a little waterside restaurant in Bebek, lunching on *lüfer,* the sublimely tasting bluefish of the Bosphorus and invoking Lady Satanaya's spirit and presence with sentiments of sweet reminiscence. We were the usual motley crew from the group which congregated in the Prince's Kensington apartment: an elderly Turkish novelist, a young American computer scientist, a bearded preacher, an aging ex-army colonel who had known the Lady in Constantinople during the British occupation.

Prince Mehmet had a way of looking at you, as if he was seeing through to some other place in yourself, a place you yourself had not yet reached. Initially it made one feel quite vulnerable, and that may have been the intention – to scare one away, perhaps, or to see what you were made of, whether you could stand the heat. It was a kind of sizing up, the way a good tailor will know if a certain cut of cloth will suit you, and if you can afford it. This assessment was not without compassion, but there were the inevitable timewasters (and heaven knows how much of his time I wasted in my naive questioning, my stubborn arguing and protesting). Not that he was averse to wasting time, but as he would point out, he had better things to waste his time on.

Mehmet was giving me that look now, and I waited. I suddenly had that feeling when swimming in the sea, when I realise with fear and panic how deep the water is beneath me, and the only solution is to surrender to the beauty of its vastness. The Prince exchanged glances with the ex-Colonel. The rest of the table were drinking white wine and chatting away, and hadn't noticed our side-conversation. The ex-Colonel gave a shrug and said quietly, with a little smile.

'Well, why not? No one will believe it anyway. If he publishes, it'll be like a novel. Anyway, these things will get out eventually. Go on, why not?

After all, it was all so long ago.'

Mehmet separated a piece of glistening white flesh from the grilled fish on his plate and held it on his fork, appraising it with complete satisfaction for a moment before popping it in his mouth.

'The best fish there is, *lüfer,* perhaps better even than salmon. On a par with turbot, some would argue, but thankfully their seasons are different. Jacob, come and see me when we get back to the hotel. I have something which might be of interest.' And with that his attention returned to the fish on his plate.

We were staying in the Pera Palas Hotel, long before its recent 'refurbishment' in which the delightful birdcage lift, with its mahogany, mirrors and brass fittings was retired, relegated to the status of a museum piece, and accommodation became only affordable for Russian oligarchs, Texan widows and Hollywood first wives – and long, long after its heyday with the opening of the Orient Express rail service from Paris, and later, the glamorous period of the Allied occupation and the early years of the Republic. The grand old building was now something of a dowager, a beauty grown old, deserted by her lovers, with few remaining who remembered her glory days. But Prince Mehmet remembered, and had insisted we put up there, with its enormous enamelled cast iron baths, the huge chrome taps worn to the brass, the musical plumbing, the threadbare Hereke rugs on creaking oak floors, and the vast mahogany wardrobes and bedsteads. We were transported into the nostalgia of European noir, enjoying the views over the Golden Horn, riding that beautiful birdcage lift, and drinking rakı in the dimly lit bar with its heavy velvet drapes, a grand piano tinkling in the background.

I knocked on room no. 232.

'*Buyurun!*' the loud call in Turkish to enter was now familiar.

He was sitting in bed, propped up by numerous pillows and reading an Agatha Christie novel. The room smelt strongly of bergamot cologne and Maltepe cigarettes. He pointed to a battered portmanteau on a marble topped mahogany dresser opposite.

'Would you be so kind and bring me that bag?'

I brought it over, a heavy leather holdall with a strong handle and fastened with a brass clasp and lock. Mehmet fished around in his pocket for the violet crochet-work purse where he kept his change, extracted a small key and opened the bag.

Inside was another trove of papers and diaries.

'As I said, something which might be of interest to you. It was among the luggage which Lady Satanaya left long ago, a trunk and some bags, stored in my brother's house. He had been using the trunk as a table. Most of the stuff, clothes and books, he gave to the *eskici*. But he thought I should have these personal papers. I haven't had time to look through them properly, but the diaries cover the war years, and the letters... well, the letters are mostly between the two of them, his to her, and, strangely, hers to him. I believe he returned them to her when he got married. Why he didn't destroy them is anyone's guess, but, well, make of them what you will.'

'He?' I said.

'Oh, the Turkish officer of course. The one who appeared at the Beyt. Oh dear, it's another long story. But you'll see if you get through all this. What you have to understand is, with a man like Mustafa...'

And then the Prince launched into a disquisition on this man Mustafa, how he was a true man of destiny. He talked about his influences, the changes that came about through him, and the changes still coming to the world. And Mustafa's connections with the *'Büyükler'*.

'These "great ones,"' he explained, 'through whom the destinies of nations, and the world are guided – people you would never recognise for what they are, unless you were one of them, the real dervishes, the true mystics, the 'joined-up' people, not the ones in robes and hats who call themselves sufis and sheykhs, not the *'inşallahs'* and the *'maşallahs'*, though some of these too might be among them. One never knows who they are.'

Mehmet paused. He raised his eyebrows and gave me a teasing, slightly mocking look, as if testing my credulity.

'You won't find any mention of him and Lady Satanaya anywhere outside these papers – she was his yeast, she was what made him rise – and you don't taste the yeast if the loaf has been well made. But the evidence, the proof as they say, is in the eating.'

Mehmet noticed that I was struggling to make sense of what he said.

'Come on, Jacob,' he added, 'by now you must see that none of this accidental. That there is some purpose, some intelligent evolution at play here. Nothing happens in this world without the intention of man. But we have to ask, which man? And what is his real nature?'

Mehmet pushed the bundle of papers and notebooks towards me.

'Anyway, I'm sure you'll have your work cut out unravelling this lot. Here, now take it all away, I need to rest before the evening. And don't be in too much of a hurry. You have all the time in the world.'

Jacob Merdiven de la Scala

APPENDIX I
Recipes from Takla's cookbook

1. Uncle Mesut's Lentil Soup (Chapter 7) – (for 10-12 persons)

INGREDIENTS:
1 kilogramme of red split lentils
3 medium onions, diced small
2 large carrots, cut in thin matchsticks
2 medium potatoes, thin matchsticks
3 green peppers sliced in small matchsticks
3 large tomatoes cut into small dice

meat stock – preferably chicken, or vegetable stock if preferred
half a handful of oregano
half a handful of thyme
fresh flat leaf parsley – 2 large handfuls roughly chopped
salt/pepper

flour
butter
lemons

THE METHOD:
Sort the lentils first to remove any stones. Then wash the lentils well in cold water and drain. Fill a large *kazan* with 5 litres of water and/or stock, and place over the fire.

Next add: lentils, carrot and potato, chopped parsley, diced onion, green pepper, salt and pepper.

Bring the mixture to the boil, lower the heat and simmer gently for a good hour, stirring from time to time and carefully skimming off any scum which rises to the surface.

In another pan, melt 3 or 4 ozs butter over the fire, and add enough flour to make a liquid roux. Cook this until it begins to go pale golden brown (but not burn), then add water and combine well and cook until smooth. Add this butter/flour mixture to the lentils and stir in well and let it cook into the soup a while, until the lentils have disintegrated. Finally, adjust the seasoning to taste, and serve with quarters of lemon on the side.

This soup needs to be given a good stir before each serving. The lemon, squeezed over the soup in each bowl, is an essential part of this dish.

2. Clotilde's Recipe for Pheasant with Chanterelles in White Wine and Cream Sauce (Chapter 9)

First shoot your pheasant, and hang it by the neck in a cool, dry, airy place, below 5C, for between two and four weeks depending on taste.

Pluck and gut the bird, setting aside the liver and heart for pâté. Rinse well, taking particular care to remove all intestinal matter, and dry.

In a decent-sized frying pan, melt some butter and saute the bird all over to a golden colour, then place in a roasting tray.

Slice an onion very thinly and longitudinally and fry in the same pan until softening, but not browning. Next deglaze the pan with a half a glass (150ml) of medium-dry white wine. Add twice that amount of good chicken or veal stock and bring back to simmer. Add stock and onion to the pheasant in the tray.

Season with salt and a little freshly ground black pepper, a small pinch of mace or nutmeg, a quarter teaspoon of lemon zest (no pith), a bunch of fresh thyme, a bayleaf, two or three crushed juniper berries and half a teaspoon of sugar.

Roast a medium-sized bird in a hot oven, about 180C, for half an hour, then lower the heat to around 150C, and turn the bird breast-side down; cover the tray and continue to cook for a further 45 minutes. Then remove the cover, turn the bird right side up again and cook for a further 15 minutes at 180C. Remember, a big old cock pheasant will take longer to cook than a tender young hen, so adjust cooking times accordingly.

When cooked, remove from the oven and bone the bird, laying the meat in decent portions in an oven-proof serving dish deep enough to hold sauce as well. Cover, and keep in a warm place. Try and discover and remove any lead shot at this stage. Also, remove the spines from the drumstick meat, or don't serve if badly bruised and broken.

Take the bones and pan juices and boil up with extra stock if necessary, sufficient for a generous sauce, when reduced and infused. Strain and keep.

Having earlier cleaned any earth or pine needles from the chanterelles with a soft brush, carefully tear the fungi into pieces as big as a 50 centimes coin, that is, about 2.5 cm. Melt some butter in a frying pan and gently sauté the chanterelles, adding a little salt. Turn up the heat and when sizzling, add a tablespoon of brandy and gradually add as much of the reduced cooking juices and stock as needed for the sauce, and combine with thick cream until it begins to thicken. Then pour the sauce over the pheasant meat which is waiting patiently, relaxing in the warm serving dish. Bring to the table immediately.

This dish can be made substituting field mushrooms in place of chanterelles. If using dried wild fungi, wash and pre-soak in cold water, and add the soaking juices to the cooking stock. The soaked fungi can then be sliced thinly and sauteed as described above.

3. Venison Casserole (Chapter 23)

'One of the bright young things, whose father owned estates in the mountains, had provided the Beyt with a couple of deer, so the feast had centred round a vast casserole of venison… The dish was served with mounds of mashed potatoes and platters of red cabbage cooked with apple and raisins.'

The deer were quartered into shoulders and haunches, and roasted in trays with onions, tomatoes, red wine and rich meat stock, with wild thyme from the hillside and juniper berries. First the joints were given a short period roasting in a hot oven, and then after adding the fungi, dried ceps and field mushrooms soaked in brandy, the meat was cooked long and slow at a lower heat until the flesh, while easily carved away from the bones, retained a moist tenderness enfused with earthy forest flavours.

4. Yayla Çorbası (Chapter 41)

Yayla Çorbası is the universal soup of the Anatolian steppe, named for the high pastures – *yayla* – where the nomad herders bring their flocks in the warm months of the year. The ingredients are readily available: cracked wheat and chickpeas – both of which were first domesticated in this region; dried herbs, dairy products and eggs from their accompanying animals.

The common name is *Yoğurt Çorbası* – yogurt soup. The İstanbullus use rice, although in Central Anatolia where it is called Toyga soup, bulgur is added. In eastern Turkey it is made with cooked chickpeas and whole wheat that has been soaked overnight. The basic principle of combining yogurt, eggs and flour with meat stock, then flavouring with dried mint and butter remains the same for all three versions. Dried mint is always used, never fresh mint, and is cooked in browning butter before being poured over the soup and stirred in just before serving.

A version of this soup includes onion juice and chopped spinach root, as well as tiny *köfte* – meat balls made with soaked wheat and minced lamb seasoned with salt and pepper.

Shireen's cook, Nevin, showed Satanaya the way she cooked *Yayla Çorbası*, the eastern version. She had soaked the wheat and chickpeas overnight, and pre-cooked the chickpeas without salt, boiling until soft, then removing the skins while still warm.

In a heavy pan she combined strained yogurt, egg yolks and plain flour, working the mixture until it was smooth. She slowly added the meat stock, stirring the mixture continuously over a low heat. As it came to the boil she removed the saucepan from the heat and added chick peas and soaked wheat, salt and ground black pepper.

'We must take it off the heat while adding salt, otherwise it might curdle' said Nevin.

She placed the pot back on a corner of the stove and still stirring she let it cook slowly, with just a hint of a simmer, until the flour was cooked through.

In a small pan she melted a good spoonful of fresh village butter, and when it began to foam, she added a handful of fine dried mint. She let it a sizzle a little in the hot fat, then poured it over the soup, and stirred it in. It was ready for the table.

Ingredients for Yayla Çorbası

1 litre of stock, chicken or lamb.
1 large egg
1 heaped tablespoon of flour
3 heaped tablespoons of yogurt, preferably strained or goat's yogurt

either:
a tablespoon of white rice
or
a tablespoon of coarse bulgur
or
a handful of soaked wheat

and:
a handful of cooked chickpeas/garbanzos
salt and pepper
a large tablespoon of butter
a desertspoon of dried mint

APPENDIX II

The Russo-Ottoman War of 1877-78 and the Siege of Plevna

Bulgaria was part of the Ottoman Empire for nearly five hundred years. In 1876, encouraged by Russia, its Christian population broke out in open rebellion against the authorities. The revolt was severely suppressed, with atrocities widely and graphically reported in the European press, bringing grave censure on Turkey from the European public. The Russian Tsar Alexander II had been waiting for such an excuse: claiming exasperation at the Turks' behaviour, in April 1877 he had declared a 'holy war', a crusade to free the Christians from the yoke of their heathen oppressors. Others saw this simply as the Tsar's wish to establish control over the eastern Mediterranean as a prelude to Russian expansion beyond Central Asia into India. In a very short time, having gotten assurances of neutrality from Austria-Hungary, and an alliance with the Principality of Rumania, the Russians invaded Turkey with two great armies, one entering through the Caucasus, and the other, a force of 200,000 men under the command of the Tsar's brother Grand Duke Nicholas, coming down through Rumania.

The small town of Plevna lay some twenty miles south of the Danube, in a deep valley surrounded by steep hills covered with vineyards and orchards and ripening corn. Plevna itself was quite vulnerable, having no fortifications or garrison. Yet the natural topography of its setting within craggy ridges and rocky terrain, ravines and rough escarpments, meant it could be defended effectively from the high ground surrounding the town on all sides. Plevna's importance lay in its strategic position. The road which the Russian army would need to take on its route to Constantinople lay through the town to the bridge over the River Vid which passed by two miles to the west. Whichever army commanded the heights of Plevna commanded the town, the road and the bridge.

The Russian force in the west had made easy headway, taking a big Turkish fortress on the Danube at Nikopol twenty miles to the north of Plevna, and a small force had taken the Shipka Pass in the Balkans to the south east.

In the meantime, the Turkish general, Osman Pasha, alerted to the impending threat, and responding to a telegram from the Sultan Abdul Hamid II, force-marched his troops to the defense of Plevna. They covered the one hundred and twenty miles from his headquarters in Widden on the Danube to Plevna in a space of six days, arriving in late July. Immediately they set to building the defences. They mounted cannon on the encircling heights and dug in row upon row of trenches. Two great redoubts, each capable of holding a thousand soldiers, were built on a ridge at the village of Grivitza to the east of Plevna. In the town itself the Turks amassed ammunition, stores and water which were distributed to the surrounding fortifications. Reinforcements were continually arriving.

Barely ten days later the Russians made the first assault. With 35,000 troops they attacked the newly-built redoubts. But the Russian infantry, like most European armies of the time, were armed with single shot weapons of a design fast becoming outmoded. They made a frontal assault on the Turkish positions, and were expecting to win the day by massively outnumbering their enemy. The Turks, however, had recently been equipped with the latest quick-loading rifle, the Peabody-Martini, a weapon with deadly accuracy over a range as great as a kilometre. In addition, the Sipahis, the Turkish cavalry, who had exchanged their mounts for defensive trench positions, carried the new repeating rifle which became famous in the American Wild West, the Winchester. The Turks, with long range accuracy and rapid fire capability made mincemeat of the enemy front line. Although the massive Russian attack eventually achieved some successes, the Turks counterattacked and won the day, suffering only 1,000 casualties to the Russians 4,000.

And so it proceeded through summer into autumn, with each assault more savage than the last, and each defence more determined. Back and forth, month after bloody month until winter, the Russians fought a war of attrition against the numerically smaller but strategically advantaged Turkish defence. Reinforcements, in particular from their Rumanian allies, brought the Russian strength up to 140,000 troops, while the Turks never had more than 30,000 men in the field. The Tsar himself came to view the proceedings as his brother's guest, from a safe hillside seat out of the line of fire.

Osman Pasha was denied permission from Constantinople to abandon the field and retreat, in spite of the inevitable hopelessness of the situation.

Finally in late October the Russians had completely invested the town. The Turks were trapped. Food and water supplies dwindled. Brave attempts were made to break the siege from within and eventually Osman Pasha was wounded and the Turks surrendered.

The heroic resistance of the Turkish general and his army had captured the imagination of the Western press who reported the seige on a daily basis, swinging public opinion back in favour of the Ottomans. The Western Powers also took note of the casualties – 40,000 Russians and Romanians to 10,000 Turks, and began to re-equip their armies with the modern weapons of mass destruction in preparation for the great bloodbath of 1914.

Russian forces continued their march south, halting in January 1878 at the seaside village of San Stefano on the Marmara Sea, a few miles outside Constantinople (modern day Yeşilköy, site of Atatürk Airport). Only the arrival of the British navy's fleet of battleships dissuaded the Russians from entering the city. A truce led to the Treaty of San Stefano, its terms modified later that summer at the Congress of Berlin, which gave Bulgaria a degree of independence as a principality within the Ottoman Empire.

The subsequent restructuring of the Balkan states in the interests of the Great Powers of Britain, Russia and Austria-Hungary, with the continuing dissintegration of the Ottoman European lands, laid the seeds for the later conflicts of the Balkan Wars of 1912-13 and World War I.

An Ark in the Flood of Time
If you wish to read further of the life of Satanaya, a sequel, 'An Ark in the Flood of Time', is due to be published in late 2019/early 2020.

'An Ark in the Flood of Time' continues the story of Satanaya in Constantinople where she becomes lady's companion and governess in the household of a noble Ottoman family, and later acquires a partnership in a hotel. As her life unfolds in this great metropolis Satanaya becomes inextricably linked to the struggles of the time, in her relationships with a number of notable political and military figures throughout the Balkan Wars, World War 1 and the Turkish War of Independence.

For publication date and where to purchase 'An Ark in the Flood of Time' please see website: www.christopherryan.co.uk or contact author via email: info@christopherryan.co.uk

ALSO BY CHRISTOPHER RYAN
The Story of the Damascus Drum
Daud is a successful trader from the island of Arwad, Takla a young cook in the famous Convent of Seydnaya, and Shams, an old billy goat from the hills above Damascus. The Damascus Drum takes them on a journey in time, space, and beyond through the Syrian landscape of the 19th century, the old Syria that still lay close to the surface before recent catastrophes.

It is a journey of love and self-discovery, an adventure replete with entertaining storytellers recounting tales of mystery and love, villainous villains and hospitable goatherds, clerics both wicked and wise, memorable feasts and a lot of goats....

As a Syrian reader, now displaced in Turkey, writes: *"Stigmatized by ISIS; devastated by pro-Assad militias and opportunist paramilitary groups; nobody could remember the wonderful aspects of Syria before such a savage crazy war. The Story of The Damascus Drum draws a portrait of the Syria which I can recognize as my own country and really miss. The country which was the cradle of civilization and has contributed a lot to the progress of human history. This novel goes back to ages I have never witnessed; but which my imagination has already visited and lived in."*
Ruba Khadamaljamei, translator at Syria TV تلفزيون سوريا

382

Praise for 'The Story of the Damascus Drum'

'A journey of self-discovery and rebirth… sympathetic characters who reach out to the living even after their death, as does Shams the Billy Goat as the skin of the drum that awakens the hearts of all who hear…a work of Sufi Realism and a beguiling tale… I highly recommend this book.'
David Paquiot, SUFI Journal, Washington D.C.

'A fabulous adventure story, scented with magical realism, resonating with a talking goatskin drum… set among the monuments of Syria, and the old khans and mountainous hinterland of Damascus in a timeless Levant… part of that ancient Near Eastern tradition that buried valued spiritual teachings within a fast-paced plot.'
Barnaby Rogerson, Eland Books, London.

'A delightful and quirky independent book, it catapults us directly into the old world of Damascus, far away from rockets and mortar bombs and deaths of civilians … a magical piece of escapism with a lesson to teach the weary 21st century soul.'
Marion James, Sunday Zaman, Istanbul.

'… how much I've enjoyed reading THE DAMASCUS DRUM… is unique, profoundly human, funny, wise and it's a good tale.'
Sebastian Ritscher, MOHRBOOKS AG Literary Agency, Zürich

Also available in German translation as 'Die Damaszener Trommel' from www.chalice-verlag.de